I0823325

THROUGH OUR TEETH

Also by Pamela N. Harris

When You Look Like Us

This Town Is on Fire

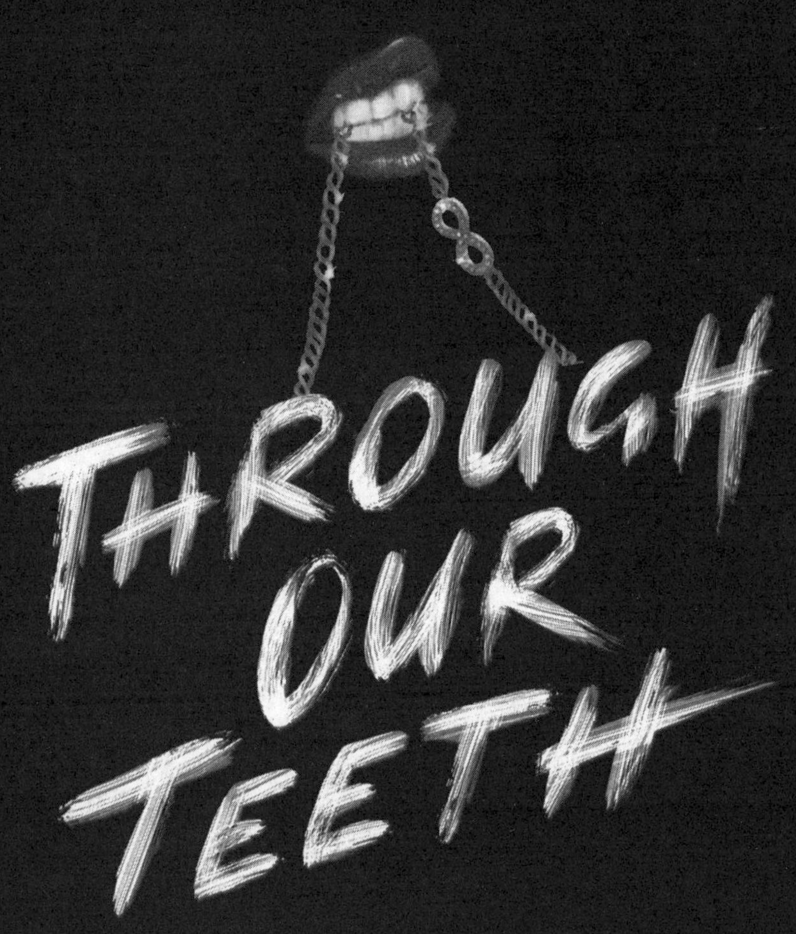

PAMELA N. HARRIS

Quill Tree Books
An Imprint of HarperCollins*Publishers*

HarperCollins Children's Books,
a division of HarperCollins Publishers, 195 Broadway, New York, NY 10007

HarperCollins Publishers,
Macken House, 39/40 Mayor Street Upper, Dublin 1, D01 C9W8, Ireland

Quill Tree Books is an imprint of HarperCollins Publishers.

Through Our Teeth

harpercollins.com

Library of Congress Control Number: 2025941305
ISBN 978-0-06-321267-1

Typography by Carla Weise
25 26 27 28 29 LBC 5 4 3 2 1

First Edition

FOR THE BLACK GIRLS HOLDING IT ALL TOGETHER WHILE QUIETLY FALLING APART—I SEE YOU.

ONE

IT'S HALLOWEEN AND THE GOONS ARE OUT tonight. Claws sinking into the sand, fists thumping against chests to the blaring beat. Flames from the bonfire reflecting the mischief in their smiles. And that's if they're not wearing masks. There are lots of masks out here. Half masks, light-up masks, overhead masks. Masks that leave tiny openings for eyes to show there's a human behind them. The goons laugh and dance and vibe with each other to prove they're having an amazing time. The faces behind these masks are my classmates. My friends. At least, they used to be.

Everyone's surprised to see me here, as though the Halloween bonfire at Huntington Beach hasn't been a tradition since our grandparents did the bump and hustle down our hallowed school halls. It always had to be at Huntington, which the official website boasted as being part of a sixty-acre park that trailed the beautiful James River. But the reviews painted a clearer picture of what to expect. Contamination, rude lifeguards, unsavory people—the perfect storm for a little high school debauchery. So each year, we traveled a half hour away from our quaint little bubble in York County, Virginia, to become a few of those *unsavory people.* A group of seniors always took the lead on the festivities, securing the playlist, firewood, and alcohol. Especially the alcohol. Whoever oversaw the bonfire was a bigger deal than being prom king or queen. It told everyone that, yes, you were indeed the shit. We hate you but want to be you at the same time. This was supposed to be my year planning the Halloween party. To be both feared and admired by my peers. But . . . shit happens.

My first hour at the bonfire consisted of gaped mouths and wide eyes and hugging. So much hugging. A bunch of *I miss you*s even though they still see me at school. Repeats of *Where have you been?*, as if I've somehow disappeared. I take it all in with a huge grin, though. Try to be the Liv Porter they knew and loved and hated before my world blew up six months ago. I'm wearing my own mask tonight—and on the prowl for a certain someone.

Jace Martinez is not that certain someone, yet he strides toward me and my red Solo cup, bobbing his head to the *boom, boom, boom* from the Bluetooth speakers. He's decked out in crushed-velvet pants and a matching jacket, both with a leopard-print trim. He also carries a cane and tops off the costume with a wide-brimmed hat. Lord help me, this fool's dressed like a pimp. Once he's within arm's reach, he breaks out into a hair-raising body roll that has me searching for an exit.

Thankfully, he stops whatever he was doing to rub his eyes and peer at me. "Am I seeing things or has Liv Porter graced us on this beach?"

"Do you know you look like a pimp?" I ask.

Jace doesn't deserve my pleasantries. He's been on my shit list since we partnered up for a world history project back in ninth grade. I did all the research on the Ottoman Empire, but he insisted on doing most of the talking for our presentation. He even wore a toga, though people usually wore kaftans during that era. He still got an A for effort and charisma, whereas I got a B-plus for giving him that much wiggle room.

"Nailed it." He dusts off his shoulder with genuine pride. "And you are . . ."

He looks me over in my navy-blue newsboy cap, matching cropped long-sleeved shirt, and high-rise jeans. There's also my necklace. The silver chain with the infinity symbol pendant. But that's more part of my daily uniform than costume.

He snaps his fingers. "Either Chloe or Halle Bailey. Those singing twins? I'd peg you for more of a Chloe. She's a bit more diva than Disney princess, know what I mean?"

I blink at him so he'll know that I don't. "They're not twins," I tell him. "And I'm Janet Jackson from *Poetic Justice*. She had box braids instead of Marley twists, but—"

“Same difference,” Jace finishes for me, even though there isn’t an ounce of truth to that comment. “But yeah, Janet Jackson was definitely going to be my next guess.” He peeks into my cup. “Don’t tell me you got the cheap shit.”

“I got whatever they were serving.”

“Don’t worry. Someone went on a drink run. They’ll hook you right up.”

I pinch my face up into a fake smile. “Okay, Jace.”

“Surprised you’re here, yo. After Hope . . . you know. Then that face-plant thing at your track meet, I just knew your ass was going to be homeschooled.” He laughs, oblivious to his multiple levels of insensitivity. Not only did he mention one of the most humiliating moments of my life, but he also brought up Hope’s name without an ounce of sorrow. It’s been only six months since she’s been gone. Too soon for her name to be tossed out like leftovers, especially from someone as insignificant as Jace Martinez.

Instead of flinging the rest of my drink in his face, I preserve my energy for a more formidable opponent. “It’s senior year. I wanted to go through all the usual rites of passage. Prom, senior prank. Humoring you at this party when there are hundreds of other people more worthy of my time.” I give him another flash of a smile.

Jace’s mouth pinches up at the corners. Not quite committing to the smile as he assesses my chi. “Wait, are you . . . ? We’re cool, right? You’re just fucking with me.”

I sip my drink and allow the silence to stretch. My girl Tia, with her perfect timing, struts over to us, all decked out in a lavender mermaid gown with a sequined white floral pattern and a puffy tulle corsage on one side of the halter straps. Her natural curls have been pressed and flat-ironed into feathery, eighties waves—though they'd frizzed some because of the lingering October humidity. She even tops it off with a tiara and gives me a Miss America wave. I give her a curtsy, and she throws her head back with a haughty laugh.

"Now, now. No need for all that. I'm one of the people. Just more glamorous and painstakingly beautiful." She does a weird combo of cockney and Southern belle accents, but I'm pretty sure she thinks she sounds British.

"Okay. Check out Carrie." Jace surveys her with a nod.

Tia drops all airs and clucks at him. "Are you serious? Does it look like I have a bucket of pig's blood all over me?" She spins around and allows him to see the fake Polaroids of blurred-out nudie shots I helped safety pin to her dress before we got here. After a moment, she turns back around, and Jace still looks befuddled as fuck. "I'm the one and only Vanessa Williams, reclaiming her Miss America title post-*Penthouse* scandal."

Jace's mouth twists to one side. "Who the hell is Vanessa Williams?"

Tia huffs and gives me an exasperated look. I laugh and shrug. I told her that while I trust the intelligence of our classmates, she may be going a little too far in the pop culture vault to make a political statement. And yes, this is coming from the girl who's dressed as a nineties character from John Singleton's third-best film. But Tia was adamant, dammit. She had a rough time last school year. We both did. Her with those leaked photos, and me with panic attacks and . . . Hope. Tia and I flew in different flocks, but our catastrophes made us birds of a feather. We clung to each other throughout the summer, and we haven't let go once since our senior year began. I'm bummed that I missed being front row to all of Tia's class and sass throughout the years, but at least I get to appreciate the time we have before we both leave the nest.

"I can't believe I'm explaining myself to someone walking 'round here looking like a pimp," Tia says to me.

"That's because I am a pimp," Jace says, plucking at one of his velvet sleeves.

"Boy, and you saying that with your whole chest?" Tia asks, aghast. She shakes her head and hands him her cup. "Be my little feminist-in-training and get me something else to drink."

Jace looks down at the cup, eyebrows furrowing like, *What are drinks?* He finally sighs and nods. "Hopefully the good shit's here. I'll be back," he says as he trudges away.

I'm not sure if that's a promise or a threat.

Tia and I glance at each other, then crack up laughing.

"Girl," she says, linking her arm through mine. "I came over here to save you but got roasted in the process."

"Jace ain't had to roast nothing. You're already hot."

"I better be. Have you ever tried walking through sand with heels? It is not for the faint of heart. My ass better be as tight as freshly done cornrows by the time the night is over."

A warm breeze brushes through us and kicks up sand. Some of our classmates take it as a sign to whoop and dance harder.

Tia looks up at the dark sky. "Ugh, it looks like it's gonna rain. Do you think it's gonna rain?"

I gaze up at the sky as if I can see the pending raindrops. I can't, obviously, but still—the air smells earthier than usual. That thick, wet scent of moisture rising from the ground that seems to permeate right before a storm. "Probably."

Tia chews on her bottom lip, and there's a wistfulness behind her eyes like she stumbled into a memory and isn't sure how to return. I squeeze her closer to me to bring her back.

"It's okay," I say. "It'll probably just be a little sprinkle. Not enough to rain on everyone's fun."

"It's not that. It's . . . Sierra. She always loved the rain. Said it was the only thing loud enough to silence all the ghosts."

I don't know what to say, so instead I just rest my head on her shoulder and allow her to sit in the moment. Tia never really talks about her older sister, at least not in the time that we became tight. She died about five years ago. Rather, she was killed five years ago. I was too young to know what exactly happened, aside from a few news clips that my parents promptly turned off whenever I entered the room. I remember bits and pieces, though. There was a fight between Sierra and their mother. Police were called to deescalate and ended up fatally shooting Sierra. There were talks about mental illness. About police reform and cries for counselors to join police on certain calls. Those talks quieted over the years and . . . here we were. Drinking cheap beer on a contaminated beach with unsavory people.

"Well, bring on the rain, then," I say finally. "It's perfect for Halloween—and it'll be like Sierra's partying with us."

Tia gives a faint smile, then lets out a groan. "Why the rain gotta be blowing up my spot like that? Doesn't Mother Nature know this is the first time I've been able to get *the* Liv Porter out of her house in months?"

And just like that, she's her old sassy self.

"It's fine. I'm having a good time," I lie. I give a sly glance over her shoulder. If it does rain, I need to find *him* first. That'll be hard to do if there's a washout. My eyes land on two girls who joined the track team as freshmen last year. They give me an overly eager wave. I return it with a more subtle nod. *Keep there*, I tell them through my weak skills of telepathy. I can't handle any more *Holy shits* and *How are yous*. I can't handle more classmates throwing their arms around me without consent. And, as though the crowd can read my energy, more bodies began to descend closer to the fire, until I feel like I'm in the thick of a swarm.

I find myself gripping tighter to Tia's arms again as I take a few slow breaths. Try to mitigate the shakes before they even begin. I can't afford to be shaky tonight.

"You okay?" Tia asks, patting one of my hands.

I blow out a steady breath and nod just as Erica Matthews struts past us holding a cordless mic. "Can I get everyone's attention for just a moment? Just gather around the bonfire, please?" she asks.

"Who the hell gave that girl a mic?" Tia mutters.

I shrug as the rest of the Sedgefield High swim team gather behind her to face us, and I want to dive headfirst into the flames. This is about to be some bullshit. Erica is only swim team captain now because Hope's gone. If moving on was a competition, Erica won. She benefited the most from Hope's death, climbing up the rankings and getting scouted by colleges. Colleges that had their eyes on Hope first. If she's gonna give some tearless sob story about how much she misses Hope, I might just push her into the flames with me.

"I'm so happy we're all here tonight," Erica says into the mic as more partygoers gather closer to the fire. "And we all know who would be the loudest one here tonight. The lovely, incomparable, and sorely missed, Hope Jackson."

I forget all about my mindful breathing and groan. If there were a hundred eyes on me before, I'm sure there are thousands now. Tia wraps her arm around my waist, shielding me as much as she can from their scrutiny. If only I could wrap her completely around me and hibernate until spring.

"As most of you know, Hope has been gone a little over six months now," Erica continues, "but it feels like only yesterday that she was screaming in my ear, 'Lean in to the stroke, Matthews.'"

The swim team giggles. They're the only ones who do. Guess we had to be there. My eyes gaze across all their faces, searching for signs of sincerity, when they land on Sherie Jacobs and linger.

The tallest and palest among them, she stands there looking like a literal cavewoman with her dusty-blond hair pulled up into a bone barrette. I wait for her to look up at me. Offer an apologetic shrug for not giving me a heads-up about this charade. She owes me that much.

Sherie was homeschooled up until ninth grade, and she and Hope grew close after hanging out at some summer swim camp for middle schoolers. In fact, it was Hope who convinced Sherie to enroll in our high school. Swim with the big leagues to get scouted by huge universities. The transition was awkward, nay, brutal. Case in point, she showed up the first day of high school with a Powerpuff Girls lunch box. I thought I'd do her a solid, let her know that nobody carried those anymore. She came into the cafeteria the next day with a Bluey lunch box instead. Still, Hope wanted to take her under her wing, which meant that I took her under my wing. Which, in turn, meant that nobody fucked with her. But after Hope died, Sherie latched on to her precious swim team and left me adrift.

I squint my eyes at Sherie and use the force or whatever to get her to glance at me. But she just smooths down her leopard-print, shapeless shift dress as if she's passing time for this speech to be over.

"This school year has been tough without her."

Oh my God, Erica is still going.

"And Lord knows the past few months of school were tough on Hope."

"No shit," Tia says, her voice now above a mutter. She wants to remind everyone of their hypocrisy. Of the lies they spewed about Hope in the hallways, and especially online. Tia dealt with it herself last year with her nudes, but they went for Hope's neck.

Erica clears her throat and tries to find her spot in her memorized monologue. Clearly, she didn't expect this to be a call-and-response-type deal. "So, um . . . we should . . . I hope we make our loss also our gain."

The fuck?

"That we remember that words hurt. That people hurt. And that hurt people hurt people. . . ."

A snort rips through the crowd, and there's a collective gasp. Yes, Erica is spewing bumper sticker vomit, but we're not supposed to laugh. At least, not aloud. Heads swivel until we find the culprit: Kizzy Chan. Her costume is deceivingly ethereal, all soft blues and sheer fabrics and looking like the most beautiful genie to ever float out of a lamp. But *soft* and *delicate* are the last words I'd use to describe Kizzy. She is another former friend of mine and Hope's—more so Hope. They got tight after their time at Keystone Behavioral Center two summers ago. Hope went for her depression; Kizzy for being a bitch. That's what Kizzy says, anyway. I suspect it has something to do with her anger. I once saw this girl flip out on a Subway cashier for taking too long to make her sandwich. A meltdown over a tuna melt. Spending time with her meant getting your calves ready to walk on eggshells.

Kizzy finally notices that she's pulled the attention away from the swim team and stops laughing. "My apologies." She holds up her wine cooler. "Continue."

"Thank you." Erica rolls her eyes but presses on. "All this is to say that I would love us to use this year to become better versions of ourselves. Not just for Hope, but for each other. Let's live up to her name."

Gag.

"If you don't mind, I'd love for us to pay our respects and give Hope a moment of silence." Erica bows her head, and the swim team follows suit, though Sherie lags because of fiddling with her bone barrette. Some of the other partygoers tilt their heads, too. A group of guys on the other side of the bonfire pour out some of their beer onto the sand, which is stupid, because Hope hated beer. Nobody here really knew her. Maybe not even me.

As the moment of silence drags into several moments, someone starts humming a tune. High pitched and whiny, trying to hold on to a note that's beyond their reach. Heads lift to find the source and, of course, it's Kizzy Chan.

She stops humming and closes her eyes. "'It's so haaaaarrrd, to say goodbyyyyye, to yesterdaaaay,'" she croons into her bottle, delivering an atrocious cover of the Boyz II Men oldie. Someone tries to take the drink from her, but Kizzy twists away and sings even more off-key.

"You better get your girl," Tia says to me, amusement tickling the back of her throat.

Kizzy finally loses her bottle to Wonder Woman, or someone

dressed like her. Kizzy throws up her hands and surrenders. "My bad. My bad!"

I shake my head. "She's not my girl. Not anymore." She's just someone else who ghosted me right after Hope died.

Erica murmurs a thank-you into the microphone and, gratefully, the music picks up again. The crowd disperses and reenters their evening of dancing and debauchery. The swim team heads off to wherever the hell they were before their interruption. I can't believe they allowed Erica to be their spokesperson. This is the same girl who Hope said started a campaign for the swim team to not wear the green ribbons the school counselors were passing out during Mental Health Awareness Month. *They clash with our warm-up sets*, she supposedly had said. Yet now she was the poster child for "love thy neighbor." As Sherie passes me, she gives me a meek wave with her index finger. I nod at her. Just once. That's enough for now.

"Mighty funny how Brendan pulled a vanishing act during the dedication to his girlfriend," Tia says as she unwraps her arm from me.

I catch a chill. Maybe because I no longer have Tia's body heat to rely on. Maybe because it really is about to rain. Definitely not because the sound of Brendan's name does things to me that it shouldn't do. There are thousands of Brendans in the world, but everyone at Sedgefield High knows that Brendan Jean is *the* Brendan. No last name needed. He's the quintessential tall, dark, and handsome guy but all for valid reasons.

Tall: At six foot four inches, Brendan stands a clear foot above me and is the power forward for the mighty Sedgefield Stingrays.

Dark: His dad was born in Haiti—and when he says anything in Haitian Creole, a girl loses an item of clothing.

Handsome: His eyes are shaped like almonds, and he has this dip in his chin that's not quite a cleft, not quite a dimple, but something far more powerful. And when he smiles, his face splits into two, and you can see that chip in one of his bottom teeth that he got when he fell after thwarting a game of double Dutch during third-grade recess.

Not that I've been paying attention or anything.

I play it cool and flip my twists behind my shoulder. "Is he even here? I figured he'd think he was too good to show up."

Okay, so I know Brendan will be here. Brendan's the certain someone I've been looking for, but Tia can't know that. She considers getting me out the house a badge of honor, and I want to give her that W. Besides, I'm not looking to catch up with Brendan. He and I have unfinished business. Business that I don't want Tia to have any part in. Keeping her in the dark is the safest thing for her.

Tia smirks. "Please. Brendan is not trying to miss a party. He went on a beer run, but I'm sure he's back now appealing to the masses."

Makes sense. Of course Brendan would be on the bonfire-planning crew. Everyone loves him, and he has all the qualities to charm a liquor store clerk. Everyone wants to get on the good side of the future NBA star. There's talk he'll get drafted a year after he graduates. Sooner if eligibility rules change. There was a time when he wanted Hope and me to look at colleges in North Carolina and Connecticut so he could ball out and we'd still be nearby. There was a time when Hope designed tattoos that Brendan wanted all three of us to get as soon as the last of us turned eighteen—three puzzle pieces that all fit together. There was a time when you'd look to his right, you'd see me, and to his left, you'd see Hope.

Then, Brendan Jean was my best friend. Now, he might be a murderer.

"I'll be back," I say. Tia's already on the verge of shimmying away from me to join others on the makeshift dance floor.

"And lose your place here on the sand?" She gives me a teasing smile. "For real, though. Where you going?"

I hold up my almost empty cup. "To get lit," I say.

Tia squeals in delight and blows me a kiss before joining the fray of writhing bodies near the bonfire. I watch her for a moment longer, vibing and laughing like the queen she is. Damn, I wish I could be next to her. Doing silly TikTok dances and singing loudly with the music and just enjoying the hell out of my last Halloween bonfire as a Sedgefield Stingray. I just want to be young and dumb for one final night. But Brendan Jean took that away from me.

I kick up sand on my black boots as I trek across the beach and toward the parking lot. That's where all the drinks and coolers are, so maybe that's where I'll find my former best friend. I make my way past the volleyball net, where a few classmates seem to be having their own side party. The skunky scent of marijuana envelops them as they talk and laugh and dance, and I try to quicken my pace before someone tries to pull me into their fray.

"Hey, Liv."

Too late. Two familiar figures sitting on the outskirts of the mini-party wave me over. Coko and Sy'rai. My girls. Or maybe just Hope's girls. We've lost touch over the past six months, too. While it's good to see them, I'd prefer to play this game of catch-up when I'm not already on a mission. Still, I push out a smile and inch my way toward them. They're both in leg warmers. Coko tops hers with a sparkly purple-and-green leotard, while Sy'rai has a tutu in matching colors. They both wear wigs with ombres of turquoise, purple, and pink, and the ends of their hair are joined together forming a colorful arch above them.

"We're Satin and Chenille," Coko says, eyeing me eyeing them. "From the Trolls movies."

I nod, impressed. "Which one is which?"

Coko and Sy'rai give each other a knowing smile.

"We haven't figured that out," Coko says.

"Well, you're both definitely winning the costume contest," I tell them.

"Oh, we decided to scrap that this year. Figured it was too cheugy to continue. Sorry." Coko looks me up and down. "I know you were a fan."

Okay, so they called me over here to fire shots. I refuse to take the bait, though. I raise one shoulder into a shrug. "Hey, your party. Your call." It was supposed to be our party, our call, but sometime over the summer they lost my phone number. And vice versa. Looking at them now, pinching their overly glittered faces at me under the moonlight, makes me wonder why I ever had their numbers in the first place. Why I'd spend countless hours texting them into the night and still have more to say when I saw them the next morning. Why I thought I ruled the world alongside them, and Hope, and Kizzy, and even Sherie, but standing in front of them now, I felt as though the sky was pressing down on me and pushing me through the sand.

I hitch a thumb over my shoulder. "Good seeing y'all. I was heading to the bathroom, so—"

"You rolled up with Tia Shepherd?" Sy'rai finally speaks.

I almost jump at the sound of her voice. My ears were getting accustomed to Coko throwing all the shade.

"Yeah?" I didn't mean to make it a question. That was surely only going to invite more drama.

As expected, Coko and Sy'rai exchange another look, this one a smirk.

"She's good people," I snap. "She's had my back this summer. More than I can say about anyone else."

"Come on, Liv." Coko tries tilting her head, but her attached wig prevents it. "You the one that always called that child thirsty. I mean, look at her costume. Subtle much?"

A snicker escapes Sy'rai's mouth before she covers it with her hand. Coko joins in. Their shoulders vibrating up and down as they trade silent barbs about Tia. For a moment, I see myself sitting in between them. Cracking up about some other girl's costume. Throwing petty jabs if anyone outside our circle dared to walk up and say hi to us. It all felt so long ago, but also just like yesterday. I fight the urge to vomit right on their leg warmers.

"Next time you want to talk about how parched someone is, maybe spend less money on the discount bin at Claire's. Broke-ass JoJo Siwas." I didn't realize I said the last part out loud until Sy'rai gasped. Oh well. I turn on my heel and continue my mission.

"Emo bitch," Coko says, loud enough for me to hear, but I keep walking. Fuck them. Fuck this sand ruining my Prada combat boots. Fuck this party. I just need to do what I came here to do so that I can be finished with it all. Find Brendan.

It's not like he'll be hard to miss. Just find the tallest Black dude with a circle of groupies around him. As I get closer to the parking lot, though, another tall Black guy leaps from the cooler that he's been using as his chair and jogs over to me.

Dayvon Jenkins. Brendan's boy, Hope's neighbor, and my . . . I'm not sure what he is to me. He's not sure, either, as his face alters between confusion and contentment with every step he takes toward me.

"Hey," he says once he's close enough. He smiles, and it makes his eyes pinch. And yep, he's still cute. His thick hair is pulled back into immaculate stitch braids, which puts his clear, tanned skin on full display. He wears a smoking jacket à la Hugh Hefner, which works well for his sleepy, bedroom eyes and broad chest.

Any other hetero girl would get weak in the knees from being this close to Dayvon, so, clearly, there's something wrong with me. Dayvon's just never made me feel like there was.

"I'm surprised you're here." He shakes his head quickly. "I mean, I'm glad you're here. Just didn't . . . expect you."

"Yeah. Well, free drinks." I don't know why I say that. Everyone knows I'm not a huge drinker. And as much as it would be nice to shoot the shit and catch up with Dayvon, fuck this party. I can't with any more interruptions. I lift on my toes to peer over his shoulder, and it's not until he scratches his head that I realize how much of an ass I'm being.

"Sorry," I say as I settle back on my heels. "I'm a bit rusty at these events now."

Dayvon's mouth curves up into a small smile. "Same old, same old. Get drunk, get crunk, get home."

"Oh, is that all? You might have to school me on the art of getting *crunk*. I think the last person who mentioned it was my great-uncle at the family cookout."

Dayvon throws back his head and laughs. That's one good thing about him. He's never too cool to cackle. "Wow. You got jokes? How about we refill your cup and you can talk about my mama next?"

I don't have the heart to ditch him. You know how some people have a punchable face? Dayvon's the complete opposite. He has the face of someone you just want to feed heart-sprinkled cupcakes to. I don't have to search for an escape plan because at that moment, near the cars, a huddle of boys behind Dayvon start pumping their fists and chanting in dude-bro fashion. *Go, go, go*, like frat guys at a kegger. Asher Cohen's the loudest of them all because Asher Cohen is always the loudest in any room. His dark brown hair is slicked back with an obscene amount of hair gel, and he bangs his chest under his clear raincoat. Underneath the coat is a pin-striped suit. Great. He's Patrick Bateman from *American Psycho*. And here I thought Jace Martinez had the douchiest costume of the night.

One of the guys, with a hairline about two inches farther back than it should be at his age, breaks from the crowd and hurls about a foot away from Dayvon and me. Nice.

"Cleanup, aisle five!"

I know that husky voice from anywhere. The chorus of laughter that follows only confirms my suspicion: Brendan. Nobody else can get away with something that corny except Brendan. He gets away with everything. The huddle parts for him as he walks over to the guy with the receding hairline and pats him on the back.

"You good, bruh?" he asks. Even leaning forward, he towers over the guy. The guy mumbles something incoherent before taking another chug from his beer bottle. Brendan laughs as the guy bows to the applause from the crowd. It's only when the drunken dude trips back over to the huddle that Brendan looks up . . . and spots me.

I take a deep breath. So does he.

The night has officially begun.

TWO

FOR ABOUT FIVE SECONDS, THE MUSIC STOPS AND everyone freezes mid–fist bump or two-step. It's just Brendan's eyes trailing me. My eyes trailing him. As though we haven't seen each other for months. And in a way, we haven't. After Hope, our Venn diagram of friends split into two drifting circles. Him with his boys and his fans. Me with Tia, my meds, and my head in the books. Anything to push through the start of my senior year.

But now . . . here we are.

Let me pause for a moment. Talk a bit about this boy in front of me and the dead girl in between us. Me, Hope, and Brendan. A trio for as long as I've known the word *trio.* We were six years old and the only Black kids in Brendan's mom's after-school childcare program.

She ran it out of her house and treated it like an academic enrichment program. Whenever it was time to rotate learning centers, Hope, Brendan, and I gravitated to each other like planets, moons, and stars. After a while, Mrs. Jean grew bored of trying to break up the solar system.

We were inseparable ever since. The summer before high school is when the cracks began to surface. Hope was away at camp again, and Brendan was spending a lot of time at my house. Mrs. Jean was on husband number three by then. Brendan didn't tell me much about him yet, but I knew things were rocky enough that he'd rather mow the grass with my dad in ninety-degree weather than go home. In between yard work, he'd find his way to me. We'd film silly TikToks, or play *Tomb Raider*, or simply vibe to whatever song we were feeling at the moment. I started to look forward to those moments. Where it was just me and Brendan. And slowly but instantly, I also started caring about how I looked when he came over. Gone were the baggy sweats and sloppy buns—the second half of the summer became all about tennis skirts and corkscrew curls.

Then there was that one moment. Brendan and I were mouthing the lyrics to Silk Sonic's "Leave the Door Open" for another one of our ridiculous videos. He was giving a horrific Bruno Mars interpretation when his hand found my cheek and we froze. Both forgetting the lyrics. Both forgetting that we were even filming. His hand lingered, and my heart drummed all the way up to my throat. Then, as though someone else took over my body, my mouth turned into his palm . . . and I kissed it. I kissed his fucking hand. Brendan didn't say anything. He didn't move. Just stared at me in a way that made me feel like the delicious dinner he'd been thinking about all day.

Then my dad entered the family room and we separated as quickly as cheap Velcro.

"Ready to tackle the rosebushes today?" my dad asked Brendan, oblivious as all get out.

"I have to tell you something," Hope said to me on the night before our first day of high school. We were coordinating our 'fits for the week, but she paused out of the blue with this intro to a confession. It worked for me, though. I'd been trying to find a way to break the ice about Brendan. I'd been dying to tell someone how he made my insides all gummy when he smiled at me. How I'd started to enjoy the smell of his sweat when he entered my house after doing yard work. How he kept reaching for my hand when my parents weren't looking, quietly raising his eyebrows at me. *You're feeling something, too*, his eyes seemed to say.

And I did. Oh God, I did. I'd been too shy to talk about it, but maybe all I needed was an extra push from my best girlfriend to send me over the edge.

"Me, too," I said, and I could feel my face get warm at the admission.

"Okay. Me first." Hope dropped my jeans to the floor, then crawled next to me on my bed. She wrapped her arms around my stomach and tackled me against the pillows. We giggled as we untangled our limbs until we settled into our normal chilling position—me on my back, Hope's head snuggled on top of my chest. "I think I'm gonna ask Brendan out."

My heart froze, then shattered into one hundred pieces. I prayed that Hope didn't hear the explosion. "Wh-what?" I managed, trying to keep my voice composed but ultimately failing.

"I know!" Hope shifted away from me and snatched a pillow from under her head before smothering her face with it and squealing. She caught her breath and peeked back at me. "I can't believe it! That's weird, right? It's stupid weird."

I opened my mouth to form a response, but, thankfully, she kept going.

"I mean, it's Brendan. The guy who used to fart along to 'Pop! Goes the Weasel' when we were kids. But . . . I don't know, Liv. This summer, his voice has gotten deeper and his shoulders are all big, and he's just so . . . manly. And when the hell did he get so cute? Doesn't he look like Ralph Angel from *Queen Sugar*?" She squealed again, and I forced a smile. A smile that didn't reach my eyes.

"But you've been at swim camp all summer," was all I could say.

Hope propped the pillow underneath her again and gave me a conspiratorial smile. "We snuck phone calls like every night. We even FaceTimed a few times. And, Liv? He blew me kisses through the phone before we had to hang up. Like actual kisses."

She gave a dreamy sigh, and I wanted to die. Right then and

there. Just stop breathing so I didn't have to hear any more about this courtship. While Brendan was holding hands with me, he was virtually smooching Hope at practically the same time. Why didn't he tell me he talked to her every night? He saw me almost every day this summer, you'd think it would come up. Unless . . . unless he was catching feelings with her and didn't know how to tell me.

"It's weird, right?"

I wasn't sure when she started talking again, but she was staring at me. Eyes begging for my approval.

"I know jumping from friends to lovers can be tricky, but people also say that the best relationships have a strong friendship as the foundation. Right?"

Wow, she was really into him. I could hear it in her voice. It was full of rainbows and flowers, dripping with sugary optimism that she usually saved for gushing about that actor Trevor Jackson. I hadn't seen Hope get excited about someone in real life in . . . never. I hadn't seen Hope get this excited about a lot of things, and I felt this strange urge to hold on to this moment and pull it out on one of her darker days. Even if that meant my heart would remain shattered.

"Lovers?" I asked, scrunching my nose, then proceeded to gag.

Hope playfully shoved me, and I shoved her back. We kept this up for a while, until her head found her way on top of my chest again. We lay there in silence for what felt like an hour, almost like we knew this would be the last normal moment between us and wanted to savor it.

"We're gonna be okay, Liv," Hope said, as though sensing my fears.

I wanted to believe her, even as the floor seemed to crumble underneath us.

Now, standing at the beach across from Brendan, the sand beneath my feet feels just as shaky.

"Liv Porter," Brendan says as the music replays and everyone resumes moving. "Look at you."

"Yeah. Look at me." I raise my Solo cup to him and take a tiny sip. He watches me with the wonder of someone seeing a shooting star for the first time. My cheeks get warm.

Someone clears his throat, and I remember Dayvon to my right. Asher's also here now. When the hell did he walk over? Brendan blinks and notices them, too.

"You wanted more to drink, right?" Dayvon reminds me. He takes a few steps until he's in front of me, partially blocking Brendan from my view.

"What you sipping on?" Brendan's closer now, bumping his arm against Dayvon's shoulder and nudging him aside.

"Hopefully, not this anymore."

I hold up my cup, and Brendan takes it from me. Sniffs it and makes a face.

"I was going to find her something fruity," Dayvon says. He gives me a smile to pick up where we left off.

"You go do that, then." Brendan hands my cup to Dayvon and holds out a hand to me. "Come holla at me real quick."

I look down at his hand and try to remember the last time we've touched. Just the thought sends my stomach into a frenzy. So I stop thinking and shove my hand into his. There are no fireworks or shooting cannons. Just familiarity. Like slipping on an old but favorite T-shirt.

Brendan steers me away, and I give an apologetic smile to Dayvon, whose left holding my cup with a small grimace. Asher says something in Dayvon's ear, then cackles like the idiot he is. Dayvon stares at me for a beat more, his expression as hard to read as a William Faulkner novel. He finally trudges in the opposite direction with Asher close on his heels.

Brendan leads me back down the beach to one of the empty lifeguard towers and releases my hand. Who told him to do that? He leans against one of the wooden beams and smiles at me.

"I don't know why you're smiling," I say. "That was stupid rude."

"What was stupid rude?"

I nudge my head toward the drinks and parking lot.

Brendan blows air between his lips. "Those my boys. I can punch them in the eye and five minutes later, we're dapping each other up."

"Asher? Yeah. But Dayvon?" I make a face and tell him I'm not highly convinced.

"I can call Day over and ask him. That's what you want? Give my boy a chance to strike out again?" He waves his hands and starts to call Dayvon's name. I pull his arms down and try to cover his mouth, though I have to get on my tippy-toes to make any ground. He laughs and steps back from me.

"I hate you," I say. "And he didn't necessarily strike out. Double dates are awkward, especially ones where you keep being all up in our grill."

"Hey, I was just trying to break the ice. Plus, I'm not the one who kept pulling you into the bathroom to strategize or whatever. That was all . . ." He can't even start to form her name. *Hope.* It's stuck somewhere in his throat and can't get past his Adam's apple. He gives me a sheepish grin and reaches for one of my twists instead. "Still a fan of the nineties, I see. How many white folks here asked if you were Moesha?"

I laugh, and the looming tension between us dissipates. "Like eighty percent. A handful of your Black friends called me Brandy, too, though. Don't let the melanin fool you." I tug at the bottom of his basketball jersey. "I see you didn't have to go far for your costume."

"You know I'm not into the whole dressing-up thing." Brendan shrugs. "Besides, lots of kids want to be basketball players when they grow up."

"Lots of kids want to be Brendan Jean when they grow up," I correct.

It's true. Brendan's magic on the court. Unlike anything I've ever seen. He moves and leaps with the grace of a Julliard dancer yet manages to ram the ball into the hoop with so much fervor that he's snapped the rim on more than one occasion. College scouts had their eye on him when he was in eighth grade playing JV ball. Now, NBA teams are chomping at the bit for him to turn nineteen and become eligible for the draft.

A small smile escapes his lips as he pounds his fist against the beam to the music. "Check out Olivia Porter. Crawling out from her hole with guns blazing."

My face falls. "I wasn't in a hole."

"Well, you weren't around."

"Just because I haven't been to parties or swooning at your practices doesn't mean I haven't been around. I've just been doing my own thing."

Brendan stops smiling, too, realizing we're no longer joking. "I know you, Liv. You're the first one at a party and the last to leave. Since when did 'doing my own thing' mean becoming a recluse?"

"Since my best friend's skull cracked on the concrete next to her pool." The words come out louder and harsher than I intended them to, and I swear Brendan shrinks several inches. He's probably never heard Hope's death described in such a blunt way. I'm sure when he was questioned by the police, they cushioned it with velvet and feathers. Saying things like "Hope has *passed*" due to an "unfortunate *incident*." Just . . . no. Hope's dead because her head split open like a coconut.

"Liv." He breathes out my name like he's trying to grasp on to some former version of me. "Can you . . . not? She was your best friend. My girlfriend." There's something behind his eyes. Something sad. I'm not sure if I've seen Brendan look remotely sad in the six months since Hope's death. Always in defense mode. Quick to tell people he wasn't there and he never touched her and she was the crazy one. An odd tactic for the grieving boyfriend. But now, when it's just me and him and the James River, his guard is crumbling.

I need to remember why I'm here. I take a deep breath and dial down my anger. "Sorry. It's just . . . I didn't like your word choice."

"*My* word choice?"

"You said I was in a hole, B. We technically know someone in a hole now." On instinct, I pinch the infinity pendant on my necklace.

Brendan looks at the necklace, looks at me, then nods in concession. "Noted. I won't use that word again. I'll just call you a hermit instead."

"Hermits still have phones," I say. "You could've reached out if you were so concerned."

"And a phone works two ways."

The audacity of this boy. Clearly, his budding fame has already gone to his head. "I think we both know that reaching out to you was a little complicated."

"Woooow." Brendan blinks a few times as if I'm just coming into focus. "Couldn't have the accused murderer ruining your reputation, right? Forget that he went through the checkout line with you the first time you had to buy tampons. Or that he cosplayed

Legend of Zelda with you for Comic Con three years in a row."

I hug myself. "I don't remember you being accused of anything, Brendan. The police ruled Hope's death as suicide."

"Exactly!" Brendan takes a beat when his voice carries out to the sea. "So, can we stop doing this, please? This weird song and dance? I miss my friend. Can I speak to my friend tonight?"

There go those sad eyes again. I look at them, and we're thirteen years old, and I'm trying to cheer him up after Kiara Morris broke up with him for having quote-unquote Kylie Jenner lips.

She's mad because she doesn't have any lips, I told him. *When people sketch her, they use a hyphen for her mouth.*

Hope even drew a picture of Kiara to prove my point. Gave Kiara stink waves around her armpits to boot. Brendan laughed until he peed himself.

He's right. I miss my friend, too.

The sky rumbles and rivals the hip-hop bass line playing in the background. Brendan looks up and whistles. "Fuuuck. It seems like it's about to throw down. I don't remember hearing that it was going to rain."

"You know how Virginia does," I say. "Rain one minute, sunshine and birds tweeting the next."

"And don't even get started about wintertime. Seventy degrees one day and seven degrees twelve hours later. You think we're getting snow this year? Damn, I hope we don't get snow."

"'In winter nothing more dreary, in summer nothing more divine.'"

Brendan raises a curious eyebrow.

"It's from *Wuthering Heights*," I say.

He nods, the recognition tugging at both eyebrows now. "I ain't hear anyone mention that book in a minute."

He's thinking about Hope again without saying her name. Last year, Hope carried around that novel like an accessory. I didn't get it—her attachment to the characters, the words, the mood. She talked about it so much that certain passages got stuck in my head like a pop song. But that was Hope. Taking the unconventional thing and making it *the* thing. Look at Sherie. Hell, look at me.

Brendan hisses through his teeth as he laughs. "We're old as shit," he says. "Talking about the weather like we're rubbing arthritis cream on our knees."

He pinches my ear and gives it a playful tug. We're kids again—him joking about my small ears and me eating up those small moments when he touched me.

I take tiny steps toward him until my cheek is pressed against his chest. I don't wrap my arms around him. Still, he gets it. He envelops me inside his long arms, and I could stay like this. In his cocoon with the river behind us and everything in front of us. If only it was that simple.

"You know," Brendan begins as he rests his chin on top of my hat, "I loved your duet with Monica." He erupts in laughter as I push him away.

"I hate you," I say again. He sings the chorus to "The Boy Is Mine," and I kick sand at him. But I laugh, too. I can't help it.

He points at me. "Your hands are still empty. Where's Dayvon with your drink?"

"I think he's mad at us. We kinda ditched him."

Brendan swats away any notion that anyone could possibly stay mad at him. "He'll be all right. Come on, let's find something ourselves, then."

He reaches for me again, and as much as I want to take his hand, I can't. I know what happens next if I do. I sought him out specifically for the what's next. It all feels wrong at the moment. Talking to him for just a few minutes made me miss the days when we talked for hours about nothing and everything. While I was group chatting with my girls, Brendan and I had our own text thread. Sharing jokes and dreams and even nightmares. Things I wanted to tell Hope but knew that only Brendan would get. Right now, Brendan and I seem like we can fix whatever tear was in our friendship—and I want to keep the possibility open. Keep hope in a life beyond Hope.

"You know what?" I say finally. "I'm good. I've kept you away from your fans for too long."

Brendan smirks. "It ain't like that. And even if it was, they could wait. We still have some catching up to do."

Damn. He's not going away easily. It's almost like he wants me to go through with everything tonight.

"I agree," I say. "But I need to . . . take care of something. I'll find you."

He tucks his chin to his chest and pouts. "How I know you ain't trying to ghost me?"

I give him a small smile, keep my lips together when all I want to do is shout at him, *Go! Run away!* "I guess you'll just have to take my word for it," I say, turning around before I change my mind . . .

And crash right into Kizzy Chan and her wine cooler.

"What. The. Fuck," she says, even though I'm the one dripping wet. "Are you a toddler? Do you have no sense of direction?"

"Sorry," I mumble, shaking out my limbs like a drunken dog.

"You cool?" Brendan asks me.

"Is she cool?" Kizzy snaps. "This was the last Jamaican Me Happy in the cooler, and you're asking if *she's* cool?"

"It's basically a bottle of juice, Kizzy. Stop acting like somebody knocked over your Cîroc."

She blinks at him. "Well, if anyone knows something about knocking things over . . ."

Brendan's face darkens. "Come again?"

Kizzy raises both eyebrows, more amused than fearful. She even takes a step toward Brendan. "I said—"

"It's cool," I say, before it goes any further. "It's all cool. Everyone's cool. Especially me." I take off my hat and dab my shirt with it.

Kizzy rolls her eyes, and even while she's pissed, she's stunning in her *I Dream of Jeannie* knockoff. Her high cheekbones and narrow hips could make muumuus look runway ready.

"Hey, look." I point at some girl in a naughty referee costume farther down the beach. She giggles as she does what I assume is dancing. "I think she has a Jamaican Me Happy—and her bottle still looks full."

Kizzy purses her lips. I can tell she wants to say something, but the idea of a fresh drink is too tempting. "Uh-huh," she finally mutters. "You should find something dry to wear." She raises an eyebrow at me before heading toward the naughty referee.

"I can't stand that girl," Brendan says. "She doesn't pay attention to where she's going then acts like we're the ones who fucked up her night. I don't even know why Hope—" He stops, his anger trampling over the eggshells we've been tiptoeing on since we were reacquainted tonight.

Kizzy says something in Naughty Referee's ear. The girl blushes and covers her mouth with her hand. She's so preoccupied with Kizzy's words that she doesn't realize that Kizzy slips the drink right out of her hand. Kizzy catches me watching her and then raises the bottle at me. Cheers.

"You want to get out of here?" I ask, glancing at Brendan again.

His eyes shift to me. "What did you have in mind?"

THREE

THREE YEARS AGO

THE ONLY THING WORSE THAN BEING A FRESHMAN in high school is being a freshman in high school listening to a lecture on self-care and wellness. Okay, maybe a lecture on safe sex and abstinence would be more cringe-worthy, but I definitely can't connect to all this crystal-collecting, woo-sah mess. I don't care about being present enough to smell the kid farting next to me when I'm still figuring out the best way to get from English on the first floor to art on the second floor before the tardy bell rings.

I glance over at Hope, sitting to my left. She looks down at her phone, which she has hidden on her lap underneath her desk. A small smile spills on one side of her mouth, and I almost reach for my phone to see if I've missed something in our group chat. But then I notice Brendan at the desk behind her, fingers flying over the phone on his lap. I don't think there's a text waiting for me—not from the flirty smile on Hope's lips. I'm still getting used to that. Not being part of their conversations. They've only been together for two weeks, the same amount of time we've been in high school, and I still can't work out where I fit into our trio.

Hope catches me looking at her, then scrunches her nose and nods toward the lead school counselor, Mrs. Sanchez, who's demonstrating some finger-tapping maneuver that's supposed to ground you, whatever the hell that means. "Relax, relate, release," Hope mouths to me, and I can just hear the thick country accent she's imitating. It's classic Whitley Gilbert from *A Different World*. Our moms hooked us onto the old sitcom, and one of our favorite episodes is when a therapist teaches that phrase to Whitley to help her get over an ex. Mimicking that line in our most atrocious Southern belle accents became our thing for an entire summer.

I snicker at the memory, feeling settled again about my place in the triangle. Hope and I still had our own inside jokes, so Brendan can send her a corny meme. It's not going to change anything.

"Okay, now that we know how to take care of ourselves," Mrs. Sanchez continues, "let's talk about how to take care of others. It's important for you all to know the signs of when your friends and classmates are not feeling well. I'm not talking about having a cold or a fever, I'm talking about not feeling well here . . ." She touches her chest. "Or here." Her other hand touches her forehead.

"So . . . I'm supposed to know when my boy has heartburn or migraines, too?" Asher asks from the back of the classroom, sending the rest of us into fits of laughter.

"Asher," our English teacher, Ms. Donaldson, warns from behind her desk.

Not only was he rude to her guest, but he was also interrupting her grading time.

"My bad, my bad," Asher says. "I'm following you, Mrs. Sanchez."

Mrs. Sanchez nods at him as though she really needed his permission to continue. "That was a good guess, but I'm talking about how we're feeling emotionally and mentally. Feelings of depression or suicidal ideation can feel like such an intimate experience, but many times, there are signs right in front of us. Who knows of something your friend might do that could indicate they need help? That they're thinking of maybe ending their life?" Her eyes roam across the room until they land on a short, curvy girl with Afro puffs and glitter eyeshadow. "Tia, right? What are your thoughts?"

A hush rolls throughout the classroom as a few of us exchange nervous glances. Everyone knew not to talk about this kind of stuff with Tia Shepherd. Not after what happened to her sister almost two years ago. The story always changes, depending on who you ask. I heard an old church lady gossiping in the grocery store that Sierra watched too many horror movies, then snapped on her mom. The police ended up shooting her with a butcher knife in her hand. Then there was that one boy in my seventh-grade gym class who insisted that his cousin used to do Sierra's hair. His cousin said that Sierra used to show up at appointments with a different serial killer biography each time, and constantly talked about how much she hated her mom. *What if she wanted to eat her mom like Jeffrey Dahmer ate his victims?* the boy, who thankfully moved away last summer, had asked.

Granted, Mrs. Sanchez is just getting to know us all this year but . . . York County isn't *that* big. She had to know talking about anything related to this mental illness stuff was off-limits for Tia Shepherd.

"Um . . ." Tia shifted in her seat, and I wanted to ask for a pass to the bathroom or clinic. Anywhere but here in the thick of this awkwardness. "Maybe they want to start giving their things away?"

"Good, Tia," Mrs. Sanchez said, a little too enthusiastic to be talking about signs of suicide. "Yes, giving away possessions can be a sign that someone is thinking of ending their life, but it certainly isn't the only one. Who else has any ideas?"

With that, Tia broke the ice. One by one, my classmates raise their hands to answer the question, and I relax in my seat. My shoulders slump and remind me of the whole "relax, relate, release" line, so I turn to Hope to give her my best Whitley impression. Except . . . Hope's distracted. Brendan's leaning forward now, practically draped on top of his desk to say something in Hope's ear. He's moved on from the cloak of texting—now he's sharing his messages up close and personal. Hope giggles and squirms a little in her seat. What in the world could he be saying to her that makes her whole body respond like that? A regular ol' joke isn't going to make Hope squirm. She only gets wiggly like that when she's excited, like when a shirtless pic of her favorite actor drops online. Wait—has Hope seen Brendan shirtless? Has Hope seen Brendan shirtless while they were alone? How often have they been alone together? It's only been two weeks. Far too short a time to be seeing each other shirtless while being alone. In a bedroom. And if their shirts are off, it's only a matter of time that their pants are off, too. And if everything is coming off then—holy shit! Are Hope and Brendan having *sex*?

"Olivia?"

My name snaps me out of the hole I've been sinking into, and I find Mrs. Sanchez's eyes on me—as well as half of the class's. My cheeks get warm and it's my time to squirm.

"Yes?" I ask.

"I was waiting for your answer," Mrs. Sanchez says.

Okay, now my cheeks are on fire. My answer? My answer to what? I can't look like I'm not paying attention. Mrs. Sanchez and Ms. Donaldson don't know me that well. They don't know that I'm actually a good student who makes good grades and usually reads more than the assigned pages for homework out of pure curiosity. I take a deep breath and try again.

"That was my answer," I say. "Yes."

Mrs. Sanchez raises an eyebrow as a few snickers rumble behind me. "All right. Well, listening to emo music is not necessarily a sign of depression or suicide, though many people do find solace in its lyrics. Personally, Dashboard Confessional has pulled me out of a few dark spaces."

The snickers evolve into laughter. Lots of it, coming for me at all angles. I want to join in, but I don't know if they're laughing at Mrs. Sanchez's interesting taste of music, or if they're laughing at me and my cluelessness. The loudest laughter comes from Tia Shepherd, who turns in her desk and laughs toward my face. Is this girl seriously laughing at me? When the entire class, including me, kept a lid on her family drama in front of the school counselor for *her* sake?

I find myself raising my hand just as Mrs. Sanchez switches the PowerPoint slide.

"Yes, Olivia?"

"Violence," I say, folding my hands together. "Is violence a sign of depression or other mental illnesses?"

Mrs. Sanchez tilts her head in thought. "Sure, abnormal aggressive behavior can be a sign that something is wrong."

"Abnormally aggressive?" My palms start to sweat, but I keep going. "Like attacking your own mother? That would suggest some deep psychological damage, right?"

"Oooh," someone bellows behind me and, once again, the class is in an uproar.

This time, though, they're not laughing at me. They're laughing with me. Only I'm not laughing—at least, not really. Especially when I see Tia pull her hoodie over her puffs and slouch farther into her seat, as though those simple acts can make her disappear.

Hope slaps my arm, but when I look over at her, she has this bemused grin on her face. *Who are you, and what have you done with my best friend?*

"Savage," Brendan says to me, as he covers his mouth and laughs along with everyone else.

Both of their eyes are on me. They're no longer in their private bubble.

It took about three minutes for Mrs. Sanchez to calm everyone down. Two of those minutes I spent talking to Ms. Donaldson out in the hallway.

"I know we're just getting to know each other," she said to me. "But something tells me that you're better than this."

I'd nodded, wanting to agree with her but knowing deep down there was uncertainty. I'd like to be the better person, but I'd also prefer everyone to laugh at someone else than at me. I'd much prefer for my two best friends to include me in their moments.

The bell rings, letting us know that the period is over. Everyone scurries out of class, but I take my time to gather my things. I glance over at Tia, hoping that she takes a little longer, too. I want to apologize, and it's easier to do so when there's no audience. But Tia's on the move. So fast, in fact, that she leaves behind her notebook. It must've slipped off her desk as she rushed out, too preoccupied to feel it fall by her feet. I should grab it for her. Maybe find her at lunch to return it and give her my apology then.

"Liv." Hope waits for me at the door with an impatient, yet

playful, raised eyebrow. "You coming, or are you trying to be late to art again?"

Brendan peeks his head back into the classroom. "You taking art is like me tryna take AP Calculus. The math ain't mathing, bruh."

They waited for me. They both waited for me. They didn't remember to wait for me yesterday, or the day before, but they're waiting for me now. I slip my backpack on one of my shoulders and step over Tia's notebook.

"The day you take AP Calculus is the day I know to say my prayers because the end is near."

Brendan and Hope laugh as I make my way in between them. The three of us walking in perfect harmony with each other, ready to take on the rest of the day.

FOUR

NOW

"SHUT THE FUCK UP," BRENDAN SAYS AS WE DRIVE to the empty house almost an hour later, my headlights spilling across one of the limestone walls facing us. And there's a lot of limestone. Mom was inspired by the homes in Tuscany when she designed this model. Everything from the terra-cotta roof tile to the marble accents over the windows takes me back to three springs ago, when Hope and I walked around Lucca, Italy. Eating gelatos, throwing flirty smiles at the local men, and feeling very grown—though neither of us had our learner's permit yet, and Hope had only started having a period a few months before that trip. Still, nobody could tell us nothing in our Dolce & Gabbana Half Print sunglasses.

"Shut the fuck up," Brendan says again as I put the car in park on top of the gravel road in front of the home. It's supposed to be a circular driveway with stone finishing around a flower bed in the center, but the builders haven't poured the concrete yet. When they do, it'll be the cherry on top of an already delicious house.

"Yep. It's my mom's biggest project yet after starting her own architectural firm," I say, nodding as if I had anything to do with Mom's success. I'm not too cute to admit I'm proud of her, though. It's tough for a woman to climb the ranks in a male-driven industry, especially a Black woman. She'd made a name for herself in her old firm but kept getting overlooked for partner. So she left and started her own shit and now makes beautiful creations like the home in front of us.

"Mrs. Porter making them stacks on stacks on stacks." Brendan squints his eyes and leans forward, trying to get a better look at this mammoth of a house. "Where's the garage?

"In the back. There's two of them. One holds three cars and the other holds two."

Brendan blinks and shakes his head, as if he's trying to compute what I just said. "Five cars? Plus this big-ass driveway? How many people they expect to live up in here?"

"I think Mom said it can have up to seven bedrooms, depending on the features the buyer wants to include. Five and a half bathrooms total. But it's a little over thirteen thousand square feet, so if it were me, I'd nix that seventh bedroom for a bigger loft on the top floor."

"*But it's only thirteen thousand square feet*," Brendan mocks, his voice high and nasally and nothing like mine. He then shakes his head again and laughs. "Fuck you."

I clutch my chest and pretend to be appalled. "Fuck *me*? You asked me about the living space, right?"

"If only you can hear yourself sometimes."

"I hear myself every day. Voice of an angel. That's why I walk around looking and feeling blessed and highly favored." I give Brendan a smug smile, and he returns it. We fall into our pokes and jabs as easily as bad habits. That's what we are to each other. A fix we can't easily shake. "You want to check out the house or naw?"

Brendan scrunches his nose like my question stinks but unfastens his seat belt. I knew he couldn't resist. Something thuds in my car as I cut off the engine and my blood turns to ice.

"That doesn't sound good," Brendan says.

No, it doesn't. But the more we linger on the topic, the more he'll want to check it out. "My dad borrowed my car to go to his bowling league the other night," I say. "He left his crap in my trunk." I roll my eyes to show my annoyance.

"I can't believe a man who wears Louis Vuitton slippers around his house is that corny." He shakes his head in mock disgust, then slips out the car.

I sigh, and my blood thaws—then I'm right behind him. He places both hands on top of his head and lets out a whistle as he's able to take in the full scope of the home. It takes up a massive amount of land, which is why Mom couldn't build it in an already established residential area. She found a plot on the outskirts of Williamsburg, about an hour away from Huntington Beach and in a county more known for farms and pumpkin festivals than traffic lights and fast-food restaurants. There's a shopping center with a Target and Starbucks about ten miles out, but for the most part, you have to drive through an insane number of woods just to get here. The owner of this house is going to be someone who loves to entertain but who also loves their privacy. And it is *private.* Which makes it a perfect spot for tonight.

I glance back at my car, and nothing seems amiss. I hold back my sigh of relief. "Once you sign your contract and become a Laker, this can be your vacation home. Unless you'd want something even bigger," I say as I step onto the loggia. Not the front porch. I made the mistake of calling it that in front of Mom, and she corrected me in a thick Italian accent that bordered on offensive.

Brendan smirks. "Come on now. It's Warriors or bust for me."

I cross my arms across my chest and give him a look.

"But you know, I ain't trying to hang up the phone on nobody just yet," he finishes.

"I bet. Come on. Let's check out the inside." I punch numbers onto the keypad on the front door, then push it open.

"Welcome home," a feminine, automatic voice says in greetings.

Brendan flinches and holds up both fists.

I laugh at him. "Relax. It's just part of the smart-home system the contractor convinced my mom to install." I tap the touchscreen of the system panel on the wall of the entrance. After a few moments, the lights of the great room and adjoining kitchen flicker on.

"Daaaamn," Brendan says as he scans the space. He marvels at the marble kitchen island. Whistles at the portico behind the double doors on the other side of the great room. Gawks at the two-story ceiling with the exposed beams. On the top floor, there's a loft that overlooks the entire great room. Like royalty looking down on the peasants.

I love seeing this house through his eyes. I was just like him the first time I saw it only somewhat finished, but now I expect it to be grand with every visit. I give it the same indifference as a sunny day in summer. Like, of course the weather is supposed to be nice. But there's something about his enthusiasm, his innocence, that I want to bottle and sip on during my lowest moments. I can watch him be this giddy for hours . . . but I don't have hours.

I balance the difficult act of giving him a rushed tour without making him feel like we're in a rush. We bypass the study, laundry room, and family room to take a closer look at the walk-in pantry, dining room, and primary suite. On the upper level, I let him check out the loft and covered balcony—and pause for him to flub a few lines from the balcony scene of *Romeo and Juliet*. There are four other bedrooms he was dying to see, but I told him later. We'd have time. Then I lead him down to the basement level, though this space is far too fancy to be considered *just* a finished basement. It's pretty much its own living quarters, with a snack bar, rec room, exercise room, media room, and a room to do with whatever the hell you want, though Mom envisions setting it up as either an office or spare bedroom. I take Brendan past all this with zero flair, because I know what he truly wants to see.

"And this," I say, tapping my hand on the smart-home panel next to the door, "is the indoor basketball court."

Lights illuminate across the ceiling in one sweeping motion.

Brendan's face slackens with awe as he takes a few steps onto the court. "Sheesh," he says, nearly out of breath. As though his astonishment is so vast that it eats up his whole chest. He walks to the center and rubs the top of his head with both hands again, spinning around slowly.

"Well," I say, watching him with the same awe he has for the court, "what do you think?"

"What do I think?" he repeats in disbelief. "I think draw up the paperwork. I'm moving into this bitch tonight."

"I thought you always wanted to leave VA, though."

"Shit, not if this is what Virginia has to offer." He bounces an invisible ball and dribbles it between his legs. "Besides, during my gap year, you know I'd still want to be within driving distance of home. Leaving was more of—" Brendan winces like he stubs his toe but then shakes it off. He jumps and shoots his invisible ball from the half-court line. Then roars into his hands like some rowdy fans in the stands.

"You can say her name," I say, cutting into his cheers.

Brendan pauses and looks at me.

I almost lose my nerve but push forward. "You're not going to burst into flames if you do. Or drop dead on the spot."

Brendan chews on something in his mouth. His cheek? His tongue? Maybe his words. "True," he says finally. "But you do realize that you didn't say her name, either." He tilts his head to one side, challenging me.

I think about withdrawing, but I need to be up for anything tonight. Pushing him might make the rest of the night go easier. I cross my arms across my chest. "Hope," I say, so quiet that it barely registers in my throat. I swallow and try again. "Hope." Firmer this time.

Brendan claps his hands together, the sarcasm reverberating with each slap.

"Hope." I'm louder, working to overpower his applause. "Hope!"

Brendan stops clapping. "All right. You proved your point."

"Hope!" I can't stop now. I'm an engine, and Hope's name is my fuel. "Hope. Hope. *Hope!*"

"All right!" Brendan's voice booms off the walls, and my jaws clench shut. "What the fuck is wrong with you? Should you have even driven us here? How much did you have to drink?"

He's staring at me like half my mind is spilling on the floor between us. I force a weak smile and sigh. "Apparently, not enough." I grab one of the basketballs from a cart against the wall and toss it to Brendan. "Here, have some fun with an actual ball. I'm going to grab the beers I stole from the party."

Brendan bounces the ball once, twice. Eyeballing me the whole time. "You know what I think? You're starting to take all that emo music a little too seriously. Next thing I know, you're going to shave all your hair, get a nose ring, and ask everyone to call you Willow Smith."

I sigh through my nose, pushing out all the tension that was in the air before. "Like you weren't bopping to Willow during the pandemic like everyone else."

"I have no idea what you're talking—" Brendan erupts into the first lines of "Meet Me at Our Spot," dribbling the ball to the beat.

I laugh and shake my head as he continues to sing—off pitch but full of conviction. "Sing it, B," I coax. This only compels him to sing even more off tune as he proceeds to dribble down the court.

"I'm getting refreshments!" I call out to him as he pretends to block a pass. I hurry toward my oversized purse by the door and pull out two cans of lukewarm beer. I pop the tops and glance over my shoulder. Brendan jumps up and dunks the ball, hanging from the rim as he croons out the chorus. He really doesn't need anything else to drink.

But I made a promise.

I dig into my purse again until my hand grazes a small envelope. I open it and eye the crushed powdery contents inside and let out a shaky breath. *I can do this, I can do this. No, I* will *do this. For Hope.*

I stop thinking and pour the powder into one of the cans before shoving the envelope back into my bag.

"Where's the applause?"

Brendan is over me quicker than I can blink. I jump and almost drop our drinks.

"Did I scare you?"

I force a smile. "From your inability to stay on-key? Yes."

Brendan laughs and takes one of the beers from my hand before I can even pass it to him. Leaving me with the tainted one.

"Wait," I say, my voice echoing off the walls. "I already drank from that one."

Brendan scans my face, waiting for the punch line. "Oookay," he says finally. "You caught the new strand of Covid or something?"

"Better safe than sorry, right?" I swap our cans. "Besides, I don't know where those lips have been."

"I mean, you can find out." He says it so quickly, so quietly, that I almost miss it. But then he stares at me. No, not just stares, he *researches* me as though he wants to take in every slope, every curve, every inch of my body. The air in the room gets thin as I try to wrap my head around it all. Brendan wants to kiss me. Brendan Jean wants to kiss me. Brendan Jean is standing an inch away from me wanting to do things to me in this empty house. Things that I've wanted to do with him since I was thirteen years old, if I'm being honest with myself.

I take in a breath, then it comes out my nose like *Fuuuuuuuck*.

But no. *No.* That's not what tonight is for. I push out a smile. "I'm sure you say that to all the ladies." I take a small sip of my beer even though my throat is too tight to swallow it.

Brendan's face falls just a little bit. So quick that the average person wouldn't notice the shift. But I'm well-versed in the mannerisms of Brendan Jean and he definitely looked . . . disappointed. He raises the can of beer to his lips and pauses to sniff it.

"Ugh, I hate the cheap shit," he mutters before taking a sip. And then another. And then a huge gulp.

I squeeze my fingers around my can until it crinkles from the pressure. The can pops between us, but Brendan keeps drinking. And I keep letting him.

"Yeah," I force out. The more I talk, the less guilty I'll feel. At least, I hope so. "That's what Jace said, too."

Brendan makes a face like he just tasted something even fouler than the beer. "Jace? You talked to that idiot tonight?"

"Not for long." I watch as he takes another swallow. "I mean, he *is* an idiot."

"You know he likes you, right?"

It's my turn to pull a face. "I'm not spending my senior year up under Jace Martin-ass's arm."

Brendan doesn't laugh, even though he assigned that nickname to Jace after my world history presentation debacle. "So what's a guy gotta do to get you under his arm, then?"

I sigh aloud this time. I can't help it. "Don't do that, Brendan."

"Do what?" He lifts a hand and strokes one of my twists, letting it loop around one of his fingers. "Do this?"

He steps closer, and my hand slaps his away. It moves before I tell it to, but maybe that's a good thing. Maybe my impulses are on point tonight.

"Whoa," Brendan says, and I can hear the hurt in that one syllable.

"My bad. I just thought that . . . I mean, was I reading tonight wrong? You brought me out here so we could be alone, right?"

Something cuts off inside me. "And what? That automatically means I was about to give you some? B, you dated my best friend for two years! How would that make me look? Sleeping with my dead best friend's boyfriend?"

"Hey, hey, hey." Brendan pats the air between us with one hand. "Nobody said anything about sex. Did I think we were vibing at the party? Yes. Did I think we were going to keep vibing here? Yes. That don't mean we have to take our clothes off. I just . . . I just wanted to be close to you. I missed you."

I press a hand against my chest, shielding his words from my heart. "But Hope—"

"Was my ex-girlfriend when she died," Brendan finishes for me. "But you've been *my* best friend long before me and Hope were anything. Maybe there was a small part of me that thought we could've been something more and I fucked it up but . . . I don't know. I thought we'd have time to figure things out." He gives a half-hearted shrug. "I dropped the ball, though. I gave you too much space for too long. I should've reached out sooner. I should've been there for you."

I squeeze my eyes close just for a moment, and when I open them, I'm not dreaming. Brendan's still looking down at me, his eyes as warm and sincere as a puppy's. He's saying the words that I've always wanted him to say since we were thirteen years old, but why now? Why tonight?

I want to ask him, but at that moment, Brendan frowns and

turns toward the doors. "You hear that?"

I blink. My heart couldn't be pounding *that* loudly. "Hear what?"

He looks up at the ceiling as if he could see the main floor. "I thought . . . you locked the doors behind us, right?"

"Nobody's coming through here," I reassure him. "The only people who know this place exists are on my mom's team. It's far off the main roads."

Brendan still frowns at something above us, and he's slipping through my fingers.

"I missed you, too," I blurt out.

Brendan's eyes are on me again. A smile oozes from his lips. "No shit," he says before taking another swig of his beer. His Adam's apple bobs up and down as he chokes down the brew. I can see it traveling down his esophagus, doing its thing before settling into his stomach.

The sweet moment that just passed between us flashes through my head like a slideshow: *I missed you. I thought we'd have time to figure things out.* His finger twirling around my twists. Then, a new moment. My hand pressed against his cheek. Him bending over, brushing his lips against mine . . . I can't. Dammit, I can't. I reach up and slap the can from his mouth.

"What the hell?" Brendan jumps back just as the can crashes against the floor, gold liquid geysering up at us.

"You shouldn't drink that fast." My fingers twitch. I clutch my can tighter and ball my other hand into a fist. "Plus, I thought I saw a fly on it."

Brendan frowns down at my fist. "You didn't take your meds,

did you?" His voice is soft but still punches me in the gut. We weren't talking when I got my anxiety diagnosis, right after my freak-out at my final track meet. But still—he kept up with me. He still cared about me.

"I . . ." I stop myself. If I keep going, I'll tell him that this is a mistake. That tonight is a mistake. I'll shove him toward the door and tell him to leave. Before it's too late. But it already is. "I . . . I'll be right back."

He says something, but I'm already out the door. I scurry past all the bells and whistles on this floor until I'm on the other end of the house. The bathroom is connected to the spare room down here. I rush inside and lean against the sink, taking in slow, steady breaths. Brendan is right. This is the first day I haven't taken my meds in four months, and my anxiety's hammering at the door outside my brain, threatening to break the hinges if I don't let it inside and take over. I continue my breathing, but I'm not winning this battle. I dig into my back pocket and pull out my emergency stash. Three Xanax pills sealed in a plastic snack bag. I pop one into my mouth just as my phone buzzes next to the sink.

I let out a genuine yelp and almost choke up my pill. I hope it isn't who I think it is. Checking in to see if I'm doing my part of the plan tonight. I don't even know how to answer: *Yeah, but wait* . . . Wait for what? It's not like I can stop now . . . right? Right? Thankfully, Tia's name is on my screen.

Did I lose you boo? Did Jace kidnap you? You know I have a PhD in ass whoopin.

I smile at her text as my thumb trembles over my keypad. I want to tell her I'm okay, but first I need to get okay. Let the Xanax do its magic. I push the phone back into my pocket, run the cold water, and shove both hands underneath the faucet. Splash the water on my face and scrub as hard as I can. I don't even bother to glance at myself in the mirror. If I do, I'll see someone weak staring back at me. Someone who made a promise and who's about to break it. I'll see a traitor.

Damn. That's it, then. I won't do this. I'll tell Brendan we need to leave. Take him home, then binge-watch old episodes of *Love & Hip Hop* over at Tia's. That's the perfect ending to this mindfuck of a night.

I shake the water off my hands and search for a napkin or a towel but, of course, don't find either. Cursing under my breath, I lift my shirt and pat my face with the inside of it.

"Liv," someone hisses.

I gasp, and my shirt falls from my face. Brendan stares in the doorway of the bathroom, staring at me with his eyes as large as basketballs.

"Jesus, B. What the f—?"

Brendan holds a finger up to his mouth and hushes me—and that simple act sends a chill right down my spine. "Someone's here," he mouths. "Come on." He reaches for my hand.

"My hand's aren't dry," I say automatically—because what the hell else are you supposed to say when you're in pending danger? The imminent doom must not have reached my nervous system yet.

Brendan just snatches my hand and pulls me out of the bathroom, guiding me through the adjoining spare room and toward the main rec room area. We pause at the threshold. "Does that lead outside?" he whispers to me, pointing toward a sliding glass door.

I blink at the door, trying to remember where my car is parked from this location of the house. What did Brendan hear exactly? Was it actually something, or is the spiked drink getting to him? Did I give him too much?

"Liv," Brendan hisses again, shaking my hand. "Will that take us back to your car?"

I shake my head a few times, jostling myself to the present. "Yeah," I say finally. "It's a covered patio, but if we go over a hill, it will lead us back around to the main entrance. Brendan, what's going on?"

He doesn't answer me—just makes a beeline toward the glass door. As he yanks the handle to slide it open, a tall, masked figure appears and fills the doorway, blocking us in. My heart sputters before leaping up to my throat. *No, no, no.* Before I can say anything, Brendan lifts a fist and clocks the figure on the side of the head. I squeak and cover my mouth with both hands as the figure tumbles to the ground. Brendan doesn't hesitate to grab my hand again and pull me in the opposite direction, his heroism on autopilot.

"Let's get to the stairs," he says, dragging me behind him. Everything's so quick, so frantic. I barely have time to catch my breath.

"Brendan," I say as we propel toward the stairs. "Brendan, wait."

I stop in my tracks and yank my hand away from him. Clutch it against my chest to help myself breathe. To help myself think.

Brendan turns to look at me, confusion clouding his face. "What are you doing?"

"I just need to—" Something moves behind Brendan. Something shadowy. I blink once, twice, and another masked figure comes into shape. They creep from behind the stairs, wearing oversized coveralls and a Donald Trump mask tilted awkwardly over their head. Trump places a gloved finger against their plastic lips, and every hair on my body stands in attention.

"Brendan!" I cry out.

Brendan whips around just as Trump presses a stun gun right against Brendan's rib cage. Brendan convulses as the gun buzzes against him, then tumbles, his forehead knocking against the banister with a sickening *CRACK* before he hits the floor.

My hands are over my mouth again, trying to keep the bile from escaping. Trump peeks up at me and moves in my direction. I step away from them, almost tripping over my own two feet.

"What . . . what did you do?" I ask.

Trump lets out a breath as a gloved hand reaches up to the mask and yanks it off. Kizzy puffs air from her mouth to blow her matted bangs away from her forehead. She then shakes her head at me. "What you couldn't do."

FIVE

TRUMP'S FACE GLARES AT ME AS IT DANGLES FROM Kizzy's hand, not to be outmatched by Kizzy's grimace.

"We didn't say anything about knocking him out," I cry out. I rush over to Brendan and kneel next to his head. There's a bump next to his right temple that's puffy and scarlet and rising. I touch it gingerly, then wince as if I could feel the pain. "Jesus, Kiz."

"Hey, all I did was zap him to subdue him. It's not my fault he fell the wrong way."

I press my head against Brendan's chest and strain my ears. A beat. Two beats. Good. *Good.* I let out a sigh, then frown at Kizzy. "What the hell were you thinking?"

"Whether I should be snarky and shout 'TIMBER' before he hit the floor." She shrugs. "But only white people do that shit in movies."

She thinks this is a joke. Brendan's lying on the floor with a possible concussion, and she's joking about being a villain in some stupid action movie. I climb to my feet and get right in her face. "You're too early."

Kizzy doesn't flinch. "No, I'm not. You were moving too slow."

I shake my head. "I gave him more than enough melatonin. He would've been out in five more minutes, tops."

"I don't believe you."

"I said I would, didn't I?"

"You're kind of flaky, Liv."

"Flaky? I got him here. Just like I said I would."

"Yeah, but only after I put pressure on you at the party. Now you have three seconds to get the hell out of my face before you join your boo thing on the floor." Her fingers squeeze around the stun gun, but that's not what gets me. It's the way her eyes narrow and look right through me. As if she's no longer seeing me as her former friend. She only sees a splinter in her plan that she'll cut out without thinking twice.

I wisely take a step back and glance down at Brendan to avoid her gaze. "You could've killed him."

"And?"

The way she says it is so flippant. Like I just accused her of burning toast. "And? Kizzy, we didn't say anything about killing him."

"And what *did* we say, Liv? Because whenever I even mention Brendan's name you get all spacey. Like you disappear to some tired-ass rom-com where you and him get married and buy this big-ass house and have Black ashy babies."

"Seriously? Go to he—"

Her hands ram against my chest, shoving me so hard that I trip over Brendan's legs and topple to the floor. She hovers over me, her eyes squinting so deeply that I wait for lasers to shoot out of them. I hold up both hands, remind her *she* has the weapon. Not me.

"Let's relax," I tell her. "We're in this together, remember?"

"Then *act* like it. I saw you run away to the bathroom like a little bitch. What was your plan? To tell him everything? To call the cops and bust me as soon as I climbed out the trunk of your car? To pin this shit all on me so you could come out clean and have your happily ever after?" She shoves her bobbed hair behind an ear, then takes a moment to look at my hands. Shit, they're trembling again. "The hell's your problem? Did you take your meds?"

Wow, am I that transparent? I climb off Brendan and return to my feet. "They take a minute to kick in."

Kizzy cocks her head to the side and studies me. "Is there something you're not telling me?"

"Like what?"

She shrugs. "I don't know. Like maybe you're nervous. Like maybe you filled in Tia and she's on her way to get you and Captain Fuckface out of here." She nods her head toward Brendan, in case I didn't know who she was referring to.

I take a deep breath and consider my next words with the attention of a surgeon making her first incision. Kizzy's a bulging artery—any tiny nick and it'll be a bloodbath in here. "Tia doesn't know anything. Nobody knows anything. I wouldn't do that to you. I wouldn't do that to Hope."

Her face softens at the mention of Hope's name. "Good." She shakes her hair out from behind her ear. "And I was obviously joking about the killing-him thing. You're so sensitive. Now let's—"

"Christ on a cracker!"

Kizzy and I scream and jump. I spin on my heels and see Sherie standing behind me, an Abe Lincoln mask dangling in her hand and a rosy splotch puffing up on her chalky cheek. Upon seeing our terror, Sherie screams as well.

"What? *What?*" she cries out.

My and Kizzy's screams die out when we realize it's just Sherie and her corniness entering the fray and not some actual crazed, masked man with stale vocabulary.

"Fuck," Kizzy breathes out, clutching her chest. "Couldn't you make a more graceful entrance?"

"I'm sorry if I forgot how to be refined after being coldcocked by a giant." Sherie shifts her jaw and grazes her cheek before wincing. "Besides—who else would it be? Unless you both forgot I was here."

Kizzy and I pass a guilt-riddled look between each other. Sherie catches our exchange and pauses.

"Wait a minute—you two forgot I was here?"

"No!"

"Nooo."

Kizzy and I harmonize together, laying on the earnestness so thick that it changes the octaves in our voices. Sherie folds her arms across her chest and tucks her bottom lip into her mouth.

"I was stuck in a trunk with you for like an hour. Of course I didn't forget you," Kizzy adds.

"And I was just about to check on you," I try. "You know, after we handled . . ." I peek down at Brendan.

Sherie finally notices him, and her hands drop back to her sides. "Did you kill him?"

There's concern in her voice that was noticeably missing from Kizzy's. This reassures me.

"Why does everyone keep saying that?" Kizzy throws up her hands with annoyance.

"He's alive," I tell Sherie. "He took a really hard hit to the head, though."

"And so did Sherie, but look at her. She's a soldier," Kizzy says. "Now let's get his punk ass back to the basketball court before he wakes up."

Kizzy grabs at his feet, and I make my way toward his head. I graze my fingertips against the bump on his head. He hasn't stirred even once. What if he has a concussion? I don't think people with concussions are supposed to sleep.

"Come on, Liv!"

I snap out of it and tuck my fingers under Brendan's armpits.

"On the count of three," Kizzy says. She counts us off, and we both try hoisting him up, but Brendan's built like a boulder in quicksand.

"Fuuuck," Kizzy says in between grunts.

I try to respond, but Brendan's weight renders me speechless. We both take a break and step back to catch our breaths.

Kizzy frowns over at Sherie. "Um, hello?"

"Um, *hello*," Sherie says back, holding up one of her lanky arms that probably weighs as much as one of Brendan's eyelids.

I look down at Brendan, then toward the basketball court. It feels a mile away. Then it hits me. "Hold on," I say, rushing toward the bonus room.

"The hell is she going?" I hear Kizzy ask.

I reach the spare room and find exactly what I'm looking for. I head to the oak desk in the corner and grab a hold of the leather swivel chair behind it. I wheel it through the room and back to the corridor where Kizzy, Sherie, and Brendan wait for me.

"There," I say, stopping the chair near Brendan. "Now we won't have to carry him back to the court."

Kizzy stares at the chair and nods, impressed. I breathe a sigh of relief. Maybe this'll get her off my back some.

"Um . . ." Sherie raises her hand like a shy student in class. "Don't get me wrong, I appreciate the ingenuity, Liv, but . . . won't we still have to lift him to get him onto the chair?"

I blink a few times. Shit.

Kizzy stares at the chair. "Not exactly. Roll him onto his side. Sherie, go get the gym bag."

Sherie scurries up the stairs, and Kizzy starts digging into Brendan's pockets. I frown at her. She finally pulls Brendan's phone from the pocket of his jeans.

"Insurance policy," she says, waving the phone at me before slipping it into one of her pockets. I nod, then get on my knees, push Brendan's shoulder and torso until my muscles twitch. Finally, he's on his side. Kizzy topples the chair on its side, and I jump.

"A warning would be nice," I say.

"I'm thinking as I go."

Sherie reappears with a gym bag that she could easily fold herself into. It practically anchors her to the floor.

"Come on. Let's tie him to the chair." She snaps her fingers at Sherie and, on command, Sherie digs into the bag and pulls out rope.

Okay, I'm still lost. "Why are we . . . ?"

"Just do it as best as you can."

Kizzy shoves the chair right against Brendan's back until it looks like the chair's spooning him. We start at his legs, wrapping the rope around and around until we get to his torso. Kizzy reaches under his body, and I hand her the rope. She threads it under him, and we do this again and again until the chair is sealed against his whole body.

"Okay, we need to knot this a few times. Just to make sure everything is secure," she instructs.

Kizzy pulls the rope into a tight knot behind Brendan's back. I form one behind Brendan's knees. Not as tight as Kizzy's, but hopefully convincing enough.

Kizzy gives the rope a hard yank. "Okay, good. Now, let's push him upright with the chair. The wheels should help us get him up easier now."

I lift an eyebrow at her.

"I pay attention in science class, okay?" she says. She nods at Sherie to join us.

We position ourselves at the top of the chair and Kizzy counts off. As soon as she reaches three, I take a breath and help them pry the back of the chair from the floor. The muscles in my arm twitch again, but I keep straining. Sherie's labored breaths next to my ear let me know I'm not the only weakling. Finally, *finally*, the chair snatches upright, gliding away with Brendan for a few centimeters. But he remains secured to it, like he's up for crucifixion.

We all take deep breaths and admire our work.

"Not bad," I say.

"Well, I did come up with it." Kizzy's face pinches into a smile, just for a moment. As though her cheek muscles don't quite know how to experience joy. But I get it. Hope didn't tell me much about her time at the residential center, but she did mention something about Kizzy. How she has scars that nobody can really see. I think I can, though. They're imprinted in the way that Kizzy stomps instead of walks, crushing skulls and hearts before someone can do the same to her.

Kizzy wheels Brendan to the basketball court with Sherie and me close behind. She pushes him up against the pole under one of the hoops, then looks over at Sherie. Raises an eyebrow. Sherie does the same in return.

Kizzy huffs in frustration. "You're going to pass me the shit or naw?" I wince. We haven't been as close as we used to be since we lost Hope, but we did spend the past few weeks scheming together. Yet she still talks to Sherie like some random bitch who cut her in line at Target.

"Oh! My bad!" Sherie rushes over and hands Kizzy the bag. Kizzy snatches it from her, sets it on the floor, and begins to rummage through it. When Sherie catches my eye, I smile. She rolls her eyes lazily, then smiles back. Our silent eff-you to Kizzy Chan.

Kizzy continues searching through the bag, determination swirling all around her like a broken halo. She pulls out items one at a time with a heavy clunk against the floor. Power cord. *Clunk.* Pedal. *Clunk.* Laser-gun thing. *Clunk.*

Wait . . . pedal? Laser-gun thing? "What is all of this?" I ask. "Where are the permanent markers?"

Sherie looks over at Kizzy as if she's waiting for permission. Sherie usually just *does,* not waits. Whatever this is can't be good.

"Yeah, about that," Kizzy says. "We had a change of plans." She gives Sherie a pointed look and attaches the laser-gun thing to the power cord.

I frown at them in confusion. "And you didn't tell me? I thought we were in this together."

"Well, girl groups sometimes venture off and do their own things before reuniting for the Super Bowl. In this case, we were Beyoncé and Kelly." Kizzy waves a finger between her and Sherie. "And you just happened to be the other one who was there."

Sherie presses her palm against her chest in shock and awe. "You think I'm a Beyoncé?"

"Girl, you're not even a Kelly. I'm speaking in metaphors." With a half-hearted flick of her wrist toward Sherie, Kizzy turns back to me. "We figured scribbling on his face wasn't a heavy enough consequence. He didn't copy someone's homework, Liv. He *murdered* someone."

My nails dig into my palms at her last words. *He* murdered *someone.* We weren't tap-dancing around it anymore tonight. We're throwing the accusation out there like a grenade and won't be able to put the pin back in.

Still, I try. "Well, we don't *really* know if he killed anyone."

Kizzy and Sherie exchange another look. Even though it's not meant for me, I read right through it. They think I'm flaking out. They expected me to flake out, which is why they changed things without letting me know.

"I mean, I thought the purpose is to see if he's telling the truth. That he was really at the movies and not there that night."

"And you think that a marker's going to scare him straight?" Kizzy asks.

"It's not just the marker on his face," I try again. "It's embarrassing the shit out of him. Tying the basketball star up on his playground. Recording him being helpless and marked up and posting it on social media for all his fans to see."

"Yeah, well, permanent marker isn't so permanent. And neither is the internet. Even if Brendan doesn't find a way to scrub the video, people will still twist the story and turn him into a martyr somehow." Kizzy pulls out a power supply box from the bag and, damn, that bag is fucking bottomless.

"Plus, when you think about it, drawing something on his face is really kind of juvenile," Sherie adds. "Kids do that at slumber parties. Of course, I've only ever been to one slumber party . . ." Her words fade into oblivion. We know which slumber party she's talking about. We were all there. All of us, except Hope. Our guest of honor.

Kizzy coughs and breaks through the awkwardness. She lugs the power supply box over to one of the walls and plugs it into an outlet.

Pressure builds in my head. I press my hand against it to try to push it back. "What's going on?" I think I know the answer. I just need one of them to say it.

"Remember when Kizzy dated that girl Nikki?" Sherie asks.

I stare at her. I only started speaking to Kizzy again a few weeks ago. I don't even remember her favorite color.

"Afro puffs? Has the Harley Quinn tattoo down her whole arm?"

Sherie's words take the form of something I can hold on to. I remember seeing this Nubian goddess from community college popping up at some of my friends' parties, tatting up anyone who had forty bucks to spare. Until she inked the daughter of someone on the school board. The phantom tattoo artist vanished . . . but then resurfaced in Kiz's bed, I guess.

"She let me borrow her kit for the night," Kizzy says. She picks up what I now know for sure is a tattoo gun, frowns as she tries to adjust her fingers around it. "We only have black ink, though. Nothing fancy."

I shake my head so much my neck gets a cramp. "No," I say. "Kiz, what are you thinking?"

"I'm thinking I'm going to fuck up his face, and hopefully the rest of his life. Let everyone know who he is." The needle hums to life and she smiles, admiring it.

The pressure drums against my forehead. "Do you even know how to use that?"

Kizzy shrugs. "I've seen Nikki do it enough times to give it a go. And it doesn't have to be perfect on a murderer's face." She studies Brendan and grabs his chin, moving his head back and forth.

He's still not awake. Why isn't he awake?

"Hmm, what do you guys think? Forehead or cheeks? I think we have more of a canvas on his forehead, but cheeks seem more personal, you know?" She lets his head drop and snaps her fingers. "I know. Let's put 'G' on one cheek, 'F' on the other, and then 'KILLER' right across the forehead."

She has to be kidding. I turn to Sherie to see if she'll let me in on the joke, but her forehead crinkles as she studies Brendan's face. "I don't know. If we do it like that, it'll read: 'KILLER GIRLFRIEND.' That sounds like a Lifetime movie. One of the trashy ones."

That's it? That's her contribution to this bullshit?

"Yeah, you're right . . . unless!" Kizzy raises her finger as though she wants to shout: *Eureka!* "We go for 'I KILLED' on the forehead, and then do 'HOPE' on the cheeks. What do you think?"

Sherie chews her lip and then nods. "Wordy, but it'll work."

Kizzy lifts her eyebrows at me, eyes full of optimism. "Liv?"

I could choke her. I could wrap my hands around her neck and clutch it until her eyes and tongue pop out. Knock out Sherie if I need to. Then I can wheel Brendan out of here and get the answers I want from him one-on-one.

"I think you've both fucking lost it." The words tumble from my head and right out of my mouth. But the pressure in my head is gone.

Kizzy's forehead falls, and she's back to her normal, pissed-off self. "Come again?"

"I mean, we all have," I say, more polite now. "If we do this before getting his side of the story, we've all lost it. We'd be criminals. Even more than we are now."

"Oh, like he isn't a criminal?" Kizzy asks.

"Are you kidding me right now?" I dart my eyes between Kizzy and Sherie. "Are you both going to stand here and pretend that it's not a huge fucking deal to basically brand a Black man? Do you even know the historical trauma that carries?"

"Of course I know. I'm Black, too, bitch," Kizzy says.

"You're half Black, Kiz. Your last name is Chan," Sherie says.

"That makes me a double minority, then! Triple if you pile on me being a girl. You know how much shit society puts on females. That's the whole reason why I have a Trump mask tonight and not a Kamala Harris one."

"And you're a lesbian," Sherie adds.

We blink at her, and she shrugs. "I mean, if we're talking about intersectionality, we can't forget sexuality."

"Fine!" I throw up both hands in frustration. "Kizzy, you have four cards stacked against you, then. With that much 'wokeness,' you should understand why this is a dumbass idea."

"You know, I might've considered that for a half second, and then I remembered . . . *Fuck* Brendan Jean." She practically spits out his name. "Fuck this guy who lured my best friend up onto her own roof. Who tried to charm her into getting back together with him. And when Hope didn't buy into his bullshit, he shoved her and watched her crack her goddamn skull against the concrete like it was nothing."

I swallow, but nothing goes down. I glance at Brendan, see the helpless guy tied to the chair, but even restrained and slumped over, he looks a thousand feet tall. "I get it, Kiz."

"Do you? Do you really? Because Hope is rotting in the ground, and you're still protecting him. I thought she was your friend."

"She was my *best* friend!" I erupt, squaring off against Kizzy.

We're chest to chest, and neither of are backing down. It's sophomore year all over again and we're fighting for Hope's attention.

"You guys . . . ," Sherie says.

"Then remember it," Kizzy snaps.

"I do remember. I remember everything."

I remember how Hope didn't look like herself at the viewing. Her skin pale to the point of looking ashy, as if the beautician didn't know the right hues to use on her sepia-toned skin. Her lips didn't curve into that smirk that showed she was always prepped to share something provocative. I even remember the guy who never showed up to see how un-Hope-like she looked at the viewing. The guy who didn't even show up to the funeral. The guy who was more concerned about looking innocent than being a grieving ex-boyfriend. That guy just happens to be unconscious in this gym.

"I'll never forget her, okay? I couldn't if I tried."

"You guys . . . ," Sherie says again.

Kizzy sucks her teeth at me. "Seems like you stop trying every time you lay your eyes on Sedgefield's golden boy."

I see myself ramming my fist down her throat until she shits out my knuckles. And the way her eyes smile at me, she knows that's what I want to do. She stands there, arms folded. *Bring it on.*

"You guys!"

"What, Sherie? Damn!" Kizzy demands.

We both look at her, and she holds up a shaky finger toward Brendan, who's starting to stir. He groans as his head rolls from side to side. Trying to lift it.

My legs spasm, not sure whether to run away or stay put and see what happens.

"What the hell?" Kizzy glares at me. "I knew you should've given him your Xanax instead of that natural crap."

"I couldn't, Kiz. He was drinking too much. We're not trying to kill the guy."

The side of Kizzy's mouth pulls downward. Her thinking face. Her *Maybe that's not a bad idea* face. Then she ruffles her hair, and the thought fades like a drifting cloud. "We didn't consider his mass. Bigger people always need more of something before it does anything."

"I gave him like three times the dose."

"Obviously that wasn't enough."

"So now what?" I ask.

This wasn't part of the plan. Brendan is supposed to be unconscious long enough for us to set everything in motion. Nothing's in place. Not me or the tripod or the masks. But . . . this hiccup might actually be a good thing.

"Do we call it off now?" I try not to sound too eager. I pinch at the infinity pendant dangling from my neck for guidance. "I'm not in position—and he might be too pissed now to confess anything. Maybe we just leave and let him figure out how to get himself free?"

Brendan's groans get louder as his head lifts an inch. I flinch, debating whether I should run to him or off somewhere into the shadows.

"Say something!" I hiss to Kizzy.

"Wha . . . Who's there?" Brendan slurs . . . right before Sherie shrieks and punches him in the face.

SIX

I WATCH IN STIFLED HORROR AS BRENDAN'S HEAD snaps back then falls forward, his chin poking his chest.

"What the hell was that?" Kizzy demands, stealing the words right from my mouth.

"I panicked," Sherie explains, rubbing her knuckles. "I thought we needed to knock him back out."

Brendan stops moving for now, but the groans don't stop. Sherie's tiny fist didn't do too much damage.

"Okay," Kizzy says, mostly under her breath. She nods a few times, working out a puzzle in her mind. "Okay, we need to move. Part two starts now. Liv." She motions for me to join Brendan under the hoop.

My stomach twists into a knot. "Are we sure we want to do this?

I can hide out on the top level. You could tell him you have me locked up somewhere or—"

"We talked about this," Kizzy says. "Immediacy is key. He might need more motivation to talk. Now . . ." She snaps her fingers at me like I'm a Pomeranian with a short attention span.

I turn to Sherie and look for signs that she's just as hesitant about everything as me.

"Don't worry," she says, the additional rope suddenly appearing in her hands. "We won't hurt you." She adds a soft smile. She hates this part just as much as me, but she's moving forward. I still remember what she told us that first day when our plan started to materialize. *She saved me.* Hope saved Sherie—and she hinted at something more than just social obscurity. Hope pulled her out of some dark place, and now here she is, doing the same for Hope. Shedding light on her death.

It's obvious I'm losing my potential ally. I nod, then sit on the floor underneath the hoop. I don't make eye contact with Sherie as she wraps the rope around me, sealing me against the pole.

"I won't do it too tight," she says, knotting up the rope behind me.

"Thank you," I mumble.

"Rough up some of her braids," Kizzy demands. "Maybe jostle her shirt some."

Sherie and I look at her.

"It needs to be convincing, right? Go on." She pulls her Trump mask back over her head as Sherie ruffles the top of my head. I can feel my real hair pulling out of the twists. Four hours and five hundred bucks to get my hair installed, and Sherie makes it look like my second cousin twisted some cheap bundles into my hair during a lunch break. She then reaches for my shirt, and her hand gets dangerously close to my necklace.

"Careful," I say, snappier than I intended.

"Sorry," she mouths. She makes sure to reach under the necklace to squeeze a handful of my shirt into a fist. Just like someone yoked me up.

Sherie backs away as Kizzy swivels Brendan in his chair so that he's facing me. Once again, she snaps her fingers. This time at Sherie, who quickly slips her Abe Lincoln mask back over her head.

"We ready?" Trump looks at me, then at Lincoln.

I give a tiny nod, and Lincoln gives a thumbs-up. Trump nods and pulls out a plastic yellow megaphone from the gym bag. It was a present for her little brother's birthday, she told us. Now it'll be a key piece in getting Brendan to confess. How ironic that something that brought a kid joy will potentially reveal pain.

Kizzy presses a button on the megaphone, and a siren blares. She holds the megaphone right next to Brendan's face. Brendan startles, his head snapping upright as he starts to blink.

"What the . . . ?" he croaks. He blinks a few more times, clearing the fog out of his head. He looks up at Kizzy in her Trump gear, and his head jerks like he just got punched again. "Who are you? What is this?"

Kizzy flutters her gloved fingers in his direction. His eyes land on Sherie with her Lincoln mask. She squares up at him, making her five-foot-ten stature seem even taller.

"Asher?" His eyes bounce between Sherie and Kizzy, Kizzy and Sherie. "Asher, I'm not about the corny-ass Halloween pranks this year. I told you that already."

Kizzy and Sherie stare at him wordlessly, which makes the room feel even colder. Darker, even, despite the fluorescent lights. I see his mind working. Him trying to decide if this is a joke or not. Him sizing up Kizzy and Sherie in case he needs to fight. His eyes finally land on me. Looking tousled and scared, tied up on the floor across from him.

"Liv?" He says my name all soft and tender like a chant. "Liv, what's going on? Are you okay? Did they hurt you?"

"Yeah," I squeak out. My throat tries to close on me. "I'm okay . . . for now." I peek at Kizzy and Sherie, probably looking like fear to Brendan, but, really, I'm looking for acceptance. Reassurance that I'm playing my part okay.

"You fuckers," Brendan hisses to Kizzy and Sherie. "Don't worry, Liv. I'm going to get us out of here." He struggles in his seat and tries to shift toward me, but the ropes are too tight. Too effective. He barely budges an inch.

Kizzy presses the megaphone against Trump's plastic mouth. "*Need some help there?*" The words come out distorted—a cross between an alien and a robot.

Brendan stops struggling and studies her. "You're not Asher."

"*No shit.*"

"Then who are you? What the fuck is this?"

"*Doomsday.*"

Brendan's face crinkles in confusion. "Look, I'm not sure what you're on, but if the problem is me, then deal with me. Let Liv go. If you hurt her, if you put another finger on her, I'll—"

"*You'll what?*" Kizzy leans over until she's directly in his face. "*You'll WHAT? Kill us like you killed your girlfriend?*"

Brendan's mouth twitches at one of the corners. Everything clicks for him in that moment. He knows what this is all about. "You're one of those assholes, huh? What you call yourselves again? Keep Hope Alive–ers? Little too late for that shit."

Kizzy smacks Brendan across the face, and it cracks through the air. Someone cries out, and it takes a second to realize it's me. Brendan spits on the floor, then rubs a tongue across his bloody bottom lip.

"I'm okay, Liv," he says to me, then glares at Kizzy. "Want to try that again when I'm not tied up?"

"*Nah. This is so much more fun.*" Kizzy raises her hand, but I look away before she connects with his face. The smack echoes and travels through my whole body.

"Dammit!" Brendan barks. "What point are you trying to make? You beat me because the cops didn't? How does that make any kind of sense?"

"*Don't be a dick. You know they pulled strings for you.*"

Brendan scoffs. "I got a little too much melanin for that, homey."

"*Yeah, and so did your girlfriend. Which is why they were so quick to rule it a suicide instead of finding any dirt on you.*"

"They called it a suicide because I wasn't fucking there! The only person on that roof that night was Hope. Hope did that shit to herself! She gave up and left her parents, her friends, and . . ." Brendan squeezes his eyes closed just for a moment to stop his sentence in his tracks, but it doesn't matter. We all know what he wants to say. He thinks Hope left him. The pain on his face shouts it for him. Pain that he's been hiding from everyone, until tonight.

"*Aww, you must miss her, huh?*" Kizzy asks. Even through the voice distortion, I can tell that she's not buying any of Brendan's heartache. "*Is that why you beat the shit out of her when she was still here?*"

Brendan takes a deep breath. "I never put a hand on her."

Kizzy nods her head to Sherie, and Sherie passes her a phone. Kizzy stabs at the screen, then holds it up to Brendan's face. "*What the hell do you call this,?*"

Brendan looks down at his lap. I know what she's showing him. It's the selfie Hope took last spring. Her bottom lip bloody, just like Brendan's is now. Her left cheekbone raised and ruby red. I still remember the text message she sent me along with this pic:

Look what this muthafucka did, Liv. Now do you believe me?

Now do you believe me? Those five words stunned me more than the picture itself. They sketched how she felt about our friendship. That she had to prove something for my loyalty. She had to earn it. Then a few days later, she was gone—eliminating all future conversations we needed to have.

"I've seen that picture before," he says to his lap. "But I'm telling you just like I told the cops—I never touched her. Ever. I could never do something like that."

Kizzy sucks her teeth and scrolls through the phone again. "*'Bitch, I'll fuckin kill you.' Does that text sound familiar to you?*"

Brendan shakes his head slowly. Not in denial but in disbelief. "We said that type of shit to each other all the time when we were fighting. It wasn't right, but it was . . . it was all we knew. You don't know the full story."

"*Oh, we have the full story,*" Kizzy continues. "*You're the victim of Hope's lies, and she's the stupid bitch who wants to tear a Black man down. Isn't that what your fans think? Your friends? Your family?*"

Brendan sighs through his nose. "Look, I can't control what other people think—"

"'*Hope's a thirsty bitch,*'" Kizzy reads from her phone. "'*Already bagged a future NBA star and now spreading lies about him to get even more attention. Hashtag ThirstyThot.*'"

"I told you. People do too much online," Brendan insists.

"'*That Hope trick is a Great Value Megan Thee Stallion,*'" Kizzy continues. "'*No talent, flatter booty, and more trifling lies about Black men.*'"

"Look, I don't know half the people posting that ignorant shit!"

"*Oh, shall we get to the people you* do *know?*" Kizzy scrolls through her phone with her thumb. "*Hold on, let me find the quote from your grandma about Hope being another fast-ass girl chasing fame . . .*"

"Enough!" Brendan's voice booms throughout the gym and knocks me out of the past.

My tongue runs across my lip, and I taste a hint of blood. I'd been gnawing on it as Kizzy read through the comments, biting down on flesh so that the words would sting a little less.

"Of course, my family would have my back," Brendan keeps at it. "But that was before . . . before Hope hurt herself—"

"*Before you killed her*," Kizzy corrects.

Brendan flinches, then purses his lips together. Seals them shut. Refusing to correct himself—refusing to use those words.

"*Okay. Fuck this.*" Kizzy storms over to me, and before I can question her with my eyes, her gloved palm connects with my face. I hear the slap before I feel it. But when I do, it's like fire ants crawling up my cheek, and I can't get them off.

"Liv!" Brendan tries to throw himself out of the chair, but it's no point. "Are you okay?"

I take in a shaky breath. Open my mouth to answer, but then Kizzy's fist connects against it. My top front teeth sink into my bottom lip, ripping the tiny nick there into a crater. That's going to hurt a lot later, but something else stings more right now. I look up at Kizzy through wet, blurry eyes—only I don't see her. Just Trump.

"Okay!" Brendan chokes. "Okay, okay! Back to me! What do you want? You're pissed at my family for defending me, right?"

Kizzy moves closer to Brendan again, and my shoulders slump in relief. I glance up at Sherie, who has a fist pressed against Lincoln's rubber mask. She shakes her head, relaying her shock to me. But her astonishment isn't going to get me out of these damn ropes.

"My family aren't monsters, okay?" Brendan continues. "*I'm* not a monster. My moms raised me right. I talk a lot of shit, but I'd never lay my hands on a woman."

Kizzy throws back her head and lets out a brief, sharp laugh. "*Your mom?*" she asks once she regains composure. "*You really want to talk about your mom? The same lady who's been married three times and allowed her last husband to beat her so badly that she lost hearing in one of her ears?*"

This is the part where I throw up, vomit splashing onto my lap and dripping onto the floor underneath me. But when I look down, my lap is dry. So is my mouth. I told Kizzy and Sherie this in confidence. My contribution to the intel we were gathering on Brendan. It was supposed to be used as evidence, not ammunition. But here goes Kizzy, fully locked and loaded.

"How did you . . . ?" His eyes float from Kizzy to Sherie to me. They stay on me. "You told them that?"

My lips part and the air stings my bloody lip.

"Liv, you fucking told them?" He won't stop staring at me.

"*Doesn't matter who told us.*" Even with the distortion, the amusement drips from Kizzy's voice as clear as a sunny day.

"What is this?" Brendan frowns at me, then looks at Kizzy

again. "What the fuck is going on here?"

"*What's going on is that your mom couldn't control her ex-husband from being an abusive prick, so what makes you think she could stop you from following stepdaddy's footprints?*"

"Leave. My mom. Out of this!" Brendan starts at Kizzy, but his legs are too restrained to get any momentum. Kizzy laughs again as Brendan tries his best to . . . I'm not even sure what he wants to do to her, but the way his eyes burn, I know it's something awful. And I can't fully blame him.

He gives up and rests his chin against his chest. "You son of a bitch," he chokes. "You have no idea, no clue, what that did to my family." His shoulders heave up and down, up and down. For a moment, I think he's crying. But when he lifts his head, his eyes are full of malice, not tears.

"*And what do you think you did to Hope's family?*"

Brendan's jaw clenches again. "Stop," he says through his teeth.

"*You know they still set a plate for her at dinnertime? That they haven't changed the sheets from her bed yet because they're afraid they'll forget how she smelled?*"

I look at Kizzy, try to call her bluff. All her tells are hidden behind the mask. Is it really that bad in their home? The Jacksons used to be a second set of parents for me, but I can't even think of the last time I set foot in their house. I thought they needed distance . . . but maybe I'm the one who needed it more.

"*Answer me!*" she shouts to Brendan.

Brendan lifts one shoulder and then the other. "What for? You already have the answers, right?" He glances at me again, and I will myself not to react. For once, I'm glad my hands are tied behind me so he won't see them tremble.

Kizzy nods. "*You're right. And soon, everyone will have the answers whenever they look at your face.*" She snaps her fingers and, on cue, Sherie hands her the tattoo gun.

Brendan's face slackens and his skin grows paler. Gaunter. This close to passing out again. "The fuck are you doing?"

Kizzy doesn't respond. Just switches on the power box. She turns the dial way higher than it probably should be. I whine and shuffle underneath my ropes, but Kizzy holds up the tattoo gun toward me. *Him or you*, she seems to tell me. Jesus, him or me.

"What the fuck did you do, Liv?" Brendan squirms in his chair. "Who are they? Tell me now and we can get out of here!" He turns back to Kizzy as she moves toward him. "Liv, don't let them fucking do this to me. Liv. Liv!"

"Wait!" I cry out. My heart *thud, thud, thuds* in my chest—about to shatter my rib cage. Kizzy pauses and looks up at the ceiling. So does Sherie. So does Brendan. It's not my heart making all that noise. It's the sound of a door slamming shut.

I suck in a breath. "Someone else is here."

SEVEN

BRENDAN'S EYES KEEP SCANNING THE CEILING. "Someone's here?" he asks, somewhat hushed. As though he doesn't want to jinx anything. Footsteps pitter-patter above us and his eyebrows quirk up. "Someone's here!" He takes a deep breath and bellows out a hearty: "HEY!"

Kizzy rushes over and covers his mouth with her hand. Brendan struggles against her, then takes a gigantic chomp on her fingers. Kizzy pulls back her hand with a gasp, then slaps Brendan across the face again. Brendan's not fazed—he keeps hollering.

"Um, hello?" Kizzy barks toward Sherie, not even bothering with the megaphone anymore. She hurries behind Brendan and attempts to cover his mouth again, this time with the crook of her arm.

Sherie shakes her head a few times to wake up, then rushes to grab something out of the gym bag. She pulls out a handkerchief and masking tape, then runs over to Kizzy and Brendan. They work together to shove the handkerchief into Brendan's mouth, but Brendan doesn't make it easy. He grunts and thrashes at every turn. Kizzy snatches the tape from Sherie and manages to wind it around Brendan's jaw as he tries to headbutt them.

"Watch his nose," I cry out. "Don't cover his nose!"

"Shut up," Kizzy hisses at me. Brendan's grumblings become muffled, and she bites off the end of the tape. She and Sherie step back, breathless but satisfied. Kizzy then turns toward me, Trump's head cocked to one side above her shoulders. "Okay, you're coming with me."

"Me?" I attempt to point to myself, but my hands are out of commission.

"Yes, bitch. It's your mom's property. It makes sense for you to be here, just in case." She digs in the pocket of her coveralls and pulls out a Swiss Army Knife. Where the hell did *that* come from? Kizzy's dangerous enough with a stun gun and tattoo needle, and now we're adding tools meant for slicing and puncturing to the mix.

She saws through the rope behind my back, and the twine loosens around me before plopping down onto my lap. I pull my hands around to my front and roll them at the wrists. They're asleep, tingling all the way through my fingertips. But at least they're not trembling.

"Come on!" Kizzy orders, and I climb to my feet. She glances over at Sherie. "You stay here with him."

"Are you sure?" Sherie asks, then cups a hand over her rubber mouth. She peeks at Brendan before scurrying closer to us. "Are you sure?" she whispers to us. "What if he escapes?"

"He won't. He's tied up."

"I mean, yeah. But he's a big guy. What if he hulks up and the rope pops off him like undersized clothes?"

Kizzy huffs in annoyance, then shoves the Swiss Army Knife into Sherie's hand. "Then use this."

"Kizzy," I murmur, just in case Brendan might hear me.

Kizzy rolls her head, and I know her eyes are rolling underneath her mask. "She's not going to need it. It's just to shut her up. Now. Let's. Go."

She storms toward the doors, and I hesitate. Glance at Brendan.

"I'll be back," I say to him, trying to sound comforting even though my voice is weak. As expected, Brendan doesn't even look at me. He knows something's foul. I reek of it. I pat Sherie on the arm, hoping my reassurance works on her. She grips onto my fingers and keeps me in place.

"I'm scared," she whispers to me.

I can't see her face, but I know what it's doing. She's gnawing on her lip. Her eyes are round like pearls. The same frozen features as the night we found out about Hope.

"I just wanted to find out the truth for Hope. But Brendan's still not saying anything. What if . . . what if he's telling the truth?

What if we're wrong and we did all this for nothing? And the person up there's going to bust us, and we're all going to jail for being wrong."

I almost pull her into a tight hug, but she's still in her mask. She's still "holding me hostage." Brendan already suspects enough.

"It's okay," I whisper back to her. "We'll get rid of whoever's up there, then the night will be over. I'll talk to her." I tilt my head toward the door where Kizzy just exited. "Tell her we're both not sure anymore. It'll be two against one, so she'll have to listen."

Sherie sighs, then lets me go. I give her one final reassuring nod before chasing after Kizzy. Her rushed steps let me know it'll take more than just talking to her. She's a dog with a bone, and I may have to risk a few fingers to pull it away from her.

We climb up the stairs to the main level of the house, the rain pounding against the windows and glass doors the soundtrack to our stroll. I knew it was going to throw down tonight, but not like this. I can't help but think of Hope and her book *Wuthering Heights*. The thunderstorm that symbolized Heathcliff's rage after Catherine humiliates him. Wonder if Kizzy's rage is any match. I also think about our classmates at the bonfire. About everyone scurrying to their cars to get away from the rain, maybe even pausing to find me or Kizzy or Sherie. They'll be looking for Brendan. Of course they'll be looking for Brendan.

And Tia. I never texted her back. She was going to catch a ride home with someone else anyway. She figured I would ditch the party early since I was only dipping my toe back into social waters.

But I know she's probably worried about me. Wondering if I made it home. Once we get rid of whoever's up here, I'll need to text her back. After convincing Kizzy to call the night off—even if it takes me shoving her back into the trunk of my car until she chills the fuck out.

We reach the foyer on the main level and look around the great room and kitchen. The only things that greet us are hardwood floors and marble countertops.

"What the hell?" Kizzy whispers as she takes off her mask and tosses it next to the fireplace. "You heard something too, right?"

"Maybe it was thunder," I try, wandering around the kitchen island. "Or maybe one of the builders left his tools and stopped by to grab them." I think about one of the bottom drawers in the kitchen. The one the builders use as a catchall for hand tools.

Kizzy pokes her head inside the study next to the main entrance. She shakes her head. Nothing there. "Was it the front door that closed or something else?"

"I don't know, Kiz. I was downstairs with you, remember? Getting the shit knocked out of me." I rub my tongue across the sore on my lip, and she doesn't even flinch.

"I told you—we had to be convincing."

"Not that convincing. The slap would've sufficed. Unless . . . you've always wanted to hit me and used tonight as an excuse."

Kizzy rolls her eyes. "That's right. Make tonight about you." She wiggles the front doorknob and pauses. "It's not locked."

Wind blows against the windows, and it's like I can feel it travel down my spine. I go back to an hour or so ago. When I came in with Brendan. Did I lock the door behind us? I can't remember. "Did you and Sherie lock the door after you came in?"

"Yes." She thinks. "I mean, no. I don't know. We came in through the patio at the basement level. The one you left unlocked. Were there any other doors unlocked?"

"There's like a thousand doors that lead outside, Kiz. I didn't have time to check each one."

"Well, maybe that was something you should've considered before you kidnapped the town's basketball star."

This bitch. She is not about to pin everything on me. Not when I didn't even want to take it this far. "It's not like I acted alone."

"Yeah, and the one part you had was to secure the location. You couldn't even do that."

"Oh, I only had one part? Forget luring Brendan to the location. Forget getting tied up and knocked around."

Again with her eye-rolling. "Jesus, will you move on? I barely hit you."

"You weren't supposed to hit me at all!"

Thunder cracks through the sky outside, and the whole house shudders. It gives Kizzy and me a moment to catch our breaths. Turn the temperature down.

"Okay." Kizzy speaks calmer now, taming the wild animal across from her. "Okay. Let's finish checking everything out. I'll go this way." She hitches a thumb behind her. "Get a look at the deck attached to the primary bedroom. You check out both garages and the mudroom. Then we meet back here."

I nod. This sounds like a solid plan. Except . . . "And then?"

Kizzy blinks at me. "Then we finish what we started. Nothing's changed."

That's both what I figured and what I dreaded. Before I can protest, Kizzy turns and begins her search. I sigh and head toward the mudroom. I made a promise to Sherie that this night will be over, and I planned on keeping it. If we both gang up against Kizzy, she won't have any choice but to let Brendan go. Of course, I'll have to explain my role in everything to him. But he has things to explain to me, too. That's how this whole mess got started. Too many secrets. I stroke my infinity pendant and wonder how it might feel to let some of those secrets go. Wonder if I'm even ready to let those secrets go. I squeeze the pendant tighter, wanting it to dig into my flesh so I can feel anything but budding guilt.

I reach for my phone. The need to text Tia is overwhelming. She's been my rock these past few months. The anchor that keeps me steady. If I can just explain what happened so far, what was supposed to happen later, she'll understand. She'll know how to get me out of this.

"'Sup?"

My phone slips from my hand as I stop in my tracks. Dayvon stands in the mudroom, next to one of the doors leading to the garage. His damp smoking jacket clinging to his arms and chest.

"My bad," he says with a weak smile. "I didn't mean to scare you."

So he says, but *shit*. I press my hand against my chest to calm my heart down. He blinks at me, and I realize that I've been staring at him like he's a zombie.

"Um, let me get that for you." He bends over to grab my phone and hands it to me, his crooked grin still not leaving his face.

I take the phone, and it almost slips from my hand again because the trembles have started. That Xanax should've kicked in by now.

"Yeah. Uh, thank you," I say. I take a beat and remember more words. "What are you . . . where did you come from? I didn't see another car."

"Yeah, I just got here." Dayvon rubs a hand over his wet stitch rows. "The rain's not playing out there. I guess the road leading up here hasn't been paved yet, so all that dirt turned into mud. Our tires got stuck, and we basically had to trek about a mile just to get here. Whoever buys this place must be a fan of scary movies."

I look down at his shoes, and they're caked in mud. My mom is going to kill me for ruining her Brazilian cherry floors. He smiles at me again but . . . his answers only create more questions. Why the hell is he here? And how the hell did he know I was here? But when my lips move again, all I can manage is: "Who's *we*?"

Dayvon gives me a puzzled look as if I'm the one who showed up to his mom's new construction site without an invitation. "I thought you . . . B said that you—"

"You talked to Brendan?" Panic rises in my throat. "When?"

His eyebrows shift, the question mark in between his eyes mold into an exclamation point. "You okay, Liv?" His eyes land on my cut lip. "What happened to you?"

Before I can answer, laughter spills out of the great room. The fuck is going on? I push past Dayvon and rush back through the kitchen. I stop at the island when I see Kizzy in the great room. She leans against one of the walls, laughing at Asher as he squeaks around the great room in his soggy shoes, dramatically miming someone skiing or climbing or doing something with a lot of effort. He's still in his Patrick Bateman raincoat. Guess it was worth dressing up like an asshole when there's a storm going on.

"What's happening here?" I ask, not sure whether to keep my eyes on Kizzy or Asher.

Asher stops his performance and pushes his wet hair away from his eyes. "Hey! My people!" He runs over and picks me up before spinning me around. He's cold and wet, and I need him to stop. He puts me down before I can fuss, then slaps a hand on Dayvon's back.

"Sorry, I had to clown you about the mud," Asher says to him. "My boy looked like Atreyu trying to drag his horse out of the quicksand." He moves in slow motion again, pretending to huff and puff as he labors through fake mud. He then breaks out into laughter again.

I frown at Kizzy, who's still giggling.

"From *The Neverending Story,*" she explains to me, in between laughs.

"I know who Atreyu is," I snap.

Asher and Kizzy stop laughing and stare at me. I try to push out a smile but can't because, what the fuck is going on? "I'm sorry, I'm a bit confused. Did you invite them, Kiz?"

"Brendan invited them. And I told them that they just missed him." Kizzy raises her eyebrows at me as if she's trying to jog my memory.

"Oh. Right, right. He's gone," I say. "Which is good because this isn't even his place to be inviting company over like that."

Asher scoffs out a laugh. "Not yours, either."

"You know what I mean," I say, trying my best to hide my annoyance. I never really liked Asher's smarmy ass, but all my friends did. He's like the creepy household cat that everyone else adores for being an asshole, and who likes to hiss at me because I'm the only one who'll admit he's an asshole.

"It's not like that," Dayvon says, reading the room. "When you guys dipped, he dropped us a pin."

"Why?" I demand.

Dayvon blinks a few times, my tone clearly not what was expected on the menu. "We always do that kind of shit. Keep tabs on each other in case the parents start sniffing around and we need to come up with a cover. Anyways, the bonfire ended early because of the storm, Asher came up with the wise idea to join you guys and keep the party going. I wasn't down for it because I figured you two wanted to be . . . alone." He looks at me, then down at his feet, and someone's stomach rumbles. As though it isn't awkward enough.

"Oh, okay, Day," Asher says, tapping his knuckles against the marble island as though he's trying to inspect the authenticity. "It's not like I had to twist your arm to come and cockblock."

Dayvon's hickory-brown cheeks turn about two shades rosier—and from the way my face gets hot, I'm sure we're twinning.

"It ain't even like that," he insists. "You brought drinks from the party and everything, Ash. You wanted to turn up here. This is all on you."

"Yet, you still trekked your Black ass through a torrential downpour to cockblock." Kizzy nods, impressed. "It's giving stalker status."

Dayvon's mouth twists to one side. "Ain't nobody stalking anybody. Like I said, I rode with Asher, and he pretty much said we were coming here."

"Uber, Lyft, taxis . . ." Kizzy counts them off on her fingers. "Probably a bazillion other options, but yeah. Go off. I'm not mad at you."

"Kizzy." I give her a warning look, then an apologetic smile at Dayvon.

Dayvon shakes his head at me. *Ain't no thing.* He's someone else who's used to Kizzy's bullshit.

"Ah shit, I left the drinks back in the car." Asher slaps his hand on his damp forehead like we weren't dealing with bigger issues at the moment. Feeling three pairs of annoyed eyes on him, he gives a sheepish grin. Double-takes when he spots me. "The hell happened to your face, girl?"

On cue, I tuck my bottom lip into my mouth. Bad move. The

sting hits me like salt in a wound. "Nothing. I just tripped coming up the stairs."

"See? Liv is turning up already! Wait a minute, you said B left?" Asher asks, swinging one of the dangling light fixtures above the kitchen island. He's like a toddler on caffeine. "When?"

"What you mean *when*?" Kizzy asks. "Obviously before you two broke in here."

"We didn't break in. The front door was unlocked," Dayvon clarifies.

"Yeah, because that'll hold up to a jury, *Dayvon Jenkins*—holder of the Blackest name of all time." Kizzy laughs at her own joke. "You really need to consider changing that on job applications."

Dayvon smiles at Kizzy, but I can see him gnawing on the inside of his cheek. He's annoyed. He has a right to be because, hell, Kizzy's annoying. I have an overwhelming urge to be near him. As if my proximity can take some of her bite away. But I can't be near Dayvon right now. I need Dayvon to leave so that I can leave.

"Yeah, but how long ago?" Asher again. We all turn to look at him and try to follow his train of thought. He rolls his eyes. "There's only one road to get here. Day and I didn't see anyone else on the way up—except for some abandoned truck deep in the woods."

"Abandoned truck?" Kizzy repeats, then gives me a pointed look. *Why is there an abandoned truck near us, Liv?*

"One of the builders," I say, as though I'm reassuring everyone and not just her. "Sometimes they'll leave their trucks here and carpool with each other."

"The hell with the builders, yo. Where's Brendan?" Asher asks.

"I'm not his fucking babysitter," Kizzy says. "All I know is he was gone before I got here." She gives me an innocent look, tossing the hot potato to me.

Asher and Dayvon turn to me for an explanation.

"We got into a fight," I blurt out. "I mean, nothing physical." Shit, why did I add that? They're already wondering about my lip. "We were arguing. We had a different idea about how tonight was going to go. So, I kicked him to the curb and called Kizzy up. You know, for emotional support."

Asher spits out a laugh. "Kizzy? Emotional support? Yeah, go ahead and invite Putin while you're at it."

Kizzy gives him the finger.

"And what? This gas station uniform was supposed to make you more snuggly?" Asher tugs at Kizzy's sleeve, and she slaps his hand away.

"But Brendan rolled with you, right?" Dayvon asks me, ignoring their drama. "So how did he leave? We only saw your car out there."

My hands are at it again. Fumbling like they need something to grip onto. I tuck them into my pits to steady them, but nothing on me feels even right now. "Okay," is all I can manage.

"I let him take my car," Kizzy says. "When did we enter a *Knives Out* murder mystery? Y'all done with your interrogation?"

She looks at me and laughs. A deep, labored laugh. Like someone on a marathon becoming deliriously happy to see the finish line. I join to make the laughter seem less manic.

"Okay, you two are being fucking nutty." Asher pulls out his phone. "I'm texting B to see what really happened."

"Don't be such a bitch," Kizzy says with an eye roll. "A little thunderstorm is suddenly making you suspicious of everything? If we're so scary, then leave."

Asher looks up from his phone. "As much as I loathe your company, Kiz, my car's in a bit of a predicament at the moment. Or did you forget?" He points down at his muddy shoes.

"Then call Triple A," Kizzy snaps back.

Asher mimics her in a high-pitched voice, running low in his arsenal of witty comebacks.

"I'll drive you guys," I chime in. Triple A can take ages. Brendan is not going to keep quiet for that long. "My dad made sure to get me tires with wet road traction. He has this insane fear of me being abandoned on the side of the road during a storm. Which I guess isn't so insane after all."

"You don't have to do that," Dayvon says. "It's too dangerous."

"Yeah, *you* don't have to do that, Liv," Kizzy says sharply.

She thinks I'm trying to leave on purpose. She thinks I'm trying to ditch her and Sherie and leave them holding the bag. Or maybe even that I'll go get help. Which, no lie, has crossed my mind . . .

"I can take them. I'm a better driver."

"Yeah, but I know my car."

"And a car's a fucking car. Doesn't matter who's driving it."

I frown. "So a seventy-year-old can drive just as well as a thirty-year-old?"

Kizzy shrugs. "My nai nai still drives herself to bingo."

"Yo, what's that?" Dayvon points toward the fireplace. To a lump on the floor. Kizzy's Trump mask. This girl forgot to hide it while humoring Asher. My heart drops to the floor and rolls right next to it.

"That?" Kizzy picks up the mask and scrutinizes it like it's the first time she's ever laid eyes on it. "Looks like a Trump mask."

"Why the hell is there a Trump mask in here?" Dayvon asks.

Kizzy looks at me, and I look at her. We argue with our eyes, warning the other to come up with an answer.

"Obviously someone left it," I say, losing the game.

"Who? I thought it was just you and B here?"

"Kizzy brought a friend." I look at her again. Take that.

"You kick it with someone who wanted to rock a Trump mask?" Dayvon asks her.

"Apparently," Kizzy says, more to me than to Dayvon. "You know, for irony. They left with Brendan."

Dayvon frowns at her and it's clear that he's not following her story. He doesn't get a chance to ask another question because Kizzy's pocket starts ringing. She looks down at it and her skin grows pale right in front of us.

"Hey." Asher steps forward, his phone pressed to his ear. I

forgot all about him. "Why do you have Brendan's phone in your pocket?"

Kizzy's jaw clenches as she and Asher engage in a stare-off. The phone keeps ringing, slicing through the air.

"I found it," she says, her mouth barely separating.

"You found it?" Asher repeats. "Before or after he took off with your MAGA-loving friend?"

This is it. This is the end. We might as well put all our cards on the table. Explain to Asher and Dayvon what we were trying to do. There's no way we're getting out of this, and poor Sherie is down there wondering if the night is already over.

"Just say what you want to say, Asher." Kizzy's staring at them with her laser eyes again. I've never been happier that she gave Sherie her pocketknife, but I can't help but wonder if the stun gun is still on her.

Brendan's phone stops ringing, and Asher lowers his. Nods slowly as if he's also considering what weapons Kizzy has in her pockets. "Okay." He swallows. "Tell me where Brendan is, and I'll let this go."

He's scared, and Kizzy knows it. She feeds off it. She smiles and takes a step toward Asher. Then another. And another. Asher doesn't move. He can't or else he'll look like a punk. But he keeps sneaking glances at me and Dayvon, wondering if either of us are going to tell her to stop.

"Let what go?" Kizzy asks. "You? Nobody's keeping you here, Asher." She takes another step, her hand in her pocket.

"Kizzy," I say, but she doesn't look at me. Just fiddles in her pocket.

"Yo, Kiz. Chill out," Dayvon tries. "This is getting weird."

Kizzy stops inching toward Asher and turns her head to Dayvon. He shifts a little, as though determining if he'll need to tackle her.

"All right." Asher pulls out his phone again. "Fuck this. I'm calling—"

The sky cracks above us, flashing light across all our faces. Then, after a second, it's gone. All the lights are.

The power is dead.

EIGHT

FIVE MONTHS AGO

WHEN I WAKE UP FROM THE DARKNESS, I CAN'T move and there's a bright light in my eyes. Bright enough to blind me.

"Liv?" a voice I don't recognize says. "You're all right. You're in good hands. You had a bit of a scare out there on the track, but you're okay now."

Who's talking to me, and what are they talking about? I try sitting up, but I still can't move. It's not until the penlight leaves my eyes that I take in my surroundings. I'm strapped tight to a gurney as the road underneath me jostles me back and forth. There are machines beeping and buzzing next to me, and some Indian guy with thick black hair tousled on the top of his head smiling at me as he scribbles something down on a clipboard. He looks nice enough, but what in the actual fuck?

"Dad?" I say, and my voice doesn't seem like it's coming from me. Panicked, I try to sit up again and, holy shit, why is there a ringing inside my head? "Dad!"

"Shh, Liv. I'm right here." I feel my dad's warm, calloused hand squeezing mine. Possibly the only finance bro with rough hands, but my dad has a habit of taking things apart and never putting them back together. We have a shed filled with all his unfinished projects, circuit boards and screws splayed about like spilling guts.

"Am I dead?" I ask him, because nothing feels real at the moment. Not even his hand. "Am I dying?"

"No, baby. You're not dying," Dad reassures me, but I can't help but notice him sneak a glance at the EMT on the other side of me. As though he needs to be certain himself.

"Vitals look good, Liv," the EMT says to me. "We're just taking you to the hospital to get another look at that cut on your head. Unfortunately, as you went down, your head connected with one of the hurdles."

My head? No, it wasn't my head that needed to be checked. It was my heart. It all started coming back to me now. I was stretching out on the grass, getting ready for my relay and blasting Paramore through my headphones. I needed something loud and angry. This was an important meet. The most important one, actually. And I needed to be on my A game more than anything, though I knew it would be tough after the month that I had. . . .

When I took off my headphones to remove my warm-up suit,

I heard my dad's whistle. "THE PORT-ER BLIIIIITZ," he hollered from the stands. My dad's the type of guy who never needed a mic or megaphone. His voice just has a natural bass that could carry through a hurricane.

I looked toward the stands, where I saw him waving like a madman, as though I could miss him in his bright yellow T-shirt that had one of the most unflattering pictures of me stretched across his chest. He held up his phone, which I assumed was my mom on FaceTime. She had a huge meeting that she couldn't miss, but said she would sneak out to watch my race. On the row in front of Dad sat Sherie, looking tiny and folded up into herself. I hadn't seen her much since the funeral, and her pale skin indicated she hadn't left the house a lot aside from school. Still, she showed up for me today. She gave me a small wave, then tucked her hands back into the pockets of her hoodie.

I should've been happy. Inspired, even, by the show of love for my most important meet. But instead of focusing on the people who were here, I couldn't help but notice the empty spaces next to them. Spaces where Brendan would be, holding up a sign with my name, a huge grin on his face. Spaces where Hope would be, my name written on each of her cheeks with sparkly purple glitter because she knew it was my favorite color. But Brendan was MIA, and Hope . . . Hope was dead. Hope was buried in Eagle Harbor Cemetery forever clothed in a black wrap dress she would've hated, wearing delicate diamond studs when everyone knew she was a hoops girl.

That's when the pain in my chest hit me. A sharp stab, as though someone had punched right through my rib cage with brass knuckles. The pain was so intense, so alarming, that it literally took my breath away. I gasped for air, but my lungs burned with each attempt. I clawed at my chest, scratching to let the oxygen in, but it was useless.

"You okay, Liv?" one of my teammates asked.

I couldn't answer. Just stumbled onto the track to get help. To reach my dad, who now stood up, watching me with concerned eyes. I opened my mouth to scream for help, but then the ground rushed toward me and . . . darkness.

My mom runs into my hospital partition just as the nurses finish sticking things all over my chest. I waited for them to pull out the paddles to make my heart work again, but they never grabbed them. Didn't they know that I was having a heart attack? That I was dying? My mom smothers my face inside her boobs and kisses the top of my head. When she finally pulls away, she touches the bandage on my forehead before giving my dad a fretful look.

"What in the world happened?" she asks.

"She just fell." My dad pinches the bridge of his nose, something he does to keep the tears away. "She was about to start her relay and . . . I don't know."

"You don't know?" My mom throws her hands up in exhaustion. "I miss one meet, Derek. Just one meet, and the next thing I know my daughter's rushed to the hospital."

"Baby, I'm sure the same thing would've happened if you were physically there."

"Well, did she seem sick before she left? Did she eat?" Mom turns to me now and grabs my hand. "Liv, I need you to be honest with us, okay? Did you . . . take anything?"

I snatch my hand away from her. "Mom."

"I know it's been rough without Hope, but, sweetie, if you did anything to hurt yourself, it's best that you tell me and Dad now before the doctor runs tests."

"Mom!" It's the only word I can manage. I don't know what pissed me off more—the audacity that she thinks I'm on drugs or whatever, or that she described life after Hope as just *rough*. Like her death was a test I bombed after a night of partying.

Thankfully, *thankfully*, the doctor strolls in at that moment. All cool, calm, collected like he hasn't just walked into an inquisition. He flips through his chart, then flips on a smile.

"Olivia Porter?" he asks.

"Am I dying?" I respond.

Mom sucks in a gasp and crumbles into the chair next to me. Dad clutches my shoulder.

The doctor throws back his head and laughs, in only the way a white man with a medical degree can. "Far from it. Vitals look great. Breathing is nice and clear, just how we like to hear it."

My mom exhales, and my dad's grip on my shoulder loosens. I blink and clutch my chest. Try to feel my faulty heart. My rusty lungs. "I don't . . . I don't understand. My heart stopped working.

It's done it before, but this time felt different. It felt like the end."

The doctor nods with his smug smile. "Yeah, panic attacks feel that way sometimes. I've had patients who thought they were having a heart attack. I'm going to send you home with a referral to some great local therapists to talk to you about a possible anxiety diagnosis, especially since you said you've felt this way before. Now, let's take a look at that nasty cut on your forehead to make sure you don't need any stitches."

The doctor cracks a few jokes as he pokes at the wound on my forehead, but I can't hear them. I can barely see him. All I see are my parents exchanging a look with each other. Their daughter isn't dying. Their daughter is just . . . *crazy*?

My parents let me stay home for a week. Enough time to rest, recuperate, and schedule my first appointment with some therapist named Dr. Liora Solomon. She has a thick accent that reminds me of sunny days and umbrella straws in coconuts. Plus, she has a painting by Chuck Styles of Dr. Martin Luther King Jr. and Malcolm X posing like an Outkast album cover hanging in her office. She just might win me over.

Today's my first day back at Sedgefield High. And though my mom was reluctant, Dad reminded her that there was only a week left in the school year. I could handle just one week. I believed him . . . until I set foot through the doors and everyone in the hall seemed to get real quiet. I look around, waiting for someone to greet me or even ask if I'm okay. Search for Kizzy or Sherie or

Coko or Sy'rai. But nobody says anything. No one even looks at me. In fact, they look everywhere *but* at me. As though I'm contagious and one glance my way will cause them to faint. I make my way to my locker and might as well be marching through the halls butt-naked. Even without eyes directly on me, I feel their questions. Their ridicule, even. But they wouldn't dare have any of those thoughts if I were sandwiched between Hope and Brendan.

"I got this," I say to myself as I pull out my book for first period from my locker. "It's just one week." I close my locker and see two guys I don't recognize laughing with each other but looking in my direction.

"Our bad," one of them says to me. "We didn't mean to interrupt your conversation."

"Make sure to say hello to yourself from us," the other says, and they both grow weak with laughter again. With their oily skin and oversized jeans that are scuffed and thready at the bottom from being dragged under their shoes. Who are they even? And why do they have the nerve to even speak to me? And why can't I move my mouth to ask any of these questions?

Like some kind of cocoa-buttered miracle, Tia Shepherd steps in between me and my audience of two and gives them a once-over that probably has them questioning their life choices. "Which one of you is Dungeon and which of you is Dragon?" she asks them.

The taller one scoffs. "You can only be a dragon in D&D if your Dungeon Master allows you to. Even then, being a dragon can cause serious balance issues in the play. If the dragon destroys every enemy, then everyone else would just get bored. I mean, does that sound like fun to you?"

Tia stares at him. And stares. Then stares some more. The guy scratches his ear to give his hand something to do. His friend looks down the hall, possibly searching for a subtle way to escape the awkwardness of it all.

"Wow," Tia says finally. "You just spit out the weakest bar ever and think you deserve the honor to speak to *the* Liv Porter? Don't you have a gecko somewhere to feed?"

The taller guy storms off without another word, his friend cackling close behind him. All tension leaves my body as Tia turns to me.

"Welcome back," she says with a smile, a tiny gap between her two front teeth on full display. "I see you didn't need any stitches."

I blink, then remember the cut on my forehead. "Oh, no. The doctor said it was just an abrasion." I touch the healing scar near my hairline, then quickly drop my hand. Try not to draw further attention to it. Hell, try not to draw further attention to me.

"That's what's up. Mederma will clear that right up." She walks over and hooks her arm through mine and leads me down the hall, as though we've been doing this stroll together for years. "Okay, so word on the street is that the cafeteria has Pizza Hut all this week instead of just on Thursday. I think the lunch ladies didn't feel like defrosting the chicken nuggets for the final days of school. I mean, personally, I'm a Papa Johns girl—that Shaq-a-Roni slaps, but I can fuck with some Pizza Hut. Oh, and one of the assistant principals will be out this week. You know, the pregnant one? Not because she had the baby, but apparently her husband done had a baby with another woman. Talk about Real Housewives of Sedgefield, boo."

Tia goes on and on, catching me up on what I missed while I was away as we weave in between our classmates who occasionally shoot curious glances our way. I'm probably looking just as curious. I could count on two hands how many times I've directly talked to Tia, but here she was, escorting me through the halls like my personal emotional support person. It's nice. It's a little too nice. I stop in my tracks and pull away. Tia raises her eyebrows at me.

"Forget something in your locker?" she asks.

I shake my head. "Why . . . why are you doing this?"

"Doing what?"

"This." I wave a finger in between us. "I haven't been . . . pleasant to you."

Pleasant is an understatement. I've been a straight-up bitch to Tia. I've been a straight-up bitch to lots of people. Especially Hope. Especially that last night with Hope. That's probably why my girls aren't around. They must know something went down between us that final night. I shake my head again. This time, to jostle out the memories of Hope.

"I don't deserve this." I don't even realize I said that last part out loud until Tia's eyebrows fall and her face seems to melt into something gentle.

“I’ve been there,” she says. “Hell, I’m probably still there. And . . . I know how lonely it can be.” She doesn’t directly say where *there* is, but she doesn’t need to. She’s right. We’re both in the thick of *there*. Whereas I deserve to be in it alone, she’s setting up camp right next to me. Willing to teach me how to pitch my tent and start my first fire. I blow out a shaky breath as the novelty of it all hits me. I don’t know what I need, but she seems to.

“Now come on.” She hooks her arm through mine again. “I know you’re not trying to get a tardy slip on your first day back.” She walks me to my first class and makes sure I’m settled in my seat before telling me she can meet me for lunch. I nod and as she leaves, I notice the window next to my desk. The sun peeking out in the east. The sunlight spills into the room, making it easier to see everyone and everything.

NINE

NOW

WE ALL STAND STILL FOR A MOMENT, AND THE only sound is the rain thrashing against the windows.

"That was just a flicker, right?" Asher asks finally.

We all wait to see if he's right. We keep waiting. More waiting.

"A flicker is like a few seconds," Dayvon says. "It's been more than a few seconds."

"Fuck." Asher throws up his hands. At least I think he does. It's hard to make out anything with the only light coming from the moon—and the clouds take away most of that. "So we're stuck in a power outage with Kizzy being all weird and murder-y. This is how horror movies begin. One of us is about to get sliced and diced before the opening credits."

"Don't tempt me," Kizzy mutters, moving toward one of the

windows to get a better view of the storm. It's severe out there. The kind where schools get closed early to make sure everyone's off the roads before flooding.

"Yeah, chill, Asher," Dayvon says.

"Chill?" Asher lets out a small laugh. "You're the main one who should be freaking out. The Black guy usually dies first. I mean, usually it's the *funny* Black guy, but hey. Slim pickings."

Dayvon smirks. "Shut up. Black guys are heroes now. Jordan Peele, bitch. If anything, you should be the one who's worried."

"Nobody should be worried," I say. The madness has to stop. "It's just a little power outage. I'm sure it'll be back on in no time."

"Unless this was part of your and Kizzy's plan." Asher keeps buzzing around my ear like a fruit fly. If he had the same energy toward his schoolwork, homey would be at the top of our class. "You two want to keep the lights off long enough to complete whatever satanic ritual you were up to before we got here. First, B was the sacrifice. Now us."

"Asher, you're not worthy enough to be anyone's sacrifice," Kizzy says, "In fact, I'm sure your family would hand you over to us with a bow just to get you out of their hair. But if you're this damn worried, you can peace out. Like I said before."

"One step ahead of you." Asher presses something on his phone. After a second, he frowns at it. "Yo, Day. Can you call out on your phone?"

Dayvon rummages through his pocket until he finds his phone. The light from the screen illuminates his face. "No service."

Panicked, I try my phone and see Kizzy working on hers, too. We look at each other. Kizzy shakes her head.

"Fucking perfect." Asher shoves his phone back into his pocket. "Thunderstorm. No power or cell service. Cue the cannibalistic family to barge in and torture us."

Kizzy and Dayvon both groan at Asher, telling him to shut up in their own, colorful ways. I step to the center of the room to try to bring some order. Just like I was back on the track team. Boost morale after a lousy meet.

"Okay, let's calm down," I say. "I'm sure the power will be back on shortly. When the power's on, phone service will follow. Then we can call Triple A or whomever to get you guys out of here."

"Maybe it's not a major outage," Dayvon says. "Like, it could be centralized to this house because it's new construction. All we'd need to do is mess with the electrical panel."

Asher snaps his fingers and points to him. "My man." To me. "Where's the electrical panel?"

I shrug. "I have no idea." And there goes my Ted Lasso moment.

"What? Didn't your mom, like, design this home?"

"Doesn't mean I know all the ins and outs. Your dad's an actuary. I'm not asking you to predict when I'll die."

"Based on the vibe in here?" Asher looks at his Fitbit. "I'd say in about an hour. Tops."

"All right, logistically, electrical panels are usually in garages or attics, right?" Dayvon says, ignoring Asher and his wisecracks. "I'll have a look around and see if I can find it."

"No," Kizzy and I say in unison, and Dayvon flinches.

"The . . . house is too big," I try. "It'll take you forever. It'll be best if we split up and looked."

"Yeah," Kizzy says, nodding several times. "I like that idea. Dayvon, you search the garages. Asher, you come with me—"

"The hell I am," Asher interrupts.

"And Liv," Kizzy continues, "you check out the lower level. Might be something there."

I can't really see her facial expressions, but based on her tone, I know she's raising her eyebrows. She wants me to check on Sherie and Brendan. See if Brendan duped Sherie into doing something stupid, like letting him go.

"Nah." Dayvon shakes his head. "I don't like the idea of Liv being alone. I'll search with her."

My unease forms a lump in my throat. This definitely throws a wrench into our plan. Now I'll have to think of a way to ditch him once we get to the basement level. "Okay," I say somewhat weakly. "Let's get to it, then."

We each cut on the flashlights on our phones.

"If I don't return," Asher begins, tossing his raincoat onto the floor, "Day, tell my mom I love her. Tell my dad . . . I love Mom."

"Boy, shut up." Kizzy shoves Asher toward the stairs. She glances back at me, and I can feel her nerves piercing me like a swarm of darts before she disappears.

Dayvon and I stand awkwardly in the great room, our flashlights beaming toward each other.

"Where first?" Dayvon asks, breaking the ice.

"Uh, let's try the garages."

He extends a hand toward the mudroom. "After you. My ass would just get us lost anyway. This place is stupid big."

I give him a polite smile. "That's why you didn't want to split up. You didn't know where the hell you were going." I head toward the three-car garage with him close behind, only proving my point.

"So," he says, his breath grazing the back of my neck, "Asher's Ashering."

I laugh. "When isn't Asher Ashering?"

"Fair point. But . . . you have to admit. You and Kizzy were acting a little strange."

I suck in a breath and try to keep my cool. "Were we?"

"Uhh, yeah. Having Brendan's phone, the creepy Trump mask . . . hell, you two hanging out is weird in itself."

"How is it weird? We used to always hang out." We reach the first garage, and I open the door. We take a few steps inside, and our lights swim across the vacant space. The paint fumes so new and fresh that they tickle my nose.

"*Used to* being the key phrase," Dayvon continues, walking along the perimeter of the garage. "You two haven't really kicked it since Hope . . . you know."

There it is again. Everyone's so afraid to talk about what happened to Hope. This is why tonight made sense to me initially. The more people treated Hope's death like an urban legend, the less real it felt. It's hard to grieve for an anecdote. Tonight was about her death becoming concrete. Then hopefully, finally, I could shed a tear about it like a real best friend. I had one of the only dry pairs of eyes at Hope's funeral. There's something lonely about being the only strip of dry land in a sea of tears. Something scary.

"You haven't really kicked it much with anyone after Hope, though," Dayvon says, reminding me he's here. "I tried calling you. Texted you. Even hit you up on IG, but . . . radio silence."

I stop in my tracks just as the red manual cord dangling from the center of the garage thwaps me across the face. "So, I'm not allowed to grieve? I'm supposed to laugh and smile and kiki with everyone so *they* don't feel bad about my best friend dying?"

"No, but you could allow others to grieve with you." He presses a hand to his chest. "You could've allowed *me* to grieve with you."

There goes Dayvon again. Being sweet and perfect and saying all the right things. And he *was* right. Dayvon was grieving, too. Him and Hope were friends as well. But even Dayvon has flaws behind that gentle and handsome exterior. I've seen those flaws, even if he doesn't know it. Still, there's no need to make them bigger by exposing him to my own bullshit.

"There's nothing here," I say. "Let's look at the other garage."

I'm out the door, and Dayvon jogs behind me to catch up. He gives me a few moments of silence as we walk through the mudroom again, crossing the hall to get to the second garage entrance.

"I'm sorry if I'm making things weird," Dayvon says as I open the door. "I just missed seeing you around, and I didn't know how to tell you."

I pause before walking through the threshold. Why is he doing this to me? Being the romantic lead in a Jasmine Guillory novel for me? *Me*. Doesn't he know who I am and what I've done? Even before tonight.

"I think you just did," I manage.

Dayvon raises an eyebrow. "And?"

"And what?"

A soft laugh escapes his mouth. "And . . . did you miss me?"

I take a deep breath and walk into the garage, even though I don't even remember what we're searching for. Not until I trip over a can of paint blanketed by the darkness. I curse under my breath and resume searching the room with my flashlight.

"Guess I got my answer," Dayvon mumbles, scanning the room with his light as well.

I drop my phone to my side. "Please, Dayvon. Not now."

"What? You did give me an answer. You invited Brendan here tonight. Not me."

"Yeah. Brendan's been my friend since elementary school," I remind him.

"Is that all?"

"What the . . . ? Yes! He was in love with Hope! They were the golden couple."

"Is that why you didn't shoot your shot? Because he was in love with Hope?" He moves closer to me. "Is that why you never really gave us a chance?"

I frown. "Dayvon, we went on a date. Once. It didn't work out. I thought we both knew we were better off as friends."

"Yeah, because you kept your eyes on Brendan and Hope the whole damn time!" The irritation grows in his throat. His voice so edgy that I take a few steps away from him—even though I'm the one who has a man tied up in the basement.

He senses my uneasiness, then takes a deep breath. "You didn't really try, but I know something was there. Something between us. Brendan knew. Hope knew . . . but you punked out."

I grit my teeth. What part of *not now* did he not get? Having a heart-to-heart while our mutual friend is tied up in the basement is not a good look. I usually wear velvet gloves with Dayvon, but tonight? I need to choose violence. "You're coming across real thirsty right now. A girl doesn't show interest in you and now she's a punk? She's weak? What's next? You going to call me a lesbian?"

We engage in a stare-off. Not truly able to see each other's facial expressions, but we both feel it. The anger. The pain. The exhaustion. They all dance between us.

"I think inviting your dead best friend's ex to an empty house has thirst written all over it."

Dayvon's words punch me in the chest, leaving knuckle prints right on my heart. This smug bastard. Walking around like he's Will Smith pre–Oscar slap, all golden and beloved as though he doesn't have his slip-ups. His dark moments. But all things in the dark eventually come to light.

I move closer to him. Get on my tippy-toes so my mouth is right next to his ear. "I saw you," I hiss.

Dayvon jerks back. My words have done the damage I intended them to. His breath comes out ragged as he stares at me. Studying me for the truth. Wondering what I'll do with that truth. Even worse, who might I tell.

"Liv," he starts, his voice hoarse and full of worry, "it's not what you—"

A scream screeches through the air, slicing through the silence and causing both of us to jump.

"Was that what I think it was?" he asks in a hush.

I strain my ears for confirmation but only hear the blistering rain and wind. If it was a scream, it definitely wasn't a joyous one. That person sounded frightened. That person sounded like they were fighting for their life.

"Did that come from below?" Dayvon asks again.

Fuck. Brendan. *Sherie.* Something's going down. Before I can put all the puzzle pieces together, Dayvon darts out of the garage.

"Dayvon—wait!" I chase after him. There's no telling what he'll find. I need to get there first. Make sure Sherie's okay. Make sure I have enough time to explain to Dayvon why Brendan's actually here, and bruised and tied up.

But Dayvon doesn't make it easy for me. Even though I'm the former track star, he's still the point guard on the basketball team. Usually the fastest on the court, he doesn't even let the house's confusing layout slow him down. He swings open the door to the laundry room, pivoting when he doesn't find the stairs to the ground level. He spots the entrance right next to it, and he's down the stairs in a few seconds, twisting and turning around in the rec room. Seeking the source of the scream.

"Fuck, this place is huge," he says in between breaths. "Where do you think that scream came from?"

"Maybe it's just the wind," I say, catching up to him. "But why don't you check out this side." I point to my right. Toward the office and playroom, in the exact opposite direction of the basketball court. "And I'll look over there to be safe."

Dayvon gives me a nod just as another cry cuts through the air. This one deeper, more guttural. This one obviously coming from the side of the house where the basketball court is located. Dayvon darts in that direction, and my heart drops to my stomach.

Shit, shit, shit. This can't be good.

I run after Dayvon, trying to stay in the present but thinking of several stories I can tell that won't impact my future. If only I had Kizzy's stun gun. I could slow him down, give myself a few moments to figure out what to do about him and Brendan and Asher. I can't even believe I'm thinking about hurting Dayvon. Who am I becoming?

I bump into Dayvon's back. He stops in his tracks as soon as he reaches the threshold of the basketball court. Oh God. It's over. I swallow and step around him. Get ready to rip off the Band-Aid.

Only the wound is too deep for that.

Sherie's on the floor. Face down. Mask off. A tiny trail of blood spilling from her head. I cry out and slap both hands over my mouth, trying to keep the bile down.

"I . . . I didn't do it."

It's only then I notice someone else in the room. A pair of legs stand next to Sherie's body. My eyes scan up and follow the light from Dayvon's phone. Brendan. Staring back at us, wide-eyed. Gripping Sherie's mask. No ropes in sight.

Oh shit.

TEN

"I DIDN'T DO IT!" BRENDAN'S STILL SHOUTING, both hands high above his head. His eyes darting and full of panic. The wild eyes of a guy who might have bashed a girl's head in.

"What the hell's going on?" Dayvon's voice is razor-thin. Almost squeaky.

Brendan blinks at him through the phone light. "Day?"

"They said you left," Dayvon continues. "What happened? What did you do?"

"I didn't!" Brendan's voice booms. "I told you . . . I found her like this."

"Is she . . . ?" I can't finish the question. Dead is finite, an abrupt stop. I already lost Hope. I just found my way back to Sherie. She can't be . . . I shut my eyes for a few seconds, but when

I reopen them, she's just lying there. Still. I lose my footing. Fall against Dayvon's arm as he reaches out with this free hand to steady me. It doesn't work, though. Everything's still tilted.

Footsteps hammer behind me, then screech to a stop. Kizzy and Asher wedge in between Dayvon and me. Kizzy sucks in a wet breath when her eyes land on Sherie. Sherie on the floor. Sherie on the floor bleeding.

"Brendan?" Asher asks. His eyes shoot between Brendan and Sherie. "Brendan, what the fuck, yo? What happened?"

"He was supposed to be gone," Dayvon says. "But we found him here. With . . . her." He looks down at his feet so he doesn't have to look at Sherie.

"Is she dead?" I ask, finally able to say the word. It lingers at the back of my tongue, and I lean against the doorframe. I still can't right myself.

Kizzy crumples in half, burying her face in her knees as she coughs. I can't tell if she's panting or crying. She won't let anyone see.

"What the hell is happening?" Asher grabs at his hair.

I need to move. I need to get my feet to work. I take a deep breath before pushing myself off the doorframe. Wiggle my toes in my boots to ground me, then run over to Sherie and kneel next to her. I peel her blond hair away from the matted blood on her forehead. Her eyes stare back at me. Her eyes stare *through* me. Not blinking. Not moving. I press two fingers against her neck and check for a pulse. Nothing. I move to another section of her neck but still feel nothing. No breaths. No beats. Just stillness. A cry hiccups out of me as I fall flat on my butt. Brendan edges away from me and paces back and forth. He shouts several curses into the air as he continues to pace.

"Again, what the fuck is happening?" Asher demands. He turns to Kizzy, panicked. "Sherie was your friend with the Trump mask? The one who was supposed to take Brendan home?"

Kizzy springs back up to her feet as if her power switch just clicked on. She charges toward Brendan and shoves him in his back. Brendan propels several inches away, tripping over his feet.

"You killed her!" she screams at him. "You *killed* her!" She clenches her fists and starts walloping Brendan, trying to connect anywhere on his body. His chest, his arms, his chin. Brendan dodges as many as he can, but Kizzy's too quick. Too wiry. He finally gathers Kizzy up in a bear hug and lifts her off the floor.

"Stop—stop!" he pleads as Kizzy kicks his knees.

Dayvon rushes over and pries Kizzy away from Brendan, carrying her across the room.

"Let me go!" Kizzy demands, trying to leap away from Dayvon. "He's the one you need to restrain. He's the murderer! First Hope—now Sherie!"

"Me?" Brendan slaps his chest so hard that it booms throughout the room. "I'm the murderer when you bitches tied me up and tried to carve up my face?"

"Wait, what?" Asher rubs his forehead. "They, like, kidnapped you? The girls?"

Brendan's nostrils flare, in and out. He doesn't know how to answer the question. On one hand, he'd look like a coward. Some wimp who let three girls get the best of him. On the other hand, though, he needs this story to prove his innocence.

"Is that why you killed Sherie? Because she wanted to maim you?" Asher asks.

Brendan scoffs in irritation. "Sherie was the sane one out of all of them. She cut me loose. I was leaving when I heard her scream."

Kizzy barks out a laugh. "How fucking convenient."

Dayvon gives her a disappointed look as he uses his body to form a wall between her and Brendan.

Brendan stops and glares at her. "And where were you?"

"I was with Asher, asshole. We were trying to get the power back on."

"Well . . ." Asher stretches out the word. "We did get separated. You were already down the stairs when I ran down."

"Yeah, because I was trying to get away from your skeevy ass. You were trying to smash, and I was looking for the electrical panel. I left you to be productive!"

"Then maybe caught Sherie cutting Brendan loose?" Asher adds.

Kizzy starts cussing him out, and Asher and Brendan dish it right back. Dayvon tries to control the masses, but something Asher says haunts me. *Cutting* Brendan loose. Kizzy gave Sherie the knife. With how edgy everyone's being right now, none of them should get a hold of that weapon. I dig through Sherie's pockets with gentle hands. I don't want to disturb her—her body deserves respect.

"Enough!" Dayvon booms, cutting through all the noise. "Enough of this blame game shit. Someone is dead here, okay? *Dead*. We'll let the cops figure out the logistics. But we need to get the power on to make the call and get some help."

"He needs to be tied back up, though," Kizzy says, stabbing a finger in Brendan's direction. "I don't trust his ass."

Brendan scoffs. "Want to tell everyone how I got this?" He points at the bump on his head. "Huh? What about you, Liv?"

He turns in my direction, and I scramble back on all fours like a crab. Brendan pauses, face bunched up in confusion. "Are you serious right now?" he asks. "You're cowering from me? When it was your conniving ass that lured me here?"

"The Swiss Army Knife is gone," I announce to everyone, but keep my eyes on Brendan. "You said she cut you loose, but the knife is gone. What you'd do with it?"

Brendan's frown shifts from confusion to disgust. "How the fuck am I supposed to know? I told you—I tried to bounce. Only reason I'm still here is because I thought she needed help."

"So, it was an accident?" Asher tries. "You wrestled her for the knife after she freed you. She slipped and busted her head. That's okay, B. They attacked you. That's considered self-defense."

Brendan grits his teeth, his jawline throbbing in anger. "You, too, Ash?" he says, lips barely moving.

"Just saying. It's not a good look getting called into questioning for the death of two girls. At least with this one, it's pretty open and shut."

"With this one? You think I had something to do with Hope, too? You're supposed to be my boy."

"I am your boy. I'm just saying . . ." Asher looks between Kizzy and me. "They obviously had some compelling evidence to say that you did."

Brendan flashes me a heated look, and I glance down at Sherie, scooch closer to her. As though I'm expecting her to pop up and tell us all to keep it down. As though she's trying to sleep. If only.

"Empty your pockets," Kizzy says. "If you're claiming you didn't snatch the knife from her, then empty your pockets."

"Empty yours," Brendan snaps. "I can already think of at least one weapon you have on you. What else?"

"It's obvious I'd have something for protection. I'm a girl who—"

"Now you're playing the gender card." Brendan throws his head back in annoyance.

"I'm a girl," Kizzy continues, louder now, "in a fucked-up town where men get away with murder just because they can bounce a ball. You tower over all of us. Why do you need a weapon? So empty. Your. Pockets."

Brendan smirks, then looks over at Asher for backup. Asher looks down at the floor. Brendan tries Dayvon next, but Dayvon gives him a small shrug.

"Don't see what the big deal is," Dayvon says. "Just do it so we can move on."

"Fuck this," Brendan says, sweeping the room with his glare. "Fuck all y'all. I'm out of here." He storms toward the door but trips over Sherie's arm in the process. She jostles like a fish out of water, and I look away. I can't see her like that. Brendan glances down at her like he wants to apologize, then tightens his jaw and continues his march.

Dayvon moves in front of the threshold and blocks him.

"What you doing, Day?" Brendan asks. The question comes out thick with warning.

Dayvon takes a breath as if he's trying to amp himself up. "Someone's dead. It might be a good idea for us all to stay put until the cops come."

"Yeah, well, I'm a victim, too. I'd rather take my chances with going to the cops directly instead of waiting for them to get here."

Dayvon shakes his head. "That's not a good look, B. We should stick together."

"I'm not sticking with these bitches, bruh."

I feel Dayvon's eyes on me, searching for answers, but I can't look up at him. I can't look at anyone, not even Sherie. Poor Sherie. She shouldn't even be here tonight. Kizzy and I worked on her for days, but Sherie was the holdout. She kept telling us, *Hope wouldn't want this. Hope loved Brendan.* But I turned that sentiment around on her.

"If Hope really loved Brendan," I said, sitting next to her on my bed, "doesn't he owe it to her to be honest? And if he hasn't been honest before, all we're doing is giving him a gentle push. Nobody's going to really get hurt. You told us that Hope saved your life, remember? Don't you want to save her memory?" I remember placing my hand on top of hers. Her hands were always cold, no matter the season. But I enveloped them into mine and dealt with the clamminess to make her a promise: *I got you. We got this.*

Look at us now.

"I can't answer for them," Dayvon says, pulling me from my memory. "But they can explain themselves to the cops. Just like you."

"Day, I ain't playing. Move out my way," Brendan says.

"No."

"Move out my way or I'll move you."

"Do what you gotta do, bruh."

Brendan huffs, then tries to push past Dayvon, but Dayvon pushes him back. Their sneakers squeak and glide across the floor as they struggle. Kizzy and Asher rush over to break them up—or to keep Brendan in. I squeeze my eyes closed. If I squeeze them tight enough, I'll be home when I reopen them. In my bed under my favorite comforter. And this whole night would've been a dream. Or maybe it's the night before Halloween and the Ghost of Halloween Present pays me a visit to warn me of how tonight might go.

When I open them, though, everyone's still scuffling, and Sherie still lies next to me. Lifeless. Except . . . except now there's something underneath her. I lean closer and a folded-up sheet of paper pokes out from under her chest. I didn't notice it before. Brendan must've jostled her body just enough that it's now visible.

With trembling fingers, I slip the paper from up under her and unfold it. It looks like a social media post, but it's too dark to truly tell. I hold my phone light up to it and see that it's a screenshot. It's Sherie's response to someone on Instagram:

> **CharliesAngel212:** So what if the girl was a lil cuckoo for Cocoa Puffs at times. She said what she said. I'm gonna need yall to start believin Black women. #KeepHopeAlive #Hedidit
>
> **SherieAndFree:** LOL, love that cereal. Srsly tho, appreciate the support, but let's not make this a Black and white thing. I was Hope's best friend. She didn't see color.

Sherie's comment is circled with red marker. An arrow points to it with the words *YOU KILLED HER* in all caps underneath. I suck in a breath and choke from it.

"You guys," I strain, but they're still arguing. Still scuffling. I climb to my feet and face them. "*You guys!*"

Everyone stops what they're doing to turn and look at me. I hold the paper out to them, and it trembles in their direction. "I don't think this was an accident."

ELEVEN

IT'S LIKE A BOMB HAS GONE OFF IN THE BASKET-ball court. Everyone screams at each other, fingers pointing in all directions after I share what was written on the note. I stare at it now as chaos blooms around me: *YOU KILLED HER.* The words are clear. Concise. Not really open to interpretation, yet . . . I have lots of questions.

"Let me see this." Kizzy snatches it out of my hand and almost gives me a paper cut. She holds her phone light against it as she reads everything. The same words I read aloud to everyone. Maybe she thinks if she sees it with her own eyes, it'll all start to make sense. She sucks at her teeth. "What the hell is she LOLing at? And, okay, *best* friend. Hope just had a high tolerance for her."

Asher stops pacing. "Yo, *that's* what you're tripping over?"

"I'm just saying. I hate when people lie for clicks and likes."

"You mad about who was Hope's BFF?" It's Asher's turn to snatch the paper. He stabs at it with his index finger. "'You. Killed. Her.' It's all right there. We have Hope's murderer lying dead in front of us, and now *she's* been murdered. It's the exact opposite of the circle of life. The shit they didn't sing about in *The Lion King*."

Kizzy smirks. "Sherie didn't kill Hope."

"How do you know that?"

"First of all, Sherie Jacobs doesn't even know how to kill a housefly. Second of all, we all know that he killed Hope." She flashes her light in Brendan's face.

"We're still on that?" Brendan asks, shielding his eyes from the light. "One of your friends was killed tonight, yet you're still pressed on that false narrative."

"Just like you're pressed on murdering my friends."

"Kiz," I beg. Sherie's body is barely cold, so it hardly seems appropriate to make jokes about whatever's happened to her.

"What?" Kizzy takes her time to look at each of us like she's pleading her case to a jury. "Think about it. Brendan needed the heat off him, so he tried to set up Sherie—the formerly home-schooled outcast who remained in Hope's shadow. It's a little too on the nose, Brendan. Even for you."

"Yet, you delivered a succinct stereotype of Sherie," Brendan says. "I thought she was supposed to be your friend, and you're writing her off like some loser sidekick."

Instead of a snarky comeback, Kizzy says nothing. Just looks down at Sherie, as though she's now realizing her death is a fact and not a hypothesis. Her body even shifts a little. Her shoulders slump, and her head lowers, like the weight of Sherie's death is finally hitting her.

"Besides," Brendan continues, "I didn't even know Sherie was going to be here to set her up. When the hell would I have time to print out some old-ass IG post? I barely had time to grab a con—" He stops like his sentence just slammed into a brick wall. Silence fills the room.

"A condom," Asher finishes. "Brendan had to get a condom from me before he ditched the bonfire. He had sex on the brain, not murder."

I can't see everyone, but I definitely feel their eyes on me. The clear understanding that Brendan Jean expected to have sex with me. Me, his oldest friend. As well as the best friend of his dead ex. I suddenly feel very naked, so I wrap my arms around myself to be less exposed.

Brendan shakes out his arms, waving off his former thoughts of getting horizontal with me. "But you know who did have time? Liv."

My eyes just about fall out of my head. "Are you fucking serious right now?"

"Funny how nobody saw that note on Sherie except you."

"Ay. Chill, B," Dayvon says, and I really wish he didn't.

If Brendan was angry before, his rage is white-hot now. I'm getting burned just being near him.

"Chill? You don't think she's crazy enough to do it? Do you even know the shit they tried to pull with me before y'all got here?"

"Exactly," I snap, the word ripping out of my body. "If I lured you in here to confess to murdering Hope, why the hell would I kill Sherie for it? Make it make sense."

Brendan shrugs, unfazed by my argument. "That's my point. You turn on your friends on a dime. What makes her any different?"

"Maybe because Sherie doesn't have a history of beating Hope," Kizzy says, sidling up next to me. I want to reach out and hold her hand, but she doesn't like that kind of stuff. Still, her next to me is enough.

Brendan steps toward us, ready to make another point, when Dayvon cuts in front of him.

"I think we're overlooking the big picture right now," Dayvon says. "Someone in here thinks Sherie had something to do with Hope. Someone might've killed Sherie because they think she had something to do with Hope. And that someone is either one of us, or somewhere else in this house."

The words seem to sink into all of us at once, and a hush sweeps across the room. I look toward the open door. All I see is blackness. All I hear is rain pounding against the windows. Rain that could mask the footsteps of another uninvited guest.

"I'm calling the cops," I say, picking up my phone from the floor.

"We don't have service," Dayvon reminds me.

"New construction sites always have spotty service. But sometimes if you find the right spot, you—"

Kizzy smacks the phone out of my hand, and it clatters against the floor. She hovers over me, one hand clenched into a fist, and shadows cloud her face.

"What the hell, Kiz?" I ask, keeping my tone measured so she won't hear the rising fear. I bend down slowly and pick up my phone.

"I get it. We need to call the cops. Someone obviously hurt Sherie . . ."

"Someone *killed* Sherie," Brendan snaps. "The girl hasn't been breathing this whole time."

Kizzy kneels next to me. "I'm just saying, Liv. Before we call them, maybe we need to get our stories straight." Her eyes shift toward Brendan. Fuck. She's right. The first question the cops are going to ask is: *What are you doing here?* I look at Sherie, then to the phone in my hand. Back to Sherie. Loyal Sherie. She didn't want to do any of that tattooing shit. I know she didn't. But Kizzy probably told her that was the only way we'd get real answers, so she rolled with it. That's how she was. Fucking faithful to a fault. Like that time in tenth grade when our chemistry teacher caught me cheating on a quiz. I stayed up the night before on FaceTime, binge-watching *The Boys* with Brendan and tripping off his commentary instead of studying. Sherie made a huge production of leaning forward in her desk to copy the answers from the kid in front of her. Both our asses ended up in detention. It was our first time hanging out without Hope around. She told me all about Chappell Roan, and I told her how to cuss someone out with just a look. No matter how much Sherie contorted her face, she always ended up looking like she was entering a surprise party. We laughed so hard we ended up in detention for another day.

Damn. I had almost forgotten about that. That rare silly moment shared only between us.

"Forget this," Dayvon says, dragging me out of the memory. "I say let's call. Some of us may have different providers. One of us should be able to get through."

At that, he and Asher start trying to call out on their phones. Pacing the room, lifting the phones in the air to get a signal.

Brendan snaps his fingers at Kizzy. "My phone."

Kizzy doesn't take her eyes off me, piling the pressure on extra thick.

"Brendan's still alive," I say. "The most important thing is finding out what happened to Sherie. That's what they'll focus on."

"Sure," Kizzy says. "They'll believe the two Black girls over the superstar. It worked so well last time."

"Now," Brendan demands. There's an edge to his voice. Any second, someone's going off a cliff. Kizzy senses it, too. She pulls his phone from her pocket and shoves it into his hand. Brendan turns on his heel and leaves us next to our dead friend.

"We might need to go up to the top floor," Dayvon says. "I'm not getting shit down here."

"Fuck that." Asher looks up at the raindrops pounding against the windows. "I say we get out of here. Use Liv's car to get to mine."

"Your car is stuck, bruh," Dayvon reminds him. "And the way it's throwing down out there, Liv's can get stuck, too—good tread or not."

"We could still get a better signal out there. And, call me crazy, but I'd rather take my chances in the rain and mud than inside this haunted house with a deranged killer."

I resist the urge to cover Sherie's ear. It's pointless, but I hate the way everyone's talking about her like an outcome instead of an actual person.

"Asher's right," Brendan says. "Let's bounce." He doesn't wait for anyone else to respond. Just struts to the door like the natural leader he is, with Asher trailing after him.

"You guys coming?" Dayvon asks Kizzy and me.

Kizzy sighs as she stands. "Guess so. Come on, Liv. We can talk more in the car."

I look down at Sherie. "We're just leaving her?"

"It's not like she can come with us."

"Kizzy? Really?" Dayvon says. Then to me, softer: "We're leaving *for* her, Liv. The sooner we get out, the sooner we can get someone here to figure out what's happened to her. Isn't that what you want?"

I do. I really do. But it still feels wrong to leave her by herself—cold and alone on the hardwood floor. "Okay." I stand finally. "But I want to find her a blanket."

"All right." Dayvon rests his hand on my back. "Where can we find a blanket?"

I think about the spare room down here. The armoire against the wall. Mom usually kept extra blankets and towels in spaces like that. She always said you can never have enough decorations—in case the interior designer had a last-minute change in vision. I leave the court with Dayvon next to me. He pauses to look back at Kizzy, who still stands next to Sherie.

"You coming?" he asks her.

Kizzy doesn't respond. Just stares down at Sherie with her arms folded across her chest. Taking in Sherie's stillness.

"Give her a minute," I say.

She needs it. Those two were never peas in a pod, but as soon as Hope pulled Sherie into the fold, Kizzy's inner guard dog extended to her, too. Kizzy could talk shit about Sherie, but if some random bitch tried to? Heads would roll. As Dayvon and I walk toward the office space, we pass Brendan and Asher struggling with the patio door.

"What's going on?" Dayvon asks.

"This shit's not budging," Asher says, out of breath.

"What you mean it's not budging?"

"Exactly what he said." Brendan kicks at the glass door. "It was open like a minute ago."

He's right.

"Is there another door down here?" Dayvon asks me.

I close my eyes for a moment and try to remember the floor

plan. "Yeah, there's a covered deck attached to the spare room." I open my eyes and point in the direction I was heading.

Dayvon nods. "Okay. I'll go check that out. You guys go up to the main level. If all else fails, we'll just go through the front door. Same way we came in."

Brendan and Asher scurry up the stairs before I even take a step in that direction. Chivalry is dead when there's a potential murderer among us. By the time I reach the main level, Brendan and Asher are tugging and cussing at the front door.

"That one's stuck, too?" I ask.

"It's more than stuck," Brendan says, stepping back and scowling at the door. "It's locked."

"But it won't let us unlock it," Asher continues. "It's like the dead bolt is frozen shut."

"What do you . . . ?" Before I even finish the question, the answer settles in my gut with a loud thump. I remember touring this place with Mom right after the IT guys installed the smart-home features. "State of the art," the head guy kept saying. "Just one simple tap can turn this bad boy into one giant panic room."

"Why would we need that?" I remember asking.

The guy shrugged. "You know. The world be cray-cray."

Mom and I had exchanged a look, all *Boys and their toys*. Knowing nobody would ever actually need such a feature. Except Mom never told the guy that aloud. I don't remember her telling him to disable anything.

"Oh no," I say to myself as I rush over to the smart-home panel by the door. Just as I expected, the system is down. The backup power generator isn't scheduled to be installed for another month. Still, I helplessly poke at the screen. "Oh no. Oh no. Oh no."

"Stop saying that," Asher demands. He turns to Brendan. "Why the fuck does she keep saying that?"

"Liv." Brendan steps up next to me. The closest he's been to me since this whole night began to unravel. "What's wrong?"

I slap the smart-home screen and rest my hands on top of my head. Try to think. *Think, Liv, think.* But I'm not a tech person. I don't even use that ChatGPT stuff for homework.

"Liv!" Brendan snaps me out of it.

I take a deep breath. "The smart home—it's in default mode."

Brendan waves a hand at me, urging me to continue. "Meaning . . . ?"

"Meaning"—I swallow—"we're in a tomb."

TWELVE

BRENDAN'S AT THE FRONT DOOR AGAIN, CLAWING and kicking at it. As if his sheer will can bust it open. My breathing is rushed and shallow, like I'm gulping air through a straw. Being trapped does that to you, even if you're basically inside a McMansion. Doesn't matter if your coffin is six feet or sixty, it's still a coffin. I try to steady my breath. Do the box breathing my therapist taught me: Inhale for four seconds, hold for four seconds, exhale for four seconds. But the air keeps coming in tiny sips. My lungs are already preserving the oxygen, rationing it like a granola bar on a deserted island. Wait, when *is* the last time I ate something? When will I eat again? Nobody is expected to be here until Monday—that's over forty-eight hours from now. Can you survive not eating for forty-eight hours? The questions send tremors down to my fingertips, and I know what's happening. I can feel the panic rearing its ugly head, ready for a full-blown strike. I reach into my back pocket for another Xanax, but my hand is suddenly too big. Or my pocket shrank about six inches. My fingers twist and fumble but can't reach the small packet.

"Hold up, did you just say tomb?" Asher's next to me. I think he's next to me. He sounds like he's underwater, his words leaving his mouth in muffled bursts that do nothing to relieve this feeling that all the air is being sucked out of the room. That we're all underwater now.

I stumble back and bump against something. A console table? A coatrack? But none of those things belong in the ocean. Asher floats in front of me. Opens his mouth to shout at me but only a stream of bubbles escapes. They dance toward me, tiny ripples trailing them, and I grab for the oxygen mask on my face. But it isn't there. It's never been there. My lungs burn, dying for another breath, but if I breathe in, I'll drown. I'll drown. I'll drown.

I'm drowning.

Soon, a hand is pressed against my stomach and Brendan is in front of me. His mouth moves, too, but I can't hear him. I'm dying. The hand on my stomach jostles as another hand anchors my shoulder. Brendan's closer now, and his words take form of something I can hold on to.

"Breathe, Liv," he says, louder now. "Breathe into your belly. Make my hand move." His fingers tickle my stomach, letting me know he's right here.

I nod weakly but do as I'm told. The first breath is tentative, still expecting to choke on water. But when that doesn't happen, I try again. Deeper this time. The third time even deeper. Brendan's hand begins to move in and out with each breath, and soon, I feel the floor underneath me again. I smell the blend of gum and beer on Brendan's breath. Hear him breathing right alongside me. See Asher's eyes studying us, all squinted with confusion. After a few more moments of grounding myself, Brendan nods and gives my shoulder one last gentle squeeze before backing away. It takes everything in me not to reach for him. To feel his hands on me again, but we have bigger issues than my complicated emotions.

Brendan gives a final kick to the front door and spins around. He spots the glass door on the other side of the great room and makes a beeline for that. Yanks at the door handle, but it doesn't budge. He barks out a curse.

"Sooo, now that whatever that was is over," Asher begins, "Liv, why the hell did your mom design a house like a fucking tomb? Was she planning on the goddamn apocalypse?"

"Her partners are all into the tech boom." I feel the strong urge to defend my mom, even through exhaustion. I had been able to ward off a complete panic attack, but the traces of one took a lot out of me. "They figured the potential buyer would want extra security since we're in the middle of nowhere."

"But what do you do when the threat is inside the house with you?" Brendan looks at me without looking at me. And here we are. Back to square one.

"I . . . I didn't plan for any of this," I say.

"Yeah. *This*." Brendan waves a finger at the glass door. "But we both know that none of us would be in this fucking mausoleum if you weren't being a sneaky link." It was as though he hadn't pulled me back from the brink just moments ago. As though he didn't do and say all the right things to keep me from crumbling. He's thrown off his mask and turned into this brooding figure in front of me, and I can't help but wonder if this is what Hope must've dealt with behind closed doors.

I hug myself. "You can leave a mausoleum," I mumble. "It's the place that houses the tombs."

Brendan sucks at his teeth, and I can imagine the scowl eating up the top half of his face.

"Why aren't y'all in the car yet?" Kizzy's upstairs now, her phone light bouncing over all of us.

"The hell were you?" Asher demands.

"Putting a blanket on Sherie. Liv never came back. Your turn."

None of us say anything.

"Why are you still here?" Kizzy says, slower now.

"Liv's mom is in a doomsday cult." Asher again.

"Fuck off, Asher." I turn toward Kizzy. "The power outage put the smart-home system into lockdown mode. We'll be fine once the power turns back on."

"When will that be?" Kizzy asks.

I frown at her. "I assume once the rain slacks." Like, what the hell?

"Y'all try the windows?" Kizzy's too distracted to register my annoyance. Something's up with her.

Brendan snaps his finger and points at her before running to one of the windows in the kitchen. Asher tries another.

I shake my head. "The window locks are part of the smart system."

Nobody listens to me, the girl who was here when the smart-home system was installed. The boys keep trying to pry open the kitchen windows. Kizzy even has her hands on one of the windows in the great room. Grunts fill the air, all to no avail. I massage the back of my neck and roll my head from side to side, hoping this will help me snap out of my post-panic weariness.

"There's no point." Brendan shakes out his arms. "This place is like fucking Alcatraz."

"And that's what I tried to tell you all," I say under my breath. Not low enough, though, because Brendan whips around.

"At least we're trying something. We're not standing here giving commentary like some loser watching the Met Gala red carpet."

I blink at him. "That was oddly specific."

"*You're* oddly specific, Liv."

If this were any other situation, I'd laugh my ass off. *I'm oddly specific?* What the actual fuck? But tensions are high, and my friend is dead—and I can't trust any of these assholes in this room. Too much sarcasm might make someone go full on Billy and Stu from *Scream* on all of us. So I bite my bottom lip and keep quiet.

"This is bullshit," Asher yells. "There's no way this is it. There has to be some way to override the system."

"Yeah. Once the power's back on," Kizzy says. At least someone's listening to me.

"Fuck that." Asher picks up a barstool from the island and hoists it over his head.

I wince before the inevitable. "Asher, I wouldn't—"

But he would, and he does. He crashes the barstool against the glass door, and the chair breaks in half, the seat separating from its legs.

"What the hell kind of cheap furniture is this?" he asks.

"It's not the furniture," I say. "It's the glass. They're impact-resistant. All of them."

"From what? Bullet holes?"

I sigh. This situation is exhausting as it is—then there's Asher. At least my annoyance is outweighing my depletion for the moment. I might even have enough energy to smack him on the back of his head. "There are other dangers out there besides madmen. The windows are built to hold up against hurricanes."

"Let's try something heavier." Brendan searches around the great room and kitchen.

"Heavier than a gale-force wind?" I ask.

"Jesus, Liv. Shut up! Let me try something."

I take a step back and hold up my arms. He's spiraling. We all are. I need to remember to keep my mouth shut. But I can't help but feel irritated by the way they're just shitting all over my mom's hard work. By the way they're not listening to me in the first place. There was a time when my word was bond. When I could tell everyone that the sky was purple, and they rolled with it for the hell of it. That Liv seems to be buried right next to Hope.

Brendan grabs the leather ottoman in front of the sectional and heaves it into his arms. Mom was very particular about that piece of furniture. She wanted it to look like a flea market find but with the price tag of heirloom leather. Her interior designer purchased it from a family-owned tannery in Italy. She'd pass out if she saw how Brendan's manhandling it right now.

"Come on, Ash," he grunts as the wooden frame pokes at his rib cage. "Let's SWAT this shit. Go full battering ram."

Kizzy backs up next to me, as if she can sense the disaster that's about to strike. Asher grabs the other side of the ottoman, and he and Brendan go full speed toward the glass door. I close my eyes before impact. But I don't hear the drastic sound of glass exploding into a million pieces. Instead, something tinkles like wind chimes fighting against a flurry.

When I open my eyes, the ottoman is on the floor and a web of cracked glass the size of a bowling ball is now at the center of the door.

"That's it?" Asher scratches the back of his head. "Why isn't it, like, shattering?"

Kizzy blows out a breath filled with irritation. "Liv said it was impact-resistant, not impact-tolerant. The glass can get disrupted, but it's not going to leave the frame."

I raise my eyebrows, impressed. Kizzy wasn't lying when she said she paid attention in science class. Brendan and Asher try to poke and shove at the cracked glass, because they obviously suck at science. Also, they're guys. Guys always need to be the smartest people in the room, even when they're the dumbest. At least Dayvon gives me my flowers when I'm spot-on about anything. Speaking of which . . .

I scan the room. Right, left. Right, left. "Hey," I say. "Where's Dayvon?"

The room goes still for a moment before necks begin twisting and craning in all directions. It takes a moment for everyone else to realize he's not here. That he hasn't been here.

"Ay yo, Day!" Brendan calls out. Asher and Kizzy fall in line, calling on him like a parent demanding their child come downstairs and eat.

"Hold on." I raise a hand, and everyone quiets down. We listen. Nothing but the rain, which at least has settled to steady knocks instead of incessant pounding.

"He said he was going to check another door downstairs. Maybe he got out." The hope hugs the last words from Asher's mouth.

Brendan shakes his head. "He's not like that. He wouldn't just bounce without getting us first. Maybe something stopped him before he could get out."

"Like what?" Kizzy's closer to me now. I've never seen her this scared. This meek. I allow my arm to rub against hers to remind her I'm here with her.

"More like who." Brendan points his giant index finger at Kizzy. "You were the one down there with him last."

Kizzy rocks back on her heels. "I didn't see him. I grabbed a blanket for Sherie and came right up. Just figured he was up here with y'all."

"We were all shouting his name, Kiz. He didn't answer."

"He might not have heard us. It's a big-ass house."

"It's an *empty* big-ass house! Voices carry!" Brendan booms, as if to prove a point.

I look over at Kizzy, to see if I can find any cracks underneath her surface—even in the dark. But her face is scrunched up in genuine confusion. "The rain could've drowned out our voices," I try. "I'm sure he'll catch up with us. He said the floor plan was confusing. He probably just got turned around. Also, our parents know the bonfire ended from the rain. Someone's bound to come look for us."

"Something tells me you didn't tell your mom you'd be using her property as a torture chamber, right?" Brendan says.

Oop, he got me there. Of course I didn't tell my parents where I'd really be. They think I'm spending the night over at Tia's after the bonfire. But Tia . . . Tia has to come look for me. Except I never texted her to let her know where I was. That wasn't part of the plan. Kizzy, Sherie, and I didn't take into account contingencies like a fucking rainstorm knocking out the power. Damn, is there really no way out of this?

A dry laugh escapes Brendan. "Fine. Guess I'll go down there and see what's up. I swear to God, Kiz, if anything's wrong with my boy—"

"Your *boy*?" The fire returns to Kizzy's voice. "You've been clowning him all night."

"I was agitated. Trauma will do that to you."

"Fuck your trauma," Kizzy mocks. "What about at the bonfire? Was it that traumatic to see Liv and him undressing each other with their eyes?"

"Kiz!" I snap. This is neither the time nor the place for some sophomoric love-triangle shit.

Brendan's here but gone—chilling out somewhere between pissed and dejected. Finally, he shakes his head a few times. "I know what you're doing. You're stalling. I'm going to go find Day."

"Oh, hell no." Asher grabs Brendan's arm. "You're not leaving me here with Carrie and the Bride of Chucky. From now on, we move as a unit."

"You really scared to stay here with two girls, bruh?"

"Did you or did you not say these girls yoked you up before I got here, *bruh*?"

As Brendan ruminates over Asher's question, light flickers in the corner of my eyes. And then again. And again. It can't be lightning. Lightning is too unpredictable to have that much of a steady tempo.

"Fine," Brendan says through gritted teeth. "Let's all roll together. That way we can keep an eye on each other."

"Wait," I say. I follow the flashing light up to the top level. I point a finger up to the loft overlooking the great room. "What's that?"

Everyone gathers close to me to see what I'm seeing.

"The fuck?" Asher asks in awe.

"Maybe it's Dayvon," Brendan says.

Kizzy frowns at him. "Doing what? Turning into the Green Lantern?"

"He could be using his phone to signal for help," Brendan snaps back.

"How about we stop hypothesizing and find out?" My suggestion is met with silence, but when I move toward the stairs, they all follow.

"Hold on," Brendan says. "I'll lead. Asher, you take the rear."

"Said no girl ever," Asher mumbles as he files in behind Kizzy. Even now, his mind can't help but go into the gutter.

I'm right on Brendan's tail as he climbs the stairs. I don't know how to feel about him wanting to head us off. Supported, maybe. Surprised that he wants to be chivalrous even after everything that's happened tonight. Then again, he might think that being first will make it easier to jump out of the way of danger, leaving me to take the ax to the forehead. You never know with Brendan. I haven't been able to read him since we were fourteen years old.

We reach the loft on the third level and try to find the source of the flashing light.

"I think it's coming from there." Brendan points a finger toward one of the bedrooms. There are four up here, but the one he IDs is the last room of a long, dark hallway. As though it would be any other choice tonight.

"This is the part where I say that one of us should've brought a weapon," Asher whispers.

He's right. I think about that tool drawer in the kitchen. A screwdriver can turn into a shank with the right amount of vigor.

"I'm one step ahead of you." Kizzy pulls out her stun gun.

"Okay, why haven't we removed the weapon from the psycho yet?" Asher asks.

"Hand it over," Brendan demands. "I'm in the front. Whoever's back there will get to me first."

"Hold on. Let me think about it." Kizzy scratches her forehead with her middle finger.

Brendan huffs in annoyance, then leads us down the hallway. Even with the pulsing light and our phones, the darkness seems to gobble us up. My hand itches to grab on to Brendan's, but he can't see that I'm scared. My panic attack was enough ammunition to use against me if he wanted. Brendan pauses just as we reach the last bedroom and cranes his neck back and forth.

"All right," he mutters, psyching himself up like an injured hero in an action movie. "Let's do this." He thrusts himself into the room, and I hold the line. His response will determine my next move: fight, flee, or freeze. The seconds drip like we're preparing cold-brew coffee. I move my ear closer to the door, listening for sounds of a struggle.

"What in the . . . ?" Brendan finally says.

Kizzy, Asher, and I look at each other for a sign of how to respond.

"Um, you guys. Come see this shit."

I push myself through the door with Kizzy and Asher close behind me and suck in a breath.

"What in the . . . ?" I mumble, not immediately aware that I just repeated Brendan verbatim. But really, there's nothing else to say. I can barely see the textured wallpaper my mom spent weeks deciding on. Instead, the walls are plastered with social media printouts. Similar to the one found underneath Sherie. We all take a spot along the wall, holding our phone lights up to the papers like we're perusing through an art gallery. Only this gallery consists of hundreds and hundreds of comments about Hope. The nasty ones. My phone light captures some of the lowlights:

> Trifling bitch.
>
> Lying ass ho.
>
> We know that ho is cray.
>
> Maybe she hit him first. That's what her ass gets.
>
> Just kill yourself, bish.

I squeeze my eyes closed on that one. I don't understand. I never understood. No matter how pissed you are at someone, what goes on in your own brain to urge someone to take their own life? Hope got hundreds of messages just like that after she shared that pic of her battered face. Even more after she was found dead. It was like her death wasn't enough—they wanted to haunt her in the afterlife, too.

I reopen my eyes only to feel that they're lined with tears. I rub at them a little too hard with the back of my hand when I'm reminded about the strobing light. The thing that sent us up here in the first place. I turn to the center of the room. On a card table, there's a laptop projecting an image on the wall in front of it. The image runs on a loop, blinking over and over and rooting into my brain. Brendan, Kizzy, and Asher stand in the middle of the room, staring at the image as if they're all in a trance. Maybe they are. Maybe I am, too. We stare at a black-and-white picture of some white guy with a goatee. A dangling hand holds a square prism in front of his forehead. Right below the image are the following words:

"Of course I'm crazy, but that doesn't mean I'm wrong."—Robert Anton Wilson

THIRTEEN

IT'S ASHER'S CLAPPING THAT SNAPS ME AWAY from the picture. The words. And the meaning behind those words. A slow clap. Four singular pops, almost like gunshots, that cause my shoulders to jerk each time, each one hitting a nerve.

"Nice," Asher says once his applause ends. "Well done, ladies. The production quality is a bit Tubi instead of summer blockbuster, but you get a B-plus for effort. Also, who the fuck is Robert Anton Wilson?"

I blink a few times, but the images, the words, still float in front of my eyes. "What are you talking about?" I ask.

Asher waves a hand around the room. "This grand proclamation of respecting mental health. Don't worry. We hear you, sista." He holds up a fist in feigned solidarity.

"Watch yourself," Kizzy snaps. "And I didn't have anything to do with this shit."

Asher laughs. "Yeah. Okay."

"What's your proof?"

Asher walks to the wall with the projected image and slaps his hands over one word: *crazy*. "Think only two of you fit into that category. Given that you tortured B, then killed your buddy right after."

"I didn't kill Sherie," I almost shriek, pissed that I even have to say those words. "And I also didn't do any of this."

Brendan clucks his tongue, and Kizzy and I look at him.

"Great. What's your bullshit rebuttal?" Kizzy asks.

"Not really bullshit." Brendan shrugs one shoulder. "This *was* both your plan to get me here. And this *is* Liv's mom's property. Plus, Liv didn't show me this room during our tour."

"Thirteen thousand square feet," I remind him. "My apologies for not showing you every nook and cranny."

"And this room just happened to be one of those nooks?"

"Okay. Screw this." Kizzy marches over to the laptop and stabs at the keyboard. The projection mode disappears, and she flips it upright. "We want to know who's screwing us? Maybe this laptop will tell us something."

That's actually a brilliant idea. We crowd behind Kizzy as she opens the file explorer, clicking on various folder icons. Brendan's arm bumps against mine, so he takes a step away. Just in case I might stab him, I guess.

"Nothing in the folders," Kizzy mutters, and continues to search. "Let's try the internet searches. That might come up even with the power out." She clicks on the Google Chrome icon and scans the search history. Still nothing. This has to be a brand-new laptop that hasn't seen a lot of traffic yet.

Asher smirks. "Again. How convenient."

"Hold on. Open the deleted files," Brendan says.

Kizzy gives one nod. Too much enthusiasm would suggest she's siding with Brendan and she's not even trying to go there. She finds the deleted files folder and there's a subfolder inside. One labeled "Dirt."

"Jackpot?" Kizzy asks, not sounding too sure of herself. She clicks on it, and a window with tiny picture icons pops up on the screen.

"The fuck?" Brendan asks, speaking for all of us.

Kizzy clicks on the first pic to make it bigger. My heart does a pole vault up to my throat. It's me. I'm staring right at me. I'm leaning against my locker at school and looking down at my phone. Completely immersed in whatever's on my screen and completely unaware that someone's taking a candid of me. Brendan and Asher give me a sideways glance. Their eyes want to say something, but their mouths don't know how to form it. Kizzy clicks the arrow onto the next screen and again, me. This time I'm sitting on the bleachers in the school's gym with my chin resting in my hands. It had to be from our first pep rally of the school year. I can tell because my hair is slicked up into a top bun. I was going to wash it that night because I was getting my braids put in the next day. The braids I have now.

"Kizzy?" I ask, though I'm not even sure what I'm asking. I just need to hear my voice as evidence that this is all real. I place my hand on top of my stomach, right where Brendan's was a few minutes ago. I take several deep breaths until they reach my belly. I refuse to let the panic set in again. Especially not now, when more than anything I need to be alert.

Kizzy keeps clicking. Me. Me. Me. Opening my car door. Eating a fry in the cafeteria. Talking to my track coach. Probably the time I was begging to rejoin the team, assuring her that I'm controlling my stress and taking my meds. An intimate moment. All of them, though, were intimate. Taken with my assumption of privacy. Of freedom.

"Looks like you have a fan," Asher says to me.

"More like a stalker," Kizzy corrects. It's not until like the tenth picture or so that my face is no longer on the screen. Kizzy's up there now, bending over to tie her shoe in the school hallway. Kizzy jerks back and bumps into me.

"What is this?" She whips around and looks at us. "Who's doing this?"

Brendan nudges her aside and takes over. Clicking through more candid shots of Kizzy going about her business at school. A few clicks in, we get images of Sherie. My breath catches as I see her. Mid-laugh. Mid–hair flip. Mid-life. I focus on breathing to keep the tears away. There's no time for that. Not when some creep has been taking inventory of our actions. And it only gets creepier. There's a picture outside my bedroom window. Me, reaching for the blinds to close them. The tops of Kizzy's and Sherie's heads are partially visible. But it's them. I know it's them. This was about two weeks ago, when the plan started taking shape. Right after Brendan was announced to be on some national preseason watch-list, and we thought enough was fucking enough.

"See!" Kizzy's indignation makes me jump. "I told you we weren't doing any of this. Whoever's doing this has been following us for weeks. Funny how neither of you are popping up in this folder." She trades accusatory glances between Brendan and Asher.

"You might want to hold that thought," Brendan says. On the laptop now is a screenshot of one of the articles about him from six months ago: BASKETBALL STAR SUSPECTED OF GIRLFRIEND'S DEATH. Several words and names from the article are highlighted: *Hope. Fall. Alibi. NBA.* Brendan's picture is at the center of the article. His face was blurred out due to being underage, but everyone knew it was him. It's the one he took for the team last year. Cheesing at the camera in his uniform with a basketball tucked under his arm. Except cartoon devil horns have been drawn onto his head and a giant *X* is covering his face.

"Oookay," Asher says. "So it's safe to say that this person's *not* a fan of Brendan. I'd go as far as to say that they wouldn't mind if you got hit by a Mack truck."

Brendan glares at him over his shoulder. "Yeah. And I don't see anything in this folder about you."

"Really, B? I'm trying to fly on private jets with you to Mykonos once you get signed. Why the hell would I want to off my meal ticket?"

Brendan gives a half-hearted smirk and returns to the screen because, really, how can he argue with that? He clicks past more articles about him and soon there are screenshots from social media about Hope. A lot of these look familiar. The girls and I perused most of them while we were trying to find the most damning evidence against Brendan. And many of them are up on the wall in this room. Brendan has no problem sifting through these quickly. His jaw clenches as he whips through the images, pulsing with each click. I almost want to tell him to stop before his head explodes when my eye catches on something that doesn't look like it's from IG or TikTok.

"Wait," I say to Brendan as he clicks ahead to the next image. "Go back."

To my surprise, Brendan doesn't grunt or cause a fuss. He simply goes back like I asked. It's a screenshot of a text message exchange. White and blue bubbles trailing down the page.

White Bubble: Why are you doing this? Why aren't you talking to me???

White Bubble: Hello???

White Bubble: You really about to leave me on read?

Blue Bubble: K, I'm this close to blocking you.

White Bubble: Okay, I'll stop. Just promise you'll call me later???

Silence seeps into the room, and everyone's body language shifts. Shoulders scrunch. Knuckles crack. Heads tilt in curiosity, trying to make sense of the exchange.

"You gonna tell us who you were messaging, Kiz?" Brendan finally asks.

Kizzy touches her chest. "Me? How do you know that was me? Lots of people's names begin with K." She sounds far from convincing. She doesn't raise her voice, and there's no snark to her rebuttal. If anything, the words leave her lips laconically.

"Yeah, but you're the only K who has pictures of themselves in this folder. That would be one hell of a coincidence."

"Coincidences happen all the time," Kizzy insists. "And if I was texting whoever this psycho is that's been stalking me and Liv, why would I willingly suggest looking through the computer?"

Brendan shrugs. "I don't know, Kiz. You're the crazy one."

"That's a little insensitive," I say.

Kizzy glances at me, gratitude spilling over the shadows across her face.

"Now's not the time to be all *woke*," Asher basically spits out. "Kizzy was in a crazy home. Facts are facts."

"I was an inpatient at a mental health care facility, asshole," Kizzy snaps. "Have some respect. Hope was there, too."

"Hope killed herself. You're proving my point! If they didn't take the crazy out of her, then—"

"Asher, shut the fuck up," Brendan says.

His voice is calm. Even. Which makes it all the more intimidating.

Which is also why Asher promptly shuts the fuck up.

"And if you don't want to tell us who you were texting," Brendan continues, flipping through the images, "we'll just have to see if the laptop will."

Kizzy hugs herself and looks down at the floor as Brendan keeps clicking. She doesn't look up at me, even though I know she feels me staring at her. It *was* her in those messages. But who the hell was she writing? Maybe there's a fourth person she pulled into our plan. She didn't tell Sherie or me because she knew we'd object. Knew this person might go off the rails. But who?

"Shit," Brendan hisses, and snaps me out of my own head.

I look back at the laptop, and my lungs forget how to work. Hope's on the screen. But not real Hope. Dead Hope. Hope lying in her coffin, with makeup that makes her skin look ashy instead of bronze. Her hair straightened in the way that she hated but her mother loved. Her eyes closed with a deep furrow in between her brows, as though she's concentrating really hard to stay dead. As though she doesn't understand how this death thing works.

Brendan slaps the laptop closed and paces back and forth. He bumps into me, into Asher, into the wall. But his body's on autopilot. Then it hits me. Brendan didn't attend Hope's funeral. He's never seen her body. I heard his lawyers advised him not to go, but Hope's parents made sure to set up security outside the church in case he tried to slither inside. It was the talk of the repast. Instead of sharing stories about Hope in between bites of baked ham and lemon chess pie (Hope's favorite), people were whispering whether Brendan or someone in his family would make an appearance. He wrecked Hope while she was alive, and he wrecked her passing, too.

Kizzy, Asher, and I stand in silence as Brendan makes rounds across the room. He shakes out his hands, rolls his neck, just like he does before a big game. All that's missing is his headphones blasting an angry hip-hop song.

"Okay," I say. I have to be the rational one here. As his former best friend, I still feel obligated to make him happy. To calm him down. "We know whoever this is was obviously at the funeral. Isn't there a way to find out the owner of a digital image. Looking through metadata or whatever?"

Asher scoffs. "All right, show of hands of whoever knows how to do that shit." He looks around the room and the lack of hands in the air. "That's what I thought. We can google how to do it, but we're all in a fucking dead zone right now."

"Okay," I say again, and nod. I can't give this up. Not yet. I look back down at the laptop and snap my fingers. "Licensing! Can't we look through the Microsoft software and see if—"

"Microsoft isn't installed," Kizzy says, finally looking up again. "The laptop's basically a shell. Whoever left it here didn't invest much time in it. It's as if they bought it for the sole purpose of fucking with us."

"But they're not that smart," I try. "We found the deleted photos. The screenshots. They didn't cover their tracks that well."

"How do you know that they *didn't* want us to find them?" Kizzy asks.

I chew on that thought. She's right. Nothing installed on the laptop except a Canva image to display the Robert Anton Wilson quote. No footprints left on the internet, either, from what we can tell without a connection. This person just wouldn't be all laissez-faire about deleted files.

"Okay, fuck this." Asher holds up his phone. "Everyone hand over their phones."

My breath hitches in my throat so quickly that I cough. It takes me a moment to get it all out, but when my coughing fit is over, Asher's still looking at me.

"To you? Why?" I ask.

"Not to me. To all of us. We don't have access to the internet right now, but we have access to our texts. Our photos. If somebody in here's responsible for killing Sherie and leaving all these psycho messages on the walls, there would be traces of it on our phones. So, let's put it all out on the table and see who we can trust." He knocks the laptop down to the floor and plops his phone on the card table in its place. He looks around at all of us, expectedly.

"This isn't fair," I say. "Not all of us are here. What about Dayvon?"

"If we go through all our shit and don't find anything, then obviously we'll realize it's the missing Black dude playing reindeer games." He nods his head at the table. "Let's have it. No time to delete stuff."

Brendan huffs and sets his phone next to Asher's. "I don't have nothing to hide." He looks pointedly at me. Then at Kizzy.

Kizzy and I glance at each other. Seeing who'll flinch or give in first.

"What's the worst that we'll find?" Brendan asks. "Your plans to make me confess to something I didn't do? Sorry to break it to you, but that's already out the window."

Kizzy's jaw clenches in defiance. "We were never stupid enough to text about our plans. But maybe you guys were stupid enough to talk about yours." She sets her phone on the table and scurries back like a bomb might go off. Soon, all eyes are on me. Waiting. Expecting me to fall into line.

"Liv?" Kizzy says, as though waking me up from a nap. "You're up."

I look down at the phone in my hand, and it burns right through my palm. Threatening to set this whole house on fire if I do something as stupid as letting them touch it. I shove it into my back pocket, then look up at my former friends.

"No."

FOURTEEN

I'VE MALFUNCTIONED. THERE'S A CONSTANT whirring in my skull as my brain works to guess how I can get out of this one. Kizzy takes a step toward me and cocks her head. She's puzzled. She's trying to solve me. Good luck with that.

Brendan slams his foot down, and my heart pounds against my rib cage. Gripping my chest, I look down at Brendan's foot. The laptop is crunched underneath it, and the whirring has stopped. The laptop was crashing, and now it's out for the count. I was never malfunctioning. I guess that's a good thing.

"Hold on." Asher rubs a knuckle into his ear. "Did you just say no?"

I almost look back down at the laptop, hoping that a better answer will pop out of its crushed circuit board. But hanging my head means I'm spineless. Hanging my head means I'm guilty. I straighten my back and lift my chin in the air.

"It's my property. I have a right to say no," I say.

"Uh, no you don't," Asher insists.

"People have a right to privacy. Besides, we'd only be wasting time."

"Finding out who murdered Sherie is wasting time?" Brendan asks.

I flinch but shake my head to get myself together. He's not throwing me off. "No, but we'd be better served to find Dayvon. Or find the electrical panel. That way we can get out of here and get the cops. Let *them* play detective."

"Because they've done such a fine job already," Kizzy says, shooting a look at Brendan.

Brendan smirks at her. "You're loving how much she's stalling, huh? That way we don't have to find out who you were texting, *K*."

"I know it's dark, so I'll spell it out. My. Phone's. On the. Table. I have nothing to hide." She folds her arms across herself again, very much trying too hard.

"Okay." Asher walks over to the card table with the rest of the phones. "Liv's right about one thing—we're wasting time. So instead of us spending hours looking for evidence, why don't we just share the darkest thing on them. That way we can cut to the chase and mitigate any pending embarrassment. I'll go first." He pauses and takes a breath. "Dick pics. Lots of them. Different angles. Different backgrounds. Different . . . stages, if you will."

"Ash." Brendan rubs his forehead in disgust for all of us. "We got it, man. You don't have to keep going."

"I'm just putting it out there. I'll go ahead and show them all to you now if that'll—"

"If you show me even one pimple on your penis, I swear you'll be without it for the rest of your life," Kizzy warns.

Asher tips his head in consideration. "The penis or the pimple?"

Kizzy starts at him, but Brendan steps in between them.

"Okay, I'll go," he says. He looks down at this phone as if he's trying to remember every illicit piece of evidence in there. "I'm a flirt. There's a lot of . . . risqué exchanges between me and a few other girls during the time I was with Hope."

My chest heats up like an incinerator, and I'm pissed at it for betraying me. After everything, the thought of Brendan flirting with another girl gives me heartburn. Even after he fell in love with my best friend. Even after he was accused of murdering her. Even after he's shown multiple shades of asshole tonight. I should be focused on who's out to get us, but my heart is still hardwired to feel something for him. To question if he meant the things he said and planned for me earlier tonight, or if this was all part of his schtick. Was I just another toy for him?

"News flash: Brendan Jean interacts with skanks and hoes." Kizzy's voice drips with sarcasm.

"And," Brendan interjects, "I laughed."

The rest of us wait for an explanation.

"Dayvon found out first. About . . . Hope," he continues. We all knew that. Dayvon lives down the street from the Jacksons. He was over there all the time for cookouts and dinners or any other occasion where he could grab a plate of food. He was practically another son to the Jacksons. Yet another reason why Brendan and Dayvon's friendship always included an asterisk. Brendan knew that Dayvon was the son the Jacksons always wanted, and no amount of NBA buzz could truly replace that.

"When he hit me up about her death, I laughed." Brendan shakes his head and gathers himself. "I mean, not actually laughed. I sent a GIF of guys falling out on the floor laughing."

"The fuck?" Kizzy asks, stealing my exact words.

"I thought he was joking. I *wanted* him to be joking. I didn't know what to say, so that's what I sent." Brendan slaps his fist into his palm, over and over. More skittish than scary. "I was going to delete it, but I knew Dayvon wouldn't delete it on his end. And then if he had that when I didn't, people would wonder what I was trying to hide."

"That was a lot of calculating for someone who claims to be innocent," Kizzy says.

I agree. This whole night I've been on a seesaw. Earlier, I was up in the clouds. Seeing the old Brendan. The guy who was my best friend. The guy who could make my palms sweat with a simple quirk of his eyebrows. But the night has evolved and painted a different person. Someone with a wicked streak. Someone menacing. Someone with enough rage to bruise Hope's face, or worse. The majority of tonight have been full of lows—but this? Sharing our phone's dark secrets? This won't add any levity.

"Yeah, well, I knew there were a lot of assholes out here like you," Brendan shoots back at Kizzy. "There. I've shared. What about you?"

Kizzy shifts from foot to foot, like she's prepping herself before leaping out of a plane. "Fine. I've talked a lot of shit about you to Hope."

Brendan scoffs. "You talk a lot of shit about me to me."

"I pride myself on being transparent," Kizzy says. "But I guess if you look at my texts, it was a lot of me convincing Hope to dump you. And a lot of accusations that something was going on . . . between you two." She looks between me and Brendan.

She might as well have punched me with that look.

"What?" I demand.

"I told Hope she needed to keep an eye on both of you because you two flirt. A lot. You think it's some cute, secret language you share but it verged on verbal humping. And . . . I may have mentioned to her that y'all hooked up at the Cupid Dance."

Asher lets out a surprised laugh as Brendan cusses to himself.

"That's a lie!" I shout over Asher's cackles. "I went to that dance with Dayvon. Hope's the one who set us up."

Kizzy sighs, exhausted. "You know you weren't into Dayvon like that."

"Um, he wasn't into *me* like that." I pound my chest to prove a point, but only hurt myself in the process. "He's the one who . . ." I don't drown out. I sink. I know what I saw. Dayvon knows what

I saw that night. But it doesn't feel right putting him on blast. Not while he's not in the room to defend himself.

"I had to take a piss. When I went out in the hall, I saw you two up against the lockers," Kizzy continues.

"We were arguing," Brendan barks. "I was telling her to stop being weird." He refuses to look at me. Not wanting to see the hurt across my face from hearing those words again. But just like that, it's eight months ago and I'm in the school's hallway. Me pushing against his chest. Him grabbing my wrists. Both screaming "Let me go" even while we couldn't keep our hands off each other.

But we didn't kiss. We didn't cross any lines. We were both devoted to Hope.

"You know what happened after that, right?" Brendan's tirade snaps me back to the dark bedroom. "You know that your reckless mouth created a domino effect, right?" His voice cracks.

It's true. After the dance, Brendan and Hope had their final breakup. *The* breakup. A month later, when she wouldn't take him back, Hope took pictures of her black-and-blue face. All from Brendan, she said—and she posted them. She went online instead of to the cops. She knew the cops wouldn't believe her, but she thought she'd have the public on her side. She thought a tarnished reputation would be punishment enough for Brendan. But the public turned against *her*. Hailed Brendan as a prince and her a wicked witch. A few weeks later, she was dead.

"You asked me what's the worst thing on my phone, so there it is," Kizzy says. She works hard to show that she doesn't feel guilty.

Arms still crossed. Chin lifted with indignance. But she can't keep still. She bounces from foot to foot like she's avoiding a land mine. Only thing, though, is that her actions already blew up our world.

I shake my head in disappointment. "Why didn't you just ask me what happened? Why did you run off and tell Hope before you got my side?" Hope seemed distant right before her death, especially with me. Every interaction with her felt like a test. As though I needed to prove that I'd always stick around. But all her actions did was push me further and further away—or made me want to push her. Especially that last night. That awful, *awful* night.

Kizzy shrugs. "Hope was my friend."

With those four words, she ripped out my heart and took a bite out of it. "I thought we were friends, too."

She doesn't answer for a moment. Then two more moments. Then three. I wonder if she's running through the stages of our friendship, just like I am. Evaluating the reality and the fiction. Trying to remember what we actually meant to each other before Hope's death. Maybe I'm seeing rainbows when all she's experienced were storms. It's like our friendship is an optical illusion and I see two faces, but she only notices a candlestick.

"Thanks for sharing your dark secret that destroyed a thousand relationships," Asher says, always the tactful one. "I believe there's only one person left for show-and-tell." He and Brendan look at me. They haven't forgotten about me.

My mouth feels incredibly dry, so I lick my lips. Prepping them to move and say something. Anything. "Okay, as you all know, after Hope died, I had that incident at my last track meet."

"You mean when everyone thought your heart gave out, but it was only a wimpy-ass panic attack—and your team had to forfeit a potential championship?"

I stab Asher with my eyes. That's like the hundredth inappropriate comment he's made about mental health tonight. "Panic attacks are nothing to joke about. And maybe if you were a bit more mindful about your mental wellness, you'd be less of a jerk and people could stomach being around you."

"But then you'd have to share me, Liv. We all know how well you do with sharing." He nods toward Brendan.

Brendan and Kizzy both whip out a "Shut up, Asher," and Kizzy waves her hand to continue.

"So anyways," I say, and take a breath. "I started seeing my therapist, and one of the things we discussed was for me to start journaling. That way I didn't have to bottle up my feelings. When I hold everything in all the time, it comes out like . . . well, like what happened to me at the championship meet. I started journaling in between my sessions, but I didn't trust having a physical copy of anything. My parents have been high-key snooping on me. I think they're worried that I'm going to follow behind Hope because we're . . ." I wince and try again. "We *were* so close. So yeah, I started journaling in my Notes app. Most of it is incoherent except to me but still, there's a lot of my private thoughts in there."

I finish, and something lifts off my shoulders. The phone feels dense in my pocket, but at least I can breathe a lot better in this room. Brendan steps closer to me, and for a moment, I think he's about to hug me. My heart races at the thought because, what am I supposed to do? Hug him back? Push him away? I don't even know how I'm supposed to feel about him right now.

"Bullshit," he says.

My laugh comes out as a hiccup. "Excuse me?" I ask.

"You don't want to hand over your phone because of diary entries?"

"It's journaling," I correct. "And it's private. I don't even tell my therapist everything I write, and she doesn't make me."

"Yeah, but she might if you're a suspect in a murder," Brendan says. "And if she doesn't, the police will subpoena you and all your shit is going to be out in the open anyways."

"I'll take my chances if the time comes, then."

"Liv, I fucking know you!" Brendan's voice cracks again, and I can't tell if it's from the sheer volume or frustration. "You're not going to go against everyone else just because of some random thoughts about crushes, or how your parents are getting on your nerves. If that was it, you would've been the first one to put your phone on the table. Never mind, you would've been the second."

I frown. "What does that even mean?"

"It means you're a fucking follower." His breath is on my forehead now, and it's scorching with anger. "You thought you were hot shit. That the world revolved around you, but the only reason it did was because Hope was next to you. The only thing I believe that came from your mouth is your parents think you're going to kill yourself, too. You would hold in your piss until Hope announced she had to go to the bathroom. That's how it's always been."

My hands ball into fists, and I ram them both against his chest, hoping to crack something. "Shut up," I practically scream.

"Then give me your phone."

"No!"

Brendan whips his hand toward my pockets. I push him away again, and Kizzy pushes him a third time before he can make his way back to me.

"Don't touch her. Ever," she warns him.

"She's hiding something, Kiz." Brendan waves a hand at me. "You and I both know it."

"All I know is if you start getting handsy again, there's going to be a problem."

Brendan sucks at his teeth. "Kill that noise."

"Try me, Brendan. I really want you to try me."

"Hey, hey, hey!" Asher gets in between them. "Let's turn down the temp in here, okay?"

Brendan and Kizzy continue sparring, their accusations and name-calling blurring together so much that they seem like they're speaking another language. But they're distracted. All of them. So, I leave.

I don't just leave. I run.

I sprint out the bedroom and down the dark hall. I don't use my phone light. If I do, they'll see me. I'm in the loft and a few steps from the stairs by the time I hear Asher cry out: "She's gone, guys!" Fuck.

The stairs are the obvious choice. Not only will they hear me, but they'll see me, too. That's the thing about grand staircases. Too much space to make a quick getaway. I dash into the bedroom closest to the stairs when the idea hits me: the dumbwaiter.

I thought it was the stupidest fucking thing when my mom told me about it. This is a luxury home, not a plantation. Nobody needed to send a tray of hominy grits and freshly squeezed orange juice upstairs to their *massa*. Mom went on to list the benefits of installing one. Not just for food but for laundry. Which is why she made sure that she'd install one to go past the laundry room on the main level.

I squeeze into the bedroom closet as I hear footsteps out in the loft behind me. I feel for the wall and pray I don't have to pull out my phone light. Finally, I feel the small handle poking out of the wall panel. I breathe a sigh of relief as I yank open the hidden door. An empty cabin waits for me. Thank God the contractor didn't install the shelves inside yet, or I may not be able to squeeze in. I fold myself into the dumbwaiter and reach for the button then remember . . . no power. *Shit*.

"You see her?" I hear Brendan ask from the loft.

I can't just hide in here forever. Someone's bound to find me. So I grab the manual pulley outside the cabin and pull. And pull. I feel like I'm pulling an anchor out of water, but I don't stop. This is my only way down. It actually might be a good thing. If the power were on, they would hear the motor. They would find me in no time. And I need *more* time.

"Come on," I urge under my breath, begging for my arms to be stronger. Work harder. I slide past the laundry room. Good. Just one more floor. I grunt and feel my hair curling up at the roots. The sweat working its way through my kinks. It's okay. It'll be worth it.

Just when I think my muscles are about to burn through my skin, the cabin stops with a thud, and there's no more leverage in the pulley. I made it. I'm at the basement level. I breathe a sigh of relief and rest against the back wall of the cabin. It's so quiet that it sounds like I'm breathing into a microphone. But if that's the only thing I'm hearing, then I must be alone.

I pull out my phone, realizing it's safe enough now to shine a light. I need to. The darkness is suffocating and equal to what I assume being buried alive feels like. I open my Photos app and click on Albums. I scroll down past all the usual ones—friends, family, and favorites—until I reach the Utilities section and click on the Hidden option. The one that only opens with my Face ID.

Even with just the phone screen as my lighting, it recognizes my face. The folder opens, and I stare at a picture of Hope. Face down on the pavement a few feet from her pool. A pond of blood surrounding her head like red mist.

With shaky thumbs, I press Delete. Go to my Recently Deleted album and press Delete again. Poof.

FIFTEEN

EIGHT MONTHS AGO

THEY ALL WANT A PIECE OF US.

The DJ's in the pocket, sliding in one hit song after the other. Feeding from the energy of the crowd. The school's gym has morphed into Cupid's house party. Red, pink, and white gossamer streamers are strewn across the walls, and plastic hearts dangle from the ceiling. A disco ball hangs from the center of the room, reflecting heart patterns over our skin. In the thick of it all, there's me and Hope. Hope and me. Writhing our bodies to the music. Holding hands and shouting lyrics to each other with everyone watching. Everyone's trying to join our private party, but only our inner circle gets the invite. Kizzy twirls around us, bumping her hips against ours to the beat. Sherie floats like she usually does, arms moving toward the ceiling as though reaching for the song lyrics. Coko and Sy'rai slip in and out, wrapping their arms around my and Hope's waists occasionally to add to the groove. Forget Cupid's house party. This dance belongs to us.

The music leaks into something with a slower tempo, and Hope fans herself.

"Girl," she says to me. "I need to sit. Plus, somebody's antiperspirant has expired, and I'm not trying to walk around smelling like onion rings."

"I told Sy to stop buying the store-brand deodorant," Coko says, still pulling Sy'rai close to her to get her to slow dance.

"Girl, bye. My shit's clinical strength," Sy'rai insists.

I laugh and link my arm through Hope's and lead her back toward our table. The crowd parts for us and makes a clear path. I can't even remember the last time either of us had to say "Excuse me." Everyone just knows to get out of the way.

Brendan and Dayvon sit at our table, looking toward the dance floor and laughing at something or someone. Dayvon notices me, and his eyes basically flicker. He stands and pulls out my seat. I give him a polite smile as I sit, and he helps to scooch me under the table. He's been taking this date thing seriously all night. He rented out a stretch Hummer, bought me a corsage. About two weeks ago he wanted to know my dress's exact shade of green so his tie could match. He's a keeper . . . except I'm not sure if I want to hold on to him.

"What were y'all laughing at?" Hope's on Brendan's lap, rubbing the nape of his neck with her fingertips. He has both arms around her waist. They're always like this. Hands on each other at all times. It would be annoying if it seemed forced, but they just naturally fall into that rhythm. Interlocking fingers, palms on lower backs, chin on top of head. They're like puzzle pieces snapping into place when they're next to each other.

Brendan and Dayvon exchange a look and laugh again.

"Nothing. Just Ash, man," Brendan says, shaking his head. "That dude's a nut." He looks out onto the dance floor again, and I follow his eyes. I spot Asher, wearing a powder-blue tux just like one of those idiots in that *Dumb and Dumber* movie. He's behind Tia Shepherd, thrusting his hips in her direction as she bends over and twerks to the beat. He looks over at our table again and holds up devil horns in one hand.

I turn back around, and Brendan's still chuckling. "I don't get it," I say. "Why the blue tux?"

Brendan shrugs. "I don't know. Because he's Ash."

"Ash is going to Ash," Dayvon adds.

Now it's my and Hope's turn to exchange a look. "They're not laughing at his tux," Hope says to me. Then pinches Brendan's neck.

"Ow! Babe, what the hell?"

"Why's he dancing with Tia?" Hope demands.

"It's a dance, bae. That's what people do."

Hope points a warning finger. "I swear to God, B, if y'all are planning on messing with that girl—"

"We're not. I promise." Brendan holds up both hands. "Asher's just being stupid. I didn't put him up to anything."

I shake my head, and Brendan catches me.

"Okay, go ahead," he says to me. "Your turn. Let me have it."

"I think Hope gave it to you enough." I look at Dayvon. "And what's so funny to you? Did you see her pictures?"

Dayvon's eyes get big. It's not a fair question. Pictures of Tia's bare breasts popped up on Threads and IG right before winter break, and when they came down, everyone was DMing each other the screenshots. It was wrong, but it's like seeing footage of a celebrity taking their last breaths. We knew we shouldn't look, but curiosity sometimes gets the best of us.

"Nope. No, ma'am. I did not," Dayvon says.

Brendan cracks up again, and Hope climbs off him. "Come on, don't be like that." He reaches for her, but Hope slaps his hand away as she takes her own seat.

"I don't get it," Hope says. "Why aren't you clowning the loser who posted her pics?"

"Ain't nobody fucking with Taj like that," Brendan insists. "But, and I say this with all due respect, she knew that Taj was sus when she sent him those nudes."

"So that gave him a right to show them to everyone?" Hope asks.

"Of course not. But he wouldn't have anything to post if she didn't send them in the first place."

"Y'all acting like that girl hasn't been through enough," Hope says. She's talking about Tia's sister. The one who snapped on her mom before the police killed her. Sure, it's a sad story, though I'm not sure what it has to do with Tia sending nudes to randos years later. Like, where was that chapter in the trauma handbook? Hope looks at me, waiting for me to chime in. But . . . Brendan kinda has a point. I'm not sending my goodies to anyone, especially not Taj Houston. I never understood the appeal. I don't even go around eating just anyone's mac and cheese, so what would I look like trusting someone enough to keep naked pics of me on lock? Hell naw.

"Sooo . . ." Dayvon taps his finger against his cup. "How about them Bears?"

We all look at each other, then bust out laughing.

"You are mad corny, Day," Hope says. "The Bears? Who rockin' with the Bears if they not from Chicago?"

Dayvon shrugs. "I don't know, man. Shit was getting heated, and I felt like I was breaking out in hives or something."

Hope raises her eyebrows at me.

I frown: *What?*

She raises her eyebrows even higher until she looks like a girl possessed. I swallow my irritation. I know what she's doing. She does this all the time. Drop not-so-subtle hints of how I'm supposed to "human" like I couldn't possibly function without her. Like I need her as my guide dog.

"Hey, Dayvon," I say, following suit as always. "What football team do you like anyway?"

Hope gives me a small smile, clearly pleased with my conversation attempt. Dayvon, on the other hand, looks like I just asked him to tell me the meaning of life.

"Oh! Um . . ." More tapping against his cup. Damn, you would think we never had a single conversation before. "I'm more into college ball than the NFL. Georgia always holds it down, so I'm usually rooting for them."

I nod. "Yeah. The Bulldogs typically bring it."

Brendan snorts.

"What?" I ask.

"What you mean 'what'? When's the last time you watched a Georgia game?"

"I don't know. The last time they played?"

Brendan chuckles.

"Shut up, Brendan. I can watch other sports outside of when you're on the court."

"You fell asleep during the Super Bowl."

"Nothing was happening during the first half. The clock kept stopping after every play. Besides, everybody knows that the best things about the Super Bowl are the commercials and the half-time show."

"True that," Hope says as she sips her drink.

"Oh, don't get me started on that." Brendan leans toward Dayvon. "Ask her what's her favorite halftime performance."

Dayvon blinks. "Usher? Beyoncé?" he tries.

"You would think, right? But nope." Brendan looks at me, taunting me with his eyes.

I narrow mine at him as a warning.

"Maroon 5." He leans back in his seat like he just dropped a mic.

"Who?" Dayvon asks in between laughs.

"I don't know what the big deal is." I fold my arms across my chest with indignation. "They had bops. That's why everyone wanted to work with them. Cardi B, Megan Thee Stallion, Rihanna . . ."

"Ah, Rihanna. Liv's second favorite halftime performer," Brendan says. "Even though she danced like she was on quaaludes the entire time."

"She was pregnant, fool, and still moved better than you."

"Oh, ain't nobody moving better than me." Brendan's voice gets husky, saying something without saying it. And something about his voice makes me shift in my seat. He glances me over, a small smile across his mouth like he's pleased that he caused me to squirm. Then he turns to Hope. "Ain't that right, bae?"

"That's right," Hope says with a flirty wink. "Rihanna did throw down, though." She smiles at me but it's off. Almost like someone traced it on her face.

"Maroon 5's not that bad, though," Dayvon says a year later. "I like that one song of theirs. The one with that K-pop band."

I give him a gentle smile, appreciating the effort. "That's Coldplay."

"Oh. For real? Well, what's your favorite Maroon 5 song? Maybe you can play it for me sometime."

What's my favorite Maroon 5 song? This boy is way too cute to have this weak-ass game. Maybe that's why he relies more on his dimples and hazel eyes than actual sentences.

"Maybe," I say. Then take a sip of my punch and hope someone changes the topic.

"I'm probably going to have to go onstage soon," Hope says, reading my mind. "To spotlight the couple who won the sweethearts dance." Hope is the first junior at our school to win student council president, and one of her many important tasks is to announce the couple that everyone voted to have the first dance to the live band the school hired. It was a popularity contest—one with a low-stakes reward. But hey, Sedgefield loves its traditions.

"That must be awkward," I say. "Having to introduce yourself."

Hope smooths down her hair. "What? I don't know if me and B won."

Dayvon and I both roll our eyes and laugh. For once, we're in sync tonight.

"Anyway." Hope playfully throws up a hand at us and turns to Brendan. "B, make sure you get my good side while I'm up there. I ain't sportin' this swoop bang for nothing."

Brendan pats at his breast pocket. "Shit. I don't have my phone."

Hope frowns. "I just saw you with it."

"Naw, it's not here." Brendan continues to feel through his pockets. "Don't worry. I'll find it. Go do your presidential duties. Liv, come help me get past Ms. Martin."

"You know, she'd like you, too, if you didn't sing the *Martin* theme song every time you passed her classroom," I say.

"And deny me the joy of seeing that sneer across her face?" Brendan kisses Hope on the lips as he stands.

As I push out of my chair, Dayvon stands as well. He must've gone to some gentleman's finishing school. I'll admit, it's adorable. But it's not my jam. Still, I give him a polite smile as I follow Brendan out of the gym.

Ms. Martin is at her post outside the doors, monitoring the underclassmen at a table collecting everyone's entrance tickets. She's a chaperone with a capital *C*. While other teachers use their time here to grade on their phone or catch up on faculty-lounge gossip, Ms. Martin's always on the lookout for shenanigans. Like being Sedgefield High's in-school suspension coordinator was her birthright.

She cocks an eyebrow at Brendan's audacity to just strut out of the gym without saying where he's going. "Uh, excuse me, Mr. Jean. Can I help you?"

Brendan gives her a huge grin, and I just know he's prepping to sing "Mar-tiiiiiinn!" at the top of his lungs.

"We're just looking for his phone, Ms. Martin," I intervene. "We're coming right back."

Ms. Martin gives me a nod and shoots a warning look in Brendan's direction. "Five minutes." She even holds up five fingers in case we're visual learners.

"What if we have to take a dump?" Brendan asks in my ear.

I grab Brendan's arm and guide him down the neighboring hallway, toward the main entrance of the school. "Hurry up. I'm not trying to get on this lady's bad side. I heard she makes students balance her checkbook in ISS."

Brendan frowns. "Who the hell writes checks anymore? Have you even seen a checkbook before?"

"Nope. And I'm not trying to, so tell me where you saw your phone last."

Brendan slows his stride and digs into his jacket pocket. He pulls out his phone and waves it at me.

I blink at him. "Oookay. How much did you have to drink before we got here?"

"I didn't drink." He takes a beat. "A lot. I didn't drink a lot. But the missing phone was an excuse. I was saving you."

"From what?"

"From making a fool of yourself." He tucks his phone back into his pocket. "Your weird dial is on a thousand right now."

I scoff. "Fuck you. I don't have a weird dial."

Brendan smirks at me and pretends to wind up an imaginary dial between us, with clicking sound effects and everything.

I slap his hand down. "And *that's* not weird?"

"No. That was mad weird. But that seems to be the only language you speak right now."

"Stop calling me weird!" My voice carries down the hall and right into the face of a freshman couple entering the building, looking all cute and confused in their ill-fitting tux and gown.

"Our bad," Brendan says to them. "The dance is in the gym to the left." He nudges me up against a row of lockers so we get out of their way. The couple stare at us in awe, like they just caught a Beyoncé and Jay-Z sighting, before scurrying toward the gym.

"Why you gotta scare the kids like that?" Brendan asks me. He's so close that I see his voice vibrate against his throat. Smell the bodywash on his skin. Old Spice Swagger because he's a cornball. But only I can call him that.

"Why you gotta be an asshole?"

"You're kinda being an asshole to Dayvon."

The back of my head taps against the locker. "I've been nothing but nice to Dayvon."

"Liv, you're nice to the doofy guy who bags your groceries at Food Lion. You're on a date with Day."

"So what? *Don't* be nice to him?"

"No, just be fucking . . . you!" He presses a hand against the locker, right next to my head, and takes a breath. "You're the shit, Liv Porter. You're smart and funny and do strange, sweet things like feed your fries to squirrels because you think they look hungry. You're . . . you're all that and then some, but you're bottling all that in right now. I just want you to let Dayvon see you. Let Dayvon see you like . . . like I see you."

The bass of the music in the gym reaches the lockers and quivers against my back. Only the pulsing of my heart rivals it. So loud that I know Brendan can hear it. Can feel it. I want to grab his hand and press it to my chest as punishment. So he can know what he's doing to me and feel so guilty about it that it keeps him up at night.

"Then leave me alone." It comes out as a whisper, so I swallow and try again. "If you want me to give it a shot with Dayvon, then leave me alone. Stop interrupting our conversations. Stop with the inside jokes. Stop looking at me when you think I'm not looking. Just let me go."

Brendan's whole face crinkles for a second, and I know that look. I saw it when his parents split up. I saw it when his dad didn't show up to his games. I saw it when he told me about his violent stepfather. He's hurt. He's hurt but he's trying to push it away. He even laughs now to hide it. "Let you go? I'm not holding you hostage."

"Brendan, you eat off my tray at lunch. You save a seat for me in every class we have together. You call me every damn night. If you want me to find someone, let me go."

"Stop saying that."

"Let me go," I repeat. The words need to cling to him. "Let me go."

"Liv . . ."

"Let me go!"

"You let me go!" He punches the locker next to my head. I scream and, on instinct, shove him away. He's back in an instant. Hands on my arms, pinning them to my sides. "You fucking let *me* go!"

We're struggling and I don't know why. Pulling, tugging, pushing. Looking for any reason to touch each other. To hold on to each other. I manage to scratch his neck and Brendan draws back. Touches it and winces. Then his hands are on my wrists, and his body is pressed up against mine. I don't fight it anymore. I'm too tired, so I just give in. We breathe heavily. Brendan lowers his head, and our mouths are just centimeters away from each other. I can taste everything that he's sipped on tonight. He presses his forehead against mine, and I close my eyes.

"Let me go," I repeat. This time with less authority. I curve the ending. Include ellipses to allow him to fill in the rest.

Brendan sucks in a breath. I no longer feel the music rattling my bones. Just him. Just us. "Liv." It comes out as a moan. "I—"

"What's going on down there?"

Brendan rips away from me, and my skin gets cold. Ms. Martin's at the end of the hall, her hands propped against her broad hips.

"It's all good." Brendan pulls his phone out of his pocket. "See? Found it."

Ms. Martin's eyes swap between Brendan and me. I push myself off the lockers. Give her a smile to let her know I'm okay even though my insides are trembling.

"Five minutes is up," she says finally.

"Right. We're coming." Brendan turns to me.

"Go ahead," I say. "I need to use the bathroom."

He raises his eyebrows, and his eyes ask a thousand things at once: *You sure? Are we good? What was that? That was nothing, right?*

I give one single nod in response, and Brendan ambles down the hall. He glances over his shoulder one final time before turning the corner and heading back toward the gym with Ms. Martin.

As soon as they're both out of sight, I fall back against the locker and cover my mouth with my hands. I suck in a silent gasp. Blink my eyes a thousand times to keep the tears away. One word drums through my ears like a heart under the floorboard: *Hope. Hope. Hope. Hope.* Hope is Brendan's girlfriend. Hope is my best friend. Hope doesn't deserve to be hurt.

The music has officially stopped as a voice speaks into a microphone. It's Hope fulfilling her presidential duties and making her announcement about Sedgefield High's favorite couple. This is my best friend's moment to shine, and here I am—on the outside arguing with her boyfriend about how he can never be my boyfriend. The thought alone is enough to make me vomit.

I peel myself off the lockers again, smooth down my dress, and steady my breath. Pull out my phone to inspect myself in the camera. I rake my fingers through my hair to get rid of any flyaway curls and check my makeup. Everything's on point. Except for my hands. I can't get them to stop shaking. That's been happening more and more lately. Fingers trembling like I'm in need of a caffeine fix. By the time I make it back into the gym, the live band is singing a cover of "Stay" by Rihanna and Mikky Ekko, and Hope and Brendan are slow dancing in the center of the room.

Of course they are.

The spotlight shines down on them to show how magical they are together. How flawless they look. And they really do fit together. Hope wore heels tall enough so she can perfectly wrap her hands behind Brendan's neck without it looking like she's hanging on for dear life. Brendan caresses her lower back, his fingers interlocking to keep her safe and secure. They beam at each other, sharing *I love you*s with just their eyes. Nobody else exists to them in this moment. They're so beautiful together that I could cry.

And I do.

The tears come out slow. Sporadic. As if my tear ducts are begging me to get it together, but I don't have any fight in me. I don't wipe them away. Just stare at my two best friends as they swim across the dance floor. My mind can't help but go back over two years ago. My lips on Brendan's hand that summer. If only my dad hadn't come in and interrupted. If only Brendan and I had a follow-up conversation about that moment. If only I told Hope the truth. That I had feelings for Brendan, too. That I deserve to be happy as much as she does. If only, if only, if only.

"Hey. You okay?" Dayvon's next to me. I'm not sure when he got here.

I blink and he comes into focus. "Yeah." I laugh a little. "I'm just . . . really happy for them."

I'm not sure if he buys it but he gives me a nod anyway. Even hands me a napkin. I give him a grateful smile and dab at my eyes. Right before the second verse picks up, one of the singers announces that everyone can now join the happy couple. Dayvon extends his hand to me and smiles. I sigh and shove the napkin into my bra before sliding my hand into his. Pray he doesn't notice the residual trembling. He leads me onto the dance floor, then wraps his arms around my waist. I rest my hands on his shoulders, and we sway to the music. Back and forth. Back and forth. We move well together. But that's all we do. Move. No theatrics. No heat. Just a safe, comfortable cadence.

I allow my hands to move farther up until they're behind Dayvon's neck. Even rest my cheek against his chest. He's cozy, and I need cozy right now. I close my eyes and allow myself to be in the moment. To listen for Dayvon's heartbeat. When I can't hear it over the music, I open my eyes and Brendan's staring at me. He's dancing with Hope, but his eyes are on me. And mine are on him. And we stare at each other until the song comes to an end.

Two hours later, the dance has died, Hope's nowhere to be seen, and I'm holding Kizzy back before she gets suspended again.

"I'll kill that bitch," Kizzy's hissing, pushing up against the wall that Sherie, Coko, Sy'rai, and me have formed so that none of the teachers can see her spiral.

I take a moment to glance behind me. The lights are brighter, the dance floor is empty aside from a few stragglers kicking at balloons and other discarded decorations, and the DJ is playing an upbeat pop song to torture us enough to get the hell out of here. What I don't see is some angry bitch taunting Kizzy on the other side of the room.

"Who is she even mad at?" I ask Coko.

"Girl, hell if I know. She's so lit, she probably thinks her shadow started some shit."

Coko's right. Kizzy's eyes are doing that darting thing they do when she's sipped on too much Grey Goose. "Kiz, it's okay. Let's just get home." I rest my hand on her shoulder, and she swats it away like it's on fire.

"*You* don't touch me." There's an extra emphasis on *you*. Like she wants to make it clear that I'm the last human who can help her right now. Well damn.

"Everything okay?" Tia comes up behind us, attempting to peel through the huddle.

"Does it look like it?" Coko asks, not even bothering to glance at her.

Tia's undeterred. "How can I help? You need me to distract the teachers or something?"

"We cool, okay?" I say, snappier than necessary. But the last thing we need is somebody in our ear like a telemarketer when we're trying to look out for our friend. I flick my wrist at her in full dismissal. "Off you go."

"Liv," Sherie says, with the same level of disappointment I could expect from my mom.

Tia's face falls as she gathers up the bottom of her gown and makes her exit. She walks slowly and gently, like I bruised more than just her ego. I can't linger on that, though. Not while Kizzy's a ticking time bomb. Once again, she tries to push past Sy'rai, but Sy's broad shoulders and hips make her a perfect fortress.

Sherie turns to me. "Hope."

I nod. Hope's the only one who can calm Kizzy down. She has the magic touch to turn vinegar into Moscato. Sherie wraps an arm around Kizzy's shoulder as Kizzy blows out an angry puff of air. I have another minute or so before she erupts again.

Another glance around the gym lets me know that there's no Hope in sight. As I run toward the doors, I see Brendan and Asher lingering around the exit. Cracking up over something as always.

I clear my throat, and they stare at me. Well, Asher does. Brendan stares down at my heels. He hasn't looked at me since his sweethearts dance.

"Where's Hope?" I ask, cutting to the chase.

"Bathroom," Brendan says, beating me to the finish line.

Asher's eyes ping-pong between us, smiling at the awkwardness. "She's either redoing her face or changing her tampon," he adds, because . . . Asher.

I wait a moment to see if Brendan will look up at me, but he just sips from his cup. I sigh and leave the gym. Dreading the conversation we'll need to have to clear the moldy air between us. Ms. Martin and the rest of the faculty are in the neighboring hall near the main entrance, making sure students look sober enough to leave the facility. I know Hope's not in the restroom near the gym nor the entrance. She doesn't like all the traffic and has a fear of someone listening to her pee. I take the stairs where the two halls connect—knowing Hope's in the bathroom that mostly everyone forgets about. The one sandwiched between the custodian's closet and the German classroom. Nobody hardly takes German, just like nobody hardly pays attention to the custodians. Thus, Hope's haven.

I push open the door and prep to call Hope's name when I noticed that there are two pairs of feet in the accessible stall. They squeak apart as soon as the door clicks behind me.

"Shh, someone's in here," a voice whispers. A voice that sounds a hell of a lot like Hope's.

My heart leaps in my throat, choking me so much that I can't utter anything. Those are definitely Hope's silver heels in that stall—and the other pair of shoes are definitely not Brendan's. Hope doesn't move. The other guy doesn't move. But I do.

I back out of the bathroom and scurry down the hall. I know Hope. I love Hope. I know and love her so much that I know she wouldn't want to feel humiliated. If she's stepping out on Brendan, she needs to tell me on her time. Not like this.

Still, curiosity gets the best of me. I slip into the enclave next to the custodian's closet and peek around the corner. Trying my best to conceal myself in the dim hallway. Hope comes out of the bathroom and looks around. I push myself against the wall and out of view until I hear her footsteps recede. A few moments later, the bathroom door swings open again. I wait a beat, then lean forward to peek again. I catch him adjusting his tea-green tie, the same shade as my dress. He turns, and his rows graze the nape of his neck. His black oxfords squeaking down the hall and down the stairs, presumably looking for his date.

Me.

SIXTEEN

NOW

I RUB MY THUMB ACROSS MY INFINITY PENDANT as I stare at my phone screen. Hope's picture is gone, but I've memorized the image. The way the moonlight shone on Hope's blood, making it a more cinnamon color than crimson. How her index finger extended against the pavement, pointing to something she'd never be able to reach. Even the way her coils seemed mid-drift from the night wind. It wasn't a chilly night, but the breeze came through to temper the upcoming muggy weather that summer.

My phone falls asleep, and I'm cloaked by darkness again. Shadows crawl up my skin and claw at my chest. My neck. My mouth. I need to leave. I need to get out of here before I suffocate. The rest of them might still be on the upper levels. But if they find me, it's okay. It'll be okay. They'll be pissed that I sent them on a wild-goose chase, but . . . the picture is gone. Disappeared into the ether. It should've been gone months ago. I just don't know how to let Hope go.

I sigh and lean back again, expecting to feel the cold wall of the cabin. But I don't. Something soft and warm and fleshy presses against my back. It squirms behind me, moving in and out. In and out. Like a chest taking deep breaths. And that breath tickles the back of my neck.

I'm frozen. I want to move. I want to scream, but my body forgets how to do either. *Stop it, Liv. This is just your imagination.* I squeeze my eyes closed and take in a shaky breath. The flesh is still behind me. No longer warm. Clammy now, like someone who got locked out of their house in the rain. I challenge myself. Turn my head ever so slightly to inspect the cabin. To make sure that I'm actually alone. My cheek bumps against a mouth, then a nose. I jerk back, and Hope's smiling at me. As much as she can. Half her face is a bloody pulp of meat and bones. Her skin is translucent, and I can see the blue veins in her arms. Veins that are no longer pumping blood. She lifts one of those arms around me, settling in for an icy embrace.

The scream finally erupts from my mouth as I kick out the door in front of me and throw myself out of the cabin. My palms slap against the floor before I fall on my face. I don't even feel it. The pain. My heart's pumping too fast to receive it. I scramble until I'm on my feet to get farther away from the dumbwaiter. When

I know I'm several feet away, I whip around and flash my phone light into the cabin.

Empty. Just like it was when I first entered. That's when it all sets in. The nausea. The relief. The throbbing tenderness in my forehead. I lurch forward and dry heave toward the floor. Nothing comes out, but my stomach still clenches, trying to push up something. After a few failed attempts, I press a hand on my belly and just breathe.

Breathe in. One, two, three, four.

Hold. One, two, three, four.

Breathe out. One, two, three, four.

My heart rate dissolves to drizzle instead of thunder, and I pull myself upright again. Dr. Solomon told me this could be a side effect from my benzos. Hallucinations. She also said my mind could play tricks with me during a panic attack. Either way, my body chemistry's all wrong. Taking that Xanax later than usual has got me all the way fucked up. I wave my phone light around so I can get familiar with my surroundings. Just a cold, barren room with no furniture or windows. I close my eyes and remember the floor plan. Above me is the laundry room, which means I must be in one of the storage rooms. There are three down here. One to store cold items, and the other two for whatever. Mom and the interior designer decided not to furnish these spaces so potential buyers could see how much square feet they have to store decorations, old clothes, dead bodies. Plus, they wanted to make sure they didn't block the . . .

I suck in a breath. That's right! I remember. I allow my phone light to guide me as I rush through one of the doorways. I enter the adjoining storage space. And there, on the opposite wall, is the motherfucking electrical panel. Hell yeah! I can fiddle around with it. Get the power going so we can all leave and call for help. That has to be enough for everyone to forgive me for not handing over my phone. Maybe they'll even forget that I was being weird about it all.

I run for the panel. This night is almost over. I can smell the wet grass and feel the rain on my skin. Before I reach the wall, my foot catches on something, and I stumble forward. My phone slips out of my hand, and my shoulder smashes into the wall.

"What the . . . ?" I rub my aching shoulder and search for my phone in the darkness. It fell flashlight side down, but I spot a small orb of light next to my boot. As I bend over to pick up my phone, the light cascades across a hand on the floor.

I gasp and fall backward, landing flat on my butt. I take a few deep breaths. *She's not here, Liv,* I say to myself. *Hope's not really here. She hasn't been here for six months.* With shaking hands, I lift my phone and pray that my mind is playing tricks on me again. The light beams on the hand again. I swallow and continue scanning and reach a head now. A head full of stitch rows.

"Day?" I say under my breath.

I crawl closer to him and use my light to trace over the rest of his body. His *body.* It lies on its side with its back to me, completely still.

"Dayvon?" I shine my light to the front of him, and his eyes stare straight ahead. Hazel and empty. There's a pool of blood spilling from somewhere in his torso, and a closer look shows a puncture in his smoking jacket, right under his rib cage.

A cry comes up from my gut. A sob even. This can't be real. He was just with me. He was right next to me. And now? I reach out my hand to try to touch his arm, but it won't complete the act. Just trembles right above him. My hand retreats and presses against my mouth as I cry some more.

"I'm sorry," I say in between my fingers. I don't know why, but it keeps coming out. Over and over. If I say it enough, he'll hear it. He'll roll over, sit up, and dust his jacket off. He has to, because this? This is senseless. First Sherie, and now Dayvon? My heart can't handle any more.

"Liv?" a voice croaks.

At that, I leap to my feet. Scan the room with my light. On the opposite wall, Asher is crouched on the floor. He squints from the light, but I still see that his eyelids are bright pink. Raw.

"When did you get here?" I ask, fear rising in my chest like bile. "How long have you been here?"

He wobbles up to his feet, holding a hand up to protect his eyes. A hand with blood drenching its fingers and trickling down to its palm. The skin on my arms tightens.

"I don't know," he says hoarsely. "I was searching for you and . . ." He drowns out as he looks toward Dayvon.

I inch to the doorway. Pray he doesn't notice me moving. "It's okay," I say to him. "It's okay."

He balks, this time from my words and not the light. "The fuck it is!" It comes out as a shriek, his voice sharp and razor-thin. "Look at me!" He holds up his hands. Both are bloody. "And Dayvon—"

I don't wait for his murderer's monologue. I'm close enough to the door to dart out of it.

"Liv!" he calls out, and oh my God, please don't let him be following me. Please don't let him be right behind . . .

I crash into something and stumble backward. Someone cusses. Brendan. I'd know his grumbly voice from anywhere.

"Liv, where the hell have you been?" I hear the anger dissipate from his voice as he eyeballs me, takes in my frantic energy.

"It's Dayvon," I cry out. "Dayvon's . . . gone. And Asher—" I can't say it. I can't finish. Kizzy runs up behind Brendan and stops in her tracks, sensing my terror. She looks between Brendan and me.

"What's going on? Did he hurt you?" she asks me.

I shake my head with fervor. "No. No, but Asher . . . and Dayvon. And they're in there." My cries come out in splutters. I hear the sentences in my head, but they won't leave my mouth the way they're supposed to. Footsteps run up behind me.

"B." It's Asher.

Brendan's hand is on my wrist as he pulls me behind him, right next to Kizzy. All three of us face Asher, who stands across from us, wild-eyed and red-handed.

"Look, I don't know what she told you, but Dayvon's dead."

Kizzy sucks in a breath next to me and squeezes my hand. I squeeze back. I see Brendan's shoulder tense up and touch his ears briefly before melting back down to his sides.

"Why are your hands like that, Asher?" he asks.

Asher looks down at his hands and stares like they're not attached to him. "I tried to save him." He talks to his hands, not us. "I thought there was something I could do, but it was too late. He was gone." He looks up, and his face morphs from sadness to rage. "And this bitch—"

"No!" I shout. I don't give him the privilege of finishing. Not after what he did. Not to mention I'm feeling braver behind the shield of Brendan Jean. "I found him, Asher. I found him like that. And you were there with him!"

"I found him, too!" Asher reaches for his hair but then thinks twice. The blood is still there. "Come on, Brendan. I was just with you searching for this girl. She's the one who went rogue!"

"But we got separated," Kizzy shouts. "I didn't see you for a good five minutes, Asher. If not more."

My girl. I cling tighter to her hand.

"And you really think that would give me enough time to fucking kill Dayvon?"

"He's been missing for a while," Brendan says, speaking slowly as if he were talking out a math problem. "All this time, he could've already been dead."

Asher's face crumbles. "B, seriously? Why would I kill Dayvon? He's my fucking best friend!"

"I don't know!" Brendan booms back. He scrubs the top of his head. "I don't know anything, okay? Except that we keep dropping like flies, and I'm not trying to be next. So you need to tell me what the hell is going on!"

"Bro, I wish I knew." Asher is calmer now. More coherent even though his voice still shakes. I'm this close to believing he didn't touch Dayvon, but if not him, then who? "All I know is I was looking for Liv and found him like that. I tried to save him, but he was already gone. And she was down here!"

"You were here first," I protest.

Brendan's pacing now. Still making sure to stand between us girls and Asher, but he's a little farther away. Like he's toeing the line. "He can't be dead," he's muttering to himself. "Is he really dead? Where is he?"

Asher nods behind him. "In there. But . . . you don't want to see him, man. Not like that. I wish I didn't, either."

"The electrical panel's back there," I feel compelled to say.

Apparently, the sound of my voice is enough to send Asher into a rage. "Who the fuck cares? Dayvon's dead in there! I'm not messing with that panel when my best friend is lying there dead, inches away."

"Or maybe you don't want us to cut the power back on. If we did, it'll mess up the rest of your plans for the night," Kizzy says.

"Are you fu . . . I don't have any plans for the night. I wasn't supposed to even be here for the night!"

"Yeah, but you are. And now people are dying." Kizzy's on a

roll, saying everything that I'm thinking.

"Again, why would I need to kill Dayvon?"

There's something about his words that unnerves me. Not his denial of killing Dayvon but his emphasis on Dayvon. It's not preposterous that we think he killed anyone. It's preposterous for us to think he killed Dayvon, specifically.

"Because he got in your way," I think aloud. "He found the electrical panel. And if he turned on the power, the gig is up. We get out. We call for help. But you didn't want us to."

Asher laughs, but it comes out raw. Hoarse. "Yeah, because I care that much about avenging Hope's death. I didn't even think she was good enough for my boy."

"Why not?" Kizzy demands. Her loyalty to Hope runs deep.

"Because she was a liar. Not to mention a skank."

Brendan stops pacing. "The fuck did you say?"

Asher winces, knowing he's said too much. But it's not like he can eat the words back up. He hurled them out, and now it's out there for all of us to sniff.

"Ash, why'd you call her a skank?" Brendan demands.

Asher's laughter comes out weaker. "I don't know. I'm just guessing. But my bad, bro. My bad." He rubs his fingers through his hair, forgetting all about the bloodstains. His hand trembles as much as mine, and he looks so pale that he could pass as a character from *Twilight*.

"You knew," I say. It's written all over his face. "You knew about Hope and Dayvon."

The room gets still, and I swear I hear water dropping from somewhere. Unless it's someone's sweat. The room has gotten eerily warmer.

"What about Hope and Dayvon?" Brendan asks. Getting no answer from me, he turns to Kizzy. She takes a step back and throws both hands in the air. She's not touching that question with a ten-foot pole. Brendan spins back toward Asher now. His steps are slow. Measured. A shark circling its food.

"I mean, I didn't know until after she died," Asher says.

"Know. What?!" Brendan claps with each word and they echo like thunder.

Asher glances around as if he's looking for an escape. Finding no easy path, he sighs and gives a small shrug. "You know. That they smashed."

SEVENTEEN

BRENDAN'S ACROSS THE ROOM IN A SPLIT SEC-ond, and Asher lets out a strangled cry.

"Brendan, let him go!" I yank at Brendan's jersey to pry him off Asher. He has Asher crushed against the wall, his forearm pressed so close to Asher's collarbone that Asher's face blooms into the same shade as an eggplant.

"Are you telling the truth?" Brendan barks at Asher. "Was Dayvon sleeping with Hope?"

Asher gargles out something that can't be understood. He's gasping for air and losing the battle.

"You're killing him!" Kizzy slaps Brendan's back over and over. "Stop it!"

All the screaming only makes Brendan push harder. Any second now and Asher's eyes will pop out of his skull.

"Brendan." I'm softer with my approach. Rest my hand on top of his shoulder. "Brendan, let Asher go. Let's talk about this, okay? Give him a chance to talk about it." I rub his shoulder now. Tiny strokes, like I'm soothing a feral cat. I feel Brendan's muscles loosen underneath my palm. Then, with a swift move, he lets Asher go and storms across the room.

Asher slumps to the floor and gulps for air. He pats his chest to get the air in quicker. Kizzy kneels next to him and rubs his back. I'm not sure what I should do. If I check on Asher, I'll betray Brendan. If I go to Brendan, it'll look like I'm siding with a monster. So I stay right where I am and hug myself.

"Who else knew?" Brendan asks, his voice tiny and tense.

Asher coughs up phlegm and hocks it onto the floor.

"Who else knew?" Brendan's louder now.

"Who cares?" Asher leaps up to his feet, and Kizzy joins him, hand in front of his chest in case he has a death wish. "Both of them are gone now. Dayvon is literally rotting ten feet from us! Who gives a fuck if they hooked up?"

"I do!" Brendan pounds his chest. "I care. You guys have no clue. No clue how much shit that girl put me through. And to know that she was stepping out on me the entire time?" His voice breaks, and he turns away. Even now, he doesn't want anyone to see him sad. The only emotion we can be privy to tonight is his rage. Rage makes him a man. Anything else is weak.

We're all silent. The only sound present is Brendan's sniffles.

He rubs his face in a fervor, fighting to keep everything in. I'm all too familiar with the need to fight away my feelings.

"I don't think it was the entire time," I say. Maybe that will give him a little solace.

Brendan chuckles as he faces us again. "You don't think? Liv, don't act a fool. You apparently knew all about them. You're supposed to be my best friend. And you"—he nods at Asher—"I thought we were boys."

"Boys don't try to crush each other's windpipes," Asher says.

"That's not fair." I'm hung up on Brendan's comment. "You're still putting me in the middle of your and Hope's drama. You were both my best friends. You're not supposed to make me choose sides."

"You already did." Brendan spreads out his arms as if the evidence is all around us. "You kept her secret about Dayvon. You believed I put my hands on her. And you even think I killed her. I think it's clear I lost that friendship battle."

I shake my head. "It's not the same. There was no comparison between you and Hope."

"Why not?"

"Because I wanted to believe her!" I shout the words, but the volume doesn't carry the weight of them. "Do you know how tough it is for everyone to believe women? Black women, specifically? Not to mention that everyone was already looking at her all side-eyed because of her depression. I didn't want to be like everyone else. I didn't want to be that ignorant." I saw the stats on Dr. Solomon's website. The number of Black people with depression and anxiety and whatever else, versus Black people who actually received help. Hope got help, so I had to believe she was getting better. I had to believe that the meds and the time at Keystone all meant something. Because if they didn't, then what the hell am I doing? Why am I working so hard with Dr. Solomon to get my life back if everyone's still going to look at me like some broken doll?

"It's you," Asher says as he backs away from me.

I frown at him. "What are you talking about?"

"All that believing-crazy-women bullshit? You've been relaying that message all night. Did you leave a note on Dayvon after you killed him?"

"I didn't kill Dayvon. I found him."

"No, I found him." Asher points his thumb to himself. "You just happened to pop out of the darkness. What were you doing, Liv? Going back to the scene of the crime to leave your clue for your macabre scavenger hunt?"

I wait for someone to defend me. To remind Asher he's the one with literal blood on his hands. But nobody makes a peep. Even Kizzy seems to create more distance between us.

"You were pretty obsessed with Hope," Brendan continues. "And I never understood how you just happen to have her necklace."

The room tilts and, on instinct, I reach for the infinity pendant. Pinch it to make sure it's still there. "Her mom gave it to me after she died."

"Mrs. Jackson wasn't trying to give up nothing of Hope's after she died," Kizzy says. "Not even that copy of *Wuthering Heights* she carried around all the time. I asked Mrs. Jackson for it like a month after the funeral."

I look at her, and she seems to radiate green. She's still jealous. After all this time. After all we've been through the past few months, weeks. Hell, tonight.

"Well, Mrs. Jackson actually likes me."

Kizzy's head rocks back. "Fuck you. She likes me."

"And fuck you for suggesting that I'm lying about the necklace," I snap. "Are we all forgetting that Kizzy's lie is what probably got us all here in the first place? If she didn't report that fake news about me and Brendan, Hope wouldn't have hooked up with Dayvon. She wouldn't have gotten all weird and distant and broken up with Brendan. She may not even be dead if she knew she could talk to her two best friends, but no. Because of you, she thinks we betrayed her."

"I know what I saw," Kizzy hisses. "Even if you two claimed nothing happened, something was obviously going on between you two. It still is! I saw Brendan's face when he knew you were part of the plan tonight. That dude was heartbroken."

I will my neck not to swivel in Brendan's direction.

"You made me think tonight was my plan." Kizzy won't stop talking. "You made it seem like you were just following along, but really, you're playing out some sick revenge fantasy."

"Kizzy . . ." I can barely separate my jaw to speak. I'm scared if

I move it too freely, something vicious will come out. "I'm going to need you to stop right there before you say anything else stupid."

Kizzy's eyebrows rise with delight, as if she's up for the challenge. "Oh my God, you were pissed Brendan picked Hope instead of you, huh? So you got rid of Hope and wanted everyone to think Brendan did it. Two birds, one stone. But when that didn't work, you orchestrated tonight. Get rid of Brendan and anyone else who stood in your way. All this bloodshed because you couldn't get the boy."

I storm over to Kizzy and stand nose-to-nose with her. She doesn't even flinch. Just smiles. "Go ahead," she says. "Finish the job, Liv. Am I next?"

My skin prickles and burns, and I'm ready to set this whole room on fire. I clench my fists and imagine punching Kizzy right in her smirking mouth. I want to punch it until it becomes mulch, and she can't smile again.

"Whoa." Asher grabs my hand and nudges me back. "Think about this, Liv. There's still a way out of this. Another body's not going to be a good look for you."

This bastard. I shove him away. "Don't touch me." I check my hand to see if he's rubbed any of Dayvon's blood on me. "Look at me!" I spread my arms to everyone and do a 360 turn. "There's only one of us who has Dayvon's DNA all over them. I don't even have a weapon on me to do that kind of damage." I turn my jean pockets inside out so they can see. Only my car key fob and phone are present. "What about you, Asher?"

Asher scoffs and digs in his pocket, pulling out his phone and a set of keys. "There. Happy?"

"Let me see the keys," Brendan says.

Asher's head whips in his direction. "Why?"

"Because."

Asher's jaw tightens, but he hands Brendan the keys. Brendan holds up his phone light to the keys and inspects every groove.

"Death by keys," Asher says, his words drenched in sarcasm. "Not my best work but, hey, it got the job done."

After another moment, Brendan tosses the keys back to Asher. "You could've ditched the weapon."

Once again, Asher looks as if his head is about to pop. "Hold on. You still think it's me? Even after Kizzy's closing statement about Liv?"

"You're the only one with blood on you," Brendan insists, and my spine straightens just a bit. He may be pissed at me, but dammit, Brendan believes me. He knows I couldn't have done all this tonight.

"I told you why there's blood on me. You think I wanted this?"

"Okay, so let's go to the room." Brendan looks over Asher's shoulder at the dark doorway that leads to Dayvon's body.

Asher shakes his head so much that it looks like he has a twitch. "No. Nope. I'm not going back in there."

"Asher, if you didn't do it, then prove it. Let's see what happened to Dayvon. Let's see if there's anything lying around."

"No!" Asher bellows. "I'm not seeing him like that again. If you guys want to go in, then fine. But I'm going to sit this one out."

"And what? We're supposed to leave you here when we're not even sure if you did it?" Brendan grabs Asher's arm. "Stop pussy-footing and let's take a look."

"I said no!" Asher tries to squirm out of Brendan's hand, but Brendan has a tight grip. Soon, they're dancing. Twisting and turning as Brendan tries to pull Asher into the other storage room and Asher fighting with everything in him to get away.

Kizzy and I back up to the other side of the room before we catch a fist or elbow.

Through some act of God, Asher manages to trip Brendan, who plummets to the floor. Asher uses that opportunity to dart out of the storage room and toward the main rec area.

"This motherfucker," Brendan grunts. He scrambles to his feet and chases after Asher.

I'm right behind Brendan. I'm not sure if I'm supposed to save him or Asher, but my feet feel compelled to follow. I hear Asher and Brendan scrambling up the stairs, a trail of yells and curse words in their wake. I take the stairs in twos and reach the main level. Search around. The signs of struggle seem to be coming from above me. Somewhere in the loft. I take a breath and run to the grand staircase. I'm on the first stair when Kizzy grabs my arm. I didn't even hear her behind me.

"Wait," she says.

I frown down at her arm. At the audacity of her even putting her hands on me after the shit she's just pulled, and snatch away.

"Just listen, okay?" She grabs my hand. "I don't trust either one of them."

"You don't trust me, either," I say.

"No. That's not true. I just wanted to make them think that."

"You were pretty damn convincing."

"Look." She takes a breath and looks up, making sure Brendan and Asher are far out of sight. The chase is still on. "Asher's the one with Dayvon's blood on him. And everything started going off-kilter when Asher came to the house. And who just happened to call him here?"

I look up. I barely hear them now. Just a couple of muffled grunts and arguments. For all I know, they could be putting on a production for us.

"Let's get to the electrical panel," Kizzy continues. "Turn the power back on. Get to your car. Call the cops."

She makes it all seem so simple. A plus B equals C. But she forgets the part where we staged a hostage situation. Where one of our schemers got killed. Where Dayvon's body is positioned in a dark room right in front of the electrical panel.

"How do I know if I can trust you?" I ask.

Kizzy gives a gentle head shake. "You don't. But what else are you going to do?"

Damn. She's right. Chasing after Brendan and Asher won't give me anything except more accusations, probably thrown in my direction again. If we really wanted answers, we'd need to get out of this house.

"Fine." I pull away from her again. "But I need to see your hands at all times."

"Fair enough. And you need to tell me what's on your ph—"

A gush of air cascades down my body as something large tumbles just right of the staircase, hitting the floor with a sickening *thump*. Kizzy and I stare at each other, too scared to move an inch.

"What was that?" Kizzy whispers.

I swallow, the answer lodged somewhere in the pit of my throat. I hold up the phone light and shine it toward the floor next to us. Asher's face up on the floor, his four limbs contorted away from him like a crooked asterisk. I hear the moment when it clicks for Kizzy. She sucks in a breath, then lets out a scream that I've only heard in horror movies before. Mine is stuck in the same place as all my words. I shift my phone light above me and try to find an answer in the darkness.

Brendan peers down from the third-floor loft. I can't make out his face, but his hands form fists on top of the railing.

EIGHTEEN

I THINK BRENDAN'S MOUTH IS MOVING, BUT Kizzy's screams flood my ears, overpowering everything else. My cries are still lodged somewhere between my chest and the pit of my throat as I try to make sense of what I just saw.

"He's dead!" Kizzy's screams take on a coherent form. "Oh my God, he's dead. He killed him!"

"Liv!" Brendan booms from above. "I didn't do it, Liv! He fell!"

There's something off about his pleas. Like he's practiced them in a mirror, working to get just the right inflection to portray hysteria. Almost like he's done this before.

"Just like Hope fell?" I ask, finding my voice.

Brendan pauses. I still can't make out his features. Can't see if he's confused or calculating. He pushes himself away from the railing, and I hear his feet hammering against the floor. He's coming down. Holy shit, he's coming down.

"We have to go." I grab Kizzy's hand.

She's still stunned, staring at Asher's body like she hopes it'll rise.

"Kizzy, he's coming. Move!"

Kizzy nods as she comes to. She allows me to lead her away from the grand staircase, then down the set of stairs back to the basement. When we reach ground level, she pulls me toward the storage room, and I yank her back. "The electrical panel," she says.

"The doors don't lock. He'll get in," I tell her.

Brendan's footsteps rain down the stairs.

"Come on." I pull her to the right and run into the spare room. As soon as we're both in, I slam the door shut behind us and lock it.

Kizzy leans against the desk and buries her face into her hands, doing some combo of gasping and crying. There's no time for breakdowns. We're the only ones left. It's us versus him, and we need the W.

"Kizzy, get up," I say, scanning the room.

Kizzy looks up, her bangs matted against her forehead and her mascara streaked down her cheeks. "What?"

"We need to find something, anything, to use against him. To get us out of here."

"We can't. The power—"

"We can't just sit here, Kiz!" I squeeze my hands into fists and take a deep breath. Someone has to be the calm one. "Everyone's gone, okay? It's just us. So . . . just look?"

Kizzy pauses, then gives a slow nod. She gets it. Like she says, she pays attention in science class. It's all about survival of the fittest. "I'll check the bathroom," she says as she makes a sprint for the en suite. Atta girl.

I enter the walk-in closet. Nothing in there but a half-empty container of paint and coat hangers. Not even the wire ones I could fashion into a weapon. I leave the closet as Kizzy comes out of the bathroom carrying a cleaning-fluid spray bottle.

"We can sanitize the fuck out of him," she says with a half-hearted smile.

"It's something." I give her a nod for a job semi well done. I glance around, and my eyes land on another glass sliding door that leads to the covered deck upstairs.

Kizzy follows my line of vision.

"There's no point, right?" she asks. "Remember, Asher and the barstool?"

We look at each other, remembering the sickening thud Asher's body made when it hit the floor right next to us. Dammit, Asher. He was the worst, but sometimes, he wasn't. He wasn't going to save the world, but you could count on him to tell an inappropriate joke when it was on fire.

"Liv!" Brendan bangs against the bedroom door from the other side. Kizzy and I cling to each other. "Please! Open the door! I promise I didn't do it."

"Go away, Brendan!" I demand.

"He backed up and lost his footing!"

"Over a rail, Brendan? Really?"

The other side of the door gets silent. Kizzy and I peek at each other. Did he leave? Did he just walk away?

"Yeah." Brendan's voice is small now. Less conviction. "I don't know how it happened. We were scrapping. Not like *fighting* fighting, but struggling. I was searching him for weapons, and he was trying to get away. He got loose and scrambled back and then . . . he was gone." He sucks in a gravelly breath. "It happened so quick and I . . . I couldn't reach him."

Kizzy shakes her head at me: *Don't fall for it.*

"I'd believe it was an accident if there weren't already two other bodies tonight," I say.

"And I told you, I found Sherie. I didn't even see Dayvon."

There's a soft thud on the door, and I can see him resting his forehead against it.

"What do I have to do? What do I need to do for you guys to believe me?"

"Tell the truth about Hope." The words rush out of Kizzy's mouth. "This whole night started because we wanted the truth. Where were you the night Hope fell?"

More silence, and I wonder what he's doing. Cussing to himself? Holding back tears? Trying to find a way in the room?

"Just like I told the cops. I caught a late movie. I didn't get out until after midnight."

"And I still don't buy it, Brendan." Kizzy peels away from me now and moves toward the door, her anger rebuilding her confidence. "Guys like you don't go to the movies by himself. You could've just as easily bought the ticket in advance as an alibi. That bullshit excuse goes as far back as the Menendez brothers."

"I wasn't by myself," Brendan says.

Kizzy opens her mouth, but nothing comes out. She's just as confused as me. He wasn't alone. All this time, Brendan never said he wasn't alone.

"Then who?" I ask. I'm careful with how I ask. Too much sharpness, and Kizzy and Brendan might think that I'm jealous. And I'm not. I know I'm not. It would be dumb to be jealous over someone who could potentially be a murderer. And there are several bodies at this point so, oh shit, is Brendan a serial killer? I definitely am not jealous about what a serial killer does in his spare time. "Why didn't you say that before?"

"Because . . . I didn't want to be that guy. I didn't want to be the guy who was dating another girl when his ex was going through something. I knew she was dealing with some heavy shit. She was just as angry and erratic as she was right before she had to go to Keystone. But I was tired. I was so fucking tired. I wanted to be her man, not her therapist. I didn't have the energy to soothe her anymore. And then she spread those lies about me hitting her . . ." Brendan disappears. I can still hear him breathing on the other side of the door, but he's gone. Floating through the memory of their last breakup. "I couldn't anymore. I was ready to move on, but I didn't want to be that guy."

Kizzy scoffs. "So, you'd much rather be the guy who was accused of killing his ex?"

"I guess so," Brendan says, the words lifting slightly as though he just had this revelation. "I think I was hoping the truth would come out. And I wouldn't have to put my date through all this mess. I saw the shit Hope had to deal with after our breakup, I didn't want her to deal with it, either. I couldn't see that again."

He keeps referring to this girl as just his "date" or "her." He won't speak her name. Even now, when he's trying to proclaim his innocence, he's trying to protect her. Where was that protection for me when everyone abandoned me after my panic attack at my last track meet? Or when everyone kept accusing me of being a murderer tonight? If we were best friends like he claimed we were, that loyalty should've been there. He should've seen it, even when it seemed like I was against him. This new girl must be really special.

"If you want us to believe you," I say, feeling certainty swell in my chest, "then let us go." I think back to the Cupid Dance. *Let me go. Let me go.* It's time he did.

Brendan gives a dry laugh. "Let y'all go? I couldn't even if I wanted to. We're all locked in here, remember?"

"If you didn't do any of this tonight," I continue, "then go to the electrical panel, cut on the power, and let us all go."

Silence. Kizzy and I glance at each other.

"Then you'll believe me? Then you'll have my back when the

cops arrive?" Brendan asks finally.

That seems like a loaded question. My biggest pet peeve, though, is watching a movie where a character confronts the villain after gathering evidence that they are, in fact, a villain. Instead of playing coy until they get to safety, that character decides to tell the villain their plans: *I know what you did, and I'm going to the cops.* Just do it, bruh. Keep your plans close to your chest.

"Yeah," I say. "Help us get help, and we'll come out."

Brendan sighs. Or maybe he huffs. "Okay. I'll be back."

Kizzy and I wait until we no longer hear Brendan's breaths right outside the door.

"You think he's gone? You think he's doing it really?" Kizzy asks.

I shrug, and my shoulders feel like I've been doing lateral raises with fifty-pound dumbbells. "I guess we'll find out." Still, I can't just sit here. I walk to the sliding door and give the handle a sharp tug. Of course, it doesn't budge.

"You think he's telling the truth?" Kizzy again. "That he really was on a date? If so, why didn't that girl step up and validate his alibi?"

"Because she never needed to. The police didn't feel the need to investigate any further. Do you have a bobby pin?"

Kizzy frowns and ruffles her short bob, sending her straight tresses flying in every direction. "Does it look like I have a bobby pin? Why?"

I lean over to inspect the door handle. "I'm going to try to pick this lock."

"Do you know how to pick a lock?"

I blink. "No. But everyone who's ever picked a lock had to start some place, right?"

"It just seems weird." Kizzy props herself on top of the oak desk. "He's a suspect but suddenly he was on a date? Why not mention that six months ago? It's like that device they use in theater. What's it called? Chekov's gun or something?"

I kick at the lock a few times, then huff when that does nothing. "Deus ex machina."

"It's fucking convenient, is what it is." Kizzy studies me. "And I can't tell if you want it to be true or not."

I roll my eyes. "Kizzy, I think you vocalized your theory about me enough tonight. I'm the creepy guy from *You*. The one who stalks his love interest and kills everyone around him."

"I don't really think that, Liv. I needed them to think that I was turning on you so they'd let their guard down."

"You sounded mighty convincing."

"That's because I'm an amazing actor, bitch." A smile spreads across Kizzy's face, slow and deliberate, like pouring syrup over a stack of pancakes. I cough out a laugh in spite of myself. Kizzy's as unpredictable as a snowfall in April, but that's part of the thrill. Probably why Hope was drawn to her in the first place.

"You have to admit, though, I have some great material," Kizzy continues. "You, Hope, and Brendan . . . you three were like a BLT."

I raise my eyebrows and wait for Kizzy to explain.

"Have you had just a lettuce and tomato sandwich?"

I think about it. "I'm sure vegetarians have."

"Whatever. It's fucking weird. You need the trifecta. Even when Hope and Brendan started dating, they included you in everything. That's why it never made sense."

"That we were all so close?"

"That only two of you could fall for each other." Kizzy's legs dangle off the desk. "If Brendan and Hope felt that way about each other, how could you and Brendan not?"

I swallow. It's almost like Kizzy got hold of my Notes app and read through my ramblings. That's what I asked myself the first few months Hope and Brendan got serious. Why not me? I went to as many of Brendan's games as Hope. I laughed at more of his jokes. He even trusted me to edge up his hair. So why not me? It never seemed like I was supposed to ask that question, but now I know that someone else wondered it, too. Somehow that makes me feel vindicated. But that's not important anymore. Especially not now.

"I mean, but that's different," I say. "We all had room to let other people in. Look at you and Hope. Hope and Sherie. Hope and Dayvon . . ." My voice wanders as I realize that 75 percent of the people I listed are now gone.

That stat seems to hit Kizzy, too, because her face is back in her hands, and she's whimpering again.

"Hey." I walk over to her and put my hand on her back. "We're getting out of here, okay? We're going to be fine."

"'It was not the thorn bending to the honeysuckles, but the honeysuckles embracing the thorn,'" she murmurs in between her fingers.

Wuthering Heights. I know it's from that without even having to think about it. It was one of Hope's favorite passages. I can see the line now, underlined with purple ink.

"This entire night has been about her," she continues. "Even now, we're all bending to her will. Killing ourselves from it. But she never had enough space."

I frown and try to follow, but Kizzy speaks in circles. Jumping from a book to real life in one breath. I feel like I need to be strapped in to continue this ride. "Who didn't? Hope?"

Kizzy pulls her face from her hands and looks at me. Through the tears, something lingers behind her eyes. A little bit of fear, but a lot a bit of resignation. "Hope never had enough space for me." She speaks clearly now, leaving room between every other word so I can hear her. "Even though she knew I was in love with her."

NINETEEN

I CONSIDER MY NEXT FEW WORDS CAREFULLY. I automatically want to make Kizzy feel better with a healthy dose of toxic positivity: *Of course you loved Hope—and she loved you, too. You both loved each other!* That's not what she needs, though. Kizzy's not talking about the typical love you feel for a friend. The kind of love where you cry when they're sad, or laugh when they're happy, or give the stank eyes to anyone who's pissed them off. Kizzy said she was *in love* with Hope. In love is something that cuts so deep that you don't even notice you're bleeding out until you're almost gone. It's swimming in the dark, where you try to find the surface but sink closer to the ocean floor. It's bliss even when there's impending doom. Kizzy stares at me with moist, muddy eyes, and I know that she's drowned.

"Wow." It's all I can muster now. I try to conjure up more poignant words, but once again it's: "Wow." Then: "Did you tell her?"

Kizzy breaks eye contact to look at her dangling legs. "She knew."

"So you did tell her."

"I didn't have to. Hope knew she had me in her back pocket. She knew since our first group together in Keystone." She breaks into a tiny smile, as if she's back in that room with Hope. "She was sharing something about her dad. He wanted to teach her a lesson about something and was being an asshole about it—as parents tend to be sometimes. So our counselor decides this is the moment to practice empathy. For Hope to put herself in her dad's shoes. I think the counselor was a grad student or something. Not a *counselor* counselor yet, but everyone was going along with it. The rest of the group chimed in to say things they thought Hope's dad was trying to express to her. You know, to make an excuse for his behavior."

Kizzy straightens up and her voice gets deep. "*If I didn't care, I wouldn't give you a consequence. This is all out of love. I'm your father, not your friend.*"

I laugh at her impeccable imitation of Mr. Jackson's pebbly voice, like he perpetually has phlegm in his chest.

Kizzy slumps again, and her voice returns to normal. "Then it gets to me. And all I do is shrug and say, 'Fuck him.' Because *fuck him*, right? Life lessons don't have to come with a dose of venom. Just don't be an asshole. It's not rocket science. The room got all quiet. Hope stared at me with wide eyes, then let out the loudest cackle. You remember that one? That laugh that sounded like a teakettle when it reaches boil? Of course, that gets me going—which makes her keep going. Soon, the rest of the group is all nervous giggling, and that poor grad student has to call for help to get us all under control."

I smile and climb onto the desk right next to Kizzy. The way she speaks about Hope makes me want to be closer to her. The closer I am, maybe I can grab on to some of those memories and store them for myself. I want to remember Hope's laugh. I want to remember how she could change the temperature of the room with just a smile. The more I think about those moments, the more that final image of Hope, broken and bleeding on the concrete, will fade away.

"From that moment, she had me. She knew she had me." Kizzy sighs and tries to tuck her hair behind her ear, but that straight bob has a mind of its own. "She would do things. Tiny things to keep me, you know? Finding a reason to touch me when she didn't need to. Sneaking into my bed at Keystone. Letting me . . ." She trails off and my eyebrows quirk unintentionally. "It never went beyond kissing. Maybe a little bit of touching, but never too much to think she was cheating on Brendan. I knew my purpose. She just wanted to blow off some steam. Have some fun while we were away so that it would feel like we were only at camp or something."

I'm trying my best just to listen. To be here for Kizzy. But her revelations hit me like a pile of cast-iron skillets being dropped on my lap. Hope and Kizzy? So, Dayvon wasn't the first person she stepped out with. Apparently, she also had Kizzy lurking in the wings and never told me. Why didn't she think that she could tell me?

"When we got back home, I thought it was over. That what happened at Keystone, stayed at Keystone," Kizzy continues, snapping me back into the moment. But she continued to find reasons to touch me. Or to call me out of the blue to just giggle and say hello. Or leave me notes in my locker . . ."

"Notes?" That seems unlike Hope. Then again, all of this seems unlike Hope. She was sweet at times, but never sentimental. "Like what?"

"Nothing concrete or suggestive. She still had Brendan after all. But . . . I guess she wanted me to know that she was thinking about me. She always told me to throw them away. They were for my eyes only. And I did because . . . she wanted me to. But there was one I had to keep. One that seemed too special to just toss away. I carried it with me everywhere, especially after she . . ." Her teeth sinks into her bottom lip as her eyes say what her mouth can't.

"Do you have it now?" I ask.

She shakes her head. "I lost it. I'm so pissed that I lost it. I think maybe I left it in my pocket when my mom washed my clothes. Maybe she ruined it. Or maybe she saw it and just discarded it. Mom says she's okay with my *lifestyle* . . ." She adds air quotes to the final word. "But the fact that she even calls it that clearly shows that she's not."

I want to wrap an arm around Kizzy, but she's always been so hard to read. Hope was the one who translated everything between us. "What did it say?"

Kizzy peeks up at me. Is the darkness playing tricks on my eyes, or is she being . . . bashful? "Hey, Heathcliff," she says. "With three little hearts around it. She was referring to—"

"*Wuthering Heights*," I finish. "She loved that damn book."

"She *loved* that damn book," Kizzy agrees.

I can still see her copy. The cover all creased and craggy from being manhandled. Colorful tabs poking out what looked like every page to help her find her favorite lines. Hope and I even had our own inside joke based on the book. Whenever one of us really wanted something, but couldn't get it for whatever reason, we'd cry out "I am Heathcliff!" Whether it was for the last slice of pizza, or to borrow a pair of shoes, or even to pick the song we'd listen to in the car. It was a poor interpretation of the line. Catherine says it to describe this existential love she has for Heathcliff. Something that would be present long after either of them left the earth. We knew we were being ridiculous, which made it all the funnier. Kizzy took it as something literal from Hope—no wonder she asked Mrs. Jackson for Hope's copy. But I can't help but wonder if Hope took advantage of Kiz's sincerity just a little. On cue, I reach for the infinity pendant and pinch it. This meant forever for us, too, but maybe I just wasn't in on Hope's joke.

"The text exchange," I begin. "On the laptop upstairs. It was you, wasn't it? You and Hope?"

Kizzy shifts but doesn't nod. I have my answer.

"That's why you went back and told her about me and Brendan," I say as everything connects. "Brendan would be officially out of the picture, and then—"

"And then she went to Dayvon, and not me," Kizzy says, more tepid than heated. "No wonder she ghosted me after the dance. I kept checking in on her to see what she would do about you or Brendan, but crickets. That's why I planned that sleepover. That . . . *final* sleepover."

"Fuck that sleepover," I interject. It was supposed to be a night that ended in face masks and pillow fights, but we got heartache and trauma instead.

Kizzy nods. "Yeah, fuck that sleepover. It was supposed to cheer her up, but also to see where we were at with our . . . situationship. If I had known about her and Dayvon, I wouldn't have . . ." She looks around the locked bedroom that we've been sequestered into for I don't even know how long. "I would've made different choices about tonight. I went so hard because I thought Brendan had ruined our love story before it even began, but that's all it was for Hope. Fiction. Who knows who else she was stringing along."

I nod. Earlier tonight, Kizzy tried to pin everything on me. Telling everyone that I did these sinister things all because of a *boy.* But she was projecting. She wanted to plot against Brendan because *she* never got the girl. She thought Brendan took that away from her. But as I look at Kizzy's shoulders slump, I know she realizes now that she never was going to have Hope.

I bite the bullet and wrap my arm around Kizzy's shoulder. To my surprise, she doesn't flinch or shrug me off. She leans against me and allows me to comfort her in some small way.

"I may not know exactly what you're feeling," I say, "but I know how Hope could make me feel like I was the greatest thing on earth since edible cookie dough."

Kizzy lets out a soft laugh.

"When she was with you, she was *with* you. Nothing or no one else mattered. I felt like I could do anything. And I probably did do anything . . . for her." I squeeze Kizzy a little closer to me. "We all were a little duped by Hope, so don't be embarrassed by that. If anything, be embarrassed by that haircut."

Kizzy snorts and gently shoves me away from her. "Bitch. This is cutting-edge."

"Yeah. For the dominatrix circle. That's why everyone's scared of you tonight. We don't want you to pinch our nipples until we cry out our safe words."

Kizzy gasps and clutches her chest, then cracks up laughing. It comes from her ribs and escapes like Goofy on helium. It's ridiculous, but great. She should do this more often. When we get out of here, I need to find more opportunities to make her laugh like this. *If* we get out of here.

Something thuds above us. We stop laughing and look up, clinging closer together.

"What the hell was—" I don't get to finish because there's another thud. Angrier, this time. Like the Big Bad Wolf trying to blow someone's house down.

"Is that Brendan?" Kizzy asks, her voice as shaky as my hands. "Is he trying to break another window? Do you think he really tried to turn on the power?"

I listen out for more thumps, but everything's still. The only sounds are our breaths. "I don't know. But maybe we shouldn't rely on him. We need to find our own way out of here."

"How? Is there like some secret tunnel you know about?"

I sigh. "Nope. Just a dumbwaiter."

Kizzy frowns. "Okay, that's not very nice."

"The dumbwaiter's not a person. It's like an elevator for food and clothes."

The confusion has not left Kizzy's forehead. "Doesn't an elevator shut down during a power outage, too?"

"Yeah, but that one has a manual pull . . ." The image pops in my head and stops me in my tracks. Holy shit. *Holy shit*. Why didn't I think of this before?

"Liv?" Kizzy asks.

I jump off the desk and pace around the room as I paint the full picture in my head. "The dumbwaiter's not the only thing in here with a manual pulley."

Kizzy follows me with her eyes. "Oookay."

I stop pacing and smile at her. "The garage. The garage has a manual pulley that you can use in case the power craps out." I remember the cord plunking me against the head earlier tonight in the garage. With Dayvon.

Kizzy's face lifts into giddiness. "We get to the garage . . ."

"Then we get to my car," I finish for her.

Kizzy leaps from the desk. "Holy shit."

"I know."

She makes a run for the door, then stops. "What about Brendan? What if he's right by the door waiting for us?"

I see it all before it happens. Brendan, leaning against the wall. Me, opening the door. Brendan grabbing me by the throat, pressing me up against the wall while Kizzy screams for him to let me go. Shadows cover his face as I lose my breath. I don't want to see him being a monster, even in my imagination.

"Still got that stun gun?" I ask.

Kizzy digs in her pocket and pulls it out. I grab the spray bottle she left on the windowsill. A knife would be preferable, but at least I have something. I give a weak shrug. "Then let's do this."

Kizzy takes a deep breath as I join her by the door. I reach for the knob, then pause. "No lights," I mouth to her. "Follow me."

She grabs my hand and nods. I grip her fingers and return the nod: *We got this*. I twist the doorknob, nice and slow. Careful not to make any noise. The door pushes open and, thankfully, doesn't squeak. The joys of having brand-new fixtures. I peer down the dark hall and itch to reach for my phone to light the pathway. But lights will only draw Brendan to us. I'm not 100 percent convinced he killed everyone tonight, but I'd rather that be someone else's job to figure out.

We grip each other's hands as we take slow, careful steps down the hall. The moon gives us just enough light to not bump into the walls, but not enough to eat up all the shadows. Shadows that Brendan could be lurking in. I exhale once we reach the opening to the clearing. The clearing that leads to the large rec room space. On one end of the rec room is the basketball court where Sherie still lies. On the other end, Dayvon in storage. I pinch my eyes closed for a moment to get them out of my head. The best thing we can do for them right now is to escape and get justice for their deaths.

I open my eyes, and the moonlight shines on the doorframe leading to the stairs a few feet ahead of us. The plan is laid out before me. Get to the main level, then the garage. Open it up just enough to reach my car, then . . . freedom. At least something close to it. After tonight, I'm not sure if Kizzy or me will ever truly feel free. We'll always feel the need to sleep with a light on. Glance over our shoulders in public spaces. There will always be that haunting feeling that someone is watching us.

"Liv!"

Brendan's rough voice cuts through the darkness and punches me in the chest. Without a word, Kizzy and I run. Straight for the stairs. Straight for our exit. As we pound up the first few steps, Brendan's on our heels as though appearing from thin air.

"Liv, wait!" He grabs on to my shirt, jerking both Kizzy and me backward. Kizzy finds her footing and spins around, thrusting the stun gun toward Brendan. Brendan swats it away with his free hand, and the gun clatters somewhere on the floor behind him.

He still has a hold on me. As I try to pull away, I tumble on top of the stairs. Kizzy's above me, throwing punches at Brendan's head, and he grunts and grumbles as he tries to dodge them.

"Kiz," I cry out. "Go!"

I meet her eyes as I'm crushed onto the stairs under Brendan's pressure. She shakes her head and takes another swing at Brendan.

"Go!" I repeat, more forceful now. One of us needs to get out. Maybe I can fend him off and catch up with her. Or maybe I can hide until she gets help.

With a clenched jaw, Kizzy receives my message and bounds up the stairs. Brendan pushes off me just enough for me to twist around. I use that moment to spray the cleaner right in his fucking eyes.

"Ah! Shit!" he cries out, using both hands to wipe his face.

The cleaner comes out in drizzles now instead of squirts. It's emptying. I toss the bottle on the floor and spin back around. I'm on all fours as I scurry up the stairs like a wounded animal. Brendan grabs my ankle and I'm sliding back to him. My chin bounces on each stair as I descend, and I wait for a crack. Some sign that my jaw is about to snap in half.

"Liv, stop! I don't want to hurt you!"

Too fucking late for that. I'm under him again, and he flips me around so I can face him. He reaches for my face. I'm not sure if he wants to caress or smother me, so I use both hands to push his chest. Try my best to force him off me. *Let me go. Let me go.*

He manages to get ahold of both my wrists and pins them on the stairs next to my head. I thrash and kick. I don't want to die, but if I do, I'm not going without a fight.

"Fucking stop it. Stop it!" he screams.

The sheer force of it blows some of my braids from my face until I'm staring at him. Desperation in his twisted mouth and his voice on the cusp of fear. Why the hell would he be the scared one? But his expression makes me stop fighting. At least for now.

Noticing that I'm subdued, Brendan moves closer to me. "I've been trying to tell you. Trying to tell you both." His lips are now right next to one of my ears. "There's someone else in the house."

TWENTY

I'M HERE BUT NOT HERE. I'M FLOATING OVER THE staircase, watching Brendan pin me against the steps. The distress shivering out of his throat as he tells me we're not alone. We haven't been alone this whole time. It's only when Brendan shifts and my hip bone digs against the railing, pain trailing up the right side of my torso, that I'm snapped back into my body.

"What?" I breathe out.

Brendan's blinks slow down, and for a moment, it looks like he's dozed off. I try to shift away from the railing, and he jostles into alertness. "There's someone else in—"

"I heard you," I snap. "What do you mean? How do you know?"

"I went back to the storage room to work on the power. Just like you wanted me to. When I got there, someone else was already there fucking with the switches. Like smashing them or whatever."

The blood drains from my body and I catch a chill. "Who was it?" I ask.

Brendan sighs, and his grip on me loosens. "I don't know. It was dark and they were wearing a hood. When they turned around, they had on one of them fucked-up masks that Kiz and Sherie were wearing tonight."

I swallow. Even when I knew Kizzy and Sherie were behind the masks, the images were still haunting. As though a piece of them disappeared behind those rubber facades.

"I charged them, Liv. I did. But they had a bat. Swung that shit at me and caught me in the forehead." He winces as if he still feels the pain. This has to be like the third time Brendan's been hit on his head tonight. That can't be good. "So I ran. Gave them a good chase and led them up to the third floor. Tricked them into going into that bedroom with all those printouts on the walls. Then I shut them in. Propped one of those chairs from the loft underneath the doorknob to lock them in. They were pissed."

"The thudding," I say, remembering the noise that Kizzy and I heard just a few moments ago in the spare room. Whoever it was kept ramming against the door, trying to get out. At that, both Brendan and I are silent, listening out for it again. Only the rain trickles down the windows. No more thuds to be heard.

"I think they got out," Brendan whispers.

My heart rattles against my rib cage. "Kizzy," I cry out. I push Brendan off me and twist around, scramble up the stairs with him right behind me. On the main level, I turn on my phone light and scan the great room. Next, the kitchen.

"Kizzy," I hiss, hoping she'll recognize my hushed voice.

"Did you . . . cabinets?"

I look up, and Brendan is leaning against a wall in the foyer, hands on his knees as he tries to keep himself steady. "The cabinets," he repeats.

I nod and start opening the cabinets underneath the island. Completely empty, so I move on to the ones hanging high along the walls. The possibility of her hiding up here seems slim to none, but I'd rather be safe than sorry. The smell of fresh paint tickles my nose with every swinging door. Still, no Kizzy in sight. I turn around to update Brendan, and he's slumped even lower against the wall.

"You okay?" I ask, and surprise myself with the sincerity.

Brendan raises one hand and gives me a thumbs-up. "Just catching my breath."

I don't quite believe him, but arguing with him will only make him woozier. "Stay here," I say. "I'm going to check the laundry room."

Brendan grunts an okay as I run to the laundry room. The door's slightly ajar, and I slip through the crack so as not to startle Kizzy in case she's hiding. Another swing of my light tells me the room is empty aside from the washer and dryer. I can't imagine a human squeezing themselves in those spaces without fear of suffocating. The light lands on the closed door to the dumbwaiter. I did tell Kizzy about it, so she might've known to hide here in case she heard someone. I reach for the handle, then pause. What if it's not Kizzy, though? What if it's the hooded figure instead? Lying in wait, ready to strike if I blow up their spot?

My hands tremble again. I take a deep breath and shake them out. I can do this. I need to do this. I count to three inside my head. Before I can get to the last number and psych myself out, I swing the door open. Only the cables attached to the cabin are visible. I step closer and shine my light inside the shaft. The cabin is still on the basement level, right where I left it. I blow out a sigh of relief and turn around . . . only to ram into someone's chest.

A scream scratches at the back of my throat but a hand covers my mouth and stifles it.

"It's me. It's me."

I look up, and Brendan's staring down at me. My fear melts into anger as I slap his hand from my mouth.

"I told you to stay put." I want to yell at him, but all I can manage is an angry high-pitched whisper, given the circumstances.

"I thought you called me."

I blink at him. "What are you . . . ? I didn't say anything."

"Oh, my bad. I checked out the bedroom and study down here and couldn't find her." He peers over my shoulder and into the empty shaft. "What's that?"

I open my mouth to answer, but something tells me not to. Something sitting on my right shoulder, whispering in my ear: *Don't trust him.* I take a step away from him. "You checked all that in this short amount of time? You moved pretty quickly for someone with a lump on his head."

Brendan touches his head as if he's just now remembering he's injured. "Guess I'm running on adrenaline. Where else should we look?" He glances toward the shaft again. The space that can lead to a potentially deadly fall to the basement. The deadly plummet that's a mere six inches behind me.

"Maybe I should look around." I turn and try to appear as casual as possible as I close the door to the dumbwaiter, despite my fingers still shaking. I face him again and give a small smile. "You hide out here. Get yourself together just in case."

Brendan's face twists to one side. "And leave you out there by yourself with some psycho? You trippin'."

He's trying to be chivalrous, but that thing on my shoulder. That voice. It keeps tickling my ear, murmuring the word: *Danger, danger, danger!* Again and again, like an incessant alarm going off in my head.

"What about Dayvon?" I ask, trying to overpower the voice. "You said you saw some hooded figure, but Dayvon should've still been in there. I found him right under the electrical panel."

Brendan's frown is so deep that I'm sure he's going to have permanent creases on his forehead. "I mean, yeah. I'm sure he was still down there. I was trying to avoid getting murdered to pay attention to every detail of the scenery."

"That's a hell of a big piece of detail to miss," I mumble.

At that, his frown begins to fade as Brendan takes in my

skepticism. "What the hell are you asking me, Liv? Do you think I made this all up?"

I grit my teeth and try to keep myself together. If I let on that I still don't trust him, there's no telling what he'd do to me. What trap he might've set for Kizzy when she ran ahead of me. Of course, there's the logical idea that Kizzy might've gotten out. That she opened the garage and got to my car, but, *fuck*. The key. It's still on me. She can't drive anywhere without my key. Regardless, I can't check to see if she made it outside at all with Brendan hovering over me, staring at me like he could skin me alive for not believing the words coming out his mouth.

"Of course not." I let out a dry laugh. "I'm just trying to follow the story. See if I missed anything that could explain where Kizzy might be." I need to get to the garage, but I can't let him know that's where I'm going. If he knows I have a way out, he might do something drastic to keep me in.

He studies me, and I feel the need to keep still. Not move any muscle that might indicate deception.

"It's a big house," he says finally. "Maybe she went up to the third floor by now."

I nod almost too enthusiastically. "Good point. Are you okay with going up there and checking? I mean, you said you're feeling fine, and that's the last place you saw . . . that other person." I struggle for a name for the hooded figure. The stalker? The killer? The figment of Brendan's imagination?

"You want to split up?" Brendan asks.

“Just for a little bit. If we can’t find Kizzy in the next ten minutes, let’s meet back in the great room. Sound good?” I hold my breath and pray that my face looks neutral. Completely blank. It’s hard hiding when the person across from you always knows how to find you.

“Okay,” he says, and I breathe again. “Let’s go.”

I follow Brendan out of the laundry room and toward the great room. I look toward one of the garages and resist the urge to dart in that direction. I have to be patient. Wait for Brendan to disappear upstairs before I make my move. He stops walking, and I skid to a stop to avoid crashing into him again.

“If you hear anything strange,” he says, “you need to hide in the . . .” He stumbles back and blinks, trying to find some focus in the darkness.

“Brendan?”

He shakes his head a little. “Fireplace,” he tries again. “Go inside the fireplace. Hide behind the thing. The brick. The brick thing . . .”

He lurches forward and vomits on the floor. I bounce back, but shrapnel lands on my boots. Brendan covers his mouth, embarrassed.

“I’m sorry,” he says between his fingers.

I shake my head. “It’s okay. Are you o—”

He drops onto the floor, his face landing squarely in the middle of his bile. I don’t think—I move. I crouch down next to Brendan and roll him onto his side to keep him from asphyxiating. I press my ear close to his mouth to listen for signs of breathing.

"Brendan," I say softly. "Brendan, I need you to wake up, okay?" I tap his cheeks, try to get him to respond. Slap him a bit harder when he doesn't come to, the sticky residue of vomit sealing to my fingers.

Leave, the voice on my shoulder says. *Now's your chance.*

"I can't," I hear myself responding aloud, breaking those two words into three syllables as I hold in my tears. I can't leave him like this. Not lying in his own vomit. Not out in the open for someone else to finish him. I look around for someone to help. To grab a pillow for his head or a towel for his face. But I'm alone. There's only us.

"Brendan. Brendan, please." The tears spill now as I grab him by his collar and rock him. "Please. Please wake up. I can't do this by myself." I grip the top of his jersey and sob. There's only us left. Everyone else is dead. Kizzy could be, too. And now Brendan's trying to leave me. I can't do this without him, even though I tried to.

Brendan stirs underneath me, his head slowly rocking side to side. "Liv?" he chokes out.

I cough out a laugh as relief overcomes me. "Oh my God. Brendan?" I lean over and press my forehead against his.

He winces and makes a hissing noise, and I jerk back.

"Shit, I'm sorry. I'm so sorry." I rub the top of his head. "But you're okay, okay? I'm going to get you cleaned up and get you some help."

"Don't . . . don't leave me," he mumbles.

"Only for a second. I'm going to get us out of here, okay? I'm sorry. I'm sorry I didn't believe you, but I'm going to get us out of here. You hear me?"

Brendan doesn't respond. His eyes close, and his breathing slows down to a steady ebb and flow. Shit. He's sleeping—but at least he's breathing. All I need to do is get him comfortable, get to my car, and get help. Would it be okay for him to sleep for at least an hour?

"Liv."

The voice is rough and animated. Followed by hisses and pops. Chills don't just climb up my spine—they cover my whole body. Freezing me in place and making me forget how to breathe.

"*Li-iv*," the voice taunts. It doesn't seem like it's coming from a human. It's almost mechanical, like the sound a cartoon alien might make. And then it hits me: It's Kizzy's megaphone. I rest a hand over Brendan's exposed ear as though this small move can protect him from whatever shit's about to go down. Fuck, I don't even know how to protect myself from what's about to go down. I glance around the dark space and realize it's useless. I'm completely naked.

"Liv," the voice sings again, and I bite down on my lip to keep myself from screaming. "*I. Am. Heathcliff.*"

TWENTY-ONE

SEVEN MONTHS AGO

I WALK UP TO THE JACKSONS' FRONT DOOR, AND Mrs. Jackson swings it open before I can ring the bell.

"Liv," she says, sighing my name. She looks like she's been through it. It's only 5:00 p.m. and she's already in her house robe. Her usually pristine, pressed hair is full of plaits and pulled back into a low ponytail. The dark circles under her eyes are begging for cucumbers and a good night's sleep on a silk pillowcase.

"Hey," I say as I hug her. She basically melts into my arms. She's had to be strong for days it seems, and now she just wants to rest. I hug her for a few seconds longer than I planned to out of fear she'll tumble onto the floor.

Mrs. Jackson finally pulls away from me and steps aside so that I can enter her home. "I didn't think she should go to school today.

Not like this," she says as she wipes dust from the console table near the entrance. "I told Tony we should think about Keystone again, but he thinks we should wait. For what, I don't know. It's not like we don't have the money. And even if we didn't, I'd find a way if it means I can keep my daughter happy and healthy. I think he's scared what the church folk might say. Like maybe we aren't praying the 'crazy' away. Prayers are all good and well, but sometimes you need to throw some prescriptions in there, too."

Mrs. Jackson pauses and rubs her temple. The hairs there are graying. I never noticed that before. "I'm sorry. I'm talking to you like you're one of my girlfriends and not a kid."

"I'm *your* kid, though." I squeeze her hand. "If you can sit and listen to me complain about a pimple, I can listen to you vent about hypocritical church folk."

Mrs. Jackson laughs and pats my hand. There's still sadness behind her eyes, but at least I helped them twinkle a little bit.

"Where is she?" I ask.

Mrs. Jackson points to the ceiling, and I already know what that means.

"She eat anything today?"

"She picked on a peanut butter and jelly sandwich, but I'd love to see if she'd at least eat this protein bar." She pulls one out from her robe pocket. I take it, give her a salute, and climb up the stairs to prepare for battle.

Hope's bedroom is more NYC art scene than teen girl in Virginia suburbs. Everything from the decor on her walls to her comforter is a sleek black and white, aside from a few pops of teal on her pillowcases and accent pillows on top of her vanity chair. The vanity itself isn't cluttered with makeup and body spray like mine. She has a minimalist approach, keeping all her beauty products in labeled, clear containers inside her drawers. The only thing she keeps on the surface is her drawing pad—so she can doodle when she's supposed to be doing homework. And her book. *Wuthering Heights*. Sometimes I forget the title because it's just *her book*.

She asked for blackout curtains like she works the graveyard shift at a hospital, and not just a teen who likes to sleep in late on the weekends. Behind those curtains is a window that leads to the roof of the pool house. We use that roof to climb onto the main roof, where we can look down at the Jacksons' inground pool from four stories high. It's been a hangout spot for all our friends for years—mainly because her parents couldn't hear us cuss or watch us make out with each other. Also, though, I think we've always liked it because there was that element of danger. That one wrong step and we'd be French-kissing the pavement below. It's the closest we could get to being badasses without dirt wheeling on backroads. Yeah, we live in the South, but we weren't that type of bumpkin in York County.

I slip out of Hope's bedroom window and climb up to the main rooftop. Hope's lounging in a lawn chair, rocking cutoff jean shorts and a one-piece bathing suit, even though we barely entered March and I'm still cozy in a fleece jacket and sweats. I've just come from track practice and my muscles still feel heavy. Didn't even properly stretch so I could rush over here to check on her. Hope, on the other hand, is feathery light. She has her eyes closed as she sings along to an Olivia Rodrigo song blaring from her phone. No single fucks given as she vibes with the sky above her. She looks beautiful and serene and transcendent—and it's annoying as hell.

I toss the protein bar on her lap, and her eyes fly open.

"You need to eat," I say.

Hope's face cracks open into a smile as she jumps from her seat and runs over to me. "Liv!" she squeals, pulling me into a bear hug and lifting me up to my tiptoes. She tries to spin me around but I'm acutely aware of how close we are to the edge of the roof.

"Chill," I say, pulling away from her and holding her still by her shoulders. They're cold to the touch. I can see the goose bumps crawling up and down her arm. "Why you up here acting like it's August? It hasn't even cracked sixty today. Here." I take off my jacket and wrap it around Hope's shoulders.

"Olivia Porter, always looking out for me." She slips her arms through the sleeves, then gives a little twirl. Maybe to show off how cute she looks. Maybe to be extra. Who knows with Hope.

"You didn't answer my question. What are you doing up here?"

Hope shrugs. "I'm always up here."

"No. You're always up here with one of us."

"Well, I'm not really fucking with any of y'all right now." She flops back into her lawn chair and completely ignores that she just stabbed me in the heart.

"What? Why? What did I do?" In my head, I'm demanding an answer. But in reality, I sound on the cusp of needy.

Hope reaches for a joint she has resting next to her phone and takes a hit. A slow one. As if she knows I need an answer, and she wants me to wait as long as possible for it. "I don't know, Liv. Did you do something?" she asks as she puffs out smoke.

I get a pinch, right in between my shoulder blades. Like the muscles there decided all at once to clench into a ball and inflict pain. As if I have a reason to be hurt. As if I have a reason to feel guilty. I think about last month at the dance. Brendan's hands all over me. My hands all over him. Our eyes on each other as we slow danced with our respective partners. But we didn't do anything. We wouldn't do anything. Especially with Ms. Martin lurking in the halls like a shadow. Except, what if that shadow wasn't there? How far would Brendan and I have gone? I can't think about that, so, I change the topic.

"Are you seriously up here smoking while your mom is right under you?"

"She ain't coming up here."

"Smoke travels, Hope."

"And like I said, she ain't traveling her ass up here." She extends the joint to me and wiggles her eyebrows.

"No, thank you."

She groans. "Come on, Liv. Be fun. Why won't you be fun with me?"

I frown. "Do you even hear yourself right now? You're peer

pressuring me into getting high like them after-school specials our parents used to watch."

"One of us. One of us," she begins chanting.

"I said no, Hope."

She's out of her seat again. Dancing and chanting around me, all while trying to hold in her giggles.

"Hope," I warn.

"Liv," she counters. "Li-iv. Come out and plaaaayy." She tries to place the joint near my lips, and I slap her hand away. She's tickling me now with her free hand, poking in between my ribs as I try to get away. "Come on, Liv. Do it. I am Heathcliff!" She breaks into a fit of giggles, no longer able to control it.

All I can do is frown at her. It's so strange being around someone high when you're sober. It's like being at a gathering with a bunch of old people as they talk about the glorious days of cassettes and Walkmans.

"What the . . . ? That doesn't even make sense right now."

Hope only laughs more, as though that's the point. There's no reasoning with her, so I don't know why I'm trying.

"Okay. I'll take a hit if you eat the protein bar. Deal?"

Hope holds up a finger as she gets the last of her giggles out, then hands me the joint. "Deal." She flops down on her chair and goes to town on the protein bar, half of it gone with her first bite. I place the joint to my lips and pretend to take a hit. Pray that she's too distracted to notice my chest not rising. After taking a few fake puffs, I sit down on the roof right next to Hope.

"Your mom's worried about you," I say. "She's talking about Keystone again."

Hope shakes her head as she swallows another bite. "Dad's not going to make me go."

"Do you need to go?"

Hope leans in her chair and looks up at the sky. It's ridiculous how pretty she is. Even with her regular hair plaited back into two French braids and flecks of chocolate on her lip, her face is cherubic and glowy and the blueprint for dollmakers. The cramp in my neck reminds me that because of where I'm sitting, I have to look up at her. But it makes sense, really. To look up at Hope. She's always been on another level, even when we're side by side. That's why Brendan chose her.

"Brendan's not a Heathcliff," Hope says out of nowhere.

I shift, uncomfortably. Did she just read my thoughts?

"He's more of an Edgar."

I cough out a laugh. "Edgar? Isn't Edgar basically a punk? Like boring and nice . . . and too scared to fight Heathcliff?"

I don't see that as Brendan at all. He has his nice moments, but he's never dull. He's too unpredictable to be dull. Even though I feel like I know him better than anyone else on this planet, he'll do something to jolt me. Like set me up with one of his boys while also fighting the urge to kiss me. Hope keeps looking at the sky, and I hug myself, as a breeze reminds me that I no longer have my jacket.

"And what does that have to do with anything? Has Brendan

not been here to check on you?" I ask, my mouth working overtime to keep that memory away.

"I don't need anyone to check on me."

"Umm." I wave a hand around us to capture everything. The swimsuit in March. The smoking weed while her mom is home. The oddity of it all.

"Don't you get tired?" Hope asks. "Of always feeling like you can't stand on your own? Everywhere I go, it's Hope and Brendan. Hope and Brendan. Even when he's not with me. I'm like, damn. Can't I be Hope sometimes? Just Hope."

I don't answer. For so long, it's been me and Hope. Or me, Hope, and Brendan. I don't know what it feels like to be just me, except when I'm running track. For those few seconds, it's just me and the wind and the ground beneath me. For a few seconds, I'm freer than I've ever felt before. But when I hit that finish line, the thrill is gone and I'm left with tight muscles and achy lungs. That's when I miss Hope and Brendan the most. Like I need them around to breathe again.

"I don't need Brendan," she continues, then gives a tiny shrug. "But I wouldn't mind a Heathcliff."

I see Hope and Dayvon slinking out of the bathroom, being normal for the rest of the world even though they had just finished sucking each other's faces off. She still hadn't said a word to me about that, but maybe she's hinting at it now.

"Did you already find him?" I ask, treading carefully. Trying not to give much away.

"Who said anything about a him?" She reaches down and fluffs out my corkscrew curls. "You're my Heathcliff."

I laugh a little.

"I'm serious, Liv. If you had a touch more testosterone, I'd marry the fuck out of you."

Despite the cold, my cheeks get warm. I know she doesn't mean it in a romantic sense. Marrying me would mean marrying a rock. Something steady and consistent and that wouldn't call her out on her bullshit. "Brendan might have a problem with that."

She swats a hand as though pushing Brendan aside. "Brendan doesn't get me. He gets you, though. And you get me. I say let's cut out the middleman and run off together."

I blink. "Doesn't that make me the middleman? The person in between y'all's drama?"

Hope rubs the infinity pendant on the necklace I bought her two Christmases ago. It was right after Brendan and her got serious. She kept checking in to make sure I was okay. Kept trying to assure me that she wasn't going anywhere.

"You come first," she'd always say. The reassurances got so smothering that I bought her this necklace. To let her know that our friendship was forever so she'd stop beating me over the damn head about it. And maybe, just a little, so she could remember me whenever it was just her and Brendan. Sometimes I'm a petty bitch.

"Who knows? I'm so lit right now," she says with a laugh. "It doesn't matter, because I'm breaking up with B."

I look down at the joint still in my hand to make sure it's the same size. That I didn't actually take a hit because I must be tweaking right now. "Yeah right."

"Why *yeah right*?"

"Because that boy could come on to your mama and you'd still be his ride or die."

He's done far worse during his tenure as Hope's boyfriend. There was the time he forgot to thank her at the athletes' award banquet last year. And that time he let Yasmine Santana slow whine against him at Asher's pool party. Don't get me started on when he told Mr. Jackson he was a "fucking clown" (he didn't know Hope had him on speakerphone, but he wasn't necessarily dying to apologize to Mr. Jackson, either). Point is, Brendan's not winning any Boyfriend of the Year medals. Then again, Hope certainly isn't being awarded Girlfriend of the Year. Not after her actions at the dance.

"Why now?" I ask.

Hope takes the joint from me and puffs on it again. "Maybe it's better to end things now before he gets famous and steps out on me anyway. Or maybe he already has."

She glances at me, and I can't help but think she's asking me something with her eyes. Or accusing me of something. I don't look away in case she thinks I have something to hide.

"Or maybe I'm just tired of him beating the shit out of me."

If I wasn't already sitting, I'd fall onto the shingles. "In what? Uno?" I ask with a laugh.

"That's not funny, Liv."

"Neither is lying about domestic abuse."

"Who said I was lying?"

"Hope." I give her a look. "Really? Brendan? The boy who couldn't even watch Black Panther die off-screen?"

Hope cocks her head. "That's how you respond to someone hurting your best friend?"

Which one, I want to ask, because the shit she's saying about Brendan right now is high-key painful. But the way her lips purse out tells me she's not trying to be challenged.

"That's not how I would react if you were telling the truth. But this shit just came out of nowhere." I wave a hand toward her. "You don't even have any bruises. What do you want me to do?"

"Just fucking believe me!" Her scream slices the air as she darts out of her chair and toward the edge of the roof. For a moment, I think she's going to make a jump for the pool, even though it isn't logically possible to hit the water from here. Asher tossed a chair from the roof once to test the theory, and that thing broke into a thousand pieces on the concrete. Needless to say, Asher hasn't been allowed back here for quite some time. Hope just stands there, hands balling into fists before disappearing inside my jacket's sleeves.

I take a deep breath and climb to my feet. Try to figure out how to navigate this. How to navigate her when she's like this. "I'm sorry if I said the wrong thing, Hope. Just tell me. Did Brendan hit you?" My stomach clenches as I wait for an answer. If I hear anything other than no, I'll vomit. I'll vomit until I'm dehydrated and then I'll die. I let Brendan Jean in. I have a lot of friends but have only let two truly in. If I'm wrong about Brendan, then how will I know if I'm right about anyone else?

Hope rolls her head from side to side, working out whatever kinks have built up in her neck from swim practice or drawing. "No," she says finally.

I exhale and feel like I can fly off this roof. "Hope," I breathe out again. "Why would you make up some shit like that?"

"Sometimes," she says, stepping closer to the edge of the roof, "I want people to hurt as much as me."

"How about nobody gets hurt?" I suggest.

"A few cracked ribs. Broken vertebrae. Fractured skull. That'll show him, huh?" She lifts one foot and allows her toes to slip off the roof.

I don't make any sudden movements. I don't even breathe out of fear it'll startle her enough to plummet forward. "You know what else would show him?" I say calmly. Slowly. "Not having to *show* him anything. When you take away all the hype, B's just a guy. A guy who gets morning breath and acne just like the rest of them." Maybe I need to hear this, too. That Brendan Jean is simply a mere mortal. "You don't need to show him shit to be a boss bitch."

After a beat, Hope takes a step back from the edge and smiles at me. "I'm already doing that well, boo."

I don't return the smile. My heart is beating too fast to properly function. "When you get like this, Hope . . . it makes me think I should talk to your parents. That going back to Keystone isn't a bad idea."

"Then who else will keep you on your toes?" She pulls me into a hug and rests her chin on my shoulder. "I am Heathcliff." She squeezes me tighter and waits for me to say it back.

I look over her shoulder. At the concrete that was waiting for her to smash against it. I see her there, all broken and bloodied. Hands stretched out and gurgling for air. I wait for the fear to set in, but I feel something softer. Something lighter. It takes a few moments to take shape, but when it does . . . it's relief. Imagining Hope bludgeoned against the ground gives me a sense of relief.

What kind of monster am I?

TWENTY-TWO

NOW

I STILL CRADLE BRENDAN'S HEAD AS THE MEGAPHONE hisses and pops from somewhere above me. I'm too stunned to move even an inch. If I do, Hope's ghost will creep out of one of the shadows. *There's no such thing as ghosts*, I convince myself. Even after feeling Hope's breath on my neck in the dumbwaiter. But she's gone. I saw that she was gone. Even with the picture no longer on my phone, it was stored in my head. It'll stay there forever, like an inoperable tumor.

"*Come find me, Heathcliff*," the metallic voice taunts.

A guttural cry escapes my mouth as I double over, cocooning myself around Brendan's head. I don't want this. I never wanted this. I felt like I owed it to Hope to get a clearer picture of what happened between Brendan and her. If Hope really was telling the truth about their breakup and that picture of her bruised face. That maybe I owed something to Kizzy and Sherie, who were so broken, so lost without Hope, that revenge was the only thing that might put them both back together. That maybe if I spent time with Kizzy and Sherie to create this plan, some of their grief would rub off on me. It's not that I wanted the pain to stop—I needed it to begin. I needed to feel *something* about my best friend's death. Something aside from the initial release I felt from imagining it, and the confusion that overtook me when it really happened. I wanted tonight to initiate the closure. To maybe feel less guilty about feeling as free as I felt whenever I was running.

But now, I'm stuck in this house with my friends' dead bodies and my other best friend incapacitated next to me. Instead of just Hope's final moments seared in my brain, I'll make room for all theirs, too. I'll forever be haunted, all because I couldn't fucking cry at Hope's funeral.

"What should I do?" I plead into Brendan's ear. "I don't know what to do."

Brendan wiggles next to me as something croaks out of his mouth. I lean closer to him to make out any words. He grunts again, and one syllable filters from it: "Go."

I blink at him. "I can't. I can't leave you." I've had enough of leaving friends behind when they needed me. I won't do it again.

Brendan attempts to shake his head, and his closed eyes squeeze even tighter from the pain. "Go," he says again, this time more forcefully.

I'm on the verge of telling him no again, but he finds my hand. Instead of pulling me closer, he shoves it away. He means it. He needs me to go. And a small part of me knows he's right. The garages are on this floor, just several yards away from me. I can still get to my car. I can still call for help. If Brendan's able to get up, he could probably come with me.

"Can you stand?" I ask him.

Brendan doesn't answer. He's out cold again. Shit. Back to plan A. Get help and get back . . . before it's too late. I take a deep breath and climb up to my knees.

"Liv! Liv, help!"

I freeze before I get to my feet. Kizzy. A Kizzy who I've heard a few times tonight. A scared and hurt Kizzy. But is it really her? I don't know all the options on that toy megaphone. Maybe it's a recording from earlier.

"No! No, please! Pl—" Kizzy's cries are interrupted by a loud thump. I jump all the way to my feet now and grab the top of my head in frustration. Brendan down here, hurt. Kizzy somewhere up there *getting* hurt. If I leave now, one or both could be dead. I have to do something. Anything.

"Okay," I say, hyping myself up. I angrily swipe the tears away from my face. "Okay."

I can do this. No more of my friends need to get hurt tonight. I run over to the sectional and grab one of the throw pillows, then prop it under Brendan's head.

"I'll be back," I whisper to him.

I glance up to the loft on the third floor when an alarm rips through the air. Loud and squealing, like one of those alerts for a tornado on its way. I cover my ears as Brendan stirs. He gags but nothing comes out. This is bad. This is so bad. I need to move. I run to the kitchen and dig in one of the bottom drawers. The tool junk drawer. I grab the small toolkit to steal one of the screwdrivers—I can't go up there empty-handed—but underneath the toolkit, I find a hammer. Bingo.

Hammer secured in one hand, I make my way to the stairs. Pause at the sight of Asher's crumbled body just a few feet away, still staring up toward the ceiling in a state of shock.

"I'm sorry," I say to him, wishing I had something to cover his body. His discarded clear raincoat is just inches away from him, but it wouldn't be much help. His death shouldn't be on display like this. He deserves his privacy. Once I get out of this, I'll find something for him. If I get out of this.

I take the stairs one at a time, the siren getting louder and louder with each step. I hold the hammer up with both hands now, ready to woodchop any motherfucker who pops out of the shadows and comes at me. I reach the landing to the third floor and spin around, searching for the source of the noise.

"Kizzy!" I cry out. "Kizzy, I'm here! Where are you?" The tiny hairs on the back of my neck prickle, and I get the strange situation that someone is right behind me, ready to reach out and wring their hands around my throat. I turn swiftly and swing. A gush of air slaps me in the face and I'm greeted only by more shadows. I need a light, but I also need to keep both hands ready.

A hammer in one hand can cause damage, but the force from two hands can create destruction. That's what I need to do at this point. Annihilate the asshole who's been tormenting my friends all night. Who's been following us for weeks.

I turn slowly and survey my surroundings as best as I can and realize that the siren seems to be coming from one area: the bedroom with the dumbwaiter in the closet. I swallow and move toward it. The door's ajar, and swirls of red and blue lights spill out of the crack in sync with the siren. When I'm close enough, I kick the door and it swings open with so much power that I'm sure I cracked the nose of anyone who could be standing right behind it. I scurry inside, yelling at the top of my lungs and hammer held high over my head. I check behind the door. Nothing. Rotate to scan the rest of the room. The megaphone rests on the bed. Siren still blaring and the lights flashing from a plastic window near the mouthpiece. I storm over to the bed and snatch the megaphone up, switching the power off. The silence in the room is so loud that I scrub my ears to make sure they're still working.

"Kizzy!" I call out again, then strain my ears to listen for a response. The prickly sensation returns, this time at my toes. In a second, I'm on the floor, lifting the skirt of the bedspread to peer under the bed frame. It takes a moment for my eyes to adjust to the darkness, but once they do, I see that nothing and no one is down here.

Then the creaking begins.

My head snaps up so I can hear better. The creaking has evolved to a rubbing sound. The kind of rubbing that's thick and heavy and caused by friction. Like the friction of ropes or cords slipping through a carabiner. The dumbwaiter.

I climb to my feet slowly, staring toward the closet where the dumbwaiter is located. I grip the hammer so tightly to my chest that it feels like I'm hugging it. Hugging my weapon isn't helpful. I need to be ready to strike at any moment. With trembling hands, I extend my arms and allow the hammer to lead me to the closet like I'm carrying a torch in the Olympics. The creaky, rubbing noise continues even after I swing the closet door open and stare at the panel that leads to the cabin. I grit my teeth, prepping myself for whatever's about to go down. Then, with a loud thump, the cabin comes to an abrupt stop. Right behind the panel.

I take a shaky breath and reach for the cabin door. Right when my fingertips touch the crevice, I draw my hand back like it's on fire. "Stop it," I hiss to myself. There's only me. Kizzy and Brendan are in trouble, and only I can help them. I rotate my wrist, reach for the crevice again, and swing it open.

The cabin is black, hollow. Seemingly empty. Confused, I reach my hand inside and feel around. Try to forget the feeling of Hope's cold arms wrapping around my waist. My fingers graze against something flimsy. A piece of paper. I pull it out and blink my eyes a few times to see if there's anything on it. I grab my phone and hold a light against it, illuminating the purple-inked scribble:

Hey, Heathcliff.

Three hearts flutter around the words, and I know this handwriting. These doodles. I saw it all the time in a drawing pad. Hope's drawing pad. This must be her note to Kizzy that got lost.

What is it doing here now? The light outlines something else on the back of the paper. I flip it over, see more words in thick, red marker:

You shouldn't have left him alone.

I buckle at the knees and bump against the wall behind me. Oh God. *OhGodohGodohGod.*

"Brendan," I gasp aloud. I push myself out of the closet as my heart batters against my chest. Each beat sending shock waves through my entire body. *BrenDAN. BrenDAN. BrenDAN.* I dart down the stairs two at a time, despite my legs feeling like Jell-O. I'm two stairs away from the main level when I see them. Brendan, still passed out on the floor where I left him. And someone else standing over him.

The other person wears a black hoodie and matching joggers. A rubber Bill Clinton mask covers their face. Their hands are gloved, and each one holds something different. In the left hand, a bat. In the right, a small knife. Kizzy's Swiss Army Knife. The one she left with Sherie.

I haven't gone down the last two stairs yet, frozen in place by the masked figure's beady eyes glaring in my direction. We engage in a stare-off, waiting to see who'll make the first move. My heart's a jackhammer, drilling at my ribs so quickly that I feel like I'm losing oxygen to my head. I can't panic right now. I won't panic right now. I try to slow down my breaths and allow them to reach my belly. Lean against the railing to keep me upright.

"Drop the weapon," Clinton says to me. Though muffled, there's something recognizable about their voice. Something warm like a hug but edgy enough to smother you with said hug.

Breathe in. One, two, three, four.

Hold. One, two, three, four.

Breathe out. One, two, three, four.

"You first," I manage.

Clinton throws back their head and laughs. Here, in the room only illuminated by the moonlight, it's the most sinister thing I've ever seen.

"You say this like you're in a position of power. Look around, Liv. You're on the losing end." That voice. That damn voice. Without the protection of the mask, I know I'd recognize it in an instant.

They cock their head at me, and I feel like I'm under a microscope. I want to wrap my arms around my chest to get some privacy, but then I wouldn't be ready to strike.

"You still don't know who I am, huh?"

I don't answer. Just grip my hand tighter around the hammer's handle.

"Figures. You've always been self-absorbed. But I guess popular girls don't have to pay attention to things. You're used to being remembered and not remembering. To sending people away with a flick of the wrist." Clinton lets out an exasperated sigh. "Fine. Guess we're doing this old-school. Face-to-face. At this point, fuck it." They reach up and slip the mask over their head.

My jaw abruptly hits the floor.

TWENTY-THREE

THIS IS THE PART WHERE I ROLL OVER AND FEEL my damp sheets clinging against me. Where I rub all the sleep from my eyes before sitting up and stretching out the kinks and nightmares. This is supposed to be the part where I sigh in relief, knowing that this whole night has been a dream and I can appreciate the day ahead.

But I'm not at home. I haven't been asleep. And I'm standing across from Tia Shepherd, my new best friend, who is threatening to kill my former best friend. My heart's too wounded to beat fast now. It sputters along, keeping me alive more out of obligation than will.

I must look like I've seen a ghost because Tia smiles deviously at me, the once-adorable space between her front teeth now creating fangs.

"I don't . . ." I shake my head, but she's still there and I'm still here. "I don't understand."

Tia shrugs. "I think it's obvious. I'm about to kill Brendan."

My knees buckle, and this time there's no wall to save me. My butt crashes on top of one of the stairs, but I'm too stunned to let the pain set in. "Wh-why?"

Tia frowns at me like I'm a little sister who borrowed her new shoes without asking for permission. Then her eyebrows lift as though suddenly she has a grand revelation. "My bad. I didn't have time to do my thing. Last-minute change and all."

She tucks the bat in her armpit and digs inside her hoodie before pulling out a piece of paper. "I was going to leave this under him. Want to read it now?"

She waves the paper at me, but I stay on the stairs. Keep my distance.

"Fine, I'll read it for you," she says with a sigh. "'Shorties makin up shiz for clout. The thirst is real. Hashtag dontbelievethehype Hashtag groupiestho Hashtag ontodanext.'" She looks back up at me and waits for me to cringe. I already did, when Brendan posted this last March. He never mentioned Hope by name, but he never had to. We all knew. He lit the match, and the explosion came later.

"Well?" Tia asks.

I nod. "I know. I remember it."

"You remember how the hate campaign against Hope happened right after?"

"That started after Hope posted those pictures." I'm not even convincing myself with that rebuttal. But if she argues with me, it'll distract her from Brendan.

Tia scoffs. "Those fuckin' pictures. Don't even get me started with those."

"Hope wanted evidence to show—"

"I know why she took 'em!" Tia shouts. "To show that Brendan was an abusive piece of shit. But she didn't post them. She never wanted to."

I blink, stunned. This is news to me. "It was on her feed. Under her profile. Of course she posted them."

"We'll get to that." The bat's back in her hand and she points it at me. Using it as her pointer stick for her twisted lecture. "Now, we're on this asshole." She pokes Brendan with her foot, and his arm flops against the floor. "You and I both know that as soon as he pulled that passive-aggressive shit online, the trolls came out to get Hope. The pictures were supposed to stop them, but it only made them angrier. Hungrier. Feeding off this girl whose mindset and self-esteem was already to shit. And they gonna tell a girl in that state of mind to kill herself? What a bunch of fuckin' weasels."

I give a gentle nod. "Right. You're exactly right. I'm pissed, too, Tia. But you even said it—Hope killed herself. Yeah, Brendan made a dumbass comment online, but that's what dumbass boys do. He didn't kill Hope, though."

Tia tilts her head. "I never said Hope killed herself. Did Brendan stoke the flames of online hate against Hope? Yes. Did Brendan take advantage of the fact that Hope has a mental health diagnosis on record? Hell yes. Did Brendan want everyone to think Hope killed herself because of those two reasons? Fuck yeah."

I rise to my feet again. Slowly. Don't want her to think I'm trying to charge her. "Where's the proof?" I ask. "Why couldn't the police find any proof that it was a murder?"

"Are you kidding me? Bitch, why you here, then? Why were you and Kiz and Sherie running around town like some broke-ass Nancy Drews if you didn't think he did it, too?"

"Yeah, of course we thought he did it. But after tonight, I . . ." I lose my train of thought, my mind racing through tonight's events. The laptop. The pictures of Kizzy, Sherie, and me. Even the damn truck Asher saw in the woods. Tia's uncle gave her his old truck for her sixteenth birthday, but she never liked to drive it if she didn't have to. *It's giving redneck* is what she always said. That's why she was always happy to hitch a ride with me.

"It was you," I say. "You've been following us."

Why didn't I see this until now? Was I so quick to see the good in Tia so I didn't have to see the bad in myself? I was so quick to lean on her. So quick to trust her. Now look where we are.

"That's how you knew we were planning tonight. You kept tabs on us." I can't stop talking now that I've solved the equation. Hearing it aloud, though, only makes it worse. Like I'm admitting my naivety, my stupidity, to everyone.

Tia's eyes glint under the moonlight. She seems excited. Wired even. Like a kid waking up on Christmas morning. "Well, it's not like you invited me into the fold. *At boring business dinner with Mom.* Remember that text?" She pauses to chuckle. "Bitch, you didn't even know I was right outside your house."

"I wanted to keep you safe!" I'm so loud that Brendan stirs.

Tia glares down at him, fingers twitching around the weapons in her hand. No. No, I need her attention back on me.

"Tia, you mean everything to me. It was you who stood next to me when everyone else stopped calling. You kept me smiling and laughing and . . . *living.* You're my best friend. You're my only friend." My voice breaks at the revelation. It's true. Tia and I have been joined at the hip since this summer. It's gotten to the point where we can even finish each other's sentences. She's been my lighthouse in this sea of bullshit I've had to deal with over the past six months. I had to keep her shining. That's why I didn't pull her into the plan. I didn't want her to think any less of me—and I didn't want to dim her shine.

"And all it took was Hope dying to give me the time of day, huh?" Tia asks.

I chew on the inside of my cheek. It's true, but it's not like I did it on purpose. Everyone who met Hope knew she was a ball of fire. Hell, she was the sun. When you're so close to the sun, it messes up your vision. You can't see anything or anyone else.

"Is that why you did all this? Why you hurt all these people? Because I ignored you?"

Instead of her eyes, Tia rolls her whole head to one side. "You think everyone sleeps, drinks, and poops Liv. This isn't about you. It's about Hope. About how all of you screwed her over. Just like . . . just like everyone did with Sierra." Her voice breaks, and there it is. A small shard of vulnerability. All I need to do is shatter it a bit more, and the rest of us can walk out of this in one piece.

"You're right," I say. "What happened to Sierra was terrible."

"Bitch, you never even asked me what really happened to Sierra." The anger's returned and it's sharper than before. "She did everything. Everything she was supposed to do. Asked our mom for help. Even went to Keystone just like Hope. She took her meds, exercised, everything her therapist recommended. But her bipolar . . . even with all that, it was hard for her to manage sometimes. She needed a support system. People who'd have her back. Cops who were trained to recognize when someone was in a crisis instead of being so fucking trigger happy. And you know what happened after she died? The goddamn outrage I expected from her peers? Fake. News. Those motherfuckers treated her like a joke. They used her name as a verb when someone started freaking out. That's all she became at Sedgefield. A taunt when she just wanted to be seen."

I hear her, but the words aren't adding up. She's telling a story but skipped over a page. But the more I keep her talking, the more I can keep her from harming Brendan.

"I get that you're angry. You have a right to be angry about how Sierra was treated, and how everyone treated you after she died. But . . . I'm not sure what all this has to do with Hope. Or tonight.

We never teased your sister. We were only in middle school when she died. And by the time we got to Sedgefield High . . ."

I stop myself before telling the truth. Think about those presentations from the school counselor when someone would still make a snide comment about Sierra. When *I* would make those snide comments. Sedgefield loved their traditions, and one of them included making light of anything tragic. Instead of grieving, we laughed. Laughing was less painful. But this was not the time to make excuses. I don't need another reason to piss off Tia. "Just know that we were all being stupid and immature. None of us meant to disrespect you or Sierra."

Tia clicks her tongue in disappointment. "That's because you were all too busy disrespecting Hope. You ever heard the saying about history repeating itself? Well same story, different character."

I shake my head. "That's not true. Nobody fucked with Hope. We all pretty much bent to her will. What I don't get is why you even care. It's not like you two were tight." I think back at all the parties, the dances, the school games and events. Search for Tia's face in the crowd but come up empty.

"See, the thing about being on the periphery," she says, as though reading my mind, "is that you see and hear everything, and nobody even notices you being all up in their business. And I shared what I saw and heard with Hope. I owed it to her. After Taj leaked the pics I sent to him, she's the one who had my back. She'd come to my house to talk or listen to music. Or just chill.

She made sure I knew where everyone was hanging out, because my so-called friends conveniently forgot to tell me. And she never let anyone run their mouth about me when she was around."

Now it's making more sense. I did start to see Tia around more after her pictures leaked, which confused me to no end because if it were me, I'd bury my head in the sand until after graduation. And Hope did always stand up for Tia when anyone got too slick about her, even when Tia wasn't in earshot. There was something different about their relationship, but I just never paid attention. Or maybe I didn't care to.

"You weren't there during that time," Tia continues, and I hear the anger bubbling up her throat. "I mean, you were there because you were everywhere. All the parties, all the events. Everywhere. But you never checked on me. Never asked if I was okay. Just gave me tight, polite smiles whenever you saw Hope talking with me. Like you were holding back something nasty to say until I wasn't around. That's when you weren't being a complete bitch. Sometimes, you let me know just how unwanted I was. How less than I was. But you expected other people to be there for you because you had a panic attack. The nerve."

I sigh through my nose. "You're right," I say. And she is right. "I . . . I had tunnel vision. I only saw what mattered to me back then. But that's not true anymore, Tia, and that's because of you. You showed me what compassion looks like. I'm a better friend because of you. And because I'm your friend, I'm asking you to put down the weapons. Let's get out of here together and get you the help you need. I promise I'll be with you the whole time."

Tia coughs out a laugh. "Help? Like the kind my sister and Hope received? You're kidding, right? Besides, I don't need help. I need to finish."

"Finish what?" I ask, not able to hide my exasperation.

"Taking off your masks," Tia hisses at me. "I tried to show Hope your true faces right when all the backlash started on her. Pay her back for her kindness. Let her know how her so-called friends truly saw her. How you guys treated her depression like a joke or a burden. That goofy white bitch dead on the basketball court? The one Hope took in because nobody else wanted? She's one of them color-blind bitches. The one who loves to boast she has Black friends but likes to downplay that just being Black is a crime everywhere."

The note under Sherie flashes across my mind: *Let's not make this a Black and white thing.* "If that wasn't enough, I heard that leech laughing with Erica Matthews about Hope right after her bruised face was all over social media. Erica was worried about what the backlash would do to the swim team. Like, who gives a shit? Erica went on and on about it, right in the middle of physics class. We were supposed to be working on a lab, but here that heifer was ranting and worrying about the team's image. Not even caring that I was sitting right behind her. Even had the nerve to compare Hope to Sherri Papini, the bitch who pretended to disappear for like a month. And what did your girl do? The leech? She fucking laughed. Since she sucked all she could from Hope, she was already making plans about who to attach to next."

I chew on my lip, refusing to let an image of Sherie making fun of Hope eclipse all the sentimental moments between the two. "That was just Sherie. She always laughed at awkward moments. She never meant it to be hurtful."

"Bullshit! Did Hope ever tell you about the house of horrors Sherie lived in? The strict rules? No music, no TV. Shit, she couldn't even mention a boy's name without having to pray for an hour afterward. But Hope came along, and told Sherie's parents about Sedgefield's swim team. How Sherie was good enough to get a scholarship. Hope gave that leech freedom, and she couldn't even muster the confidence to defend her."

My mind races back to when tonight's plan started to click into place. *She saved me*, Sherie had said. Fuck, why didn't I ask her what she meant by that? Why didn't I ever question why I never saw Sherie's parents, or why her curfew always seemed to be an hour before ours? But it all made sense. Why Sherie was here tonight. She didn't need answers for Hope. She wanted to thank her by going along with us.

"No," I say finally. Sadly. "I didn't know any of that."

"And Kizzy?" Tia continues, like I wasn't just speaking. "She posted the pictures of Hope all bruised up, even after Hope told her she didn't want to do that. She wanted to hold on to them in case she needed to. But nooo, Kizzy just had to make a Black woman a martyr, knowing damn well she was going to become a punching bag."

My mouth gapes. All this time, I figured it was Hope. Hope never said it wasn't, and Kizzy never admitted anything. I even blamed Hope for some of those nasty messages about her. *Why the hell would you post that, Hope?* Instead of being there. Supporting her. I went ahead and flipped the hate back on her. No wonder she didn't feel safe enough to tell me it was Kizzy.

Kizzy. I heard Kizzy crying for help.

"Tia," I say, keeping my voice measured. "Where is Kizzy? Did you hurt her?"

"Who? Thirsty Heathcliff?" Tia laughs. "I know you found my laptop. Did you get a chance to see her texts to Hope? 'Why aren't you talking to me?'" She pretends to sob, then laughs again. "Bitch, maybe because you put her pics on blast before she could make a decision. Then had the nerve to block Brendan from Hope's phone without her knowing. I saw her do it. I was at Hope's house when she came there groveling. Hope was cleaning out her closet. Asked me to stop by to see if I wanted anything. I was still in Hope's closet when I saw Kizzy. She just picked up her phone once Hope left and listened to a voicemail from Brendan before deleting it. Then blocked his damn number. Like Hope couldn't make that choice on her own. Like she was made of glass or something."

I can't help but wince. As much as I'm worried and want to make sure Kizzy is okay, I wonder if we'd even be here if not for her small actions. Telling Hope about me and Dayvon. Posting those pics. Blocking Brendan when maybe a tense convo over the phone could've prevented a face-to-face blowup. A blowup that might've ended with Hope's body broken next to her pool. Kizzy's intentions were sweet, but the outcome was nothing but sour.

"And this piece of shit." Tia looks down at Brendan. "We already know his role in the fuckery. What you might not know, though, is Brendan's the one who told Taj to post my pics."

My eyes snap back to her. "What? He wouldn't do that." It doesn't make sense. My brain is analyzing Tia's words, but they don't travel to my heart. That doesn't sound like Brendan. No, that isn't Brendan.

"There's a lot about your precious Brendan you don't know."

"And how do *you* know?" Here I am. Still defending him. I don't know how not to.

"Taj told me. My parents went to his house to talk to his parents. Do you know how humiliating that is? To have a bunch of adults sitting around a living room, talking about your exposed breasts? To bring up your dead sister and how what I did was a cry for attention? Something for me to get out of Sierra's shadow? Taj was in tears when his dad laid into him. That's when he admitted it. He was talking shit to Brendan about me ghosting him or whatever, and that's when Brendan dared him to release the pics. To teach me a lesson, is how Taj put it." She shakes her head in disgust.

"My parents bought into his tears. Saying Taj was a kid who just made a mistake out of peer pressure. But me . . . *I* should've known better. Why do Brendan and Taj get to be kids, but I'm the one who should've been thinking like an adult. Fuck them. Fuck him." She kicks at Brendan's side, and I jump.

"Tia," I plead. "That's messed up. Your parents should've supported you. Still, even if it's true, Brendan didn't hold a gun to Taj to make him post anything. None of us did."

"Maybe not." She looks down at him again, disgust smeared all across her face. "No one held a gun to Brendan to put his hands on Hope, either, but I saw him do it with my own two eyes."

At that, Tia could've taken the knife in her hand and stabbed me right in the gut.

TIA

EIGHT MONTHS AGO

DO YOU KNOW WHAT'S WORSE THAN BEING dismissed by a group of uppity bitches after trying to help a fellow sister from getting suspended? How about crying alone in a musty, old pickup truck after being dismissed by uppity bitches.

There I was. Dateless at the Cupid Dance, the fucking irony. I mean, yeah, I stayed on the dance floor. Almost every asshole in there took me for a spin. I knew what they were doing. One-upping each other, tryna see how many of them could get the girl with the topless pics to grind up on them. I couldn't care less, though—I got my goddamn cardio in that night. Why else would I give someone like Asher Cohen the time of day, night, or anything else in between?

But yeah, my dateless ass was still feeling lovely that night.

Until you pulled that bougie Liv Porter shit. As though I needed a VIP pass to intercept a fight. And I tried not to let it bother me. But stupid me for expecting anything else but shade from you. You were the girl who had a whole class cackling about my dead sister, after all. I figured, though, since Hope let me in, you might, too. You wrapped Kizzy and Sherie in your arms before Hope died, so why should I be any different? I was, though. At least to you. So even though I was floating earlier that night, sometimes it takes the smallest thing to burst your bubble. Despite all the bullshit that year. Hell, for the past few years since Sierra died, I wanted to own that night. That was what Hope told me when I told her I didn't think I should go since no one asked me. *Own the night. Show everyone you're THAT bitch.* So, I did. Until another bitch reminded me of my place and sent me crashing to the floor.

Where was I, though? Oh yeah! My uncle's musty-ass Toyota Tacoma. Just sitting in the driver's seat. Wiping away the tears that I had held in until I left the gym. Blotting runny mascara off my face with an old Starbucks napkin I grabbed from the glove compartment. When I finally got myself together, I tried starting the engine to get the hell out of there, but, of course, it wouldn't switch on. As if I hadn't been through enough, now I had to ask someone for a jump just so I could flee in embarrassment. But I couldn't. Liv, I couldn't see myself asking for help. So I rested my head on the steering wheel and cried some more. How fucking pathetic was I?

That's when I heard them. Hope and Brendan. Fussing back

and forth, back and forth. Scratch that, Brendan was doing most of the fussing, while Hope was doing most of the pleading. I knew he was pissed because of how sharp his voice sounded. It had that edge to it, like those times when he cussed out referees for a bad call. That's how harsh he was—yelling at his girlfriend like she was some old guy calling a foul. They got about three cars away from me when I could finally hear his words.

"How your dumb ass gonna send away our ride like that? You disappeared on me for the last damn dance, then decided to make decisions about my transportation? I paid for that damn Hummer, too!"

I perked up, ready to hear Hope knock him down a peg or two. I never saw her take lip from anyone, so I knew damn well she wasn't going to let this fool speak to her like that. But she did, Liv. She took it all. Even apologized to that idiot. All *I'm sorry, baby* and *I can ask them to come back*. She didn't even sound like herself. She was on some serious whiny shit, like she was an R&B singer from back in the day. I couldn't believe it. Even was about to hit my horn to snap her ass out of it because, clearly, she was gone.

Then she reached out to hug him, and that piece of shit snatched her arm so hard I was surprised he didn't dislocate her shoulder. Got in her face all huffy like she was another nigga he was steppin' to. I ran out of my truck so fast. Keys in between my knuckles to gouge his fucking eyes out.

"Nu-uh, asshole," I remember hollering. "Not today, Satan!" I'm not sure how I must've looked, running and slicing my keys through the air in front of me like a machete, but it was scary enough to make Brendan jump away from Hope.

She stopped me before I could get close enough to shank him. Placed her hands on both my shoulders. "It's all good, Tia," she said. "We were just playing."

"Playing my ass," I told her. I remember my eyes stayed on him, though. I felt like I needed to watch him. There was something about the smirk on his face that set me off. You would think he'd look embarrassed for being caught, but he had this smug smile on his face like Hope was fending off one of his fans. *Sorry, no autographs today. Brendan has a cramp in his hand.*

I don't remember how we got there, but Hope ended up in the front seat of my truck with me. She was holding my hand and tracing these tiny circles on the back of it with her thumb like I was the one who needed to be soothed. Like I was the one who had just gotten yoked up by her man.

"I know it looked, like, weird," she was telling me. "But that's just Brendan. He gets passionate like that sometimes. It works in his favor on the court—and especially in the bedroom."

She waited for me to laugh, but I couldn't. I wouldn't. My mama told me what went down with Chris Brown and Rihanna all those years ago. Still can't listen to his music because of what he did to her.

"That didn't look like passion," I told Hope. "That was all rage. Does he do that a lot? Grab you like that? Has he done worse?"

I didn't like the pause she took after I asked those questions. It probably wasn't more than a few seconds, but it felt like minutes. Stretched out, bloated minutes, almost like she was buffering.

Finally, she looked at me and said, "B hasn't had the easiest life. Everything looks shiny and perfect because of who he is and what he can do, but he's been through some things. Sometimes he doesn't know how to handle all of it. Just like the grumpy old man who comes home from work and kicks the family dog because his boss took credit for his idea."

"Are you the family dog?" I asked her. I think I asked her, but sometimes I just remember giving her a look. But I had to have asked it aloud, because I remember what she said next.

"I bite back when I need to."

Two seconds later, Brendan's hanging outside a window of Asher's car, hollering for her to hurry up so they could hit up a party. She squeezed my hand and left. She left with him. When I saw them at school the next week, it was like none of it ever happened. I started to believe that maybe I blew the whole thing up in my head. Maybe I was being dramatic because I was already so emotional. But after they broke up, she told me what was up. She told me that Brendan had always been a monster, and she needed my help to prove it.

She asked me to punch her in the face.

TWENTY-FOUR

NOW

HER WORDS KEEP PIERCING ME. DRAGGING THE knife from my stomach up to my heart with each revelation. Dayvon and I did leave early with the stretch Hummer after the Cupid Dance. I told everyone I felt sick after catching him and Hope in the bathroom, and Dayvon insisted on skipping the after-party and getting me home—even after I kept protesting. Hope even agreed that she and Brendan would find another way to the party. I didn't even consider that suggestion might piss off Brendan. I was too pissed at her in the moment to care—and I could never imagine that a pissed-off Brendan would result in Hope's shoulder almost being dislocated. I think about the bruised-up picture of Hope. Of the damage she might've asked Tia to do to her to prove a point. Of the damage that Brendan must've done before to want her to prove that point. I swallow bile.

"Is that . . . is that true?" I croak. "All of it. You're telling the truth about all of it?"

Tia shrugs. "I mean, I didn't really hit her. I couldn't make myself do it—even if there were times in the past where I thought about doing it. You, too. I would've loved to have knocked you around a few times. But I'm not a violent person."

My stomach churns again as I think about all the carnage in this house alone.

Tia blinks. "Before," she adds. "I wasn't a violent person before. I told her no. I told her no like a thousand times. Next thing I know, she's ramming her face into a doorframe. Over and over until I could actually hear the squelching—"

"Tia!" I couldn't anymore. I clap my hands over my ears to keep the image of Hope hurting herself at bay. But Tia's so casual about it, like watching people mangle themselves is something she does every Wednesday.

"So, Asher . . ."

She looks at Asher's body and laughs. She's not even computing that we're having a conversation. That I'm one confession away from passing out from sheer terror. She's on her tirade and she plans on finishing it.

"What a fucking idiot. I'm so disappointed I didn't get my hands on him. I had a laundry list of reasons he should go. But he would be the guy to die by accident."

I'm still dizzy about Brendan, about Hope. About all the people in here who are no longer breathing. But I let her finish. I let her finish to keep the boy at her feet breathing. "And . . . and Dayvon?"

Her face softens. "Dayvon was a mistake. He wasn't supposed to be here. Neither was Asher, but I'm not going to lie and say I wasn't thrilled when I saw Asher. He was going to get his later anyway. But Dayvon . . . he caught me in the storage room, so he had to go. Shame. He was like a brother to Hope. I mean, they got a little incestuous near the end, but it wasn't their fault. They were both hurt by you and Brendan, so they tried to lean on each other. Couldn't get past first base though. At least that's what Hope told me. She was in love with Brendan, and Dayvon still wanted to try something with you. He was a good guy. You really missed out, Liv." She smiles at me and a knot builds in my throat.

Dayvon wasn't supposed to be here tonight. He was killed for simply being at the wrong place at the wrong time. So was Asher, essentially. Neither were Tia's direct targets, at least not tonight. Which leads me to another question.

"How did . . . how did you know we'd be here? I made sure to keep you away from this."

"Aw, how sweet." Tia pinches her nose like she's admiring a baby. "The thing about getting close to you, Liv, is that you lowered your guards. Left things out in the open because you were naive enough to think I wouldn't snoop. It was clever for you girls to use WhatsApp instead of regular texting. I mean, not too clever for me, but still. A for effort. And you really shouldn't keep passwords in your Notes app all willy-nilly. It was easy to find the code to come to the house when nobody was here. Learn the layout, all the hidden bells and whistles. I thought the storm was going to fuck up my plans, but it ended up being a blessing in disguise. I didn't even have to override the smart-home system to keep you all here. The storm . . ." She points up to the ceiling as though she controls the rain outside. "That was all Sierra. Her way of helping me silence the ghosts for good."

She smiles above her like she can see Sierra beaming down at her, applauding her for all the murder and mayhem of tonight. Before I can make a move, she looks back at me.

"See, I know what you're doing. I'm not dumb, Liv. You're trying to distract me. You think if you talk enough, I'll tell you what I did to Kizzy. That I won't hurt your little boyfriend here. But I'm going to hurt him, Liv. Just like I'm going to hurt you. I'm just saving the best for last." Her smile grows wider, and I swear the temperature has dropped like twenty degrees in here. The hammer rattles in my trembling hand.

"First, though." Tia holds up both weapons over Brendan like she's weighing them on a scale. "You have to decide. How do you want him to go?"

My chest burns from more rising bile. "Tia," I croak. "I can't do that. I won't do that."

"You don't have a choice in that, Liv. He's dying either way."

"Tia!" I'm crying now. Hot streams of tears spill down my cheeks. "Please. No more, okay? Let's stop this now."

"Pick, Liv."

"Was it all a lie?" I wipe my face with the back of my hand. "Me and you? All our moments together this past summer? Was this all a part of your plan? Because it meant something to me, Tia. You mean something to me. You still do. So please."

My breath hitches as more tears trickle. Tia's a blur now. A dark figure behind a storm. There's no light in her anymore. Still, her hands seem to waver. There's a chance I might be getting to her.

"I love you, Tia." I keep going. Keep trying. "You're better than this. You're better than me. You're right, I was an asshole to you. I regret all the years I wasted before I saw how amazing you were. I'll keep apologizing for that until I die. But please. Let's leave here together. We'll figure something out."

Tia looks down at Brendan, who's still unconscious. Completely unaware of all the commotion happening above him. Oblivious that he's this close to death's door. She sighs and drops the bat to the ground. *Yes. Thank God. ThankGod, thankGod, thankGod.*

"Fuck it," she says. Then in one swift motion, she plunges the knife toward Brendan.

TWENTY-FIVE

A SCREAM PIERCES THROUGH THE AIR. LOUD AND shrill, lasting so long that it morphs into a siren. It's not until I cover my mouth that the siren gets stifled—that I realize it's coming from me. Brendan's coughing. Gurgling. Gagging. Then he stops. Everything stops.

Tia rises to her feet and squints at me. As though she's confused by my reaction. "Sorry," she says. "I got impatient." She steps over Brendan's body. Then takes another step, and another. She's moving—closer to me. She has that same sick smile on her face. The one that gives me chills. The one she wants to be the last thing I see before I stop breathing.

I raise the hammer over my head and hurl it at her like I'm in an ax-throwing competition. It connects somewhere on her head, and she stumbles on top of Brendan. I don't have time to flinch for him. I need to move. Now! I scurry down the last two stairs and zip past Tia. Past the laundry and kitchen, and straight to the mudroom. The two-car garage is the closest, so I say a quick prayer that the door leading into the garage isn't sealed shut like the other exits. That it's not part of this smart-home malfunction, just like it wasn't when I explored it earlier tonight with Dayvon. *Please, please, please.* I grab the doorknob and give it a twist. . . .

The door opens. I cry out in relief as I push it and scramble into the darkness. I reach for my phone for light, but then I hear Tia somewhere behind me. Groaning and trying to get to her feet. I run to where I think the center of the garage is and lift my hands, searching for the dangling red cord to yank. The city inspector guy tried it out when I was with my mom. It's supposed to disengage some kind of pin that keeps the garage door locked in place.

"Come on," I whisper, feeling the air. Finally, my hand grazes a rope and my heart leaps to my throat. With a hearty tug, I hear a click. Yes. This is it. This has to be it. I run to the edge of the sliding garage door and get low, feeling for a handle. After a second, my hand bumps against the lever. I grab it tight and lift. The garage door slides open and I'm so happy, so relieved, I can cry. I slip out into the cool, damp air and gulp it all in. Ravenously, like I'm starved for it. And I am. The rain has dwindled, coming down in sprinkles instead of streams. Still, raindrops have never felt so good against my skin. If I had time, I'd lift my head. Spread my arms and twirl in it. Drink in more of the moist air until my lungs burn. But it's too soon to be grateful. I run along the perimeter of the house, slipping along the wet grass and gravel on my way. I need to get to the front. To the unpaved driveway where I left my car. My legs pump with all their might, and I haven't moved this fast since my last track practice. My form is off. My feet slam against the ground when they're supposed to kiss it. But I move and I move well.

I round the bend of this behemoth of a house and there, a few yards away, is my car. Glistening with stale and fresh raindrops and glowing underneath the moon. I move faster. My legs propelling me forward into a fierce sprint. The Porter Blitz is what my coach used to call it. Back when I ran for approval and not survival. But just like then, I feel fucking free as my boots smack against the grass then gravel. I slam against the hood of my car, not able to come to a graceful stop. Then I dig into my pockets, and my fingertips graze against my key fob. I'm doing this. I'm getting out of here.

It's not until I run around to the driver's door that I notice that my car is leaning oddly to one side. "No," I say under my breath, and look down at my front left tire.

A screwdriver pokes out of it like a pimple. I scurry to the back tire, and that one's punctured, too.

"No!" I cry out, and kick at the tire. That doesn't take away my frustration, so I kick one of the doors. Then slap the roof. I keep going, assaulting my car in a windmill of slaps and punches until it apologizes. How dare it allow itself to be vandalized. How fucking dare it.

"Liv!"

Tia's voice cuts through my attack, and I freeze. I don't even breathe in case she hears me through the rain. I see a light flashing through the night, and I duck before it travels toward me. I study Tia's feet in the tiny space underneath my car and see that she's coming closer.

"Guess you know by now there's no way out!" she yells. Her feet pause on the other side of my car. I chew on my bottom lip to keep myself from screaming. She circles around to the front of my car, and I move, duck-crawling clockwise away from her until I reach the bumper. She stops again when she's on the driver's side.

"Come on, Liv! Come back inside. It's kinda gross out, and you're scared. Don't worry. All I want to do is kill you." She laughs a little and, oh, how I wish I could tackle her. Knock her to the ground and pummel her face until her teeth are gone and my knuckles are bleeding.

Her feet walk toward the back of the car, and I'm on the move again, crawling until I'm on the passenger's side. Tia lingers at the rear and seems to search the rest of the driveway, flashing her light toward the wooded area behind us. Then her feet turn back toward the house and her light shines that way.

"Shit," she hisses before taking off back toward the house. She has to pass me, so I slip under the car. Hug the muddy gravel against my chest. The undercarriage of my car nips at my back, hanging lower because of the deflated tires. I feel like I'm in a panini press, but I try not to think about that. I'll deal with it. I'll smoosh into this ground until I know the coast is clear. Then I'll take off for the woods. Hide out there and try to get cell service. If that doesn't work, I'll get to the main road.

Just as the pieces of my plan click into place, a hand grabs one of my ankles. I jump, and the back of my head slams into the car. Then the hand starts dragging me. On instinct I use my free foot to kick at my assailant. I thrash and stomp and connect with body parts, but I'm still being dragged. Gravel digs into my stomach, my chest, my chin. I use my hands to dig into the dirt, to claw away. Muddy pebbles bury beneath my nails and one of them starts to burn so bad, that it must've popped off. I howl in pain. Soon, I feel the rain on my entire body and know that I'm no longer under my car.

"There goes Liv," Tia says as one of her knees digs into my lower back.

I cry out again.

"Always thinks she's the smartest fucking person in the room. I watch horror movies, too, though. I know all the hiding spots."

"Please," I choke out, feeling the air seep out of my chest. "I can't . . . breathe."

"It wasn't supposed to go down like this!" Tia's still shouting, ignoring my pleas. "It was supposed to be you. All those bodies in the house? All those sinister notes? You were supposed to do it all. You were supposed to turn your mother's pet project into a house of horrors. But noooo, you had to flee. You had to make me bang and scratch you all up so now, it wouldn't make sense. I need to change my plans."

Tia's knee lifts from my back, and I gasp for air. Gulping in as much as I can out of fear that I won't be able to again.

"Turn around. I want to see you." Tia claws at my shirt and jeans, and I'm flipped over. Staring up at her and her bloody eyebrow, courtesy of me and my hammer. I take a swing right at her brow bone and she cries out. I try to scramble away, but Tia recovers quickly. She grabs a fistful of my braids and lifts my head off the ground, but then slams it back into the dirt. Loud humming screeches in between my ears. I shake my head, try to shake the humming out of it, but Tia repeats the maneuver. Braids pull my head off the ground, and I'm smacked back against it. I see stars, but I don't remember it being a starry night. Tia shifts her bodyweight on top of me, binding me in between her legs. I can't move and now the panic emerges. I feel the attack clawing at my chest, clutching the pit of my throat. I want to breathe. I want to breathe through my belly just like Brendan helped me to earlier, but I can't. She won't let me.

"Why?" I cry out, hoping my anger will stifle the anxiety even while both my arms are being crushed underneath Tia's knees. "What did I do? I love Hope. I could never hurt her!"

"Bitch, you helped him. You helped Brendan!"

"What?" Now I'm enraged. I squirm and wiggle, but Tia's mass is no match for me. She benches heavier weights than some guys I know. "I couldn't. I didn't!"

"You were there!" The rage in Tia's voice counters mine. We're two angry bitches glaring at each other in the rain. "You were there the night that she died. You either saw what he did or helped him do it."

I stop squirming now. Tia isn't just weighing down on me—dread joins her. I take a shaky half breath. I want to tell her she's wrong. I want to tell her I never saw Hope that night, but Tia knows me too well now. We finish each other's sentences, after all. She nods, knowing she has me, then pulls her phone out of her back pocket. Presses her knees deeper into my arms as she leisurely taps on her screen.

"Kizzy had a sleepover the same night. Hope was supposed to be there, but she didn't make it, did she? Because she was already dead. And you . . ." She flips the phone over so I can see. It's a picture from that night. Of the girls all dressed up in their pj's in Kizzy's bedroom. "You were wearing her fucking necklace. How savage of you."

I stare at myself in the picture. At the end, arm around Sherie's thin waist. I have a tight smile on my face, and my free hand reaches up for my neck—hiding the pendant dangling from the chain around it. The infinity symbol. Hope's infinity necklace that I took from her . . . right before she hit the concrete.

TWENTY-SIX

SIX MONTHS AGO—THE NIGHT OF

I'M GOING TO KILL HER.

Hope knows that me, Kizzy, and the rest of the girls have been planning this sleepover for days. To get her out of her funk. To celebrate her. To show her that we all love her despite what the online trolls have to say. This night is supposed to be about eating pizza, painting nails, applying Korean beauty facial masks, and watching classic, Black rom-coms. We all about died when Sherie told us she's never seen nor heard of *Love & Basketball*. Hope couldn't wait to school her on the appeal of a young Omar Epps.

But Hope's MIA. She skipped out on my track meet that day, even though she promised she'd be there. She didn't answer my calls or texts. Scratch that, she did send one. When I asked if she was ready for me to pick her up, she sent a GIF of Will Smith dramatically passing out in a church. The hell was that supposed to mean? My only takeaway was that she was choosing tonight, of all nights, to be a flaky bitch. To make me work for her to attend the sleepover that was planned in her honor. That's just like her. Making a night that's supposed to be about her *be* about her.

By the time I reach the Jacksons' house, I'm cramping and starving. My period's due to start any day now, and the last thing I feel like dealing with is Hope's shenanigans. Here I am again, bending over backward to do something nice for her, when she didn't even bother to send an apology for ditching my meet. I breathe a sigh of relief when I see the Jacksons' car absent in their driveway. I'm far too hangry to put on a song and dance for them. The goal right now is to grab Hope up and shove her in the car. Get this show on the fucking road.

I walk around to the back sliding glass door and slip in. They never remember to lock it, and I know if I ring the front doorbell, Hope will make a grand production out of answering it. Taking ten minutes just to climb down the stairs and open the door. The living room and kitchen are dark, except for the range hood lights shining down on the bare stovetop. The Jacksons shut everything down for the night, expecting Hope to already be gone with her friends. If only.

I climb up the stairs and head straight for her bedroom. The only light on is a lamp on her vanity, illuminating her sketch pad. I walk over to it and see a half-drawn outline of a hand extending out of water. Another hand dangles above it, but it's not pulling the other hand to safety. Instead, the middle finger is extended, just out of the drowning hand's grasp. I flip the drawing over like it's a photo from a crime scene. All that talent, and that's what Hope chooses to draw. I blow out an irritated sigh and climb out the window, head up to the roof where I know I'll find her.

And I do. No lawn chair this time. Hope lies on a strewn-out blanket, staring up at the starless sky. Something broody and instrumental plays from her phone that sounds like the score from some wartime movie. On the other side of her is her weathered copy of *Wuthering Heights* face down and splayed open, waiting to be picked up again. She's in capri joggers and an Old Navy cropped T-shirt, not the cute, yellow Savage X Fenty romper she had bought specifically for the sleepover. I roll my neck back and forth in preparation, knowing that Hope is about to drag this thing out.

She spots me but only moves to cross her legs at the ankles. Straight chillin'. Just begging for me to snap and snatch her.

But I play it cool. "You ready?"

"For what?"

My hand flinches into a fist at my side, but I quickly unfurl it. "To go to Kizzy's? To the sleepover we've been talking about for the past week? Where we already spent tons of money to entertain you for the whole night?" The last part slips through the cracks, but she is truly, clearly, trying my patience.

Hope uncrosses her legs and sighs. "Yeah. I meant to tell you. I'm not going to make it to that." Then she picks up *Wuthering Heights* . . . and begins to read.

My jaw clenches as she pretends to read. Yes, pretend, because ain't no way this bitch is able to read in the dark—the moon isn't that bright tonight.

"Hope," I say.

More fake reading.

"Hope."

She turns a page.

That's it. I storm over to her, snatch the book, and hurl it off the roof. It lands next to the pool with a faint *thwack*.

"What the hell, Liv?" Hope's on her feet and runs to the edge of the roof. She locates her prized possession, and her shoulders drop in relief. Still, she turns and gives me the glares to end all glares. "Okay, you need to go."

My head rocks back and for a moment, I think that Hope's slapped me. But her arms are wrapped across her chest like an ACE bandage. "I'm here to take you to Kizzy's."

"And I told you—I'm. Not. Going."

"Why you gotta be like this?" All composure's gone now. My voice breaks with irritation. "We're all trying to do something nice for you and this is how you repay us?"

"Something *nice* for me?" She tosses up air quotes with her fingers. "Know what would be nice? If you all stood up for me against those assholes at school and online."

My eyes are ready to fall out of my head because—is she kidding me right now? "You told us not to engage! You said if we tried to hit them, they'd only hit back harder. That they'd start talking shit about us, too."

"I didn't think you'd fucking listen to me!" She slaps her thigh, and I wonder if she's imagining our faces. "You guys don't know what it's like. To see all those nasty things about you, day in and day out. Just one thing after the other. It never stops. But, hey, let's play truth-or-dare and braid each other's hair for the night and it'll all go away."

When she puts it like that, it makes our idea sound pedestrian. Juvenile, even. But that's not how it happened, and she knows it. I can pull up the group chat. Hope told us that the last time she felt truly free and happy is back when she used to have sleepovers in middle school. We wanted to give her that again. Freedom and happiness, so screw us for being bad friends.

I'm so angry, so pissed. So vexed, that I can't even articulate all that to Hope. Instead, I hit her with a "Fuck you, Hope."

She raises her eyebrows. Not necessarily surprised by my comment, but pleased.

"You're acting like I haven't been here to dry your tears or wash your hair. Or bring deodorant and wipes with me everywhere because I knew you'd be too out of it to take care of your personal hygiene. I even stopped answering Brendan's calls because I picked you. I always pick you! But when do you ever pick me? You knew today was important for me. You knew it was the state qualifiers and that I was a nervous wreck. But no, here you are again being all woe is me. Maybe if you hadn't posted those pictures like I said—"

Hope interrupts me with a dry laugh.

I sigh. "What I mean is, if you would've just taken those pictures to the police instead of putting them online, maybe more people would believe you. You make fun of those girls who post videos of themselves crying online, but in a way, you kind of did the same thing. If B hit you, then—"

"If?" Hope asks, her arms folding across her chest again. "Are we on that again?"

"Hope." I keep my voice leveled like I'm negotiating with a toddler to take a nap. "I . . . want to believe you. It's just weird that one day I'm saying I didn't see any bruises and then the next day, voilà, you have an injury outbreak. So yes, if Brendan put his hands on you, then fuck him. Bury him under the prison. But you might not get that chance now since you went to IG first and not to the police."

Hope eyeballs me and time stretches for so long that I scratch my nose just to do something. My stomach gets that tugging feeling of dread, like I'm at the top of a roller coaster and about to zip down to my death. Finally, Hope steps toward me like a lioness on the prowl.

"I was wrong," she says when she's two inches away from my face. "You're not my Heathcliff. You've always been his. Brendan's. And I'm done with both of you. You two can have each other. Just know that whenever you're making out with him, you're tasting every inch of me." She flitters her fingers at me, dusting the crumbs of Brendan onto my shoes.

"You know," I say, still trying to keep my composure, "I'd be sad right now if I didn't really, *seriously* fuckin' hate you." I kick the imaginary Brendan crumbs onto her bare feet.

Her smug mask falls off and reveals the bitch underneath. "I hate you more." She shoves me on my chest. "I hate you the most. I hate you so much, that I wouldn't even spit in your mouth if you were dying of thirst." She shoves me again, and I grab on to her before I lose my footing. She slaps my hands away like they're covered in dog crap.

"You're on my case because I missed one fucking meet? How about ask me why I did? Or how I am? How about not assuming that my off days are all about you? I have a life outside of you, Liv, but you act like we can't even fucking breathe without each other. As a matter of fact, take this cheap piece of shit." She starts to tug and pull at the necklace around her neck. My necklace. The one I found specifically for her.

"Stop it," I hiss. "Stop it! You're going to break it!"

"Good!"

I knock her hands aside and pull down the clasp, removing the necklace from Hope and cocooning it in both my hands like a wounded bird.

"Get out!" Hope throws a hand toward the front yard. "Tell Brendan I said go to hell. I know you're going to run back to him now. Just like you've always wanted."

"Hope."

She places a hand on her hip, waiting for me to snap at her again. Wanting me to. I'm too tired to give her the satisfaction. I shake my head and walk toward the edge of the roof to get to the pool house. She was never going to come to the sleepover. She wanted me to come here to ask if she was going, just to lay into me. Always me, never anyone else. I'm sick of being her punching bag. My foot extends to the pool house roof when I hear it:

"Liv! Liv, help!"

The terror in Hope's voice makes me look up. A few feet away, she's on the edge of the roof. Arms flapping like a hawk as she tries to regain her balance. Four stories down, the concrete is waiting to greet her. We lock eyes. Hers brimmed with panic, mine with ambivalence. Two more seconds and we'll see if she can actually make the pool. Two more seconds and she'll be reunited with her precious book. Two more seconds and it's over. One of Hope's feet slips from the ledge.

I don't move.

My hand tremors as I reach for the infinity pendant dangling from my neck. Once I get a hold of it, I squeeze it as hard as I can before tucking it into my shirt. I take a shaky breath. *Get it together*, I tell myself as I wait for the Chans to open the front door. *Get it all the way together*. My stomach chooses rebellion, and churns everything I've eaten throughout the day so far. I feel it all rolling up my chest and settling into the pit of my throat. The pressure's so nagging that I run over to a flower bush and heave. I'm able to pat my mouth dry with the back of my sleeve just as Mr. Chan swings the door open.

"There she is," he says to me with a smile.

I force one out through gritted teeth. "Hey, Mr. Chan."

"I told you, it's Tao." He steps aside to let me in, and I automatically slip off my Vans and line them up next to the door with the other pairs of shoes. "The rest of the riffraff is down in the lair." He winks and nods toward the basement door. Usually, I can go back and forth with Mr. Chan for minutes at a time. He says that not only can I take a joke, I can ball it up and toss it right back. I take this as high praise from a man with a record collection of all the comedic greats. All I can muster now, though, is a sharp laugh as I head straight for the basement.

I'm not even halfway down the stairs before Kizzy's racing up and grabbing my tote off my shoulder. "About time," she says, then peeks over my shoulder. "Where she at?"

My stomach messes with me again and I swallow hard. "She's not here already?"

"Uhh, no. I thought she was riding with you."

I let out an exaggerated sigh. "She's doing the whole playing-hard-to-get thing. Not answering my texts or the doorbell. I figured she just came here without me."

"Did you try the sliding door?"

Another swallow. "No." I crack a smile. "I'm sure she'll turn up. You know how she is."

"Well, she better. Especially because the bitch is giving out invitations all willy-nilly. Look who's here. Look, but don't look, okay?"

I blink. "Okay." I peer down the rest of the stairs and see four girls dancing in front of the flat-screen TV, trying to pick up the choreography from Beyoncé's Beychella performance. Three of them Kizzy and I personally called or texted. Coko Augustine, who's on the track team with me and who Hope calls her little sister because they both have big butts. Sy'rai Madsen, one of the managers of the swim team and Hope's puppet. Of course there's Sherie, who seems to be following along to the choreography of a Taylor Swift video instead of Beyoncé. Then, at the end of the dance line laughing and giggling in a cute, waffle-knit onesie, is Tia Shepherd.

"The hell?" I mouth to Kizzy. It's not that I didn't like Tia. I didn't really feel anything about Tia, and tonight wasn't the night to try to learn anything about her. Why the hell would Hope invite her? Better yet, why would she pick up the phone to call and invite this stranger, but not pick up for me?

Kizzy's eyes widen. *I know*, they shout at me.

"And how this heifer going to show up before the person who invited her?" she asks out the side of her mouth.

I shrug. "Maybe she doesn't understand Hope likes being fashionably late." I need to sit. Kizzy needs to let me get down the rest of the stairs so I can sit and catch my breath. I get the same tightness in my chest after Coach puts me through the ringer at track practice. I thought I had time to process everything during the drive here, but there's still some pieces floating that need to snap into place.

"My point exactly. How you gonna celebrate Hope but not

know Hope?" She frowns, all like *Duh.*

"Just let Hope deal with her when she gets here." My throat closes on the last few words. *When she gets here.* Hope isn't getting here, but maybe I sound convincing enough. I rub my chest as though I can unblock my airways. What the hell is this and why does it keep happening?

"Nah, I'm gonna nip this in the bud. Say my mama don't like people staying in her house that she don't know. But first, I'm gonna get her to take a pic of us so Hope can see what she's missing."

I think about slapping her arm and scolding her for being that shady. But any unnecessary exertion might send me tumbling to the floor.

"She might as well make herself useful," she continues.

At that, she turns and heads down the stairs. "Look who's here!" she calls out, sunshine and rainbows now.

Sherie, Coko, and Sy'rai tackle me with a group hug as I plod down to the floor. Hands fluffing out my curls. Others tugging at my Skims boxers and telling me how cute I look. I hear congrats on my performance at the meet earlier that day. All their love, all their adulation, is too much for me to handle right now. My throat tightens, and darkness creeps up around my periphery. Almost like the walls are closing in on me. This is it. This is how I die.

"Here," a voice says. The hand attached to that voice extends a bottle of water to me. "You look like you need this."

I grab the bottle without another word and down half of it

in three gulps. I feel like I've just finished a 10K, but this? This helps. Something about drinking the water mellows out my heart rate and soon, I catch my second wind. It's only when I finish the entire bottle that I see Tia looking at me, giving me a gentle wave.

"Thanks," I mutter to her, wiping dribble from my mouth with the back of my hand.

She shrugs. *No worries.* As though she hadn't just stopped me from having a heart attack.

"All right, ladies!" Kizzy announces, and I almost forgot that I was in her basement trying to act human for a sleepover. "Our Royal Highness is running late. Let's show her what she's missing so she'll bring her ass."

Sherie looks at me. "Why didn't she come with you?"

I bite the inside of my cheek and feel Hope's hot spit on my face. Her eyes burning holes in me. Her foot dangling off the roof. I scrub my eyes with the heel of my hand and paint on another smile. "You know how she is. Keeping us on our toes."

Sherie stares at me for a second longer than I'd like before joining Kizzy and the other girls in front of the bar top. I exhale and take a position right next to Sherie. Tia looks around, trying to find where she might fit in.

"Actually, Tia, do you mind taking the picture for us?" Kizzy asks.

Tia's eyebrows stitch together in confusion as she scans the room. Then something clicks. In an instant, she wears a faint smile. "Sure, girl. Just let me get my phone." As she turns to grab her phone from the couch I give Kizzy a look: *Really?* She gives me a one-shoulder shrug, then wraps her arms around Sy'rai's and Coko's necks.

"Okay, y'all ready?" Tia asks, her phone pointing at us. "Say, 'Hot-girl summer'!"

"It's not summer yet," Sherie says.

"Shut up, Sherie. We're predicting," Kizzy snaps. "Come on, girls. Let's tease Hope!"

We scooch in real close together and I try to ignore the infinity pendant tickling my clavicle. I wrap my arm around Sherie's waist and use her to keep me on my feet. Still, my other hand travels to find the pendant.

"Hot-girl summer," I call out with everyone else through clenched teeth. Then smile until my face breaks in half.

TWENTY-SEVEN

NOW

I STARE AT MY SMILING FACE IN THE PICTURE AND see that my eyes weren't at that sleepover. They were still on Hope's roof.

"Tia," I say, closing my eyes so I won't have to look at her—myself—any longer. "It's not what you think."

"It's exactly what I think." Tia shifts, and when I open my eyes, her phone is gone and the bat is back in her hands. "I think you used that sleepover as a cover, knowing damn well you left Hope bleeding out next to her pool. Just like you got Kizzy and Sherie to use the bonfire as a cover. Told Kizzy to be all loud and belligerent and Sherie to do that weak-ass memorial for Hope."

"I didn't know about the memorial," I insist. I don't know why it matters in the grand scheme of things, but it feels important for

Tia to know that. Hope would've never liked that sappy shit. Tia has to understand that I knew Hope better than that.

"Guess what, boo?" Tia's not hearing a word I'm saying. Even worse, she's looking toward me but not at me. Something's gone behind her eyes. That tiny glimmer that keeps her in touch with reality. "I learned from the best. The bonfire was my cover, too. I made sure to dance up on every knucklehead there so everyone would be like, 'Oh yeah, Tia was here the whole night wildin' out.' I know how to make a scene." She holds the bat horizontally now. "Just like how I know how to make an exit." Her chin trembles, just for a moment. But that little twitch lets me know that a small piece of her is still there.

"Tia," I try, but the bat lunges down against my windpipe and crushes it. I try to gasp for air, but there's no point. There's nothing going past my neck right now. My tongue turns to static and retreats from my mouth, hanging out limply like a slug. On instinct, my body thrashes, fighting to keep alive. I gather enough strength to wiggle my arms free from Tia's knees. My hands reach for the bat and I fight to shove it away, but Tia's pushing all her weight down on me. All one hundred and fifty pounds of flesh and muscle. She proudly calls herself thick, and I know plenty of girls would pay money for her curves. And these curves are doing damage. Tia grows fuzzy right before my eyes.

Her mouth is moving, but the only noise I hear is the blood rushing in between my ears as all my vessels threaten to pop. Her lips form words, though. Rough, shaky words that she seems to hiss out instead of speak. *I'm sorry*, it looks like. *I'm sorry. I'm sorry. I'm sorry.* I keep my eyes there. On her mouth. Her eyes are dead, but her mouth—her mouth is still with me. Everything else starts to fade away, a narrow lens that only surrounds Tia's lips. They'll be the last thing I see. I make peace with that as my hands go limp. My legs stop wiggling. My chest stops heaving. *I'm sorry. I'm sorry. I'm sorry . . .*

I start remembering our brief friendship in ripples. Traces of memories that float in and out of my head:

Tia defending me against some hallway trolls my first day back to school after the panic attack.

Tia coming over to my house with pizza later that night. "Pepperoni helps me give zero fucks," she had said.

Me and Tia lounging next to my pool in the summer, giggling over *BuzzFeed* quizzes and IG filters.

Me and Tia trying to jump on top of one of my pool floaties, and Tia belly flopping into the water with such a loud smack that I laughed myself into a coughing fit.

Us rapping vulgar lyrics along with Cardi B in my car as we waited on our drive-through order, and getting weak with laughter when the worker handed us our food in disgust.

Tia and I linking arms as we trudged into Sedgefield High on the first day of our senior year.

"Remember, you're a bad bitch," she told me.

I looked right into those onyx-brown eyes of hers. "So are you," I said, and hoped she felt my sincerity. Hoped she felt my appreciation of her and our carefree summer together.

Now, the pressure against my neck slackens. I blink my eyes a few times and expect to see clouds and light and deceased loved ones. Hope, maybe. Hope, hopefully. But I still see Tia. Eyes wide now like someone just popped the question to her. Mouth agape, no longer able to close. She looks down at her chest. Back to me. Down to her chest. Then tumbles to her side and off me. The air reenters me in a single whoosh, so fast and furious that my neck burns. I still feel Tia's bat there even though it's now on the side of me, right next to Tia. I think that I'll always feel that bat on my throat.

As everything comes into focus, I notice a figure hovering over me. I blink again and again, and Brendan comes into form. He's shirtless. One hand presses his bloody jersey against his chest, right near his shoulder. The other holds on to a damp, yellow Swiss Army Knife. Kizzy's knife. Then Tia's. Now . . . Brendan's?

I scurry from under Tia's limp legs, crab-crawling away from Brendan and bumping into my car.

"Hey! It's okay. It's okay," Brendan tells me. He traces the horror in my eyes and looks down at the knife. He tosses it to the ground and lets me see his empty, bloody hand. Winces from the pain in his shoulder. "I'm not going to hurt you. I heard you screaming. I came as fast as I could and . . ." He looks down at Tia. I look at her, too. Spot the pooling wet spot in her hoodie—right between her shoulder blades.

"Is she . . . ?" I try to ask. My throat feels broken, and my words come out in pained whispers.

Brendan kneels and puts his fingers on Tia's neck. After a few beats, he looks up at me and nods. I gag. I'm not sure why, but that's what my body chooses to do. It knows I want to cry, but it won't let me do it. Not for Tia. Not after everything Tia's done. So my stomach clenches into several knots, and I hug my knees against my chest. Curl myself into the tiniest ball that I can manage.

"It was . . . it was Tia," I say hoarsely. It feels like I've been gargling with sewing needles. "All of it." My eyes burn and I bury my face behind my knees. I won't cry. I won't cry.

"Yeah. I kept going in and out. Saw her coming at me with the knife. Felt like I was dreaming. I didn't even know that I'd been stabbed until I heard your screaming." He pauses, and I hear the gravel scuff under his shoes, like he's kicking it around bashfully. I hear it really well, actually. I look up at the sky and notice that it's stopped raining. Finally.

"I can't believe she did all this shit by herself," Brendan says. "She almost took us all out."

At that, something tugs at my chest, and I climb to my feet. The oxygen hasn't reached my brain fully yet, so I stumble against my car. Brendan rushes over to steady me.

"Kizzy," I say, grabbing on to his free arm.

His eyes widen. "Is she alive?"

"I don't know." My voice cracks, not just from the hoarseness. "I . . . I couldn't find her."

"It's okay. We'll find her together." He takes my hand, and I jerk away. Remember what Tia told me just minutes ago. That Brendan actually used this hand to hurt Hope. He registers my fear and nods understandably. "Liv, it's me. I promise, it's just me."

He reaches for my hand again, and I give myself a moment. Hope, Brendan, and I were a trio. Surely, I would've known if something as intense as abuse happened between them. And this was the hand that calmed me down a few hours ago, guiding me to breathe through my belly despite all the bullshit I got him into tonight. Even after not speaking for months, Brendan knew how to take care of me. With a sigh, I slip my hand back into his and he leads me toward the house. I see them all next to the front door, standing there waiting for me, like in a horrible nightmare. Bloodied and battered and blue. Sherie. Dayvon. Asher. Kizzy. Oh God, not Kizzy. I pull away from Brendan again and he looks at me, confused.

"I can't go in there," I say. "I'm sorry. I can't see them again."

Brendan nods. I don't have to say anything else. He gets me. "I'll look for her. Stay out here. Maybe now you can get—" He stops and frowns toward the house and my heart stops. Can he see them all standing on the loggia, too? "You see that?"

I'm too scared to look again.

He tilts his head toward one of the windows. "That's a light. Liv, I think the fucking power's back on!"

I brave a glance at the windows and, yes! One of the lights from the great room spills out onto the unpaved driveway. I rush to the front door with Brendan right behind me and type the security code into the keypad. The locks whir, then snap. I tug the knob, and the door cracks open. Brendan and I smile at each other. Our smiles are weak and weathered, but the relief's still there.

"I'll go in," he reassures me. "Stay here and call the cops. I'll be quick, okay?"

I nod, and Brendan reaches up and tugs at my earlobe. Just like when we were kids. Then dashes inside the house. I pull my phone from my pocket and dial 911. It rings. The phone actually rings.

"Nine-one-one, what's your emergency?" a high-pitched voice on the other end asks.

I laugh and cover my mouth with my hand. Hold in my sobs so that the dispatcher can hear everything clearly. I say as much as I can without sounding like a teen pulling a Halloween prank. I tell them where we're located. I tell them that I'm injured. I tell them that they're several dead bodies, and the perpetrator is one of them. That's the hard part of the call. Not crying while I mention the bodies. The dispatcher is calm, patient. Professional. She assures me that help is on the way and asks if I'd like to stay on the line, but by now my voice is so raw and ruined that I hang up.

I did it. I got help. At least for some of us.

I melt onto the top step of the loggia as my phone chimes and buzzes at all the alerts and messages I've missed while it was out of commission. A few weather alerts about the storm, as though we needed our phones to let us know. Tags from Instagram from classmates who captured me in pics at the bonfire. Texts from my mom: *Did you make it out of that storm? Are you at Tia's now?* And Tia. Another message from Tia: *What should I tell your mom?* A sweet, innocent message, but something that places me here and her somewhere else. I guess this was part of her plan to pin everything on me. I look over at my car. I can't see all of Tia. Just her shoe poking from behind one of my rear tires. I look down at my own boots. They're covered in mud and other unidentifiable wet substances that I don't want to think about. But I'll always be thinking about tonight. Just like I'll always think about that night in April. I reach for my infinity pendant, which has, miraculously, survived the night. This thing is durable. If only Hope was. If only I were.

If I were strong, I would've told Kizzy and Sherie that this plan was bullshit. That it wouldn't change anything. I would've walked up to Brendan six months ago and demanded the truth. He couldn't lie to me. Even if he lied to the Jacksons and his parents and the cops, he couldn't lie to me. I'd be able to see right through him. If I was strong, I would've stood up for Tia during her nudes scandal. I would've been a friend right after her sister died instead of a scared little girl who made jokes to stay relevant. And I would've seen through Hope's theatrics and mood swings. I would've known she was crying for help. I would've told her parents that yes, they should be worried about her. I shouldn't have cared whether Hope would talk to me again. I'd rather have Hope walking around and ignoring me every day than no Hope at all.

No Hope at all.

My throat gets tight like Tia's bat is on me again. Hope is gone. Hope is *gone.* Fuck, it finally feels real. The tears prickle at the back of my eyes just as a hand grips my shoulder. I jump, and Brendan yanks his hand away.

"Sorry," he says quickly. He takes a seat next to me on the step, moving slow and labored as his face scrunches in pain.

"They'll be here shortly," I say to him, then nod at the wound near his shoulder. "Do you need me to put pressure on that for you? Give your hand a break?"

"It's all good. Don't want you catching my cooties or anything." He flashes me that brilliant smile of his, and he's that eleven-year-old boy I shared my Nerds with again.

"No Kizzy?" I ask, dread nipping at the question. I want closure, but not the wrong kind.

Brendan's smile fades and he shakes his head. "I looked everywhere. As much as I could. The cops will be able to find her." He looks away. If he stares too long at me, we'll both arrive at the hard truth that they might not find her alive. Neither of us want to go there yet, so we stare at the wet ground instead. We probably need to talk, though. Be on the same page about what we'll tell the cops when they get here. The truth seems stranger than fiction. That we were here to find out if someone really killed our friend but ended up killing ourselves. I don't think I'll ever be able to look at Brendan the same, even after he saved my life. I know he won't see me the same. I'm the person who turned his back on him. I have a bad habit of doing that. Still, there's something Brendan said earlier tonight that I can't wrap my head around.

"Brendan," I say, still staring at the ground. "Who was it?"

"Hmm."

I take a breath and peek at him. He deserves eye contact.

"The person you took to the movies? Who was it?" I can lie to myself. That hearing who she was will further prove that Brendan was where he said he was the night that Hope died. And yes, that's important. There's still that heavy feeling in my chest, though, that Brendan found someone else. He found someone he cared about the same night the last person he cared about died. That has to be a battle. Wanting to build something new while your past keeps tearing everything down. But a part of me wants him to be happy—even if he isn't happy with me.

Brendan blows out a breath and looks like he's contemplating what he should say. I don't blame him. I wouldn't trust me, either. "I'm kinda embarrassed to say it now." He chews on his lip then shakes his head, all *Fuck it*. "Tia."

I blink. Surely, I've misunderstood him. Tia is heavy on my mind and heart right now, so everything would sound like her name. "Tia?" I ask for clarification.

"Yeah." He rubs his eyebrow. "Thank God it never had a chance to get serious, huh? I'd be screwed." He laughs then hisses in pain.

I sit and wait for the dots to connect. Tia . . . Tia was at Kizzy's house the night Hope died. She took the picture implicating me being at Hope's right before. Kizzy did get rid of her, which was awkward for the rest of us, but we moved on. We decided on *The Best Man* instead of *Love & Basketball* and got halfway through the sequel before passing out. I guess that would've given Tia time to go to the movies with Brendan, but would she be up to it? So soon after being embarrassed? And we did embarrass her. We all came together as a sister circle for Hope but voted Tia off the island. The whole thing stunk of hypocrisy, but I'm only smelling it now.

I cough to block the tears. Try to cover one function with another, but all the cough does is dislodge the tears. Once they start, they don't stop. I try to keep quiet, try to whimper softly through my nose. But holding in a sob fest is like trying to hold in a sneeze. The buildup is so heavy that everything erupts, and I'm leaking and weeping like a woman who's just been broken.

"Hey." Brendan scoots closer to me and wraps his arm around me. It has to hurt, but he deals with the pain to comfort me. "It's okay, Liv."

"It's not," I cry out. "What's wrong with me?"

"Liv, tonight was traumatic."

"No, no. Not just tonight. It's everything. B, I couldn't even cry at Hope's funeral."

"I couldn't even attend her funeral," he says, rubbing circles on my back. "You're braver than me."

"I'm not brave. I knew I was supposed to be there, so I went. The whole time I was there, I was thinking about how much track practice I'd missed to help the Jacksons. I was thinking about how I was going to make up conditioning, Brendan. Who does that?"

He doesn't answer. Just caresses me and allows me to get everything out.

"I wanted to think of anything but Hope being in that casket. Because Hope doesn't belong in a casket. She's too bright and shiny and perfect and . . . I miss her. I miss her, Brendan." My throat is still sore, but I can't stop. All these feelings, these thoughts. They've been screwed in tight with a lid and finally, they're able to breathe. *I'm* able to breathe.

"I miss her so fucking much. But I failed her."

"No, you—"

"Stop," I say, using my sleeve to wipe my wet face. "Don't make me feel better. I need to sit in this. I did fail her because she exhausted me. I pushed her away when I should've worked to understand her. I loved her, but God did I hate her sometimes."

Brendan rests his chin on top of my head, and it's just like I'm in bed under my favorite lavender comforter. I close my eyes and bury myself in the purple.

"I failed you, too," I say. "You were hurting as much as me, but I let everyone get in my head. We should've been there for each other. I should've reached out. I made everything about me. That everyone iced *me* out and pushed *me* away, but that's not true. I was the one who shut down. I was the one who didn't return calls. I was the one who wanted to be alone while I figured out this whole grieving thing, but you all were grieving." The words keep spilling out like the tears from my eyes.

Brendan sniffles, and he might be crying, too.

"You all were fucked up, and I just ditched you. Just like I did Hope. I failed you, and Kizzy, and Sherie. I even failed Coko and Sy'rai. It was easier to ignore you all instead of just dealing with the pain. And . . . and I failed Tia."

Brendan's arm around me stiffens, and his chin lifts from my head. "No the fuck you didn't."

"You don't get it, B. She was still hurting about her sister, but when Taj posted those pictures of her, I blamed her. Thought something was wrong with her even though he was the asshole. I left her hanging . . ."

"So what? You didn't owe her anything, Liv. It's not like you two were cool back then. That doesn't give her an excuse to flip out and murder our friends. The bitch went psycho because the world saw her tits."

I sigh. That's not what I meant. "No, Brendan—"

"I'm serious, Liv. You can feel bad about Hope. You can feel bad about me, but just know that we're wiping the slate clean. You ain't getting rid of me now." He pulls me closer to him as though to prove his point. "But you are not feeling sorry for this girl who tortured and killed our friends. Who manipulated you into a friendship when all the while she was stalking you. Who kept pictures of Hope dead by her pool like it was porn. Leaked nudie pics didn't cause all that. The girl already was disturbed."

Brendan's arm starts to feel heavy, pushing down on my shoulders. I'm no longer under my favorite comforter. I have three of those dental X-ray bibs wrapped around me like weighted shawls.

At first, I think it's just the dead-porn comment. Hope bleeding out by the pool. But Brendan never got to see my phone before I deleted that picture. In fact, Brendan shouldn't even have known that someone sent me that picture the night Hope died. Unless . . .

I sit up. Unwrap Brendan's arm from around my neck like I'm unraveling myself from a boa constrictor. Brendan stares at me, curiously, as I scoot away from him.

"Brendan," I say, considering my next words carefully. "How did you know there was a picture of Hope by her pool?"

Brendan blinks a few times, trying to calculate when exactly he misspoke. Or when he fucked up. "Hope by her pool?" His voice is a pitch higher. "Did I say that? I thought I mentioned the picture of Hope in her casket."

I shake my head. "No, Brendan. You didn't."

Brendan lets out a tiny laugh through his nose and opens his mouth to speak. Nothing comes out—and his eyes grow black.

TWENTY-EIGHT

SIX MONTHS AGO—THE NIGHT OF

HOPE'S ARMS ARE FLAILING—ONE FOOT DANGLING over the ledge. Seconds away from breaking all her bones against the concrete below. I wait . . . and wait. And wonder why my feet aren't moving. Why I'm not rushing to her aid. Her eyes glance over at me, full of sheer terror.

"Liv," she cries out.

That does it. I'm snapped into action, propelling toward Hope. We're magnets, she and I. If she falls, I fall. I grab her arms and pull her toward me. She collapses against me, and we fall into a hug. Our chests fall into a natural rhythm of heaving in and out together. In sync, as always. Hope starts trembling underneath my arms, and I squeeze her tighter. Rub the back of her hair. "Shh," I say to her. "I got you. I got you."

Hope lets out a chirp next to my ear, and her shoulders jiggle even more. The more she tries to hold the chirp in, the more it evolves into a squeal. A teakettle reaching boil. I frown and lean away from her. This girl is cackling like an old lady in a candy house. Luring me inside to fatten me up.

"You should've . . . your face," she says in between giggles. "I wish you could've seen your face. You were like . . ." She claps her hands against her cheeks and opens her mouth in a silent scream, à la Macaulay Culkin in *Home Alone*. Something snaps like a twig inside me, and my vision turns scarlet. I shove her away from me. Hard. This time Hope genuinely has to flap her arms to regain her balance.

"What the hell is wrong with you?" she asks.

"You're the one who almost died to pull a damn prank!" I stop myself from shoving her again.

Hope rolls her eyes. "I wasn't gonna die." She peeks over the edge of the roof. "I mean, maybe a coma. But certainly not *die*."

"Why?" I demand. "Why is that funny to you?"

"Dying's not funny to me."

"Why is hurting the people you love funny to you?" I ask. "Me? Brendan? Kizzy when she finds out you're flaking on her party?"

"Oh, and you guys don't hurt me?" She folds and unfolds her arms across her chest, as though she's alternating between catching chills and hot flashes. "And I was just playing. Things were getting intense, so I wanted to break the ice. The real question is why'd it take you so long to come to my rescue if you didn't think I was joking."

I swallow down a response. I was scared to answer. If I had waited even a second longer, Hope's joke would've taken a tragic turn, and all for what? My frustration? My curiosity? Neither of them justified letting that girl fall. Instead, I deflect. "You're sick."

She smirks. "And you're dramatic."

"You want to see dramatic?" I step closer to her so she'll see how serious I am. "Just fucking do it."

Hope flinches slightly. "What?"

"I'm tired, Hope." I draw my hands up, surrendering. "Of your false alarms. And lies. And threats. If you want to end it, just do it. But if you want help, call me."

I make my way toward the pool house but keep an eye on Hope. She glowers at me in a way that literally turning my back on her seems like a poor choice. I don't think I've ever truly seen someone glower at me before tonight.

"I'd rather call the morgue," she spits out. "If you were my only choice, then kill me now."

My foot reaches the second landing, and I lower enough until I no longer see Hope.

"You better hope I never die, bitch!" Hope's still screaming. "Because I'll haunt you forever! I'll haunt you so much that you'll wish you never met me! I hate you!"

Hope stops yelling by the time I reach my car. With trembling hands, I start the engine and pull away from the curb. She hates me? She fucking *hates* me? She's going to feel so stupid tomorrow when she wakes up and realizes she's caused all this drama. Knowing her, she won't apologize. She'll do something like bring me curly fries from Arby's because she knows they're my guilty pleasure, then will try to shoot the shit about something completely unrelated. But I don't know if I want to just shoot the shit with her. Not anymore. We said a lot of things tonight that'll be tough to forget.

As I near the stop sign at the end of Hope's street, something catches my eye. More like, someone. A shadow, maybe, crouched low next to the hedges of a neighbor's front yard. Almost like they're playing a game of hide-and-seek in the middle of the night. Waiting for someone to find them . . . unless they're not actually trying to be found.

"What the . . . ?"

A car horn pierces through the rest of my question, and I slam on the brakes before almost T-boning a dark sedan. The car honks one more time at me and a middle finger shoots out of the driver's side window as they zip past. I clutch my chest, then whip my head around. I had been so distracted that I had forgotten to actually brake at the stop sign, and now? The shadow is gone. Maybe it was never there. Hope has me all the way fucked up.

It's not my messy mind that nags at me during my drive to Kizzy's house. It's Hope's screams. *Kill me now! I'll haunt you! I hate you!* When I park in front of the Chans' house, my hands are gripping the steering wheel long after I've put the car into park. I look down and see Hope's necklace in my cup holder. My necklace now. I pick it up and cradle it in my palm. The infinity pendant was supposed to symbolize that our friendship is forever. That our love for each other is limitless. In my hand, though, it's so light and weightless that I hardly know it's there. How can something that's supposed to mean forever be so flimsy? Maybe there is a limit to everything after all.

I clasp the necklace around my neck and climb out of my car, leaving Hope's bullshit behind me with the click of the door.

It takes me longer than the others to fall asleep, though I did have a few quick dances with slumber. One minute I was watching Taye Diggs, Morris Chestnut, and their friends performing a rendition of a New Edition song on Kizzy's flat-screen TV, the next I'm staring at the back of my eyelids. After one too many nod-offs, Kizzy realizes it's time to call it a night. And we're all too aware that Hope has stood us up.

I spend what feels like hours listening to the heavy breathing and light snoring of my friends. I toss and turn on Kizzy's futon bed—the one everyone else wanted to sleep on but I somehow nabbed—replaying my conversation with Hope in my head. Why am I feeling guilty? A good friend is supposed to be honest. A good friend is supposed to call you out on your bullshit. If Hope wanted another yes man, then she chose wrong. I couldn't just go along to get along. Not anymore. It's that insight that allows my eyes to close again, and I drift off with my conscious clear.

The buzzing wakes me up. A low, consistent pulse that's so insistent, so determined, for a moment, my sleeping mind thinks I'm getting a filling in my dentist's office. Then I hear the springs squeal as Kizzy rolls over on her pullout mattress.

"Hello?" she says, her voice thick with sleep and phlegm.

I open my eyes, and it's still dark. The sun hasn't risen yet. Who in the world would be calling her right now? I reach for my own phone and check the time: 4:42 a.m. That seems mighty late for a booty call—or is it mighty early? Either way Kizzy has dated some jokers in the past, so it shouldn't be too surprising. I set my phone down and roll over. I'll hear all about it in a few hours, but now, my pillow's calling me.

"What?" Kizzy hushes into the phone. There's a sense of worry in her voice that makes the skin on my neck tense. I lift up on my elbows to see what all the fuss is about. Sherie sits up in her sleeping bag, looking just as uneasy.

"What?" Kizzy repeats. This time, there's anger. Like she wants to reach through the phone and strangle whoever's talking to her. "No. No, no, no!" She throws the phone down to the floor and wails. The kind I'd imagine someone might make if they were being burned alive. Now Sy'rai and Coko are awake. We all exchange worried glances at each other, not sure of what to say or do.

Finally, Coko climbs into the bed next to Kizzy and places a hand on her back. Kizzy shoves her off and doubles over in tears.

"Kiz, what is it?" Coko asks.

Kizzy opens and closes her mouth, blowing invisible bubbles into the air. A few sounds escape her, none of which make any sense. She takes in a deep, shaky breath, and tries again. "Hope."

All the air rushes out of the room as it hits us at the same time. Kizzy doesn't need to say anything else. The pain in that one syllable spoke volumes. Coko slaps both hands over her mouth. Sherie buries herself into her sleeping bag and the whole thing begins to quake. Sy'rai rocks back and forth on her blanket pallet on the floor. She probably feels like she's in a bad dream. We all do.

Kizzy's wails send me into a trance as the sobbing spreads across the room. It's the background noise on an app that takes you mentally somewhere else, where in actuality, you're lying on a lumpy futon and your best friend is dead. I barely register that Mr. and Mrs. Chan have rushed downstairs, comforting the group of grieving girls like they're triaging. It's not until I feel Mrs. Chan's hand on top of my shoulder that I come to. I look up, and she gives me a soft smile. Her locs are pulled up into a pile on her head and tucked securely under an extra-large satin bonnet. With her hair all up, I see the resemblance between her and Kizzy. It's all in the way their mouths pout when they're supposed to be smiling. Like if they gave you the full-on smile, you'll turn to stone from their beauty.

"It's going to be okay, baby," Mrs. Chan says as she grips my shoulder.

I trace my finger along the infinity pendant. It feels cold despite being tucked under a blanket with me. I nod at her, give her permission to move on to the next crying girl. My tears haven't come to the surface, as though they can't cosign Mrs. Chan's sentiment.

Somewhere deep inside I know things will not be okay. They won't be okay for a long time.

I got the picture of Hope the next day. I sit on my closet floor, staring at my shelves of shoes. I'm supposed to be filtering through them to see if I had an appropriate pair to wear to Hope's funeral. The Jacksons haven't set the date yet, but my mom likes to be efficient. Having a plan is the best way for her to process anything, including grief. And she was grieving. She'd constantly find reasons to excuse herself from the room whenever my dad wanted to ask me how I was doing. This morning, I caught her sitting at the kitchen island, staring at nothing, as the microwave beeped to let her know her breakfast sandwich was ready. She overheated it, of course, so I had to make her another one. When Dad would fuss about her leaving the room, I'd make excuses for her.

"She's like a daughter to her," I'd say, not being able to speak about Hope in past tense. I had to be okay so my mom would be okay, when it should be the other way around.

So I sit on my closet floor, stare at my wall of shoes, and wait for the tears to come. Wait for my moment to grieve now that I have some time alone. Instead, I notice the space between my Burberry check-pattern sneakers and my vintage Burberry rainboots. Something else is supposed to be there, but for the life of me, I don't remember what. My phone chimes on the floor next to me and interrupts my problem-solving. It's a message from an unknown number. I frown as I debate whether to open it, fearing I'd accept some kind of spyware onto my phone. Life couldn't possibly get worse, though. *The hell with it.* I open the message.

If only it were spyware.

It takes me a moment to take in the picture on my screen. At first, I assume it's a blow-up doll lying on a floor, but then I tilt my head a few times and it all comes into focus. The crop top tee lifting up against her back. The blue capri joggers. The pool of blood blooming around her head.

A moan leaves my mouth as I drop the phone to the floor. Then scurry away from it like it's holding a gun. I curl up against my wall and keep my eyes on it. Wait for it to make any sudden moves. Sleeves and belts tickle my forehead as I wheeze and tremble underneath a row of my hanging clothes. My throat tightens again. My closet starts to shrink until I'm practically in a casket. My arms reach out in front of me, trying to push away the lid so that I could gasp for air. But I don't feel a lid. Nothing is there. My mind is doing that twisted thing again and I need it to stop. Now. I clench my fist and take a few deep breaths. I'm not in a casket. The walls are not closing in. My closet is the same size as most people's bedrooms. There's plenty of air in here.

After a few moments, I take in all my clothes. My shoes. I feel the sweat on my forehead and in between my fingers. But before I can feel relieved, I remember the picture on my phone. What. The fuck. Was that? Who would send that? And why would they send it to me?

Unless . . . unless they knew I was there. Unless they sent the pic to me to prove that they knew I was there. As though I was to blame. I may not have seen Hope fall, but in a way, I pushed her. I told her to do it. I told her to stop playing games and get it done. I'm no better than the online trolls.

I let out a tiny whimper as I creep back to my phone. Slow and meticulous so as not to provoke it. When I'm close enough, I snatch it and wake up the screen. There's a message underneath the picture. A message that confirmed my fears:

Peekaboo. I saw you.

I squeeze my eyes closed for five seconds, but when I reopen them, the message is still there. So is Hope. There but not there. Only her former vessel is on my screen. I trace the outline of her back as my lip quivers. The tears prick at the back of my eyes, but I fight them. I'm not allowed to cry for her. I don't deserve to.

I glance at my closet door. My parents are both downstairs. I can run to them, show them the picture and message and . . . then what? Explain that I was there. Explain that I told Hope to kill herself, then she wound up dead. Explain the same shit to cops and put my parents through the pain of possibly losing their only child? See the look of devastation on the Jacksons' faces when they realize that they let a monster inside their home? With a few wobbly breaths, I block the number. Not before I download Hope's picture and save it in a hidden folder. *I won't stare at it,* I promise myself. I won't even look at it again. Just knowing it's there is enough. If I try to move on—if I find myself too happy making new friends or even meeting my Heathcliff—I'll remember Hope.

I'll remember what Hope did when I left her. She told me she'll haunt me forever. And that's what I deserve.

I crawl over to my shelves and shoes and scooch my Burberry sneakers and rainboots closer together, closing the space between them.

TWENTY-NINE

NOW

I KNOW I'M SUPPOSED TO PLAY IT COOL. TO SMILE and pretend I'm not seeing flaws in Brendan's story. But I don't know how to pretend with him. He always sees through my mask. He saw through it during my double date at the Cupid Dance. He saw through it during my fake hostage situation earlier tonight. And he sees through it now.

He lowers his head, and I see the wheels spinning. Trying to figure out where to turn next and when to pump the brakes. "I . . . I think you heard me wrong, Liv."

He's still on that. Still playing I-heard-the-wrong-thing card. Gaslighting 101. Tia didn't have a picture of Hope by the pool on that laptop. I did . . . I did because he sent it to me. How else would he have known about it? I assess him. He's lost a fair amount of blood, not to mention the concussion. If I have to, I can outrun him. If I have to, I can take him down.

"When did you get there?" I ask. "Before or after?"

Brendan squints at me like I'm being out of pocket. I don't let his gaze slow me down.

"Before or after?" I repeat, slower this time. He doesn't answer. Just swallows and looks down at his wounded shoulder. He's avoiding this question, and I know why. He was there. He was that goddamn shadow I saw, lurking on her street like a predator. Waiting for me to leave her alone. It wasn't just my anxiety or my fight with Hope playing tricks on me. It was never just in my head. He was there before Hope fell. He was on that roof with her. Hope didn't want to die that night. Even when she was joking about falling, I saw her eyes. Saw that glimmer of fear that maybe, just maybe, I wouldn't get to her soon enough.

"You . . . know what she was like." Brendan speaks in a hushed voice. "She wasn't happy. Nobody ever made her happy. And since she was miserable, she wanted everyone else to be miserable, too."

As he speaks, I scoot away again. Search the ground for a rock heavy enough to defend myself, but there isn't one nearby.

"I broke up with her." He looks up at me and I freeze. "Did you know that? She likes to tell people that she dumped me, but I broke up with her. A few weeks after the dance. I tried to make it work with her, but I couldn't shake the feeling."

"What feeling?" I ask hoarsely.

"The jealousy I felt seeing you up close and personal with

another dude. I thought about you more than I thought about her, and I knew that wasn't right. She didn't deserve that. So I ended things. A few days later, her black-and-blue pictures pop up on the internet." He lets out an angry huff as though he's back in that moment. "I didn't touch her. I never touched her. I honestly think the girl did it to herself."

He's right about that, but Tia said Hope had a reason. "If you broke up with her," I begin, wanting to push away thoughts of Brendan and his huge hands yanking Hope by the hair, or gripping her wrists too tightly, "why did you show up there that night? Why didn't you just keep moving on?"

"Because she was out there smearing my name!" he booms, and I flinch. "I had college scouts calling my home asking me if it was true. She was playing with my reputation. She was playing with my fucking money. I told my moms she'd never have to work a day in her life. That she'd never have to depend on another low-life man. I was going to help her retire early. She just needed to give me a year until the draft. And Hope tried to take that away from us."

He climbs to his feet. He's a bit unsteady, but he still looms larger than any other person I've ever met. I feel like an ant he's about to squash underneath his sneaker.

"She blocked me, so I couldn't call her. Couldn't be seen with her at school because my lawyer advised me not to. I had to go to her. I just wanted her to tell everyone she was lying. I told her, the sooner she cleared my name, the sooner those jackasses online would back off. And you know what she did? She spit in my face. She got on her damn tippy-toes and spat in my face." He swipes at his chin, still feeling the spit on him. "I . . . I don't know what happened next. I remember grabbing her. I remember shaking her by the shoulders. She called me a couple of names I'd like to forget. Then . . . I'm looking over the ledge and seeing her body face down on the pavement."

He scrubs the top of his head and squeezes his eyes closed. "I went down there to be sure she was . . . you know? But there was so much blood. So much fucking blood." His eyes stay closed, not able to erase the image out of his head. I know that feeling. *He* gave me that feeling.

"You took a picture," I say, my jaw barely able to separate. "You took a picture of her dying, and you sent it to me. Why would you do that?"

Brendan looks at me again, then gives me a small, desperate shrug. "I didn't believe it was real. I had to take a picture to convince myself it really happened. That yes, she's gone. And then . . . I didn't want to be alone. I had this huge piece of information. This thing that devastated the hell out of me, and I didn't know how to process it alone. So I thought about you. Of course it had to be you."

He says it dreamily, like the happy ending of an epic love story. The words any girl would want to hear, especially from Brendan Jean. But Brendan isn't proclaiming his love for me. He's implicating me in a crime he committed. He wanted to set me up. He didn't send the picture because he trusted or needed me. He was worried that I saw him that night, same as he saw me. He sent that picture to me because he's a fucking coward. Just like he's a coward for trying to use Tia as his alibi that night. Dead girls tell no tales, after all.

"We know each other so well, so I figured you'd know the text was from me, even after I blocked my number." He keeps going, and his voice sounds like silverware scraping against a plate. Each syllable makes me cringe. "But then, you never said anything. I don't know why you never said anything. So I deleted the pic and figured you did the same. That we both needed to move on somehow."

He wanders down the rest of the front steps and paces back and forth, his steps more timid than usual. Even so, his back-and-forth boxes me in, the house my only option to escape him. He pauses, as if sensing my fear, and glances at me. "You understand why I had to do it, right, Liv? All of it? She wasn't ever going to stop."

My stomach twists and turns as I imagine the scene. Hope and Brendan on that roof. Brendan shaking Hope by the shoulders and Hope wrestling away from his grasp. Brendan starting after her again, seeing red. Running after her, shoving her. Then Hope falling, falling, falling. She wails before she hits the ground. I can hear her wailing. The wailing won't stop.

But it's not Hope. It's sirens. Lots of them. Making their way to collect my friends. To collect my story. Brendan hears them, too. His eyes widen, pleading with me in a hundred different ways.

"We understand each other, Liv. You and me. This was all on Tia tonight. It was Tia's idea to get us all here. It was Tia who played this sick game and killed our friends. And, if need be . . . it was Tia on the roof that night."

My heart stutters as it tries to find its normal pace. It would be easy to tell Brendan's story to the cops. Tia admitted it all anyway. She stalked and plotted and even murdered my friends. She wanted to murder me, but Brendan saved me. He saved me, and now I'm here to tell it all.

The sirens get louder as I draw myself to my feet, make my way over to Brendan. He eyeballs me, body tense like he's waiting for a jump scare. I reach out and stroke his forearm to put him at ease, and Brendan relaxes under my touch.

"Peekaboo," I whisper to him, copying his twisted text message to me. I reach up to stroke his chin. "I see you now." I dig my nails into his flesh and claw down toward his collarbone.

"What the fuck!" Brendan cries out, swatting his good hand and knocking me to the ground—just as the first patrol car wheels up the driveway. And that's what I wanted. He's who I wanted. Let them see Brendan with all his rage.

I scurry away from Brendan, shriek like a banshee, my screams ripping at my already battered throat. "Please! No more!"

The shock on Brendan's face is textbook. The image you'd show to little kids to help them understand emotions.

"Liv?" His voice is small. Too small to come out his massive frame.

"Help!" I cry out. "Please! Help!"

His eyebrows lower from shock to resignment. He gets it. We weren't going to be telling the same stories. We were in entirely different books.

A cop rushes over to Brendan, gun raised. Telling him to put his hands up.

"He's hurt," I say. Even now, I'm protecting him. I want them to see Brendan as the villain but not the monster.

The cop nods and pulls Brendan's hand behind his back like he's handling an elderly person. "I'll get you to the EMT, but I still have to restrain you," the cop grunts to Brendan.

Brendan doesn't respond. Just winces before returning his dead gaze on me. No sadness. No anger. Just numbness. There was a time when a muted glance from Brendan would've broken my heart into a thousand pieces. But he's already damaged it enough.

A female cop crouches next to me. Assessing me. Directing me to my feet. "Are there others?" she asks.

I nod once. "In there," I rasp, pointing back at the house. "Three bodies. And one . . . one missing."

The female cop says something into her walkie talkie as she guides me to one of the ambulance vans. We have to walk past Tia's body next to my car. I turn my head away and force my eyes shut.

"It's going to be okay," the cop says as she rubs my back.

I shake my head. "No, it's not."

She gives me a sympathetic grimace as she hands me off to an

EMT. I'm poked and prodded. I'm swiped with antiseptic and wrapped with gauze. I'm cooed at and coddled like a baby in need of her mama. And it's true. I can't wait to call my parents. I need to bury my face in their chests until I no longer see my friends' bodies.

They're letting me know which hospital I'll be transported to when a voice cuts through the radio: "We have a live one in here."

"Wait!" I cry out before the technicians can close the van doors. "Please. I have to see!"

The two technicians look at each other before stepping aside. They've probably seen cases like me before. The so-called final girl. The need to see if someone else made it through to help process this trauma.

I remind myself to breathe as I stare at the front door of the house. The seconds move like molasses as I wait for signs of life. Finally, finally, more technicians come out the door carrying a stretcher—and a dazed and battered Kizzy lies on it.

I exhale and jump out of the van. My technicians know not to stop me. I run until I'm next to Kizzy's side. There's a huge gash on her head, and her eyes are glazed over, staring through the heads hovering above her.

"Kizzy," I say, working hard to make my voice clear and certain.

Her eyes shift to me, and I watch as she takes me in. Her face crumples in relief. "Liv?"

I grab her hand. "I know," I say. "But they got him. They got Brendan. He won't hurt anyone again." I speak to her slowly.

Making sure that she catches every single syllable. Making sure our stories are the same.

She studies me, then her eyebrows lift in solidarity. "Okay." She squeezes my hand tight. "Okay."

"Sorry, miss. We're going to need to examine her now," one of the techs says to me. I nod and let Kizzy go. Watch as they load her into a van. She stares at me as they dance around her.

"Okay," she mouths to me again.

I rub my hand and still feel her warmth against it. Kizzy says it's going to be okay. And for once, I believe it.

EPILOGUE

SIX WEEKS LATER

I DRIVE PAST THE SIGN WELCOMING ME TO EAGLE Harbor Cemetery and follow the winding road that cuts through the final resting places of hundreds of other souls. I used to hold my breath when I passed cemeteries out of superstition. Now, though, I make sure to inhale slowly and deliberately. I want those souls to know I'm not taking being alive for granted. One soul, especially.

I spot the red maple tree near the back of the cemetery and park alongside the curb. Last time I was here, the tree was in full bloom. Vibrant red leaves towering over Hope's gravesite, showing out for her procession. The perfect companion for someone like Hope. Loud, colorful, stunning. Now, though, the leaves have shed in preparation for winter. We're in mid-December, and the flowers have gone into hibernation. Getting their rest before mesmerizing us again when the weather warms.

It's quiet out here. Empty—save for Kizzy sitting crisscross applesauce next to Hope's gravestone. Her mouth moves as she flips through a book. I take my time walking over there. Let her have a few more moments with Hope by herself. Her mom dropped her off early for this sole purpose.

Kizzy and I have spent the past six weeks talking about Halloween night. To police officers, to lawyers. To reporters even. I liked talking to the reporters. Especially the ones from the online publications—the ones closer in age to Kizzy and me. They're the reporters who changed our narrative. The ones who saw us as survivors and not victims. The writer from *Teen Vogue* took it a step further. She called us lionesses. "Together, these phenomenal young ladies worked together to take down the largest, if not scariest, prey of them all—an entitled young male who never had to face accountability."

The local cops say they're going to look back into Hope's death, admitting they were probably too hasty in their declarations. No shit. Asher's death, initially ruled an accident, is being further investigated, too. Especially after Kizzy shared what happened to her. Tia had struck her with the bat at least three times across the head, knocking Kizzy out cold. Kizzy came to a little later. Stumbled her way downstairs with a serious head injury. She heard all the commotion going on outside so she found a hiding spot no one would suspect—the washing machine. She never closed the door all the way. That's how Brendan found her. But instead of pulling her out so we could all wait for help outside, he sealed her in. Cutting off her oxygen supply. Hoping she'd suffocate while consoling me on the loggia. Kizzy was too weak from her head injury to kick out the door, but one of the cops heard her weakly tapping against it when she was on her last breaths. And to think, I was pouring my heart out to Brendan while Kizzy's was potentially beating for the last time. As for Sherie and Dayvon, there's no denying that Tia killed them. There are people who are pissed at her about that—and rightly so. When I talk about Tia, though, I always make sure to talk about who she was beyond that night. The person underneath the mask.

"Tia's done some terrible things, and it's going to take me a long time to process why she made those choices that night," I told the writer from *Teen Vogue*. "But I don't hate her. I can't hate her. She taught me the importance of grieving. That it's okay to grieve out loud and not bottle it up. When we do that, we tend to push people away—or make decisions without fully thinking through the consequences. And now, I take my mental health more seriously. Instead of going through the motions with my therapy and meds, I'm more intentional in finding safe spaces for me and creating safe spaces for others. My generation, and the Black community in general . . . we're becoming more open to talking about these things, but we still have more work to do. I want to be a part of that work. To not toss out diagnoses like bipolar or OCD like they're confetti when there are people out there actually living and thriving with them. To remind folks that words have power—and we could use them to either hurt each other or heal. I'm choosing to be a healer."

I haven't visited Tia's gravesite yet, but I plan to. I want to make sure I have the right things to say to her. The things I didn't say that night. It won't help her now but, I don't know, maybe it'll help me.

When I reach Kizzy, she closes her book and rests a hand on top of Hope's engraved name. I scan the title: *Wuthering Heights*. Of course. I know the seams and cracks in that cover—the frayed edges on the pages inside.

"Mrs. Jackson finally gave you Hope's copy?" I ask.

Kizzy gives me a soft smile. "Yeah. I think having something to do with Hope's investigation being reopened helped her sing a different tune."

"No you don't have Mrs. Jackson hitting falsettos."

Kizzy laughs as she stands, swats dirt from her butt. She glances at the book again before tucking it into her armpit. "I still don't get what all the fuss is about."

"You know Hope. She always likes to go against the grain. Won't admit she likes Adam Silvera and Angie Thomas like the rest of us."

"*They Both Die at the End* had me in my feels." She looks down at the small shovel in my hand. "Need help?"

I shake my head. "No need for both of us getting into trouble."

"Say less." She nods toward my car. "I'll wait in there. Remember—"

"Your group therapy starts at four. I got you."

She clasps both hands together and mouths, "Thank you," before trekking over to my car. It's become our routine every Thursday. We head to Keystone, where Kizzy has her outpatient group therapy sessions, and I volunteer with the play therapists for an hour. I mostly just disinfect and replace toys for the rooms, but every now and then I'm able to interact with some of the kiddos. Allowing them to chat me up while I escort them back to the waiting room, or holding their hands and rushing them to the bathroom when they need a potty break mid-session. It's not world-changing work, but it's a start. And something about seeing those tiny kids sorting through their shit at such a young age makes me more optimistic about what's to come.

Afterward, Kizzy and I have dinner together. It's my favorite time of the week. Sometimes we talk about how group went for her—though she mostly shares the surface stuff instead of the insights (*They brought those stale-ass doughnuts again.* Or: *I'm telling you, someone in there is allergic to toothpaste.*). Often, we talk about who she's crushing on or where we are in the college application process. Mostly, though, we ignore the stares in our direction and laugh together. Loudly. Not caring about the eyeballs on us, only that we're able to laugh loudly together.

I sit down in front of Hope's gravestone and sigh. Take everything in. Listen to Kizzy closing my car door. To the breeze. To the silence. I take it all in with Hope.

"Hey," I say. My voice's finally back to normal after Tia nearly crushed my windpipe. There's more of an edge to it now. Like any moment I'll burst into tears or laughter. Either one is fine. "It's been a minute, huh? I think you know, though, that even when I'm not here, I think about you. Two weeks ago, I noticed that my braids were looking a little rough. I heard you in my ear. *Girl, if you don't take them damn braids out.* So, I took them out that night. Just so you'd leave me alone." I laugh and pat the curls on my head.

"So yeah—me and Kizzy. We're hanging out. Alone. Isn't that weird? Us spending time together without you in the middle? I don't think we knew what to talk about at first, so we started just telling stories about you. Then one day, I started complaining to Kizzy about platform sneakers. Which led to us talking about the Spice Girls, of all things. Then the next thing I know we're joking about what it would be like to live in the nineties. I shit you not—we spent like an hour talking about boy bands and flannel shirts and white boys with floppy, blond hair. Like, why was that a thing back then? Why were side bangs irresistible on guys?"

I look over at Kizzy, sitting in my car and scrolling through her phone. "She's a good one. I see why you two were so cool. But you didn't have to hide how close y'all were. Just like you didn't have to hide how close you were with Tia. There was enough of you to go around. I'm sorry if I ever made you feel like there wasn't. Like you had to choose between us. But I thank you—for bringing Kiz into my life. Sherie, too. Damn, I miss that girl. The way she danced like she was casting a spell." I rub my hand across the grass as if I'm stroking Hope's hair, then take in a deep breath. Knowing what I have to do next.

"Okay." I pull out my phone and open my Notes app. "Dr. Solomon wanted me to start journaling, and I thought it was cheesy at first. But once I got around to writing more than one word, it started feeling less affected and more natural, you know? Anyways, I was going through some of my entries, and this one stood out to me. I mean, most of them are about you, or alluding to you, but this one? I don't know. I felt like it said all the things I wanted to say to you but didn't. I have to warn you, though. I kinda ramble. Try not to roll your eyes too much."

I clear my throat, then let it out: "'I hate you. I hate you. It still haunts me that that's one of the last things I said to you. And I did. Sometimes. Not hate in the way where I despised you, or found you despicable, or wanted to drag you on a cobble road by your hair. No lie, though, sometimes you needed to be dragged. But I heard somewhere that for you to hate someone, you have to really love them. That love and hate were on different sides of the same coin. And I loved you, Hope. So much that sometimes it made my head hurt. My heart ache. My mouth dry. I loved you enough to hate you, which I guess kinda means it's the greatest love you can have. That's what gives me comfort. What helps me sleep at night. That in our last night together, you know you made me *feel*. And I know I made you feel. And I'd rather feel that pain, that rage. That hate . . . than nothing at all.'"

My voice breaks and I put my phone to sleep. "So yeah. That's that. Reading it again was like this clichéd aha moment. You helped me feel, Hope. No matter how much I didn't want to. But feelings matter. I'm sorry I didn't tend to yours as well as I could've. I'm sorry that I clung to you so tightly until you couldn't breathe, and then let you go when you needed me the most. I had a habit of doing that—either holding on too tight or shutting down. I'm working on a healthy medium. I'm going to be mindful of others' feelings as well as mine. Feelings last. Memories of those feelings can be forever—and that's all I need."

With that, I grab my hand shovel and stab it into the ground. A tiny clump of earth sprays out. I do it again and again. Spewing dirt and grass until a tiny valley appears next to Hope's gravestone. I pull the necklace from my pocket and dangle it in front of my face. The infinity pendant twinkles under the dim sunlight. Then, I place it into the dip and scoop the bits of earth over it. Once it's neatly covered, I pat the ground for good measure.

"This was always yours," I say to her. I climb to my feet and walk toward my car. Toward Kizzy. I glance over my shoulder one last time at Hope. The tree above her is bare—but on one of the branches, a single flower is still in bloom.

RESOURCES

IF YOU NEED A LITTLE LOVE AND SUPPORT IN navigating your own mental wellness journey, please check out these resources:

www.988lifeline.org
www.teenline.org
www.nami.org/your-journey/kids-teens-and-young-adults
www.thementalhealthcoalition.org/wp-content/uploads/2020/06/Black-Mental-Health-Resources-MHC.pdf

ACKNOWLEDGMENTS

I can't believe that this is my third published novel. So many feels! All my novels have a piece of me in them, and *Through Our Teeth* is no different. I've struggled with anxiety for decades; however, I wasn't formally diagnosed until I was in my graduate program studying to become a school counselor. Once I heard those words, everything clicked into place. I was able to reflect on my childhood and teen years and understand why I got stomachaches before a major presentation, or why I went into a panic after leaving my textbook in my locker. For the latter, my mom had to catch the city bus and bang on the locked school doors so that a custodian could let her inside—all so her daughter wouldn't cry the entire weekend for not being able to complete her math homework. When I finally got my diagnosis, I wondered how school and my friendships would've been different had I understood what was going on with me. Maybe if I had certain tools in place, I wouldn't have felt like the odd girl out. Thus, Liv and Kizzy and even Hope were born—to show the different shades of mental health and the resources out there.

Of course, my continued strides along this writing journey wouldn't be possible without my rock star agent, Natalie Lakosil. Thanks for helping me sketch out concrete, tangible plans to live out my dreams. To Karen Chaplin—I've so enjoyed working with you and the questions you ask to make my stories shine. You always make me feel like the expert of my novels even when I feel like I don't know what I'm doing! To Allison Weintraub, thanks for holding me down during those rare times when I couldn't reach Karen. To Jenn Vance and the Books Forward crew, thanks for helping me find my audience! To my Looking Glass Literary & Media and Quill Tree Books teams, thank you for your incessant belief in me. To Kelly McWilliams—I received an encouraging email from you when I needed it most. I don't think you realized how much that helped me to keep going with this writing thing.

On a personal note, I have to thank the usual suspects: my mom; Tamara Hunt; and cousin, Marquita Hockaday, for being my primary support team and keeping my kiddos fed and entertained so that I can hit deadlines. My children, Easton and Brooklyn, for giving Mama a reason to keep writing the stories that I do. My buddy, Racquel Henry, for being my perpetual cheerleader and a great role model (despite me being older than you!). Finally, to my Black community, thank you for the joy, the traditions, and the overall culture. Let's take better care of ourselves because we are worthy of the softest love.